On the distant planet of Kalár the two hundred year old life cycle of the Schánda once again menace the idyllic lives of the Bólani, a small tribal village of forest dwellers living in their hollowed Lándo trees.

The schánda have a two hundred year life-cycle and normally live up on the northern edges of the tundra of the planet of Kálar. They are an insect, something like a cross between a spider and a scorpion. The mating urge mutates the schánda into a massive swarm of ferocious carnivores. It doubles in size, grows the stinger and large claws in its fourth and final moult, then begins its long march from its home-ground in the North of Kálar, south to its mating grounds on the shores of the Golden Sea.

In its path live the small peaceful Bólani tribe who make their homes in living Lándo trees in the forest. Around the same time as the schánda begin their journey, the Bólani's collective unconscious, triggers nightmares. They dream of an unstoppable carnivorous procession intent on eating their way to their mating grounds, heading their way. The Bólani must gather their possessions and flee ahead of the encroaching swarm.

Their long march to the shores of the Golden Sea takes them through a series of adventures with small blood sucking insects, vicious storms, predatory birds, unfriendly villages, lakes of volcanic lava, and desert worms. Only the skill of their apprentice wizard, Morác, saves them from disaster— transforming his powers in the process.

Even when they reach the Golden Sea their problems are not over. Imprisoned by a coastal tribe and then buffeted by storms on flimsy rafts, the dynamics of the tribe are changed forever as they strive to return to their small forest village in the far North.

This is an eco-fantasy tale stretching the imagination beyond the solar system.

The Wizard of Kalar

Sasha Garrydeb

London
2011

Published in Britain in 2011
by ABC Publishers
24 Treadgold Street London W11 4BP

e-mail: abcpublishers@ntlworld.com

A CIP catalogue record for this book is available from the British Library.

ISBN 978-09548144-5-8

ABC Publishers,
Notting Dale,
London W11 4BP.

Some contextual visuals illustrating
the story's settings

The Planet Kalar

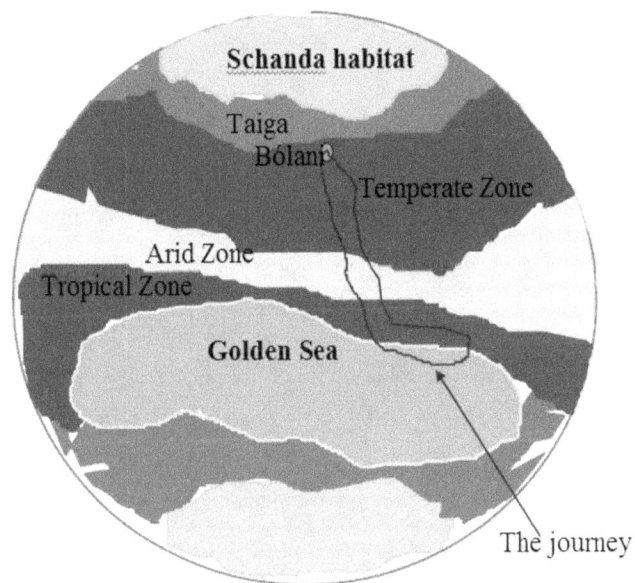

The Environs

Karti tribe
live in hills

Open plain with low
hills occupied by the Gronda tribe
who live in burrows

Nolki
tribe territory

Bolani tribe territory
The village

88 leagues across
62 leagues length

Hanum tribe

River Marka

Rimi tribe territory

The Village

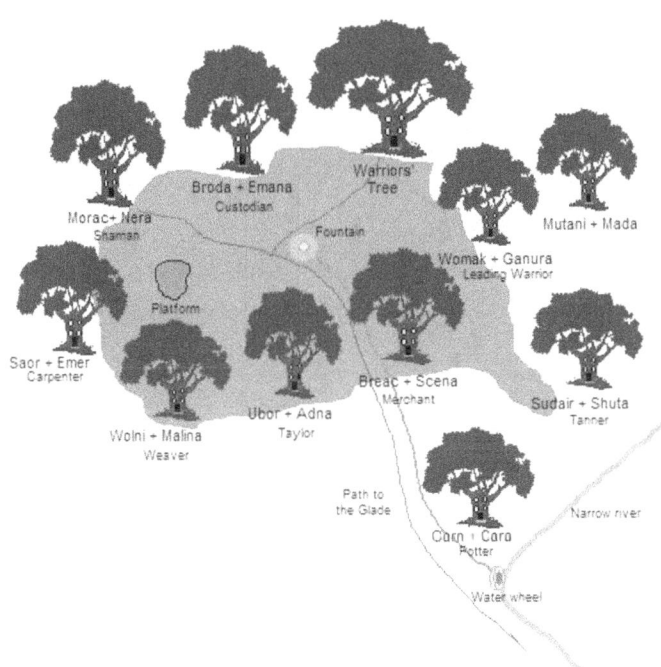

The Fauna of Kalar

Schánda

Bari

A kópi

A Wood Paloon

A Caroó

 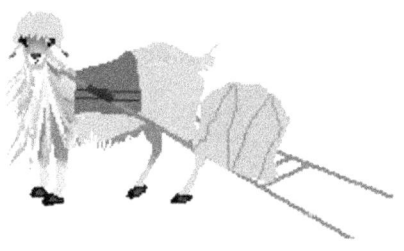

Stándy   and   Stándy + travois

 A kóira

A Dargh

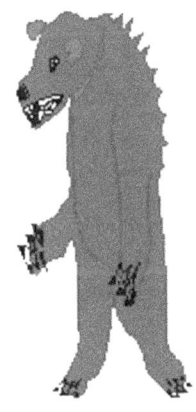

Order of March

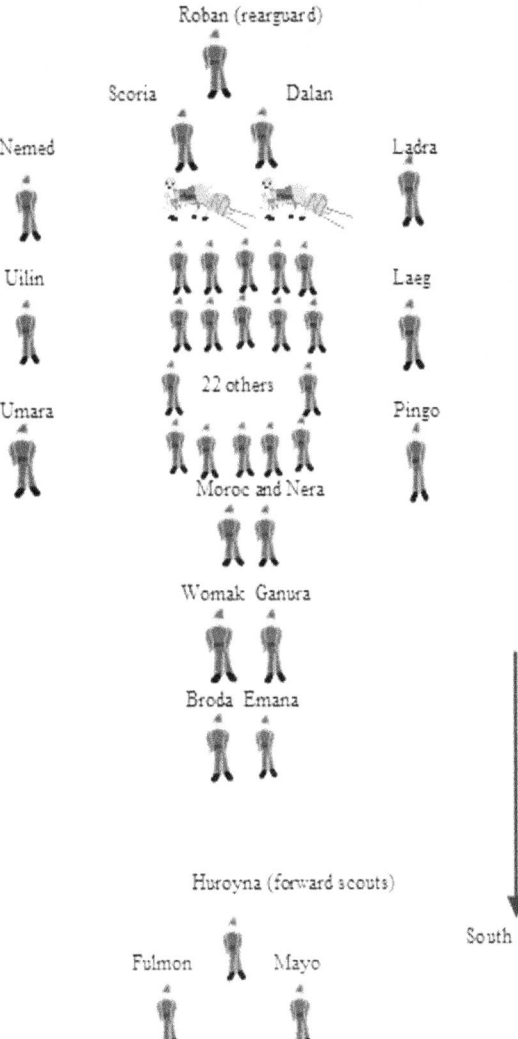

Roban (rearguard)

Scoria   Dalan

Nemed   Ladra

Uilin   Laeg

Umara   22 others   Pingo

Moroc and Nera

Womak Ganura

Broda Emana

South

Huroyna (forward scouts)

Fulmon   Mayo

1

DREAM TO THE GLADE

'I'm coming—I'm coming,' he shouted down to Néra. *Now what the Húli did the Custodian's wife want?*

Yet again she called from below, 'Émana's here to see you, come down *now* and tend to your duties.'

With a last lingering look at the fresh spring buds blossoming on his favourite bough, he sighed wistfully and climbed back inside. *She nags a bit but I'm lucky to have linked my destiny with Néra, to have got this splendid Lándo tree for our den,* the cusp of the thought fingered delicately through his overburdened mind. Before going down, he stopped to inspect himself in the long burnished mirror hanging in the corner of the night-den.

*   *   *

Earlier, he'd been overwhelmed by the intensity of the dream, forcing Morác's eyes wide open. He'd woken in a cold sweat, for a while lying damp in his perspiration. The recurring nightmare had increased in vigour; driving all further sleep from him. For the past week, each night, the same dream invaded his sleep, just beyond reach of awareness, depicting a calamity, foreshadowing frightful changes in the tranquil lives of the gentle Forest People. Yet, this dreadful dream refused to become apparent.

1

Morác's nightmares were unsettling, making him forget simple Spells. Last week he forgot the spell for speeding the growth of the salving herb, and before that he confused the spell for mending a broken love, with that of finding a lost kópi. All of Morác's unease had a knock-on effect on Néra. She was deeply attached to Morác, and when he was unhappy, she became listless and confused. That was the extent of their closeness, their bonding.

*   *   *

With the nightmare fresh, and unable to resume sleep, he'd climbed cautiously out of the double bunk without disturbing Néra; wiped himself, dressed, then ascended the narrow stairs to the top of his living tree. He needed to compose himself, to crawl out onto his favourite idling spot to wait for the suns to come up in the eastern sky. Sitting, entranced, watching dawn stealthily appear over the horizon like a thief taking the night, snatching a large bite out of the dark deep-blue sky, transforming it to richer hues, streaks of light blue, until finally the suns were ready to show. First, mighty Búla rose, her face a strong bright yellow-orange, peering over the edge, slowly as though awakening from a long deep sleep; then came Mára, smaller with a yellow countenance, heaving herself from her slumbers.

Morác perched on the hardy branch of the Lándo tree, calming himself, waiting for the day to chase the night back into the deep cavern below, to where it spent the day anticipating restitution. Never had he ceased to be enchanted by the kaleidoscope of flowing colours, watching daybreak shuffle out the night in its genial dance, ushering in the early morn. But now, the drama of the glorious dawn was occasionally broken by a discordant scream coming from his neighbours' dens, disturbing the peaceful nighttime sounds of the hamlet. Morác knew they were also having nightmares.

Soothing his green eyes with unfolding beauty in the sky—he watched. Yet the bad dream hadn't finished with him. A shudder jolted him, and the dark "beast" vaulted back into his mind. *What on Kálar is the meaning of these tortuous dreams?* He complained silently. *Why are they bedevilling me—?* Dangling his short legs over the limb, he dawdled on the branch, trying to rid himself of the "beast." A simple jest slipped into his head, pushing the "beast" into a cul-de-sac; *shamán, to the glade and mend thyself.* He smiled, fondled his red beard, as if he'd thought of a funny. He puzzled, *Now why didn't I think of that before? To the glade...to the glade,* he repeated in his thoughts. The lack of sleep tinged his judgment with a slight touch of hysteria—as it would with anyone crushed in the arms of fatigue.

Morác was the shamán in his tribe of forest dwellers, yet he was the first to admit his powers were limited. His confidence in that realm was not as strong as it should have been. Morác had apprenticed to Fándin the Elder, the former shamán of the tribe, a shamán of great renown and power. But Fándin got involved in a duel with a wandering stranger, an outsider who turned out to have far greater powers than himself. Now, he roamed the forest as a changeling; a fierce bári no one could approach, without any memory of his former self.

That was in the third season of Morác's apprenticeship, when Fándin just began to teach more interesting spells. It was a complete catastrophe for himself and the tribe. Five seasons on, the tribe was still wary of causing any offence to their neighbours, especially any wandering strangers roaming the forest. They had little protection against other's incantations.

*   *   *

For the third time Néra called again from below, 'Émana's still waiting, come *down*—tend to your *duties*.' Her voice louder, more insistent than before.

'I'm coming, I'm coming,' he called back. He took a last look in the mirror, a prize possession that had been obtained after much haggling with Bréac, the merchant. A special gift for Néra, but one he frequently tended to use. He saw she'd patched the trousers of his green tunic at the knee where he'd ripped it on a thorn. Néra was nimble with a fish-needle; the tear hardly showed. He made a mental note to ask her to replace his waistcoat, worn beyond its allotted time. A new dark brown would be agreeable; this one was beginning to show its age. He groomed his long red hair and quickly trimmed his moustache and beard. In the prime of life, and not at all displeased with his physical appearance, he turned and descended the steps into the day-den below.

Émana sat in his favourite basket chair, he observed, overweight and well into middle age. She was sipping a beaker of herbal brew. Mentally he queried again, *What on Kálar was she doing visiting so early?* 'A splendid, *early* morning to you, Émana,' he remarked pointedly, whilst inwardly admiring Néra's long red hair and trim figure. 'I see you've made yourself comfortable—of course, you're most welcome.' He went over to the table and sat.

Néra brought his morning meal, smiling at him with her hazel green eyes. Her smile made his heart skip a beat; he beamed back. She placed freshly baked wild-seed bread in front of him on a bark trencher, and a side-pot of sweet preserve.

'Now, what can I do for you Émana,' he said, spreading wild-berry preserve on to warm bread.

Néra brought a beaker of his favourite herbal brew, placing it near his wooden plate. He blew on it, and then took a sip.

Émana furrowed her brow, drew in a breath and began— 'I'm going out of my mind. I was just telling Néra. I need you to give me a potion…. I suppose Néra could do that....' she trailed off again.

Morác said kindly, 'Start at the beginning. Let me be the judge of what you need.'

She kneaded her hands nervously, 'I'm disturbing Bróda's sleep…' She cast her eyes onto the gnarled floor, and went on hesitantly, 'My sleep...is being troubled...by nightmares. I toss and turn...then Bróda has to wake me up...to stop me screaming…'

She didn't notice, but instantly she had Morác's full attention. His pointed ears stretched in her direction—not wanting to miss anything. He tried to put the question casually, 'What kind of nightmares?'

'They started...a week ago. As I fall asleep, I hear a distant snipping...that gets nearer...it gets louder and there's…there's more snipping...getting nearer still, and *louder*, turning into a crackling noise. The crackling, crunching, overwhelms my senses...I run—it always gains on me...I scream—that's when Bróda wakes me. I'm never sure what it is I'm running from—except it puts the fear of Aíne into me, may the Goddess protect me.'

'I'm going to ask Néra to make you a strong slumber potion. To add to its strength, I'll say a few words over it. That should put a stop to these nightmares. Now, take another sip of your brew to calm you.' He tried to consciously lower his raised eyebrows, and talked to her in reassuring tones. 'There you go. You pop off home. I'll have Néra bring the slumber potion to you in the afternoon.'

After Émana left, before sitting herself, Néra extended her two and a quarter cubit tall frame to its limit, trying to stretch out the annoyance she felt. 'Why didn't you admit you're having the same problem?' She looked at him reprovingly; her beautiful pointed ears quivering. 'It might even be the same dream?'

'I made a mistake in telling you,' he remonstrated. 'You worry too much my dear...and *no*; it's not the same dream.' *I really don't need to add to her worries.* 'Anyway, I'm taking my dream to the glade this morning; I can meditate its meaning there. It'll all be clear when I return.' *Néra sleeps like a baby without any dreams; that's a puzzle?*

'I hope you're right Morác,' and she left it.

He finished the last of the bread, drank the last gulp of herbal and got up from the table. 'I might as well make an early start.'

Néra made up a bag of biscuits and dried fruits for his journey to the glade, placing it on the table.

'I promise,' he told her, picking up the bag, 'when I come back, all the bad dreams will be sorted. Don't forget the potion for Émana this afternoon; you know the usual one. I probably won't get back in time.'

She nodded, put her apron over her green tunic and busily cleared away the remnants of the morning meal. At the front door, he stopped; looked back and blew a kiss. Néra turned, wiped her hands on her apron, laughed and blew one back. The parting was a daily ritual. He'd peck her on the cheek, or he blew her a tender kiss at the door.

Outside, already high in the morning sky the suns were gently reheating the forest. Morác's menacing Beast stirred restlessly within, yet he felt elated now he was heading towards the glade—to deal with it. He made his way slowly, diagonally across the grassy clearing moist with early morning dew. His neighbours' Lándo trees surrounded the open green area, acting as the hamlets focal point. Pride of place taken by their newly built fountain, standing in the middle. Others of his tribe were beginning to appear at their den entrances, going about their daily business. All variously dressed in shades of greens and browns, melding in with the forest background.

His closest right-hand neighbour came out of his dwelling. Sáor, the tribe's cheery carpenter called out, 'Starting the day a bit early, Morác?'

'Things to do—people to see. You know,' Morác responded cordially and kept walking. A kópi whistle-grunted out of sight, to the left, and he felt the delicate tendrils of its thought nuzzle him; then another. Morác had an intuitive relationship with all kópis of his tribe; they instinctively took to him, and he returned the compliment. Around the base of Bróda's Lándo tree he spied Wómak's kópis, both cautiously sniffing bark for markings. Bróda was Morác's other neighbour, to the left. Morác greeted the kópis with a high-pitched grunt; they whistled back at him, the ridges of spines on their backs quivering gently with excitement.

He heard Wómak give a high-pitched grunt at the kópis, calling them. Wómak waved at Morác from the entrance of his Lándo tree, the tree being situated to the left of the warriors' quarters. Morác waved a salutation back with his free hand. Wómak was the leading warrior of Morác's tribe, at two and a half cubits tall—a quiet giant—almost prone to surliness. A wave was going to be the limit of his expressiveness, especially this time of the morning.

Morác continued across the grassy clearing until he came to the wooden fountain. He reached into the cool water and wiped his brow with his wet hand. The fountain supplied the hamlets drinking water. On he went until in a few more strides he reached Bréac's Lándo tree. He heard Scéna, Bréac's whinging wife, shouting inside their den, berating the querulous Bréac over a perceived injustice, an annoyance she probably brought on herself by her disagreeable nature. As he skirted Bréac's tree, the Beast within spasmed, making him look back yearningly at the circle of Lándo trees surrounding the clearing, at the comfortable dens of his fellow tribesmen. He thought, *This dark stalking Beast is an abomination. I could easily have done without it. One way or another I think our comfortable lives are to end. How on Kálar am I expected to finish my sorcery studies?* Into his consciousness, from the depths of his essence, these thoughts overflowed. As yet, he was unable to tell where the Beast came from, or how it arrived, but its defilement of him was as real as the forest floor beneath his feet.

Morác picked up the loud thuds and impacts reverberating from Gárn's pottery as Gárn kneaded the day's clay on the clay-table. As he neared, the din got louder. Gárn was already preparing the clay, working away in his workshop, making the next batch of ceramics. The potter with his den and workshop were secreted away in a clearing, close by the path Morác was on, a distance from the hamlet proper. The pots were needed but there was always the fear of fire hazard from his open air kiln.

Past Gárn's, for twelve cubits, the path paralleled the narrow river. The watercourse ran from the forest, down by Gárn's and then by Súdair's tannery. In the patch between the pottery and the tannery, a number of people were early morning bathing. Morác saw three, or was it four, heads bobbing in the water. Further downstream from the swimmers, a couple of women were already washing clothing. To his left, he walked past the tall wooden water wheel, set into the riverbank—lifting the water to the wooden aqueduct transporting water through the clay pipes to the fountain. Morác waved to the bathers, who noticed him and waved back.

Every measured step took him further away from the hamlet along the half seen footpath into the canopy-covered forest. All around sounds of insects hummed reassuringly. Birds were creating their usual morning melodies, defending territories, calling for mates, hunting for food. Resin smells reassured him The Wheel of Seasons turned and spring had arrived with the sap rising strongly. The suns were stretching fingers through the gaps in the branches, fleetingly snatching at Morác through the shadows. Scattered amongst the fallen branches, light green tufts of grass showed themselves with mossy patches. Morác walked calmly along the overgrown path; a path seldom used by others going on their business. He was purposeful, heading to the glade acting as an open-air temple, sacred to his tribe. During the tribe's high ceremonials his fellow kinsfolk gathered there, led by Morác as the shamán of the tribe, officiating on their behalf. The celebrations occurred six times a season, the rest of the time they avoided the place out of respect due to a place of high power.

He entered deeper into the forest, the keenness of his senses intensifying. Past a number of fallen tree trunks to the left, laying half buried under rotting leaves and overgrown moss. To the right, he heard a couple of Wood Paloóns trilling to each other amidst the hubbub of bird chatter emanating from the forest. Around he viewed the varied green vastness of nature's rebirth, immersing himself within the vibrancy of Spring's preoccupation with growth and renewal. The season of beginnings—it would mean marriages to be performed, the young to be initiated into adulthood. He would have to officiate at the Fertility Festival. He bowed his head as he walked, to Aíne, source of all Being—both creator and creation—a closing of the sacred circle. She inspired the Wheel of Seasons to turn round the Eternal Path. But the Wheel of Seasons never travelled along the same path—each turn was different from its predecessor, as was each season. No sunrise was the same, no moonset identical—all travelled in the circumference of a larger sphere. This inspired Morác as he strode with purpose.

Emerging quietly into a clearing, he noticed a Caroó staring at him; four legged, mottled brown, large head on heavy shoulders. It turned away, knowing Morác to be friendly and continued grazing on Aíne's spring larder. Opposite, from a dense part of the forest, a pair of cold yellow eyes watched the foraging Caroó. Morác recognised a kóira eyeing its prey, readying to pounce. From a pouch around his waist he hastily drew a smidge of goddess dust and blew it at the kóira. The dust drifted across the clearing, carried by an uplifting breeze. The hungry kóira blinked a number of times at the Caroó, and then disappeared into the forest, forgetting its prey.

Looking around, Morác felt warmed by the suns; felt the suns drenching the glade with solar energy. He could see the green grass stretching upwards to the life-giving light. Morác went to a grey boulder by the Sacred Pool, placed Néra's bag of food by the base of the rock, and then sat taking his moccasins off. The pool was filled by a subterranean spring, the overflow feeding the stream. It followed the incline of the forest floor, flowing towards the hamlet, joining a bigger stream which ran by Gárn's tree and acted as the water supply. The reeds at the edge of the pool swayed gently just as they had always done. On a previous visit he laid out a number of twigs near the water's ledge, an arm's length away to Morác's right, shaping them into symbols. A few memory aids to help Morác's mind lift itself to a higher state of awareness, to soothe and smooth the energies running through his body. In preparation for the oncoming trance, Morác made himself conscious of the gathering smells passing his nostrils; the algae's mustiness mixed with water vapour burnt off the surface of the pool. He noted the little air currents drifting through the glade, smelt the heavy aroma of leaves left over from winter. The earth and grass separated into distinct odours, wafting up his nostrils; one odour deep with fertility, the other mingled with a tang of fresh spring grass, altogether a subtle bouquet tickling his senses.

The boulder he was sitting on moved into his awareness; the dark grey granite charmed there so many years ago, placed by the pool for just this purpose. Under his hands and fingers he felt the grain and hardness of the stone, pondering on the years it took to form. Thousands? Millions? Under his bare feet, his toes curled into the young grass greedily soaking up the sun, tickling his feet; this year's growth temporarily shaded out by another life-form. Then, from the depths of his mind, he sensed the emergence of the Beast. Controlling himself, he looked into the pool, gazing at his reflection staring back at him, his crystal amulet hanging from his golden necklace. It was thus the ancient legend of the Schánda sprang unbidden into his mind. He shuddered and sighed as he released his control, and the Beast came forth, gushing into his consciousness. Darkness enveloped him within its bosom. The trance proper held him. He heard the distant snipping sound...then as it got nearer, more intense snipping...nearer still, louder, turning into a crunching noise. Abruptly—Morác beheld the ancient terror of his kind. In his mind's eye he saw clearly the fierce large carnivorous insects darkening the horizon on their long bicentennial mating march, heading south to the distant Golden Sea.

In the far north, on the edges of the tundra, a seething mass of black spread itself across the wide horizon. The leaderless swarm—was on the move south. At the rear of the insect, the abdomen had a large stinger, able to settle any argument with any life-form. They were huge, cubit high poisonous creatures with large biting claws on the side of their mouths, able to crush a Bólani leg with consummate ease. They were being driven by their genes to retrace a course back to their breeding grounds on the shores of the Golden Sea.

The schánda's two hundred year life-cycle now impelled them on their long march, circumventing every obstacle, climbing, forcing, being shoved, ravenously eating any creature foolish enough to get in their way. When the schánda reach the sea, they mate, dig holes in the sand, deposit their eggs, and finally die.

2

COMMUNITY MEETING

In the glade, the previous day, Morác opened his mind to the full menace of the Schánda the Forest People were to encounter. The core of the legend revealed a horror, an unstoppable carnivorous procession intent on eating their way to their mating grounds in the South. Morác returned hurriedly, relating the event to Bróda, the tribes Custodian. He described graphically his experience and explained the implications.

Bróda, appalled the loathsome nightmares were caused by a collective unconscious memory of carnivorous insects, asked Morác, 'What on Kálar are we going to do?'

'You're the Custodian,' Morác told him. 'I want you to call an emergency meeting of the tribe.'

*   *   *

A two hundred year life-cycle was long enough for people to overlook the previous devastation in their efforts to live a normal life, select partners, and bring up younglings. Then, endure old age. When the cycle reasserted, the Schánda again trampled the life of the tribe, the horror surfacing from the subliminal rhythmic memory of the Bólani, reactivating the primed unconscious with disgusting dreams.

Morác's nightmares, the trip to the glade, the trance, were all embedded in the initiation rituals every aspiring shamán endured. The story of the Schánda was passed down through preceding soothsayers by a shrouded subliminal trigger implanted by each predecessor. Morác had been put into a deep trance by Fándin, the then tribal medicine man, who himself went into a momentary hypnotic state, automatically reciting the tradition from his forebears. He whispered the legend, implanting a hypnotic trigger. Neither bequeather nor recipient was consciously aware they had passed on the tradition.

Only when the bicentennial cycle completed its revolution did the dreams invade the primed unconscious of the Bólani tribe again. So it was, in uncountable generations the reoccurring horror embedded itself into the genetic make-up of the forest dwellers.

*   *   *

At Bróda's command, the day following Morác's trance, the tribe assembled at noon on the green, bringing three legged stools. Long ago, there had been a mighty Lándo tree standing at Morác's end of the green; it burned down after being struck by lightning. The stump was levelled and now acted as a platform for tribal meetings. Bróda sat on it, his two kópis at his feet, officiating as the tribe's Custodian, flanked on his right by Wómak, Morác on his left. Bróda stood, took a deep breath, and began— 'I've been asked to convene this meeting by our shamán, Morác. We've all been having nasty dreams lately and Morác tells me he's had a vision into what is causing those disgusting dreams. Morác will explain.'

As Bróda sat, Morác rose. A murmur went through the tribe. A bird shrieked in the distance, disturbed by panicky animals. He looked at the forty-four assembled faces, pausing, watching younglings being bounced on their mother's laps, calming his thoughts. He listened to the coughing and wheezing from the older members of the tribe, wondering if this was to be the last meeting before the impending disaster. 'Friends! I have terrible news. If the majority hadn't had the dreadful nightmares, I might be tempted to soften what I have to say with a light banter—in the circumstances, that would be wrong. We're facing the worst crisis this tribe's ever encountered. It's likely we're going to have to leave our dens, our surroundings, our comfortable existence, and flee for our lives.' He paused to let his words sink in; a sea of shocked faces stared back at him.

Stillness descended on the assembly, punctuated by the background noises coming from the disturbed forest. The gentle splash of water filled the fountain. Bróda shuffled his chair impatiently, disturbing his kópis.

'I'm sorry to be the bearer of such tidings, but we'll face this *together*, and I hope we'll find the strength to survive the ordeal. I've been to the Sacred Glade and there, all became clear to me in a vision. Coming at us from the north is a huge swarm of carnivorous insects our forefathers named the Schánda. They have deadly poisonous stingers in their tail—and if that wasn't enough, they also have powerful large claws enough to crunch a person's leg. The snipping in your dreams comes from those claws. In my vision I've seen them.' A judder went through Morác at the memory of the image.

'If there were only a few, we might try to defend our dens, but there's thousands, probably millions, spread out on a *long* wide front. The swarm knows no fear and nothing survives its voracious march. No point in hiding in our Lándo trees; they'll go through the bark. With their numbers, they'll bring the trees down. No creature that runs, walks, or crawls, can escape once they're within reach of the swarm. They leave the vegetation, but not much else.'

'Why're they coming this way?' shouted Scéna in a whining tone. 'Why can't they leave us alone?'

'Maybe they'll go round. Maybe we won't have to move at all,' added her husband, Bréac, querulously.

Morác looked stern, 'They *are* coming. The only two questions we need answered are how many days away are they? And how long we've got before we have to run? Let me be clear!

'The Schánda are on their two hundred year mating march to their breeding grounds, South on the shores of the Golden Sea. They're not after us—we're just in their way. We can't escape to either side. The breadth of their swarm is enormous; our choice is limited to fleeing Southwards, *ahead* of their march. Once we reach the Golden Sea, we will probably have to cross it—only then will we be safe.'

From the front row Súdair bellowed, 'How do you know all this?' The tribe's tanner always did have a loud voice.

In contrast, Morác said quietly, 'I can't rightly tell you. The vision in the glade seems to have opened up part of my memory; a sort of information store on what's to happen—on the Schánda and its lifecycle. I think Fándin had a touch to do with that—I can't be sure. Look! The point of this meeting is, for me to tell you, probably within a week, maybe even less, we'll have to grab what we can carry and run before the coming swarm.'

A collective groan came from the audience, followed by a sullen silence.

'*I can't leave my Stándy to those insects*,' wailed Wólni's wife, Málina. She herded tame Stándy grazing near her tree, providing all the tribe's wool. She tended her "pets" as if they were her younglings.

'I'm hoping we can take the Stándy with us,' Morác reassure her.

Suddenly, from within the crowd a high-pitched scream was heard. All eyes turned to Sáor's wife, and found Émer fallen asleep—plunging straight into a nightmare. Nobody asked *what* she had been dreaming, caused her to

15

scream. Nobody needed to—most had experienced the same dream. Émer was suitably embarrassed when shaken awake. '*I'm sorry*,' she sobbed repeatedly whilst Sáor tried to comfort her.

From another part of the crowd Gárn shouted, 'What of my pots; my kiln? How am I going to survive?'

'Would you rather stay and die with your kiln?' asked Morác. 'Who would look after Cára, your wife: and what of your three younglings? Wherever we finally settle, you can build your kiln again. The main thing is, stick together and *pull* together in this crisis.'

'How can we be sure Morác's vision is real?' That contribution came from Ádna, Úbor's wife, the tribe's tailor.

Úbor gave his wife a dig in the ribs, followed by a stern look.

'*The vision is real enough*,' Morác said angrily. 'Can you doubt your own dreams? You heard Émer just now—was her scream *real*?'

Sitting at the front, next to Súdair, her loud husband, Shúta asked Morác, 'Are we going to leave for good?' She stared directly into his eyes, seeking a truthful response.

'To be honest, I don't have all the answers—I wish I did. I can't see clearly into the future,' Morác answered her, locking eyes with her.

'Not even with your sorcerer's skills?' she parried.

'Not even with my skills,' Morác told her, looking steadily at her.

'If we don't know where we're going, how are we going to feed ourselves?' Bréac demanded. He refused to accept the need to leave.

Bróda interrupted, 'We must to put this to a vote. The afternoon's nearly gone. Morác! Have you done?'

Morác turned to Bróda, 'Almost!' He scrutinised the meeting, 'Go back to your dens, and gather only the things you can comfortably carry. Remember, we'll be trying to stay ahead of a fast moving swarm and anything you don't need will only slow you. If it slows you down—it may kill you. Bear it in mind when you include items you think you value. *Are they worth your life*? I expect we'll have to move this week; next week at the latest. Be brave and have heart. Pray to Aíne for our safe journey. Together we'll make it. Our forefathers survived, there's no reason we can't do what they managed. Over to you Custodian.' Morác sat.

Bróda rose and waited for the meeting to settle. 'I'm putting this to a vote. That's how our tribe makes decisions; anybody voting against this has to be insane. Raise your hands if you vote to go on this journey.' He looked at the hands going up. 'Those against?' A hand went up, slowly followed by another hand. 'Mútani and Máda. I think we can all understand why you voted against. At your phase of life, a long trek through unknown country can't be a prospect you'd look forward to, but we can't leave you behind, not to be eaten by those things.' He still couldn't force himself to name them. 'That settles it. We go! It's just a matter of when. If there's nothing else…' he looked at the downcast faces, 'I bring this meeting to a close.'

People rose, and started to disperse amongst a lot of complaints and chatter, aimed at no one in general. A sort of quiet hysteria hung above the settlement, dissolving through the ether into the forest. Everyone went to their dens anxious, mulling over the information given. Bróda sent Wómak to the Warriors' Tree, holding Morác back.

*   *   *

In the warriors' quarters, tempers frayed due to a lack of sleep—then overflowed into terse comments over nothing, heated arguments over even less. The warriors were attempting to fight the loathsome dreams they were having, as were most of the tribe. Their weapon: denying sleep. Unfortunately, these tactics were turning in on themselves; earlier, a few ended in bruising scraps. The warriors' quarters were bachelor quarters, which didn't help their frustration. Their Lándo tree was the largest in the settlement, a den just big enough to billet ten warriors. Currently there were eleven warriors quartered in the tree and the cramped space further aggravated the tensions.

Bróda, the Custodian of the Bólani, threw the front door open to the warriors' quarters and made his presence felt —standing square in the doorway. A hush descended as his large frame sauntered into the middle of the den. '*What the Húli's all this!*' he boomed at the assemblage. 'Nothing to do?' He glared at those present. 'We'll soon settle that. *Wómak*! Get all your men together. I'm sending you on an expedition. This is in earnest, so listen carefully. We need to know how far these schánda are from the hamlet. We especially need to know how fast they're moving and if they're heading directly for us? Is there the remotest possibility they'll *miss* the community? If they *might* miss, then by how much? Have you got all that?'

'Yes Bróda.' Wómak's surliness disappeared and he suddenly came alive. The opportunity for action drove fatigue from him. Finally they had a tangible action into which they could put their energies.

'I've consulted Morác and he says you should go north-east,' Bróda continued, 'as far as the edge of the forest, out towards the Grónda. You'll be on our traditional land all the way, but it's a long trek. If you meet others on our land, don't challenge them as you normally do, try to find out what they know; well, you know what I mean.'

'Yes Bróda.'

'And Wómak! Leave a couple of warriors behind just in case.'

'Right you are Custodian.' Wómak turned to the attentive warriors, 'You heard the Custodian! Get your things together and rations for at least a week. Fully armed and ready to move in an hour. Make your farewells short.'

Bróda left the warriors' quarters with Wómak. 'Thanks,' Wómak said. 'The inactivity was driving us crazy.'

'Thought it might be,' answered Bróda. The Custodian turned right and went back to his Lándo tree. Wómak veered to the left for his den, to say good-bye to Ganúra. The Custodian and his Deputy had dens on either side of the Warriors' Tree. It came with their respective posts.

Wómak entered his den and was pounced on by his kópis, closely followed by his wife. 'Down you two,' he commanded the kópis. They nuzzled him and then went back to their separate baskets.

Ganúra complemented Wómak physically, she was just as tall and almost as muscular, which is why they were attracted in the first place. 'You're off again on one of your jaunts,' she accused him, red hair flying as she shook her head in dismay.

'Look Ganúra! That's what I do. You knew that when you joined me. With the coming threat, I may be gone more than both you and I would care, but I have little choice in the matter.'

'Curse this for wedlock!' she exclaimed in frustration. 'I was hoping to see more of you than this. I really *miss* you, you big hulk,' she pouted, unbecoming in such a large woman. Onlookers might have expected Ganúra to grab Wómak by the scruff of the neck, march him up to the bedroom—instead of simply pouting. In a sense, it was Wómak's fault for having a strong silent nature that in turn brought out the possessive adolescent girl in Ganúra. Anyway, she would rather kiss and cuddle than fight.

Wómak stopped, went over to Ganúra, put his arm around her waist, pulled her to him and kissed his wife full on the mouth, taking her breath away and removing the sting from her reproach.

'You big lummox,' she said gently; flustered by his gruff approach.

'Now will you let me continue? I have to hurry to prepare for a week's hike. Ganúra! Please, can you prepare the rations while I dig up my weapons?'

'All right, go upstairs and find your weapons. I'll have the rations ready when you come down.'

Wómak climbed to the top den of the tree where he kept his blowpipes, knives and axes. He put his well-waxed cape and hood inside the overnight groundsheet, just in case the weather turned. He took his best blowpipe out of the cupboard, not the prettiest or most decorated, but the sturdiest and straightest. At the same time he grabbed two quivers of darts for the blowpipe. From the wall rack he took three knives, one for the sheath to tuck in his belt, one for each of his boot sheaths. Finally, he removed two axes from the rack, a mark of the seriousness with which he treated this coming trip. One axe went into his belt; the other was rolled into the groundsheet with an extra pair of moccasins and socks. He stood back and consulted his mental checklist; *Have I missed anything? No!* he decided, *I'm ready.*

Back downstairs, Ganúra readied a knapsack with his provisions. He came to her and kissed her gently.

'I'll be thinking of you all the time,' he assured her. 'What I want is for you to clear a corner of the den in the meantime, and pile there all the things we might need to take with us if we have to leave suddenly.'

'What? You mean so we're ready for the journey Morác talked of?' She was more alarmed by what she'd heard at the community meeting than she cared to admit.

'Yes! I mean for a long trip.' He looked into her face, trying to encourage her with his eyes.

'It won't come to that surely?'

'It will. You heard what Morác said. It's best to be ready.' He held her in his arms and continued in her ear, 'When you've done, throw half of the stuff away. Remember we'll have to carry that lot. Make a list of the things you're taking. Bróda can use it for the others.'

'I hope you're wrong; I really do.'

'So do I.' He released her and picked up the knapsack. 'I have to go,' he said huskily. 'I'll think of you tonight—out in the forest.'

'And I of you—'

For a moment he looked solemnly into her eyes, and then smiled reassuringly. Opening the door, he left, without looking back, to join the others. Outside, he turned right, walking briskly to the Warriors' Tree.

*   *   *

Unstoppable in their urge to trek south, to reach their mating ground, shoving, pushing, climbing over the slower ones, the relentless swarm hurried over the cold terrain, trampling everything they came across. It was a mass of hairy bodies, snippers clicking, desperately searching for food. Those that succumbed were trampled, gobbled up by those nearest, and eagerly torn to pieces, in a frantic attempt to satiate gnawing hunger. This was survival at its most primitive. Instinct dominated, driving the swarm forward to its final destination.

3

SCOUTING THE SCHÁNDA

The warriors milled around on the green outside their quarters, talking, waiting. It was late in the afternoon and the suns were beginning to dip towards the treetops. Most of them were happy to be doing; all were armed to the teeth. Wómak went among them and brought the group to order. 'I have bad news for two of you. Scória! Dalán! You're to stay behind as guards. Sorry! Bróda's orders.'

The two moved aside, out of the group, long faces showing their disappointment. They said nothing. They understood the sense of protecting the hamlet; only they'd wished it were someone else.

'Right! The rest of you, gather round.' A huddle enveloped Wómak with all the warriors squeezing in tight so as not to miss anything. They were finally going to be doing and their faces showed eagerness. 'We're heading northeast towards Grónda country. If for any reason we're separated, we meet where the Bólani, Grónda and Hánum boundaries join. Clear? If that's not possible, head back.'

The remaining nine warriors all nodded.

'I want to make sure everyone has an extra quiver of darts; so check right now.' Wómak peered at them. 'Ládra! Némed!' He glared at the two. 'I can see from your faces you haven't. Go back inside and get an extra quiver.'

The two briskly disappeared towards the door of the warriors' quarters.

'I want the rest of you to check each other's equipment, rations and the like. Make sure you're thorough.' Wómak stood back and let them get on with his orders.

Ládra and Némed quickly reappeared with their extra quivers and meekly joined the others in performing their tasks.

'All right! Fúlmon! When we leave, you take point with Máyo. I want you well out in front. If you come across anything, I'd like warning. The rest of you; keep silent and stay sharp. Robán! You bring up the rear. Right, let's go.' The ten warriors moved swiftly out in single file, the column bearing off to the right, heading out towards where Morác said the schánda were coming. During what was left of daylight they travelled well-worn paths the warriors mostly knew by heart. They moved rapidly until it was too dangerous to go any further in the descending gloom. They had gone five leagues before Wómak ordered a halt for the night. 'We've travelled long after we should have stopped,' Wómak remarked to Robán, who came to report.

'Have you noticed there's a lot more animal activity than usual in the forest?' Robán asked him.

'Strange! I was going to make the same comment. Tomorrow night we'll make camp earlier. Oh! Get one of the lads downwind to build the latrine and erect the guide rope.'

Robán called Láeg over to build the latrine and told the burly Píngo to go ahead and build the fire. Píngo was a remarkable member of the tribe. Nature had made him even larger than Wómak; an albino with a sour disposition. It was as if he was aware of being a freak despite being a bit slow in the head. He was the group's fire maker, who found it difficult to squat on his haunches on the ground, yet that is what he did in a clearing, cutting out a square of turf from the ground in front of him. He removed the turf and put it aside. Next he laid a platform of green sticks in the hole and built up a pyramid of four sticks balanced against each other. He added to the pyramidal structure with more sticks, leaving a hole to one side with enough space underneath to put lit tinder. Then he took dry grass from a pouch, trimmed dry bark into tiny pieces with a knife and buffed the trimmings into powdery tinder. He made a ball of the tinder twice the size of his fist. Using the bow and drill method, Píngo rotated a hardwood spindle on a softwood base above the tinder. This friction ignited the tinder and he placed it in the hole under the pyramid of sticks, blowing gently at first, then harder to encourage the little flame. To the tinder he added kindling, dry leaves and twigs, building up the flame within the pyramid until the pile caught hold. Main fuel followed small fuel and a surge of flames told the rest of the warriors the campfire was ready for the group's cook.

Just then, Fúlmon returned from point duty having left Máyo twenty cubits out on the perimeter of the camp as sentry. 'Yo, Fúlmon! Come and tell us what's ahead,' Wómak encouraged.

Fúlmon hurried over to where Wómak was still talking to Robán. 'I probably went further than you ordered; the way seems to be clear. Only—I think I had company, and I don't mean Máyo. I had the feeling eyes were watching me, trailing my progress. They stayed out of sight, but you know when a person's stare bores into the back of your neck. Máyo tends to agree we're being followed. We've no idea who it might be. My guess it's one of the Hánum tribe. The other weird thing is there are lots of animals heading down south, spooked.'

'Good! Thanks Fúlmon. You've done well. We were just saying the same thing.' Wómak scratched his red hair thoughtfully. 'You were followed—so close to the hamlet, hey? What are they up to? Robán, organise three sentry shifts tonight. Each watch had three sentries; two facing forward one facing where they'd come from. Now let's see what Umára's cooking up for supper, as if I didn't know.'

Uílin, Umára's tubby cooking assistant added large fuel to the fire and built a large tepee structure from three stout sticks above the fire, hanging a large pot filled with water from its top; the beginnings of a wild millet evening porridge. Umára, the trek cook believed too much meat bloated the warrior and made him sluggish on a march. His practice was to feed them a hot wild cereal porridge in the evening spiced with herbs, fungi and lichen; a hot porridge in the morning with sweet sap from the Orel tree poured over it, and a cold cereal at midday. The warriors had biscuits for the occasional snack if they desperately needed one; and if they ate those, they'd be digging into their emergency rations. After those present had eaten supper, three others took the place of the sentries so they could also eat.

'Right, now listen up.' Wómak began to settle the camp before sleep. 'Máyo, Ládra and Némed, when you've finished eating, start the lean-to. All of you check your gear, repair anything needing it. Tonight, I want you all to put a smudge of extra poison on your darts. Be careful. We won't have time when we need to use them. When you've finished, hang your packs in the nearby trees.'

The three lean-to builders went to work cutting down the poles for the group's shelter for the night. The shelter had to be built nine cubits wide, a warrior deep, and two cubits high, with an open side in the lee of the wind. Big enough to sleep seven warriors. The poles were tied together with fronds and brushwood was woven into the sidewalls. Sticks were laid criss-cross on the roof and brushwood woven into the roof frame to provide protection from the dew and rain. It was a nightly performance every time they stopped to bivouac, so everyone was expert at it. Within half an hour, the fire was doused and the camp settled. Everybody bedded down in their blankets. Wómak lay awake for a time, listening to the night sounds coming from around him. Even then, more animals were on the move than normal. He felt others nearby listening to the pseudo silence, and then a gentle snoring chorus invaded the nearby stillness.

Wómak's thoughts were with Ganúra. Each time he left her alone, he was riddled with guilt the first night out. He'd have liked to stay with her, hug her, and hold her in his arms. However, the warrior in him needed to be with his men, out here sharing their adventures, sleeping rough. As he drifted off, he was amused the contradiction was to be resolved from unexpected quarters; the threat of the schánda would soon put Ganúra beside him in the rough outdoors.

During the third sentry shift, Fúlmon threw out a loud challenge. Immediately following, Umára was heard shouting —then Uílin yelled from the other side of the camp. In short time, all the warriors had awoken and were fanning out towards the commotion. Wómak found Umára twenty cubits away from the camp, facing northwards, crouching near a tree, straining to hear the noises coming from deep in the forest.

'Fúlmon's in hot pursuit; told me to stay here,' Umára reported.

'Do you know what it was?' Wómak whispered.

'No. I heard Fúlmon yell, and then he was off. I've no idea what he's chasing.'

'He'll catch whatever it is. Once he gets wind of prey, he's like a kópi; tenacious to the point of obstinacy.'

They crouched, listening to the receding hullabaloo disturbing the nighttime forest. The distant noise stopped as suddenly as it begun. A kind of silence reclaimed the night as the two crescent moons came out from behind the clouds, lighting up the lamps of many eyes, sucking up the colours. The murky darkness abruptly illuminated, creating an eerie half-shadowy world around them. Moonlight muddled their night vision, and they could see only if they squinted hard into the dimness lit by the occasional moonbeam reaching bellow the canopy. Just then they glimpsed, moving noiselessly towards them, a blurred outline of a person lit momentarily by a moonbeam.

A quiet whistle-grunt came from the shadow, the forest recognition call of the Bólani.

'That you Fúlmon?' Wómak whispered.

'It is!' came back a voice they recognised.

Fúlmon appeared, squatting on his haunches beside Wómak. He was breathing harder than usual.

'Damned slippery, that one,' he said in an undertone.

'Any idea who it was?' Wómak asked.

'No. I thought *I* could manoeuvre in the forest; whoever it was, and I take my hat off to them, outdid me. I never got close.' The frustration was evident in his voice.

'I have a feeling we'll know soon enough,' voiced Wómak. 'Well, let's get back to the camp. The night's almost done.'

Wómak called those warriors who ran into the forest, back to the lean-to. What was left of the night went quickly, if fitfully. Dawn fingered its way through the canopy and Umára encouraged them to rise, calling the warriors to the morning meal. He mixed extra sweet sap into their porridge to boost their energy. The cook was always eager to start the day, was the first one up and always in good humour. The warriors gathered round the re-lit fire, warming themselves, gobbling the hot sweet porridge.

After they had eaten, Wómak stood and clapped for attention. 'Whoever our visitor was last night; it ought to make us more vigilant. Fúlmon! Máyo! Back on point. Keep a sharp lookout. Report every two hours. The rest of you, break camp.'

*　　*　　*

Back on the Grónda trail, the column moved with added urgency, trying to outrun any followers. They put distance between themselves and pursuers, pushing along at a steady trot, treading familiar paths. Overhead, the two suns beat strongly on the backs of the warriors. Whilst the column moved northeast, they passed animals going in the opposite direction.

At midday, they stopped for meal and rest, before pressing on. The pace picked up by early afternoon, their strides developing an easy rhythm. Since they were travelling on well-known paths, they put speed into their gait; but that would change when they hit less familiar territory.

On one of the visits from the scouts, Máyo reported they had come across tracks of a pack of kóira. Fúlmon sent him back to warn the column. The kóira hunted in packs of fifteen or more, were intelligent carnivores, and when hungry, had little fear of people. The tribe's tame kópis were a distant relative of these ferocious beasts. The danger to the column was commensurate to the hunger of the pack. The kóira might try to pick off Robán, who was bringing up the rear, so Wómak stopped the column to alert Robán he ought to keep a sharp lookout for the savage beasts.

Later in the afternoon, Wómak came across a sign from the scouts they should look into the forest to the right. An arrow made from sticks pointed to a Y branch stuck in the ground, near a tree. Wómak sent a warrior to have a look; noticing he went unusually silent. He reported back that a half eaten body of a youth lay near the stick.

Wómak went to look himself and found the mauled, mutilated corpse of a young lad. He could not have been more than fifteen. His throat had been torn out; the innards chewed and strewn around. The corpse had been stripped by the kóira of its flesh. There was little doubt that it had been the kóira's work. The signs were unmistakable. From the tracks all around, the boy had put up an immense struggle. The mangled head told the age and sex of the victim.

There had been one other person with him in the struggle, although there was no sign of the other person. Maybe she had escaped? The lightness and size of the other person's tracks, suggested it was a woman. The warriors buried the remains of the boy and Wómak said a few words to Aíne, asking her to deal kindly with the youth's lemur.

'We'd better get on,' Wómak told those present. 'I hope I don't need to tell anyone to keep their eyes peeled for these kóira. They must be hungry to have dared to go for a person. It'll be wiser not to travel at dusk, so we'll go two more leagues before pitching camp.'

That day they'd travelled twelve leagues northeast; Wómak was pleased with the progress. The problem was, the farther they went, the more difficult their passage. Paths were less used, forcing them to hack through the bushy growths. It slowed progress; and hacking through the forest was tiring work.

In contrast, the path northwest to the cave-dwelling Kárti was a highway, a flourishing trade route, selling, bartering all sorts of metal products. Everybody needed metal implements, tools, weapons. South of the Kárti were the Nólki. The Bólani traded preserves and medicines with the Nólki in exchange for coarse glass for their windows. Trade was the cord that tied the neighbours together. In comparison, the path to the Grónda, who lived on the treeless tundra, who seldom traded with, and had little contact with the Bólani, was almost non-existent. The lack of a clear path made the going tough for the column.

That night, in spite of the turning of the wheel of seasons and the onset of Spring, they felt the beginnings of a cooler change in temperature as they approached their goal. A biting northerly wind made itself felt even in the depths of the forest. They had one more night before reaching the edge of the Bólani lands on the following morning. Bólani country was a third wider than its length, measuring eighty-eight leagues by sixty-two, situated in the northerly region of the temperate zone of Kálar.

During the evening meal Umára added a sliver of rehydrated fish to each warrior's plate. It was a gesture aimed at topping up their protein requirements, lost during the day's run. All the warriors, apart from sentries, were gathered, sitting around the campfire.

Robán, second in charge to Wómak, was sitting next to him and queried the next day's plan. 'We ought to hit the Márka river at around noon?'

'That's what I'm aiming at,' Wómak told him.

'Then another seven leagues and we're at Grónda boundary.'

'That's right.'

'You think we're going to see them?'

'You mean the Schánda?'

'Yeah.' An involuntary shudder went through Robán.

Wómak said noncommittally, 'We'll see what we see.'

'At least the nightmares have stopped. Nobody's reported any since we started this trip.'

'Yeah! That's a bonus as far as I'm concerned. Look Robán; see if we can get bedded down in half an hour. We've got a big day ahead of us.'

'Right you are.'

'Sentries rotated? New sentries posted?'

'Yes, all done.'

'Good. I'm going to turn in. See you in the morning.'

With that, Wómak sauntered off to the night's lean-to and got under his cover. He lay worrying of Ganúra, of their future. A sudden melancholy overcame him and he wished it would go away. It began when Robán mentioned the schánda; it was an oppressive weight that descended on his shoulders. The strong surliness had flipped into a depressive mood, driven by the uncertainty of what was to become of him and Ganúra; their dreams; their aspirations. *"Curse this for wedlock,"* she had complained the other day. *I think she's going to look back and see a time of bliss; compared to what's coming.* With that final thought, he drifted off into the arms of oblivion.

The next morning brought the dulcet tones of Umára's voice urging them to "get it whilst it was still hot". He meant the morning meal. The third sentry-watch had been rotated, had come in, were already seated, eating. Other warriors were rolling up their bedding, dismantling the lean-tos', heading for Umára's cooking pot. The suns had risen and were making themselves felt on the canopy above. Birds were enjoying another day's courtship, letting Kálar know of their exultation.

Camp was struck in a spirit of optimism and they were soon back on the trail, the column again hacking their way through the undergrowth. Píngo took lead, his enormous height giving him extra leverage when it came to wielding an axe. The Point-Warrior often needed changing to spread the strain of cutting through the little used trail.

4

A DEATH TOO SOON

When the column of warriors departed the hamlet, Morác set out to see Bróda. He found Émana, the Custodian's wife, in a dismal vagary. Her mood swings always reacted to the behaviour of her outward looking partner. Conversely, Bróda adjusted his responses according to the business of his tribe. In peaceful times he was authoritative, kind and benign, but when a threat imposed itself, he became authoritarian and uncommunicative to her. Émana's mood then turned inwards, sinking like a stone and she would seek out others to console her.

She came to the door with a long face and told Morác, 'Sorry, I've no idea where Bróda's got to.'

'You look a bit down Émana, what's wrong?'

'*What's wrong?* You're not serious? My life is falling apart and you want to know what's wrong.'

'All our lives are falling apart, not just yours. You've got to pull yourself together and help Bróda. Weren't you listening to me at the meeting? We've got to help each other, that's the *only* way we're going to survive. Bróda's got enough on his plate without nursing you; you've got to put you own problems aside and help Bróda. For Aíne's sake, you're the Custodian's wife. The tribe looks up to you.'

At the appeal to her vanity she perked up, 'Do you think so? They look up to me? I suppose you're right—thanks Morác.'

'That's better. You're a strong woman, Émana. *Use* that inner strength. For what it's worth, I think we'll survive this calamity.' He began to turn away; her voice stopped him.

'I think Bróda said he wanted to see the carpenter. You could try there.'

'Thanks Émana. Are you prepared for the journey yet?'

'I'm just going to make a start. See you later.'

Morác crossed the green, passing to the left of the burnt out stump of the once mighty Lándo tree, reminding him of the recent meeting held there, then veered to the right for Sáor's den. The two suns were just dipping towards the treetops, preparing to enter the horizon for the night.

He noticed his fellow tribes-people dashing around on the far side of the green; others were standing about arguing. There was a lot of frantic activity boding well if it was directed towards leaving; or it could simply be a waste of time and energy. He determined to find out.

Morác noticed Émer, the cheery carpenter's wife, leaving her neighbour Wólni, heading for her den. Bróda was being let out by Sáor as Morác came up. Bróda stood aside and let Émer through; she hastily brushed past her husband.

'Hi Morác! Coming to see me?' Sáor asked.

'No! I need a word with Bróda first. I want to see you later though.'

Bróda waved a farewell at Sáor and Morác walked with him, skirting the green, going in the direction of Wómak's place.

'What can I do for you?' Bróda said good-naturedly.

'Are you aware what's happening in the forest?' Morác swept his hand in an arc.

'You mean a few panicky animals?'

'And don't you think they're trying to give us a message?'

'You're suggesting we should be on the move?'

'Have we *less* common sense than the animals? At least we ought to be ready to move as soon as the warriors return. I get the feeling no one's ready. There's a reluctance as if they're hoping this threat will disappear. Even you're not ready for the journey; I've just come from your den.'

Bróda looked angry at first, then abashed. He knew Morác was in the right.

'I've been busy,' he tried to excuse himself. Quickly changing the subject. 'If you're not too busy yourself you could go round the tribe and prompt them to get a move on. See Ganúra; she's made a list of essentials people ought to take. At this dithering rate the Schánda will be knocking on their door instead of you.'

'I was going to do that,' Morác said, peeved his former determination now had been turned into an indirect command.

'Don't take it too hard Morác. With the warriors gone, I've nobody to prevail upon—so for the moment, I've chosen you as my second authority.' Bróda was half joking, half serious.

Such is the lot of the shamán these days, Morác thought. 'Where have all the kópis gone?' Morác noticed the absence of his animal friends.

'They're with the sentries out fifty cubits facing the northeast.'

'Scória and Dalán?'

'Right!'

'Did you see if Sáor was ready?'

'That's not why I saw Sáor. I asked the carpenter to make a dozen of those long dart contraptions the Nólki are so fond of.'

'Bows and arrows?'

'We might need them on the journey. Not everyone's an expert with a blowpipe—the long dart contraptions are easier to master.'

'Are you sure? Well, it's your affair. So I'll have to go back to Sáor. Oh well! See you later.' Morác took his leave.

Bróda went to see if Ganúra was all right, maybe give her a few words of encouragement.

Morác headed towards his den, skirting the green to the left of the platform. He was looking forward to seeing Néra, having his evening meal. His stomach growled. Thus the day came to a close with warriors going full speed on reconnaissance and the rest of the people rushing around in a fretful mood, not yet believing in the calamity facing them.

Early next morning Morác crossed the green towards Gárn's pottery. As he passed Bréac's he reluctantly acknowledged he would have to interfere in the merchant's private affairs without being invited. If they were to be in close proximity on the journey, relying on each other, Bréac and his wife would have to be reconciled. Scéna's whining would have to stop and Bréac would have to cease bellyaching.

It only took a succession of minor annoyances to upset the cohesion of a travelling group—inevitably leading to disaster. They would have enough trouble staying ahead of the Schánda without having to cope with a bickering couple that really had little to complain of.

Coming round the potter's shed, Morác saw Gárn sitting on a bench with Cára, relaxing in the morning suns. Gárn held her round the shoulders, their backs against the shed wall; their three younglings playing ball in the front clearing. A girl eight seasons old and two twin boys ten seasons. A touching family scene, now under threat in the looming uncertainty.

'Hallo you two. Taking in the early suns?'

Gárn replied without any enthusiasm, 'Hallo Morác.'

'That's no way to treat a guest,' Cára rebuked him. 'Morác isn't the cause of you misery. He's here to help—aren't you?' She smiled at Morác.

The little girl came and tugged at Morác's hand, 'Uncle Morác—come and play with us,' she insisted.

Cára gave her a stern look. 'Gara! Leave Morác alone; he's come to talk to your father, haven't you?' She raised her eyebrows at Morác.

'I'll come and play in a while, when I've had a chat with your dad first,' Morác told the girl. He turned to Gárn, 'I'll do all I can to help you, but make no mistake; you must prepare to go—*by morning*. The Schánda will be here soon. Have you ever seen what a pack of kóira can do to people?'

'No.' Cára replied.

Gárn interposed, 'I have.'

'Well the kóira are polite eaters compared with the schánda. Think of the younglings and their future. You *are* their future, and the coming journey is the *road* to their future.'

Gárn removed his arm from around Cára's shoulder and stood up. 'All right. You've made your point. A bit brutally, but you've made it. We'll be ready by morning.'

'That's the way. You won't regret it.'

'Only what we can carry comfortably—right?'

'Right! We'll be moving fast; we can't take anything that'll slow us down.'

Gárn's demeanour changed and he smiled at Morác. 'I'm sorry—I apologise for my ill mannered welcome just now.'

'I know how hard you've worked to build this place up, Gárn—it's a wrench to leave, but it's for your own good; there's no other choice. The Schánda are not like anything you've ever come across; not the kóira; not the dárgh. Not like *anything*. Néra and I are no sucklings, but on no account would I stay behind to shake their claws.'

Cára disappeared into their den anticipating Gárn's next move. She knew her husband as a kind and considerate host; unlike his recent self. She knew his good nature would break through in the end.

Gárn stood looking at Morác, admiring Morác's insistence. The shamán was taking time out to cajole people into doing what was in their best interests anyway. It was a selfless act, done for the good of the community—he admired the altruism.

'Stay and have a morning meal with us. Let's make amends for the rude welcome. It's that time anyway.'

'Thanks; I will. I was going on to see Bréac, but I need fortifying for that visit.'

In no time, Cára called the kids in. Like all the Bólani tribe, they had comely pointed ears, hazel green eyes and vivid red hair. They came running, still playfully yelling and shouting at each other.

'Go to the wash-bowl and wash your hands,' Cára ordered, sending them back out. 'Morác, please come in and take your place.'

The meal was a simple affair with wild grass-seed pancakes, and lots of sweet sap from the Orel tree poured over wild berries, washed down with a herbal drink.

'That was delightful; it just hit the spot,' Morác told his hostess after the meal. 'Simply delicious.'

'If you can manage; there's more,' she insisted.

'I couldn't eat another thing. It's kind of you. Now, really; I must be going.' Morác stood up and turned to Gárn. 'Remember what I said.' He went to Cára and kissed her on the cheek. 'Thank you again for a lovely meal.' Gárn showed him to the door and Morác took his leave.

It was at times of emergencies, like the present, that Morác bemoaned the size of his tribe. If only the Bólani gestation period was shorter, they could have more young. Two years was a long time to carry a youngling, and the frequent miscarriages contributed to the inadequacy of their numbers. It made every life so precious, so much more in need of saving.

He decided to go back to Sáor before tackling Bréac, although Bréac was the closest. His excuse, he wanted to make sure Sáor understood the danger coming their way; to make sure they were getting ready. In reality, he was putting off his meeting with the two most unpleasant people in the community.

Émer opened the door with a smile, 'Good morning, Morác. What can I do for you?'

'Good morning Émer. Is Sáor around?'

'He's gone to the forest to cut wood for Bróda's things.'

'You mean the bows and arrows?'

'Who's that?' Émer's daughter Láila, called out from inside the den.

'It's Morác,' Émer told her over her shoulder. She turned back to Morác, 'Why they can't use blowpipes like the rest? I don't know. Blowpipes have always been good enough for the Bólani, until now.'

'The bows and arrows are for the likes of me who have never used a blowpipe. When do you expect him to return?'

'He said it would probably be in the afternoon.'

'I wanted to tell him to be ready to leave either tomorrow, or the next day at the latest—to be packed and prepared to go. So I'm telling you, for you to pass this on to Sáor. You're sensible people, you know we must go. You've had the dreams yourself. A look of concern replaced the polite smile on his face. We can't stay here. Our safety lies in fleeing the brutes. Do you understand?'

'I promise we'll be ready; I'll pass your message on.'

'Thanks Émer.'

Morác left Émer and hurried along the bottom of the green, past Wólni's and Úbor's, coming upon Bréac's. On approaching the door he could hear Scéna's whining voice telling Bréac she "wasn't going to listen to a lot of rubbish. It was all nonsense Morác was spreading of a threat." She "didn't believe a word of it."

Well, at least they're talking about it, thought Morác. *That's a start.*

He knocked on the door. Inside, an abrupt silence.

Bréac opened the door. 'Morác, how *nice* to see you,' he enthused with glib insincerity. 'We were just talking of you.'

'May I come in?'

'But of course. Come in; come in.'

Morác entered and found himself in a comfortable den; rugs, good furniture, with a number of the most beautiful woodcarvings he had ever seen decorously placed in prominent spots. There were various expensive knick-knacks hanging on the den wall. The impression was of a well off couple that had little to complain of. They had no younglings to lavish their energies on, so indulged themselves in gathering various expensive bric-à-bracs, surrounding themselves with things as surrogates and constantly squabbling, using contention to substitute for affection.

This was the first time in years he had been inside— preferring to avoid the many invitations. The tribe had to *deal* with the merchant; otherwise they avoided any social contact, if they could.

'Herbal?' Bréac asked.

'That would be appreciated,' Morác responded politely.

'Scéna; make us a herbal.'

'Why of course,' she said obsequiously.

Her servility was a disingenuous displacement for courteousness and quite transparent, which is why people shunned them. It was as if she and Bréac had never matured, merely impersonated the pretence of adulthood, all the time clinging onto the worst aspects of deceitful adolescence. When they weren't arguing with each other, they were often seen sniggering to one another concerning others perceived deficiencies.

Morác's shamánistic ethics prevented him from interfering in the private affairs of other people without an invitation. Fándin had made that abundantly clear at the outset of his apprenticeship, but just this once, he was going to overlook Fándin's injunction.

When Bréac and Scéna had sat at the table, poured the herbal, Morác reached for the crystal amulet hanging around his neck and fingered it gently. In his mind he began a silent incantation, *By the power of the talisman I hold in the miracle of time, from the compass points I invoke, Lord of all the sorcerers, make these two conjoin and scatter their malice asunder*. In a short while the crystal began to glow with a deep green light and a glazed look descended on Bréac and Scéna. The trance-like phase lasted just a short time whilst their mental states accommodated their readjusted personas.

'More herbal,' Scéna asked politely, with not the slightest hint of fawning.

'Yes, thank you,' Morác agreed.

Her features softened, bringing out the original reason why Bréac had asked for her hand. There was a quiet comeliness to her that benefited from her being in the prime of life, now enhanced by the removal of her former scowling appearance.

Bréac's peculiar pained expression also disappeared, to be replaced by an avuncular countenance. He now gave the impression of trust and benevolence; all trace of the quarrelsomeness having gone. Morác really felt bad interfering without invitation, but the results pleased him. He might have to reinforce the spell on the journey, at a later date; for now he was satisfied.

Morác was about to excuse himself, when he heard shouting and pandemonium coming from outside. Scéna cocked her ear, and Bréac rushed towards the door, threw it open and was outside. Morác and Scéna joined him. They saw the whole settlement running to the southwestern end, past the weaver's place. Morác swung left quickly followed by the merchant and his wife.

He caught up with the tanner, Súdair, who was running. 'What the Húli's going on? What's all the commotion?'

'Kóira,' panted Súdair out of breath.

Morác raised his voice in fearful outrage, '*So close to the hamlet?*'

He approached Wólni's. Only then did he notice most of the tribe armed with whatever they managed to grab; sticks, axes, knives. Wólni's nestled between Sáor's and Úbor's at the southern end of the green and the kóira had attacked from a totally unexpected direction.

He now could see the sentries running from the north end of the hamlet, leading the six kópis across the green, the ridge of spines quivering furiously on their backs anticipating the impending skirmish. Just then, the kópis were let off their leashes and they bounded off past Wólni's tree. Morác greeted the kópis with a high-pitched grunt as he cast his mind at them and felt their excitement, the delicate tendrils whistle-grunting. He thought at them, *Go get them!*

Morác ran after Súdair to the left, past Úbor's, to the back of Wólni's, into a large clearing fifty cubits wide as it was long. He was just in time to see the kópis at the far end, set upon a lingering kóira, reluctant to leave bits on the ground. In the distance he saw the rest of the kóira pack disappearing into the forest.

As the crowd approached, the six kópis were making a mess of the lonely kóira, tearing it to pieces. Yet the kóira managed to rip the throat of one kópi and take a chunk out of another. Howls were entangled with growling-grunts, the battle moving too swiftly for the warrior's blowpipes to follow; none of the people were able to get close enough to use their weapons.

'Whose dead kópi is that?' Bróda asked Gárn.

'I think its Úbor's,' the potter told him.

A huddle of people was gathering around the thing on the ground the kóira had been loath to leave.

'Poor Máda,' Morác heard Málina say.

'Give me a cover for her,' wailed Shúta, unable to hold her grief.

Morác reached the group—and his stomach turned at the sight. Old Máda, or what remained of her, lay half chewed on the ground where the kóira left her. Hurrying towards the group was old Mútani, Máda's husband.

Morác yelled— '*Hold him back!*'

People blocked Mútani's passage, interposing their bodies. Bróda and others took him by the arms and led him back the way he'd come. Mútani struggled half-heartedly, but he knew Máda was no more. The life-long cord that invisibly bound them—had been cut, and he felt the loss deep within. They were both old and each knew their time was limited, soon destined to follow each other across the abyss. *But why like this?* lamented Mútani.

Máda's body was covered and people turned their attention to the final struggle between the five smaller kópis and the large kóira. It was exhausted, snarling at the kópis who surrounded it. When the rush came, at a subliminal signal, all the remaining kópis went in at the same time, forcing the kóira to breathe its last breath. Its throat was torn out and the kópis settled to feed on the corpse. One or two people applauded the kóira's demise, and then went silent— in memory of Máda.

Máda's remains were gently placed on a makeshift litter, and hurriedly removed. The litter was taken to Mútani's den behind Wómak's tree; set back from the green. A number of women accompanied the remains and it was they who put the corpse in order as best they could, washed and tidied Máda for the ceremonial display. Her body was horribly savaged, but her face had mercifully survived intact.

5

SORCERY

Morác, as the tribe's shamán, accompanied the body, walking behind the women carrying the litter. After the women put the corpse in order, a few stayed on with Morác for the vigil. He stayed with Máda's corpse all night, casting benevolent spells, easing her lemur safely to the netherworld. Mútani sat quietly in a corner, his face in his hands, in a deep state of shock. Morác went over to him from time to time, putting his hand on the old man's shoulder and saying a few comforting words in his ear.

*　　*　　*

On the next morning her body was displayed in an ornate casket standing on a bier in Mútani's day-den; the sweet aroma of spices hung in the air. The entire tribe, individually, throughout the day, filed past the open casket, paying its respect, silently casting a flower at her feet. By the evening, Morác was worn out by the incantations, the various ceremonial requirements. Only late at night was he relieved by Bróda.

'By the way,' Bróda whispered, 'I've made a gong out of a burnished metal mirror and hung it on the platform in the green. If there's another emergency, I want the nearest person to rush to it and bang it as hard as they can. Will you pass this on to the people you see on your visits?'

Morác did not say a word, just nodded. Slowly, with a heavy heart, he trudged back to his den in the dark, to Néra; to what he felt was a well-deserved meal. That night, a different dream interrupted his slumbers. Kóira chased him throughout the forest; every time he tried to escape up a tree; it felt to be greased with a kind of slippery substance. Thrashing around, he was finally woken by Néra, cradling him in her arms like a baby, cooing soothing words to him.

*   *   *

A funeral procession wound its way to the tribes Sacred Glade the following day, past Gárn's pottery. At the glade Morác officiated over the *rite of declaration* given by a number of Máda's life-long friends. It was the time when all of Máda's life was described in glowing terms by people who had known her, ending in the evening with Mútani's oration on behalf of his beloved. The long ritual was to facilitate a full bereavement. A healing for those left behind; but partly to throw verbal sand into the eyes of Húli, the netherworld's guardian of the gateway, so Máda's lemur could slip past him unchallenged; unnoticed.

At the end of the day the casket was closed and taken the short distance to the holy burial ground ten cubits to the right of the glade. There it was laid to rest in a shallow grave. All of the bereaved left quietly to allow Mútani to say his last farewells. The length of the funeral was deliberate, a chance for the tribe to meld, to collectively cast out the fears that recently descended, both the nightmarish dreams, the schánda, and the forthcoming journey. Together with Mútani they all said their farewells to Máda *and* to their fears. It was with lifted hearts the tribe returned to their dens that night.

'Poor Máda,' Néra said, as she set Morác's supper before him that evening, sitting herself down to her own plate.

'It's the manner of her going that has shocked everyone. No one expected those beasts to come from the south,' explained Morác.

'Why not? They always do the unexpected, don't they?'

'But every animal is fleeing southwards—Bróda stationed the remaining warriors in the north to prevent them overrunning us.'

'Sending all those warriors north was a mistake. Two, three, and four at the most—*that's all that was needed*. It only takes two or three to look and report back.' She had a mouth full of bread and was getting angry.

'Néra! For Aíne's sake, calm down. You'll choke on your food.'

'I'm sorry. It's just Máda needn't have gone so soon. Torn to pieces like that by wild beasts.'

'The reason Bróda sent most of the warriors north was due to their inactivity, which was driving them crazy. They hadn't slept for days and were beginning to turn on each other. It's only now it seems to have been a mistake.'

'It *was* a mistake,' she insisted.

'All right! From what happened to Máda, it *was* a mistake. It thought it right at the time.'

Morác went to see Ganúra the next morning on the subject of the list of essentials she'd made up.

Ganúra opened the door, 'Morác! Come in. Nice of you to call. Pleasure or business?'

'You know it's always a pleasure to see you, but put like that—its business.'

'Well, come in. I'll make a herbal drink.'

'Bróda told me you'd made a list of essentials for the tribe, items we ought to take on the journey?'

'Here, on this parchment.' She put a beaker of cold herbal and a parchment in front of Morác, 'Bróda wants me to post this list on the notice board outside his den. Tell me what you think?'

Morác inspected the list, studying it carefully. 'This is good. I can see Wómak's influence. Food, cooking utensils, bedroll, spare clothes and a tool. No frills. This bit at the bottom: "Anything other than the above may kill you." I like that.'

'Not too strong?'

'No! In any case, Bróda will check each person carefully before we set off.'

'Maybe you could pin the list up, if you're passing Bróda's?'

'Consider it so. It's a good list Ganúra. Well done! Now I'm off to see Súdair.' He got up and went to the door accompanied by Ganúra.

'Morác! Thanks for coming. When do you think Wómak will be back?'

'A day at the most; probably late today or tomorrow.'

'Good! I miss him; take care,' she closed the door.

Morác carefully folded and placed the parchment inside his coat pocket then veered left, making for the tannery. Súdair had his tannery just outside the hamlet, by the side of the river, downstream from Gárn. The tanner needed to soak his skins before he scraped them clean, forcing him to position his tannery by the riverside. People bathed between the pottery and the tannery, and the washing was performed upstream from the tannery. Down river from the tannery a clay pipe extended from the bank, dumping the hamlet sewage into the river. The sewage was flushed through by the cleverly directed over-spill from the fountain. It was the only way to maintain hamlet hygiene.

Morác rounded Súdair's Lándo tree and was pounced on by Scuráia and Sadb, Súdair's two younglings. They were playing at being warriors. Although Scuráia felt too old for it, he was indulging his sister, leaping on Morác in ambush. The boy Scuráia, twelve seasons, was wielding a pretend blowpipe and his pretty sister, Sadb, ten seasons, had a small spear. A young kópi whistle-grunted in excitement, trying to nip at Morác's heels.

'*We got you,*' Sadb yelled, dancing round Morác, who was dancing on one foot trying to shake off the young kópi.

'I give in,' Morác said raising his hands.

'You can't raise your hands; you're dead,' Sadb insisted.

'Where's your dad,' Morác asked Scuráia, the more serious of the two.

'Down Loti,' Scuráia ordered the kópi. 'He's stretching a skin at the shed.'

Hearing her younglings talking, Shúta poked her head out of the window of the day-den.

'Hallo Morác! Come to see me?'

'Tell him mom, he can't raise his hands when he's dead,' Sadb persisted.

'Let him be,' his mother scolded her.

'I came to see both you and Súdair,' Morác told her.

'Well, he's out at the shed stretching what's left of the kóira skin the kópis killed. Why not come in and I'll give you a bit to nibble,' she waved her hand towards the door. 'Sadb! Go and fetch your father.'

Morác entered the ordered disorder of a family den. Youngling's garments on one basket chair; Shúta hurried to clear an uncleared table, 'Excuse the mess. We just finished the morning meal. I was just going to go to the river to start on the washing,' she pointed at the youngling's clothing. 'Sit here and I'll get the bread.'

The young kópi was making a fuss outside, whistling and grunting as young kópi do. A deep male voice was trying to calm him.

Súdair walked through the door, 'Morác! What a pleasant surprise. Please; don't get up.' Súdair walked over to his wife and kissed her on the cheek.

'Sit and I'll get you a drink,' she invited her husband.

Súdair sat by Morác, who moved back imperceptibly from the strong smell coming from the tanner. 'It was a moving ceremony yesterday. You were particularly diligent in following the ritual.'

Súdair was referring to the length of the service for Máda. Morác usually cut the ceremony to half; this time it went the full length. It might be the final time they used the glade; so he made it last all day.

'I'm going to miss this place,' Morác confided, breathing shallowly to avoid the tanner's smell. 'I don't just mean the place. I mean the closeness, the comfortable community, the ordered life—our glade. It's so magnificent here in the forest, surrounded by all this vibrancy. I feel so deeply intertwined into the life of the forest I can't imagine any other life. Look at me; we haven't left yet and I'm already nostalgic.'

The noise in the den was getting louder as Sadb raced around the table playing tag.

'*Can't hear myself think!*' shouted Súdair. To Morác, 'Let's take a walk.'

Both went outside, wending their way towards Súdair's shed.

'Why did you come to see us?' Súdair's short legs were in a hurry, propelling him ahead of Morác.

'I wanted to know how ready you are for the journey,' Morác said to Súdair's back.

'We haven't begun to ready yet—if that's what you mean? It might be a false alarm.'

'You don't believe that, surely? We're going to have to move as soon as the warriors return; which is probably tomorrow at the latest. That's my estimate. You've got to stop pretending it's not going to happen. You've had the dreams—haven't you?'

'Yes, but they're only dreams.'

'We can't force you to go, but you're condemning your younglings to death if you don't.'

'That's a bit harsh. You're trying to scare me?'

'You're absolutely right I'm trying to scare you. I'm trying to scare sense into you. When was the last time you saw a kóira so close to our settlement? I'll tell you; never! It's a symptom the natural order of things has been disturbed. The animals around you have enough sense to be scared, even if you're working hard at ignoring the danger.'

They reached the shed and Morác saw the stretched kóira skin. The stomach area had been badly torn by the kópis, as had the neck area. Súdair would make shoulder wraps and other things out of it. He went over and began to scrape at the skin with the blunt end of a knife.

'Is that your answer? Scraping and ignoring. Don't you care for Shúta, and your younglings?'

There followed a lengthy silence when only the water in the nearby narrow river could be heard gurgling on its way. Morác stood looking at Súdair scraping the kóira skin and suddenly felt old and tired. Súdair put down the knife and looked straight at Morác. There appeared a look of concern on Súdair's face.

'Are you all right?' Súdair asked Morác.

'It's nothing. I'm just tired, that's all.'

There was a firmness in Súdair's voice when he next spoke, 'This is my decision. We'll be ready by tomorrow morning—I promise.'

'Thank goodness—you've come to your senses.'

Both walked back to Súdair's den. Morác had been convinced he would have to argue and plead with Súdair; his sudden capitulation pleased and rejuvenated him. He bade both farewell and went on his way with a spring in his step.

He still had Úbor and Wólni to visit. But not today! He decided to leave them till tomorrow. It was well into the afternoon by the time he left Súdair and Morác wanted to spend the rest of the day with Néra. He made his way diagonally across the green, gently humming to himself, revelling in the sunshine, greedily taking in the calm before the storm to come. He stopped at the fountain and splashed his face with cool water; then picked up one of the clay beakers standing on the middle dais and swigged a couple of refreshing mouthfuls. *That's better!*

He continued on to Bróda's den, took out the parchment, smoothed it out and tacked Ganura's list to the notice board, as requested.

Back in his den that evening, ensconced in his favourite basket chair, he complained to Néra, 'I'm astounded at people's complacency. Yesterday I had to impress on Gárn it was in his interest to get ready; today I had to do the same with Súdair. Don't they have any premonition, any sense of survival?'

'We've never faced such an upheaval dear,' Néra said in a placatory tone. She stood by his chair, lightly resting a hand on his shoulder.

'Tomorrow I've probably to do the same with Wólni and Úbor. By the way; are *we* ready to go?'

'Yes; I've put everything we're taking with us in the corner over there,' she pointed to a pile.

He rose heavily and looked where she pointed, placing his hands on his hips. 'Good! At least that's one worry less.'

A gentle frown on her forehead, 'Morác! Stop and think for a moment. It's Máda's death and funeral that's taken the energy out of you, not Gárn or Súdair. The manner of her death and the length of the ceremony. Once recognise that as the cause—you'll get your second wind.' The frown turned into a soft smile.

'Hmm! You're right of course. I'm still feeling a bit shocked at the kóira being so close.' He reached out and held her lightly at arm's length. 'I didn't tell you, but the other day when I went to the glade, I had to discourage a kóira from attacking a Caroó.'

She put her hands on his. 'We've always shared our troubles, Morác. Recently you've kept your feelings to yourself. It's put a burden on your mind. Tiredness is one of the results.'

He sighed deeply. 'We've had such a quiet ordered existence here. Now this danger, fleeing, the upheavals—'

'I know my dear. We'll survive.' She took Morác's hand and held it tenderly. 'I want us to go upstairs and comfort each other—it may be our last night in this den.'

It was a different Morác who set out across the green late the following morning to see Wólni; more bounce in his step. He felt what it was to be young again. The morning was glorious, the fresh air heavy with the scent of Spring. If the day went as planned, then all the Lándo trees surrounding the green would be empty by this evening. There would be no Fertility Festival this turn of the wheel. No marriages and no initiations into adulthood. The bitter thought reminded him the warriors were expected back today and he wondered, *what kind of news would they bring? There could be no good news—but how bad was it?*

He'd have to shorten his visit to Wólni if he was to include Úbor the tailor. Morác suspected Úbor and his partner Ádna were ready for the journey. They were a pair firmly rooted in reality. Both were relatively youthful, and as yet without younglings of their own. He foresaw little trouble in ticking them off his mental list. He might have to check on Sáor, to confirm he was ready.

Málina, Wólni's partner came to the door. 'Why Morác! What a pleasant surprise. We were just saying your visit is overdue.' She had a twinkle in her eye.

'You're looking—' Morác never finished the compliment.

There was an alarming noise coming from the newly installed gong on the platform, especially loud within the confines of the forest.

'*What on Kálar is going on*?' Wólni exclaimed, appearing at the doorway.

Morác recovered his senses, '*Quick, grab a weapon* —and one for me if you can,' he managed to add.

Seeing his fellow tribesmen running towards Gárn's and Súdair's dens, Morác joined them and ran towards Úbor, who had just dashed out of his den.

'What's up?' gasped Morác as he neared Úbor. He wasn't as fit as he could be.

'No idea! Just heard the gong. Grabbed an axe to investigate.'

All three dashed off in the direction the tribe was running. Wólni pushed a stout staff into Morác's hands, retaining one for himself.

They all heard the deep unmistakable growling at the same time—it was coming from the east of Súdair's den. They all knew the deep growling of the Dárgh—and there were more than one. In the distance they spied three of the vicious brutes; one clutching something and the other disputed what it held. A third was fending off thrusts from a spear by one of the tribesmen.

6

CROSSING THE MÁRKA

The Márka river the warriors were striving to reach, started in the Kárti hills to the northwest, crossed the northeastern corner of Bólani land before disappearing into Hánum country. It may have only been twenty cubits wide but the current was strong enough to take a person if they were careless.

By noon the warriors could hear the river in the near distance. The sound of the water lifted everyone's spirits and Láeg, whose turn it was to hack through the bushes blocking the path of the column, now put all his energies into breaking out of the undergrowth to the water.

It was with a heavy sigh Láeg broke out of the undergrowth, spilling out and sprawling onto the riverbank. He found Fúlmon and Máyo sitting quietly, fishing. The scouts were taking the opportunity to stock up for their evening meal. There was already half a dozen decent sized fish flapping on the bank.

'Welcome Láeg! You made enough noise to wake the dead, getting here,' Fúlmon teased him.

The rest of the column joined Láeg on the bank. They could hear the crash of leaping fish echoing back into the forest. Excitedly they pointed at the jumping abundance, looking forward to tasting the fresh catch.

'All right, let's take a break.' Wómak told the warriors, as they settled themselves on the side of the river. 'A rest before we tackle the river. Robán; in the mean time, get the lads to check the ropes and build their rafts.'

Máyo, Ládra, Némed sat in a group and began to unpack ropes. Píngo, Robán and Láeg did the same. The third group consisted of Uílin, Umára and Fúlmon. Each group constructed a raft big enough to hold their three combined backpacks. The crossing technique was well-tried, simple, safe and effective; two people always holding a rope around the third. The method passed down from their forefathers.

As a prelude to crossing, all the warriors removed their socks, placed them in their packs and put their moccasins back on. This would give a better grip on the riverbed and dry socks on the other side. The first group's raft was loaded with backpacks, secured with ropes, and the raft placed near the edge of the riverbank ready for launch. When the time came to cross, Máyo had a rope around his waist and Ládra held the rope attached to Máyo seven cubits upstream. Némed was connected to Máyo with another rope seven cubits downstream. Némed and Ládra were also connected by a rope. The effect was a rope triangle with Máyo, Ládra and Némed at each corner.

Máyo standing between Ládra and Némed at the apex of the triangle of ropes, being the strongest of the group, waded across using a stout pole as a support, probing for rocks and holes in the riverbed. The current tugged at Máyo, but Ládra upstream, held him taut, whilst Némed was the anchor if Máyo should slip. Slowly, Máyo negotiated the current, placing each footstep with difficulty on the slippery river bottom, always facing upriver. Covered rocks below the surface were deflecting the water above, causing eddies. He especially avoided the exposed rocks that were often more slippery underfoot, knowing the riverbed might be deep at those spots. He judged the strength of the current by the standing waves all around, caused by underwater rocks deflecting the water upwards, and planted his feet firmly on the river bed, moving ever forwards.

When Máyo reached the far bank, Ládra walked towards Némed tying the rope around his own waist, then began to cross. Máyo took the strain, the rope linking Némed to Máyo acted as the safety line should Ládra slip. Máyo pulled at the rope holding Ládra and Némed played out the crossing line. In effect, Máyo pulled Ládra across, making his passage fairly simple.

Trees lined both side of the river. When Ládra crossed, Máyo tied his end to a tree. Némed grabbed the short rope attached to the raft, tied it to the upper portion of the rope wound around his waist and pulled the raft the short distance into the river. The current seized the raft, pulling Némed with it; the tree held Némed's rope taut. Máyo and Ládra tried to guide the rope. All Némed had to do was stay on his feet. He failed to do this, slipping on a rock, loosing his pole, and then letting himself float in an arc across the river. He was swung mechanically to the far bank towing the raft behind him.

Twenty-five cubits downstream of Máyo and Ládra, Némed ended up beached, wet but safe, thankful he was held tight by the rope tied to the tree. Máyo and Ládra went to help Némed onto the bank, and then collected the raft and its contents.

'That was clumsy of you,' chided Máyo.

'If you wanted a bath, you should have said,' added Ládra, smiling.

Némed soaked, was scrabbling up the bank, scowling at the witty jokes of his colleagues. 'Help me pull the raft in,' he pleaded.

The first group crossed safely bringing all their ropes. The other two groups crossed in a similar fashion with Wómak bringing up the rear, spread-eagled on the last raft, ending up the only relatively dry person in the group.

On the far bank Wómak called for order. 'Right, let's get the ropes re-packed, the water skins refilled. Umára! Hand out the midday rations. Quickly now, we need to press on whilst there's light in the day.'

Umára handed out the slices of cold wild porridge, which they ate in silence. It was mid afternoon when the column set out, again hacking its way through the undergrowth. They heard a great deal of rustling in the bushes round them as if countless animals were on the move. The going got even tougher on the other side of the Márka, needing two warriors out front to do the hacking.

A couple of hours passed before the undergrowth finally began thinning out allowing the column to put speed back into their strides. Everybody immediately noticed an abundance of animal life on that side of the Márka. In fact, it was positively crowded; all heading towards the river. That was the clearest sign they'd seen of an upset in the forest. The animals' reaction was, as if fleeing from a fire.

After they'd trodden more leagues, they had a visit from Máyo, who appeared running towards them in haste.

'*Come quickly*,' he gasped breathlessly.

Wómak tried to calm him, 'Slow down lad. What's the story?'

'*Kóira*! Fúlmon—pinned up in trees—not half a league up in front.' Máyo urged the warriors to follow him.

Wómak shouted, '*Right! Quickly, lead on—*'

The whole column hurried, following Máyo. Warriors pulled out axes, loaded darts into blowpipes on the run. Everyone had a weapon out as they neared the howling and growling. Even before they got to the scene, they could hear menacing snarling from a distance. Máyo stopped suddenly and pointed to the front, thirty cubits ahead. Standing guard were two kóira lookouts—confronting them. It was unnerving to have the beasts behaving so tactically; so people like.

Wómak held up his hand to halt the column, raised his blowpipe in one fluid motion and dropped the kóira to his left. Burly Píngo dropped the other at the same instant. Silently by hand signals, Wómak gestured the column should split to left and right in an encircling movement. Máyo detached himself from the group and headed straight for Fúlmon—stuck in a tree without his blowpipe. Five kóira were patiently sitting at the bottom waiting for him, howling in unison.

Earlier, three kóira lookouts had ambushed Fúlmon whilst Máyo was far behind. Máyo ran for it, leaving Fúlmon to scurry up a tree, dropping his blowpipe in the process. Up his tree, Fúlmon then noticed the main pack of fifteen or so were at another tree, waiting, howling like a coven of spectres from the netherworld. He strained to see who the kóira had treed, when he heard a woman scream. Her foot slipped and she was hanging from a high branch. She regained the branch by hooking one leg over it and climbing up. When the woman calmed, she spotted Fúlmon, noticing the kóira at the base of his tree. She didn't call or wave, simply stared past him wild-eyed.

Fúlmon was suspicious of this strange woman out in the deep forest by herself; it was the male die-hard in him. The woman stared through Fúlmon from time to time—with a wild frantic gaze. The two sat in their separate trees—not communicating—until the arrival of the warriors. One by one the kóira hit the ground as the darts flew. Then, moving as one, all the kóira abruptly charged away northeasterly, others being felled as they tried to escape. Since the people were coming from the southwest, the kóira ran in the opposite direction.

When the tally was made, they had killed seven, not counting the two lookouts at the beginning. Kóira had a nasty habit of playing dead and resuming their attack when the person's back was turned. It was standard practice for the warriors to slit their throats to make sure they were really dead. A gruesome and onerous task assuredly necessary for their personal safety.

Fúlmon descended from his roost and headed for Wómak. 'Am I glad to see you,' he said sheepishly. 'Caught me unawares—they did. Me, a scout too—'

Fúlmon was ashamed of being caught out and ashamed of loosing his main weapon. He couldn't look any of his colleagues in the eye with embarrassment. He knew both scouts were lucky to be alive.

'Right!' Wómak said gruffly, 'Let's see who this other person is.' To Robán, 'Post lookouts.'

Being reminded of the other person, Fúlmon's interest picked up. 'She hasn't said a word in all this time,' he complained.

All heads turned to the tree in question. The woman sat on a high branch, seemingly oblivious of the carnage below, careless of the warriors staring up at her. If she was aware it was now safe to come down, she showed no sign of it. She continued to stare out east as if she was seeing that which those on the ground could not see.

Wómak broke the silence, 'Robán! Take Píngo and see if you can bring her down. Be gentle, she seems to be in shock.'

'Right you are, Wómak.'

'There must be at least two packs of kóira,' Fúlmon mused out loud.

'What? Oh, yeah. Probably more.' Wómak nodded, breaking his gaze from the treed woman. 'You could be right.'

'It's the only explanation—' Fúlmon continued, 'I thought we'd left them on the other side of the river. It's why I wasn't looking out for the pesky things.'

'Now the kóira are gone, notice the mass of wild life stirring up around us? Where there are two packs, there's bound to be more.' Wómak fingered his axe playfully. 'The forest is alive with running things. Mark my words; it's the schánda's doing.'

There was a scream from the woman in the tree. Robán had climbed up and clung just below the branch holding the woman. She was edging out further along the branch with a wild look in her eyes. She screamed again as Robán tried to climb onto the her branch. Other warriors below had a groundsheet stretched taut underneath where the woman might fall.

Finally Robán managed to swing himself onto the same branch—the woman inched further away from him. All of a sudden there was a loud crack; the branch gave way, being unable to hold the combined weight of the occupants.

The branch slumped downwards, chunks of fibres still holding the branch momentarily before it severed completely, crashing to the forest floor. The warriors beneath, scattered, dropping the groundsheet. The woman landed on the groundsheet; the branch landed on top of her. Robán had instinctively grabbed the main tree trunk and managed to hold to it, legs dangling. He lowered himself to the lower branch and rested.

The warriors ran to the woman who had been knocked unconscious by the branch. She lay still, breathing peacefully for the first time since they encountered her.

'Help me get the branch off her,' shouted Fúlmon, himself struggling with one end.

All the warriors helped and the branch was lifted gently off the woman, and put aside. Umára hurriedly knelt beside her to check her physical condition. He was their cook and field medic. He removed a vile from his pouch; uncorked it and held it under her nose.

'Mmmmm,' moaned the woman, regaining consciousness.

'Stand back. Give her air,' Umára pleaded.

She opened her eyes, and stared wildly from side to side, all the time cowering as if they were going to hurt her.

She gave the impression of a cornered animal rather than a person who might be grateful for being rescued from the kóira.

'She's frightened out of her wits,' Wómak told the gathering. 'Let Umára deal with her. Since it's late afternoon, the rest of you might find a suitable spot nearby and pitch camp. Keep the latrine close; I don't want people being picked off. And Robán; make sure everyone retrieves their darts. Keep the sentries alert tonight.'

The warriors moved off to obey, retrieving darts, collecting firewood, chopping poles for the night's lean-to. They even built an extra lean-to for the woman in expectation of her staying. The camp was set up in a clearing ten cubits further on, nestling against a leeward incline. Píngo got the campfire going and tubby Uílin took it on himself to clean the fish the scouts caught earlier, getting the pot boiling for the wild millet. He was going to do the cooking so Umára could tend to the woman.

In the encroaching dusk, the sighs and whispers of the forest were amplified. The rustlings of the animals in the surrounding undergrowth increased. A lingering tension still hung under the canopy from the remnants of the battle with the kóira. It was in this atmosphere the warriors gathered around the campfire, leaving Umára alone to minister to the woman: it was less threatening that way. If anyone could calm the woman, Umára could. He was known to be able to talk the hind legs off a Caroó.

'Well? What do you make of her?' Némed asked his inseparable companion, Ládra, whilst they settled to eat grilled fish around the fire.

Ládra was unusually quiet, looking in the direction of the woman from time to time, between mouthfuls.

Ládra shot at Némed, 'What's she doing out here all alone?' Chew—swallow. 'Where are her people?' Again biting into his fish.

'How the Húli should I know,' Némed retorted. He was surprised Ládra asked him. 'There's a thing not right with her; I'll tell you that,' he added.

'Yeah, it's what I'm saying.'

'That kid back on the other side of the river; you think there's any connection?' asked Némed.

'Could be. Anyway, we'll soon find out. Here they come.' Ládra nodded in the direction of Umára.

7

ENDLESS TUNDRA

Umára had the woman's elbow and was leading her to the fire. She looked groggy on her feet, but the wildness in her eyes had disappeared.

'Lads, give us room.' Umára waited whilst Fúlmon and Uílin shuffled sideways to allow another log to be pulled up and turned into a bench.

The woman sat and reached out her hands to the fire, rubbing them for warmth. She kept her face turned to the blaze, as if she was afraid to look at anyone; or to be noticed. Píngo, Robán and Láeg were on sentry duty, which left seven warriors sitting around the roaring logs, eating their grilled fish and porridge.

Umára collected a bowl of porridge for the woman and himself. He ladled the porridge out and handed the woman a bowl topped with a grilled fish; she took it, looking kindly at him, and reached for a spoon.

Wómak asked Umára quietly as he sat, 'How is she?'

Wómak was startled to see the sympathetic look she had given Umára. *Another conquest for the cook,* he thought to himself. *He does have a way with people.*

'She's still unsettled from her encounter, but she knows now we mean her no harm,' Umára explained to Wómak and those who listened.

Again quietly, Wómak inquired, 'Did you find out anything; why she's in the forest all alone? Why she's on Bólani land?'

'She's a Hánum,' Umára told him. 'The youth we buried yesterday on the other side of the river was her son. It's her son Fúlmon chased the first night out in the forest. He died defending her from the kóira, so she could get away.'

'But what's she doing here?' Wómak insisted.

'She's been cast out from the tribe—for having a son out of wedlock.'

Wómak looked aghast for a moment. Then his composure reasserted. 'Did she tell you what happened?'

The woman had been listening and now interrupted, 'I had an affair with the Hánum Custodian's son.' She popped a piece of fish in her mouth. 'A boy was born; I pretended it was from my husband. Many years later, in a moment of madness and spite; I threw the fact it wasn't his child in his face. He went quiet, only a moment mind you, then threw me out; told me to take my brat with me.'

Those gathered by the campfire had been startled to here the woman speak, even more startled to hear the story.

She put a spoon of porridge in her mouth, chewed and swallowed, then continued, 'The Custodian called a tribal meeting and it voted to banish me from Hánum land. His son, himself married by this time with a family, refused to recognise my son as his. This was half a season ago.' She stopped for a pause, and more porridge.

The warriors listened, absorbed by her tale; it was far better than the usual campfire story they were accustomed to.

'We've lived on Bólani land all this time, mostly out in the north-eastern corner' the woman persevered, 'on this side of the river. Two weeks ago we had to run for our lives when a pack of kóira suddenly appeared out of nowhere. We had to leave our shelter, leave everything behind. The beasts kept following us. We've lived off the forest all this time, off our wits. We think the pack came down from Grónda country. We crossed the river; so did the pack. There's a kind of mass movement going on—of all the animals. They're frightened—of whatever's coming from the north.'

'Do you know what they're running from?' Fúlmon asked her cautiously.

'No!' She looked at Fúlmon for the first time, a spoon of porridge half way to her mouth. 'I've seen you before. We followed you.' It was a matter-of-fact statement. She wasn't boasting, simply telling him. She continued eating.

'So it was you, was it?' Fúlmon observed, giving her a meaningful glance.

'How many packs of kóira would you say are here?' Wómak needed information.

'Four, maybe more by now. Two this side of the river, two on the far side. The river doesn't seem to stop them.' She put a piece of fish in her mouth; it was said with dejection creeping into her voice. 'We thought we'd be safe on the other side; they got us anyway.' Contempt and fear forced, '*Filthy beasts!*' from her. She scraped the last bits of porridge from her bowl and quickly popped it into her mouth.

'I'm sorry!' she looked embarrassed. 'I was really hungry.'

Wómak watched her put her bowl aside. He looked directly into the woman's face, so she would know he was telling her the truth.

'Well, you're safe now. I give you my word.'

Wómak intended to keep his word no matter what. He'd taken pity on the woman despite her loose behaviour; losing her son that way, should be enough punishment for anybody.

He continued, 'We're on a recon expedition to the tree-line not far from here. When we get there, we'll look around for half a day to see what's got the animals spooked, then we'll head back. You're welcome to come along. Do you want to?'

She nodded her head quietly.

'Good! That's settled. Do you have a name?'

'I'm called Huróyna.'

'Well Huróyna, we've built a separate lean-to for you so you can rest in peace tonight. Umára will show you where you sleep.' Wómak eyed the rest of the warriors, 'It's time we turned in. Umára; a word—' He got up and strode leisurely to the lean-to, followed by Umára.

'You old miracle worker. How did you get her to open up?' Wómak asked.

'When we came across her, she was half out of her mind. She was in shock, hungry, driven silly with fear and grief. Little or no sleep; hadn't eaten for days. No wonder she reacted the way she did. She's all right now. I talked to her kindly, told her we found her boy and buried him properly. That put her mind greatly at ease. With the porridge in her and tonight's sleep, she'll be well on the way to recovery. By tomorrow she'll be a different woman.'

'I want you to look after her till we get back. Can you do that?'

'I'll need to be spelled. Láeg's a big softy. If you suggest he help me, I think we'll manage.'

'I'll see to it; thanks. I know it's going to be a difficult job. I *do* appreciate this.'

Umára went back to Huróyna and took her to her separate lean-to. The campfire was kept high all night. They heard the howling but the kóira kept their distance. The noise coming from the undergrowth continued throughout the night, and near dawn, increased in intensity. When first light finally arrived and the bird chorus was well under way, the warriors stirred themselves. A few jumped out of their blankets too quickly, as if they had been awake. Usually they were hard to rouse.

Uílin helped Umára make the morning meal and Wómak was surprised to see the woman helping Umára with the cooking. She looked rested and composed, with a spring to her step. The third sentry shift was rotated so they could get some food. Warriors were speedily gulping sweet hot porridge. Others dismantled lean-tos, burying rubbish, covering the latrine.

'Listen up,' Wómak called for order. 'By mid noon I estimate we will reach the tree-line. I want no heroics. We're here to reconnoitre, assess the speed of the schánda and head back with the information. Clear?' He watched the nods. 'Good. I want to be back at the river by tonight, at the latest. Let's tidy up and break camp.'

The scouts went forward and the column moved off in pursuit. The woman was put in the middle of the column for protection; she protested. The column came to a halt with the commotion.

Huróyna went to the front to talk to Wómak. 'I'm trying to help you,' she told him. 'I know this area like the back of my hand. I should be out with your lead scout, not stuck in the middle of the column.'

'With all you've gone through, I thought you'd want a rest,' Wómak told her.

'How can I rest with my boy's killers stalking us? I want to make sure you get where you're going, and get back safely.'

'That's my job,' Wómak told her sternly.

'Are you too stubborn to accept my help? If you're trying to locate the source of the animal's terror, you need to veer to the right more in that direction.' She pointed more to the right. 'Let me repay you for saving me, and allow me to lead you through easier paths.' A fierce look of determination spread across her face.

'Píngo! Go and call Fúlmon back.' Wómak looked at Huróyna with a growing sense of admiration. *Was this the cowering woman of yesterday? She has a fierce glow in her eyes; the glow of unbending hatred and determination.* He turned back to her. 'If Fúlmon agrees, you can go with him. If you know this area as you say you do, it would be foolish of me not to use your expertise.'

'Thank you. I'll try to guide you through the less thick brush so the going will be easier and quicker.'

They waited until burly Píngo appeared with Fúlmon and Máyo. Wómak took Fúlmon aside and talked to him in whispers, and then they came back with expressionless faces.

'Fúlmon's agreed to take you with him, but you must listen to him. Up front, he's in charge. Do you agree?'

'Yes,' she replied, still with a look of determination.

The three scouts set off, with Huróyna in front, guiding them through less dense shrub. The column followed at a distance of a quarter of a league. All around them animals were heading in the opposite direction, fleeing from the all-devouring Schánda.

They travelled like this until noon when the shrubs began to thin and the trees looked stunted. Everyone put their collars up against the fierce wind blowing from the north. The trees at the edge of the forest were evergreens, with narrower leaves, exposing far less of their surface area, hanging on more supple branches that flexed to allow heavy loads of snow to slide off harmlessly in winter. The floor of the forest at these border latitudes was already thickly settled by a sturdier vegetation that would thin out as they moved further north—until it disappeared all together. The abrupt crossover from temperate to treeless tundra without an intermediary taiga zone was an anomaly caused by the subterranean geology of the northern region of Kálar, a folding phenomenon deep below the surface.

Wómak squinting ahead saw his three scouts doing a shuffle to keep warm, waiting for the column to catch up. They were at the sparse tree-line, the northerly edge of the forest where the treeless tundra began. Out there, little grew. The Grónda hunters lived underground, in burrows dug out of the permafrost. A few stunted and twisted shrubs punctuated the bleak landscape.

'See anything out there?' asked Wómak as he came up to Fúlmon.

'Not a thing: and I have to tell you, it disturbs me,' Fúlmon replied. 'I should see movement, a tundra skater, a pulverine… There's always life out on the tundra. The stillness gives me the creeps.'

'Yeah; I can see what you mean,' Wómak agreed.

Huróyna announced, 'They've all run for it.'

Máyo ignored her and pointed to a hillock on the right two hundred cubits away. 'You see over there; I could get a better view from the top.'

'Go ahead; be extra careful. Here, take my groundsheet; it's cold out there.'

'I'm going with him,' Fúlmon declared.

Wómak nodded. The warriors spread out in a line facing the wind and the treeless tundra. Huróyna didn't say a word. From her body language, she had no desire to go out into the open, into land where she couldn't shin up a tree, exposed to any predator who could outrun her.

'It's all right Huróyna. I'm not asking you to go out there,' Wómak reassured her. 'You've done your job.'

Fúlmon and Máyo emerged from the tree-line and both loped for the hillock through the stunted grass struggling to survive the desiccating winds and the brief growing season.

Máyo got there first and scampered to the top. Fúlmon went around the hillock, out of sight of the watchers at the tree-line, and then emerged to join Máyo at the top. They looked to the north for a long while, and then scurried down the hillock slope, heading back to their waiting companions.

'Well?' Wómak demanded, clapping his hands for warmth against his shoulders.

'There's a dark thin line all across the northern horizon—and it's heading this way,' Fúlmon told him.

'Can you estimate its speed?'

'It's difficult, it doesn't seem to be moving—but that's an illusion. Can I make a suggestion?'

'Go ahead.'

'We stay here a couple of hours, with a lookout on the hillock; that way we should be able to gauge its speed. What do you think?'

'I'd like to be as far away from here as possible—but you're right. You and Máyo take turns. Wrap up well, make sure you stay warm. We may have to stay longer than two hours.'

'I'm sorry you said that.'

'By the way,' Wómak turned to Huróyna, 'how far is Hánum country?'

'A league further on to the East.' Then she looked quizzically at Wómak. 'What's that—that thing you're looking at—up there?' She pointed to the North.

'I'll explain tonight—later, round the fire.' Then he turned to Fúlmon, 'Well Fúlmon, better get to your position.'

Two hours passed—slowly—then another two. The scouts reported the dark thin line had moved, gradually—towards them.

'Do you think they'll reach here by nightfall?' Wómak asked Fúlmon.

'No, not that soon. A day or so is my best guess.'

'Right! That would put them at our hamlet in four or five days, do you agree?'

'Sounds right.'

'That's it! As far as I'm concerned, we have what we came to see. Robán? Fúlmon? Have you anything to add to this?'

Neither replied; both shook their heads.

'In that case—let's get out of this wind. We're heading back as fast as we can. Huróyna, you stay with the column—no arguments. Fúlmon, Máyo; out front.'

The column formed to set off. Fúlmon took one last look back in the direction of the Schánda—his sharp eyes picking out a couple of figures near the distant hillock.

He cried out, 'Over there, look—someone waving at us.'

Wómak stared, then waved back and beckoned to come over, whoever it was. A little later, two figures ambled over, dressed in furs from head to toes, carrying spears.

'Yo there!' yelled Wómak to the strangers.

'Hargh!' the leading one yelled back.

The strangers looked every bit the Grónda burrow-dwellers. Wómak and his group were on Bólani land; it was as neighbours they greeted each other.

'What be you doing up north?' the leader asked politely as he reached the column.

Wómak pointed at the dark mass up on the horizon. 'We came to see what the animals were running from.'

'Yes, Schánda come. All Grónda people—already in Hánum land, heading south. We last ones here, checking no one left behind. As we talk, Kárti people crossing Nólki land to west. *Everything* running, not just animals running. You mad to come here.'

'We were just leaving to warn our people,' Wómak told the Grondaman.

'You hurry,' said the fur-clad fellow. Both Gronda turned to follow their tribe's people into Hánum country.

'Good fortune!' Wómak called after them. He turned to his warriors and said, 'Right, no more time to loose—let's go.'

The column set off on a trot heading back the way they came, back to the river. They passed the spot of the battle with the kóira and found the nine carcasses stripped clean. That was the way with nature; with the forest. Others had to eat. Knowing the route helped considerably, and by dusk, they reached the river bank.

'I want to set up our night camp on this side.' Wómak began giving orders. 'Robán; get the men to pitch camp; organise the lean-to and latrine. Make sure there's a rope along the river bank near the camp. I don't want anyone falling in during the night. We cross the river at first light; that way our body heat will dry us off on the march.'

Warriors settled to catching fish, others topped up the water skins. The two lean-tos' were swiftly constructed. Píngo had a roaring fire going and Huróyna helped Umára with the cooking. The grilled fish tasted every bit as good as previously. In short order, the camp settled for the night with sentries posted.

Apart from the rush of wild life crossing the river in panic, next day, their own crossing went pretty much as the journey to the tree-line. Huróyna crossed the river on a raft, despite her protestations she could use her own two feet. They were in too much of a hurry to argue with her. The occasional dead animal floated by, drowned in its rush to cross. Once on the other side, they made swift progress. Wómak gave the orders and everybody jumped.

During the day's trek they reached the spot where they'd buried Huróyna's son. Out of respect for her grief, they allowed her time at the graveside. The warriors stayed on the path leaving her to say her farewells alone. She knelt at the spot, marked by flowers and an upright pole, and said a tender farewell to the only joy life bestowed on her; wishing everlasting peace to his lemur.

They did not linger long, continuing their hasty withdrawal, back to warn the tribe. The rest of the return journey was without incident, but the kóira packs on this side of the river kept a close watch on the column, hoping it would make a mistake. Huróyna kept Umára company during the day on the trek; in the evenings, took to talking to Fúlmon when he returned from scouting. A bond was growing between the lead scout and her, which all the warriors noticed.

On the sixth day, late in the morning, exhausted and hungry, they neared the hamlet. They heard shouting and yelling coming from it. To add to the hullabaloo, there was a loud alien gonging from somewhere.

'Quick lads, load your darts,' snapped Wómak.

The pace of the column picked up. Warriors loaded for action. The gonging became louder. It was Fúlmon who first saw the source of the trouble.

He yelled, '*Over there; Dárgh.*'

8

DEADLY DÁRGH

Morác and his two companions closed on the commotion, at last discerning what the two dárgh were disputing: their stomachs turned. A smaller female dárgh was lashing out with one paw, swiping at Súdair, whilst with the other paw she was disputing the limp bloodied body of Gárn's little girl, Gara, with a male dárgh holding on to it. Súdair was desperately jabbing his spear at the big male dárgh holding the corpse.

A third roan dárgh was striking out at Gárn, who kept trying to lunge at the animal with his spear, tears streaming down his lacerated face. The roan dárgh held a dismembered arm close to his furry chest. Gárn's gaze was fixated on the appendage and intent on prising the limb from the dárgh. Úbor threw his axe, intending to distract the dárgh from Gárn. The blade of the axe caught the dárgh on its forearm; it brushed it aside. Gárn was bleeding profusely from a great swathe of claw marks across his face and chest, obtained when he frantically tried to rescue his daughter.

'For Aíne's sake, help Gárn,' shouted Súdair, himself fighting for his life with the dárgh holding the girl's body.

As more people arrived, they began to harass the dárgh with spears, clubs, axes, and sticks; anything they'd managed to lay their hands on. The male dárgh holding the girl's corpse dropped it in a heap as the tribe joined the battle. Bróda was loading his blowpipe as fast as he could;

hitting the roan dárgh Gárn was struggling with. Gárn was on the verge of collapse with the loss of blood and Bróda sought to finish off the roan dárgh in an attempt to save Gárn's life.

Wólni was trying to hit the roan dárgh's shins with his staff, sliding under the paw sweeps. Morác tried the same tactic from the opposite direction; then gave up, retreating to a safe distance. He thought he could be more effective with the crystal amulet hanging around his neck, fingering it gently, bringing it to life. The crystal began to glow with its peculiar deep green radiance and Morác aimed his incantations at the roan dárgh, trying to muddy its primitive mind, distracting it, confusing it so Wólni's jabs would get past its guard.

Scória and Dalán arrived with the five kópis, setting them on the roan dárgh, joining Bróda in the battle with their blowpipes. Finally, the roan dárgh went down, first on its knees, dropping the bloody limb, then flat on its face into the grass, perforated with darts. Its prone body shaking with muscle spasms from the poison. The kópis rushed in to finish it off.

Then the people gave a collective "yelp" as Wómak's warriors arrived, hitting both dárgh with everything they had.

People urged on by Morác, pulled Gárn away from the battle area. They sat Gárn under a tree, where his grave wounds were tended to by Huróyna. Cára was not far away, shrieking and wailing, utterly distraught at what happened to her daughter. '*Gara—my Gara*,' she was screaming. Her twins were trying to calm her, themselves severely distressed. A few of the women had the foresight to remove the dismembered limb from near the fallen roan dárgh and wrap it in a cloth.

Soon, the two dárgh disputing the corpse were surrounded, putting up a tremendous fight. People thrust their spears, swung their staffs and clubs, to little consequence. The lack of effective weaponry until now had extended the battle unnecessarily.

Wómak and his warriors joined battle. Wómak rushed over to help Bróda, who turned his attention on the smaller female. 'Good to see you Wómak,' Bróda exclaimed in between loading another dart into his blowpipe.

'We heard the uproar coming from here and rushed as fast as we could,' Wómak reported.

Píngo hurried past Bróda and threw his mighty frame at the female dárgh, exonerating people's assertion he was supposed to be sluggish. He hit her with his right shoulder near the dárgh's right armpit, just avoiding a swipe from the left claw. In an amazing piece of acrobatics, Píngo swung on the dárgh's right biceps with his arms, and swivelling, dug his feet into the dárgh's right buttock, pushing hard. Píngo went one way and the dárgh toppled in the opposite direction. Once on the ground it didn't stand a chance. Darts, spears, axes, all took their toll; it never got up.

More darts appeared in the remaining dárgh hide as results of the reinforcements made themselves felt. Morác's incantations were directed at the standing dárgh. Axes were hurled, lodging in its hide. Still the huge dárgh male fought for life, ignoring the wounds inflicted, oblivious of the pain and dart narcotic; one seeming to cancel out the other. The greater the wounds, the more ferociously it fought, aided by its pumped adrenaline. The kópis having finished off the roan dárgh turned their attention on the one remaining. The outcome of the struggle was never in doubt; given twenty of the tribesmen were now dealing with the lone dárgh.

Wómak shouted, *'Get the spear in—that's it—push and twist.'*

Bróda yelled, *'Try to trip it with your staffs.'*

The tide of the conflict turned as warriors' poisoned darts began to have the desired impact. The remaining dárgh toppled thirty to forty darts in its hide. Spear stabs perforated the dárgh; numerous axes were lodged in the corpse. To add to the carnage, the kópis ripped innards open and were feeding.

When the fighting stopped—the visible brutality of the carnage was everywhere. Málina and Ádna were holding Cára back.

'*Gara—my Gara*,' she was screaming hysterically, over and over. She was trying to reach what was left of her little girl, struggling to free herself from the grip of the two women.

'Don't struggle so—you don't want to see her just now,' Ádna was shouting in Cára's ear.

'There's nothing you can do for her—she's at peace in the arms of Aíne,' Málina tried to console her.

Women hurried over to the corpse of the little girl and wrapped it in a groundsheet, carrying it off to be rejoined with its limb; to be cleaned for burial.

Apart from Gárn, others were wounded, though not as severely. The dárgh's razor sharp claws inflicted debilitating lesions on four of the tribe. Those that were unharmed were bandaging those that were.

Huróyna was holding Gárn's head in her lap, trying to comfort the dying man. Her eyes were watery, but she held her tears back. Around her middle, her tunic was covered in blood as she cradled him. In a way, she was holding this stranger the way she would have liked to have held her dying son. She was transferring her grief onto Gárn and was rounding off her own sorrow; trying desperately to consummate her bereavement. Umára was tending Gárn's wounds, swabbing, attempting to staunch the flow of blood; he could see it was hopeless; Gárn was near his last breath.

'Gárn; can you hear me? I'll look after Cára and the twins—I promise. Don't worry—everything will be…' he couldn't finish. Through tears, 'It'll be all right—I swear.' More tears rolled down Umára's face as the last breath went from Gárn. A smile formed at the corners of Gárn's mouth. *Did he hear me?* Thought Umára, looking at the half formed smile. *Oh, I hope so!*

Other wounded were gently being gathered under a tree, in the shade. All the women came to lend a hand in tending to the injured. Émana was taking charge, ordering the fetching of water from the fountain to clean the wounds; smearing balm on them to ease the pain. Néra was mixing balm on the spot from pots she'd hurriedly brought with her. Ganúra was tearing up linen into bandages, others were binding the wounds.

'What a bloody mess!' Wómak exclaimed to Bróda. 'Lucky we took the extra quiver of darts with us.'

'I count us lucky to have got off so lightly. If you hadn't arrived when you did, we might have had many more fatalities.'

'Yes! We did time it just right,' Wómak agreed, but there was no satisfaction in his voice.

His warriors were making makeshift stretchers so the wounded could be carried off to their dens.

Morác came to Bróda. 'I'm afraid we've lost Gárn. He's just passed away from the wounds, the loss of blood. It was shock as much as anything. Seeing his daughter mauled; not being able to rescue her. The women are shielding Cára from the news. She's half out of her mind as it is. We can tell her tomorrow.'

'Thanks Morác,' Bróda told him. 'See what you can do for Cára; try to calm her. Give her a potion to put her to sleep.'

'Néra is doing that as we speak.' Morác looked appreciatively at Wómak; 'You're a sight for sore eyes. You arrived just when we needed you most. Aíne only knows what might have happened if your men hadn't joined in when they did.'

'Glad we could help—just sorry we didn't get here sooner—to prevent this,' he swept his arm at the battlefield.

Bróda held his right hand up, and then smacked his forehead with the palm. 'I'm an old fool; I should have kept more warriors here.' Guilt spread across his face—and disappeared as quickly as it had arisen, displaced by other problems rising through his consciousness. 'Wómak! I have to know—what have you found—the schánda?'

'Bad news! The schánda are only three, maybe four days away at the rate they're going. It's a black line on the horizon. We rushed back as soon as I realised. We have to move—as soon as we can. There's no time to loose.'

'I was afraid of that. Morác! In spite of this tragedy, we have to make a move early tomorrow, latest.'

'I understand. I wish the circumstances were different; we'll have to make the best of it.'

Robán ambled over to Wómak. 'There's a Nólki waiting—'

Wómak raised his hand and stopped him. 'Tell it to the Custodian,' he commanded. Wómak was intent on restoring the chain of command, now they had returned.

Robán faced Bróda. 'There's a Nólki waiting in the hamlet. Wants to talk to who's in charge.'

'Right Wómak! Tidy things up here, get people back to their dens. We've got an early start tomorrow. Oh! Get the kópis off the dárgh; they'll poison themselves. Morác; if we're to leave early tomorrow, we're going to *have to* bury Gárn and Gara today. I don't know *how* you're going to organise that; you'll have to find a way. You see to it.' Bróda turned and put his arm round Robán's shoulder, 'Good to have you back. Where's this Nólki then? Lead on!'

The Nólki scout was standing by the fountain, a quiver of arrows at his waist, beaker in hand, staring at the commotion around him. His bow was leaning against the fountain lip. He was curious, but stayed well out of it. It wasn't his affair.

Bróda strode up to the Nólki, 'Greetings neighbour. What can we do for you?'

The Nólki shuffled his moccasin in the dirt, 'I was ordered by my Custodian to come and warn you.' He stopped, staring at the wounded being carried back.

'Warn us of what?' Bróda was being patient with the undersized scout. The Nólki were similar to the Bólani.

'The Schánda come.' The scout looked into Bróda's face to see if the news meant anything to the Bólani Custodian.

'Thank you neighbour for your news, but we are aware of the coming of the schánda.'

'Then why are you still here? We left four days ago and are almost across the Rími lands. You are still here; we assumed you didn't know.'

That was bluntly put, thought Bróda. *He's right of course. Why are we so late in moving—come to that; if the nightmares are the trigger, as Morác insists, then why were they so late in surfacing? I'm going to have to get to the bottom of this.*

He turned his attention back to the scout, 'We are moving tomorrow morning at first light; thank your Custodian for thinking of us. Would you like to eat with us?'

'No thank you! It is the middle of the afternoon. I must move fast to catch up with my people. May your path be tranquil.' The Nólki put the beaker back on the fountain dais, picked up his bow and loped off towards the South.

Bróda looked on for an instant as the Nólki disappeared, then picked up a beaker and dipped it in the fountain. He drank deeply, filling the beaker a second time. The aftermath of the battle made him excessively thirsty. 'Robán; take a couple of warriors and help Morác bury Gárn and his daughter. Tell Wómak to place sentries around the perimeter. I don't want any more surprises.'

'Yes Bróda.' Robán hurried away to carry out Bróda's orders.

Those of the tribe who finished binding wounds, clearing the battle area, nursing the wounded; found themselves heading for the fountain. They mirrored Bróda's thirst. People stood around in shock; others talked incessantly, on anything they could think of. Beakers were being filled—and quickly emptied.

Before going on sentry duty, warriors were filling their water skins, generally milling with the rest of the tribe, reacquainting themselves with friends after their absence. There was a clear need to reassert the bonds holding the hamlet together—to grieve for the fallen; to touch and be touched. No one said as much, but they all felt fortunate to be alive. First the kóira—now the dárgh. So much tragedy in such a short space of time. In a week the tribe lost three of their number to beasts of the forest; their nourishing *safe* forest.

Bróda raised his hands, requesting silence. 'Friends —dear, dear, tribes-people. I feel...partly responsible for our collective tragedy.' He looked on the ground, and then wiped his nose on a rag. 'I'm sorry!' He took a deep breath, 'If I had left more warriors here—to protect you, this might not have happened.'

A number of those present exclaimed as if in unison, 'No!' Others hurriedly came to Bróda's defence. 'You couldn't have foreseen this would happen.'

Bróda was clearly shaken by his own perceived lapse in leadership, feeling the need to acknowledge to the tribe, his failure; ask their forgiveness. The tribe on the other hand, now needed their leader more than ever. They couldn't afford to have him weaken at the outset of their collective journey. All near him reconfirmed his leadership, his "Custodianship" of the tribe. The community reassured him he had done the right thing, preferring to keep any doubts to themselves. People around him, patted him, and touched him, encouraging him.

Morác arrived at the edge of the group, coming to ask them to join in the funeral rites for Gárn and Gara. He pushed his way over to Bróda.

'Bróda; no one is blaming you. No one tries harder than you, to do what is right for our people. We need you strong—for tomorrow. Please; come and say a few words over Gárn and Gara—and throw sand into the eyes of Húli. You were his best man at his union. Who is more qualified than you to recite Gárn's supplication?'

Bróda shook his head; smiled at Morác; then at the rest of his fellow tribes-people. He stood for a long instant; gazing at the two suns dipping towards the tree line; just feeling at one with them. Their reassurances worked the change. Bróda straightened his back; then followed Morác along the river, to the glade. All those around the fountain— followed Bróda.

Standing over the graves, with warriors ringing the gathering, facing outwards on guard, Morác recited the shortened battle version of the oration to the dead. He then invited Bróda to recount the supplication for Gárn and Gara. It had been agreed, although highly unusual for the spouse to be absent, it was decided for her own benefit. Cára was with Émana, fast asleep, in the grip of a slumber potion; the twins were likewise asleep with smaller doses. They would need to be fresh in the morning for the journey.

The oration was moving, lauding all the best of the potters contribution; his devotion to his family, to his craft. Then Bróda talked of the sorrow of his brutal demise. Bróda added, 'I blamed myself just now for his death...I might as well have blamed Aíne for the turbulent times we find ourselves in. I could even blame the trees for growing, or the beasts for running. But then we would ask ourselves; what are they running from? The schánda! If anything is to blame —then I'm for blaming the schánda.'

Many murmured their approval—in blaming the schánda.

Bróda finished.

The gathering, each in turn, threw a handful of soil over the funeral wrappings containing the remains, before the two warriors filled in the grave. Father and daughter were buried together, in the same mound, side by side. Morác thought Cára would have wanted it that way. The whole tribe came to pay respects, even the four wounded stood swathed in bandages by the graveside.

Slowly in the dusk, reluctantly, the gathering returned to the hamlet. Before dispersing for the night, Bróda called for their attention when they reached the green. 'Dear tribes-people. I am duty bound to remind you—we leave our dens at first light tomorrow. Remember; take only what you can carry comfortably. Eat well before you leave and fill-up on water. Turn in early, sleep well—to your dens now.

Solemnly, the tribe dispersed to their homes, to spend their last night amongst familiar surroundings.

Bróda collected Wómak and both went towards the Warriors' Tree. Inside, both leaders waited till they had the warriors' attention. Bróda stared into each of their faces in turn, making clear the earnestness of his intent.

He began, 'Wómak told me the story of Huróyna; her tragedy. I am minded to give her a second chance in life. In times like these, we'll need every able bodied person we can gather; we've already lost three, and I see no point in dragging up her past. I want you all to solemnly swear to keep her secret; oh, we'll spin a story of her getting lost in the forest—but nothing else. What do you say lads? This means *no* gossip!' Again, he looked hard at their thoughtful features.

One nodded; followed by a cascade of nods from the others. They felt the fairness of the request—not begrudging Huróyna a second prospect in life.

Once they had all sworn to secrecy, Bróda turned to Fúlmon. 'I believe you have words to say to us?'

'Hmm,' Fúlmon cleared his throat. 'Huróyna and I have agreed—that is I've asked her...to become my partner; to agree to join me in union.' The scout looked at the dusty floor.

'Hurrah!' rose the approval from the warriors' throats.

9

LEAVE-TAKING

Above the doomed settlement, stars glimmered in the deep blue sky, with the occasional shooting star leaving a faint white tracer coursing through the heavens. The two moons outlined a thick-set silhouette sitting alone on the edge of the platform—staring into the dark—southwards. Bróda was up before any light hit the eastern horizon, brooding, pondering the best route to take. *Should we veer to the right, or to the left—or simply head as fast as we can in a straight line south? Have I covered everything?* Again he went through a mental list, ticking off items done and others needing to be done.

Many of the dens already had candle-light shining through their circular coarse glass windows. When Morác opened his front door, it was dark. He stood in the open entrance and immediately recognised the sitting silhouette on the distant platform.

Morác called out, 'Come Bróda, have a herbal—take food with us.'

Bróda waved in an off-hand manner, indicating he was deep in thought.

Morác went back inside. 'I'm going to have to keep an eye on Bróda,' he told Néra, sitting at the table.

Néra brought him a drink, and pancakes for them both; sat and spread wild-berry preserve on her pancake. Both sat quietly for an instant, eating, looking around their den, taking in the enormity of the next move, locking the atmosphere into their memories.

Near the door lay two bundles, and two back-packs for the journey. Clothing, bed-roll, a few utensils, nothing more. Their food had gone to Wólni's, to be packed on to the travois the Stándy were pulling. Morác's bundle contained a brand new bow and a quiver full of arrows. No extras to weigh them down. However, Morác included his own and Fándin's note-books to continue his Sorcerers studies—feeling it a duty to the tribe, like bringing along the bow and arrows.

Néra gulped the last of her food, drank the last of her herbal, banging the beaker on the table. 'I can't stand this,' she told Morác. 'If we're going to go; let's go.'

She rose hurriedly, eyes moist, and went to her back-pack, hoisting it onto her shoulders; picked up her bundle and opened the door.

Morác didn't say a word. He threw back the contents of his beaker, swallowed his final mouthful, and quietly put it on the table. He stood; took one last look at his den; turned to Néra and smiled.

Quietly he said, 'Let's go.'

He joined her—picked up the quiver and tied around his waist, lifted his back-pack, hung the bow on the right support; the bundle on the left support. Stood for a twitch, then went through the den entrance; turned and locked the door—in his imagination; he was coming back.

Outside, first light was making itself visible on the eastern horizon. Émana was sitting by Bróda's side, Wómak was standing facing Bróda; Bróda was exhorting Wómak to control the situation. The green was filling with tribes-people, gathered in family groups around their belongings, quivering kópis near them, waiting for Bróda to organise the order of march.

'First thing,' Bróda was telling Wómak, 'do a count —there should be thirty-nine people in total; including yourself and us. There would have been forty-two, but—we lost three. Strongest at the front; weakest at the back. All five kópis on a tight leash.'

'You sure?'

'If we weren't fleeing for our lives—I would be less brutal. As it is—I want the strongest setting the pace, the rest must try to keep up. Don't worry; I'm not going to abandon anybody. We'll review the situation tonight; after we've seen how the day's march has gone.'

'That puts Ganúra and me in the lead?'

'I'm afraid so. Look; this is how I see it.' Bróda picked up a stick and drew on the ground. 'We'll have the scouts, Fúlmon and Máyo out front, let them have my kópis; there.' He made a mark out front. 'Fúlmon asked if we'd let Huróyna go with him. I've said yes. Robán takes rearguard with two others; there.' More marks on the ground. 'Then three warriors on either side of the column for protection. Me, Émana, you, Ganúra, Morác, and Néra leading the column; there. What do you think? Oh, and the Stándy at the rear of the column, pulling travois with our food.'

Wómak looked at the drawing on the ground depicting people's positions. 'Looks like you've thought of everything. I'll go over to the people and organise it.'

'Good man. When you've got them into marching order; I'll come round and have a chat; reassure them, check their gear.'

The light was just dawning, rising over the forest roof. The rest of the Bólani gathered on the green with their belongings. Wómak went round counting. *Thirty-eight people,* he muttered to himself. He counted again; still thirty-eight.

'Who's missing?' he yelled into the gathered crowd.

People looked at each other; then looked around at their neighbours; then over at the rest. They shook their heads; then the whole tribe counted each other.

In a short while Morác went over to Wómak. 'It looks like it's Mútani. He's nowhere to be seen. My guess, it's deliberate; he wants to stay behind, with Máda.'

Wómak shook his head. 'We could spend...all day looking for him. It's a decision for Bróda.' He went back to tell the Custodian.

Bróda frowned. 'Loathe as I am to leave him—he's left me little choice. If he's done what I think he's done; I'll respect his choice.' A shudder of alarm went through Bróda's thoughts at the prospect of leaving anybody behind. 'Just to salve my conscience; send warriors to look in the obvious places—just in case he's ill. His den; the Glade; the grave. We move as soon as they get back.' As an afterthought he added, 'Impress on the lads not to dawdle. Oh, and Wómak; warn Morác that I want him to perform a sacred invocation after we've eaten tonight.'

Wómak called Robán over. 'Mútani's missing. Take two lads; check his den; the Glade, and Máda's grave. If you find him, bring him to the green. Make it snappy; we leave soon.' Then he passed on to Morác Bróda's invocation request.

Robán hurried off to carry out the orders.

Morác went over to the platform to have a word with Bróda. 'What's this Wómak tells me? You want an invocation from me for tonight?'

'If you'd be so good. Do a theatrical; get people's minds off the journey. You know what I mean.'

'I'll do my best. In the mean time, Wólni wants you to check the Stándy. Taking all the tribes food is a big responsibility.'

Both strolled to where Wólni, Málina and their son Cóer, sixteen seasons old, were harnessing the last of the Stándy to the loaded travois. The travois was Málina's brain-wave to ensure Bróda didn't leave her precious Stándy behind. The travois was two long poles joined by a platform in the middle, the wider end had two poles dragging on the ground, the narrower end fastened to a harness on the stándy's back. Tied on the platform was the food. There were fourteen Stándy's in all; put together, they were pulling quiet a large load; a vital load the tribe didn't have to carry.

Bróda smiled at Málina. 'This idea of yours, the travois; they'll make a big difference in the amount of provisions we can carry. Well done! So, why did you want to see me?'

Wólni puffed himself up a bit, 'Who's in charge of this lot....' he pointed at the Stándy, 'Umára or us?'

'Why? What's been happening? You been arguing with Umára?'

'He came over and started pulling at the fastenings...on the stándy, said he "...wanted to be sure their not loose." As if we didn't know how to load a travois securely. I ask you?'

Cóer felt embarrassed by his dad's behaviour and tried to melt into the background.

'I'll talk to him. But let me be clear. When we're on the move; you're in charge; when we stop, he takes over. He's the cook; to make sure everyone gets fair shares, he cooks for all the tribe. He shares the food out; it's only fair he's in charge of the food. That's my decision. Now I want no more disputes over silly things. How we behave to each other must change—on the march. No petty squabbling...no insults...no arguments. We have to get along; our lives depend on it. Is that clear?' Bróda said the last part loudly and looked squarely into Wólni's eyes—intent that the weaver believes him.

The weaver's puffed up attitude disappeared. His head hung, only his eyes looked into Bróda's—held there by the power of Bróda's personality.

'Yes Custodian...clear.' Wólni whispered and lowered his eyes in answer.

'We're all on edge,' Málina tried to excuse her partner. 'It'll settle once we're on the move—you'll see.'

'Yes, I know. Anyhow, thanks for the travois...I'm speaking on behalf of the whole tribe when I say that. Now; must go and see what Wómak's up to.'

Robán returned. 'Can't find Mútani anywhere,' he told Wómak. 'Looks like he's hiding. We could spend days looking for him.'

Wómak told Bróda the bad news.

'We can't afford this...not now. We're going to have to leave without him.' Bróda raised his voice above the dawn chorus coming from the forest, above the crowd chatter, *'Right; listen-up everybody*. We've searched for Mútani...but without success; he's vanished. My decision; we're leaving.

'Gather your stuff. Wómak has put you in order of march; please try and maintain that throughout the day. Súdair, Ganúra, make sure you keep the kópis on a tight leash; can't have them wondering off.

'First day will be the worst—especially for those short on exercise...and of course; the elderly. Nobody will be left behind; you have my promise. Make sure you have two pairs of socks on—that's to prevent blisters. I'm aiming for ten leagues by nightfall—more tomorrow. Remember what's behind us. That's the reason for this journey. I want to remind you there are lots of panicky animals in the forest; fleeing. We've all seen the chaos they can cause; the kóira, dárgh. Even small animals can be dangerous if panicked. We're going into lands that are foreign to us. We don't know what hazards we'll meet. We're going into—the unknown. Be extra vigilant...any questions?' Only silence greeted him.

'Morác! Say a few words for our safe journey.'

Morác strode out a way; turned to the tribe, and began, 'Aíne; mother of us all...we look to you for our safekeeping. Protect us on this journey into the unknown. Give us strength for the march; help us to get along with our fellow tribes-people. To each other—soften our voices. We will make it, if we help each other. For that we seek your support; so that we can support each other. We are the Bólani —with Aíne's help, that is our strength.'

The gathered crowd responded with one voice, '*We are the Bólani—that's our strength.*'

Morác stood still for a moment; then joined Néra in the column, behind Wómak and Ganúra—and their two kópis.

'Now; Fúlmon, head off along the path towards the Glade; we're going towards Rími country.' Bróda voice boomed, so all could hear, '*Wómak; lead on!*'

With that—the march began. Ganúra was pulled forward by their two eager kópis.

Bróda stood aside, by Úbor's den, watching the column leave; taking one last look around. He joined Robán at the rear for short period, marching alongside him. They walked in silence until they reached the Glade.

'Robán, I want you to keep an eye on blisters. People will try to ignore them and walk themselves into serious injuries. If they deal with the blisters at an early stage, it will save us having to carry them later on. You know what I'm saying?'

'Yes, Custodian. I'll keep an eye out for anyone hobbling.'

'Good man.'

As the column passed the graveyard, for an instant— he thought he saw Mútani's face peering through a bush, grinning, trying to keep out of sight. It happened so fast, fleetingly; he wasn't sure it wasn't simply a wish of his. When he tried to focus on the bush, he didn't see anything. He blinked a couple of times, shook his head, and kept going.

He patted Robán on the back, 'Keep your eyes peeled.' With that parting injunction, he quickened his pace.

Bróda went to the head of the column, and led the way from the Glade. *Into the unknown; Aíne? If you're watching, I add my personal prayer for us. I put our tribe into your benevolent hands; look after us.* Bróda's silent prayer was a way of clearing his thoughts; leaving everything behind, in his mind. A closing.

The Bólani column made good progress throughout the morning, heading south. True, after a while the weaker members began grumbling; the pace was too quick; their loads too heavy; was it really necessary to have gone today? On it went like that—in that vain.

Those who had no thought of grumbling laughed and joked, conversing with their neighbours, as if they were out on a pleasant Springtime jaunt through the forest. At the front of the column, Wómak and Ganúra were of the latter disposition, as were Sáor and Émer; Wólni on the other hand, near the rear, was one of the grumblers.

He was trying to stir up Bréac, who wasn't having any of it. Wólni couldn't understand why Bréac was so cheery, so uncharacteristically optimistic. It was as if he was talking to Bréac's twin brother, diametrical opposite in character to the old Bréac. Even worse; Scéna had changed into a quiet accommodating woman, nauseatingly pleasant as far as Wólni was concerned. He finally gave up in disgust, and by mid-day had moved to the other side of the column from Bréac and Scéna.

Shúta couldn't help overhearing Wólni trying to rouse Bréac. Urging her two kids along, she asked Súdair, her partner, 'Why is Wólni being such a pain to Bréac? He's never been like that. It's usually the other way round; Bréac usually inciting Wólni. It's as if they've switched roles.'

'Listen precious,' Súdair tried to explain, hanging onto his young kópi. 'Wólni never really thought the trek would happen. He expected Wómak to come round and tell him, "it's all been a mistake...forget it...get on with your life." He's just discovered reality; and he doesn't like it. So, he's turned the tables on Bréac. Still; he can't understand why Bréac isn't taking the bait—neither can I for that matter. A strange thing going on there.'

Bróda called a halt at mid-day. Look-outs were posted. They stopped in a clearing for a rest and a bite of something cold to eat, handed out by the two cooks, Umára and Uílin. Thirsts were quenched, stomachs satisfied, if not exactly filled. It revived those would-be mutineers, belaying their rebellion. Those who were positively enjoying the trek were exhilarated by the sustenance, eager to be off again.

Bróda went round the tribe encouraging people. 'That's it, we're doing fine; making good progress,' he said repeatedly to family groups. 'Change your socks—make sure you're wearing two pairs. Soon be stopping for the night,' he told those looking over tired. They included Émer's and Málina's elderly parents.

As they were ready to move off, Máyo came back to tell Bróda the path to the Rími village was clear and he'd seen no sign of danger ahead.

'*You hear that!*' Bróda shouted to the tribes-people. 'We've got easy going ahead and nothing to fear...so let's move off, now, at a good pace.'

Máyo sped ahead to join the other scouts. The column reformed into marching order. Bróda moved off at a goodly pace, setting an example.

The afternoon's trek took them increasingly through lush evergreen forest. Either side of the column were animals streaming south though a variety of broadleaf trees. The Springtime bird chatter was shrill, mirroring the panicky rushing animals below. Extensively buttressed roots were a peculiarity of the trees they were passing, providing portals through which smaller animals scurried. Sun-streaks lit up the surrounding forest, highlighting the various shades of greens, browns.

The column hiked on at a steady pace, people at the rear herding the Stándy dragging the travois. Uneventfully, they marched on late into afternoon when they came out into an open space. Bróda, seeing the scouts waiting in the middle of the clearing; stopped the group. Fúlmon had the two kópi on leads.

'There's no better camping space further on,' Fúlmon told Bróda.

Bróda's kópi were nuzzling him, happy to see him. Fúlmon pulled them back. Bróda looked around, and then ordered the pitching of the night camp. Having given the orders, he turned his attention to serious stroking of his kópis.

The clearing half reminded Morác of the tribe's Glade back near their hamlet...their deserted hamlet. He sighed...then got a grip on himself. *This won't do. I must look forward, not back. We've a long way to go and I've to be a strength for the people, not gape back on what's gone.* He straightened his shoulders and went off to the trees to look for stout poles with which to make A-frame beds for Néra and himself. Others of the tribe did likewise. Wood was gathered for the fire. The cooks busied themselves, gathering utensils, water; leaving Píngo to light the camp fire.

Within a short span, a roaring fire was blazing in the middle of the camp. The panicky animals would steer clear of such a pyrotechnic display. The cooks began complaining the flames were too high and the fire had to be dampened, allowing the pots to be hung. By the time the food was ready, tired people had found spots where they built their A-frame beds. Logs were rolled up close so people could sit by the fire. The food dished out; everyone ate in silence. Half way through the meal, as the food revived the weary travellers, conversations began. By the time the plates were emptied, laughter and babble filled the evening air. People relaxed, making light of the days trek. It hadn't been such a bad day after all.

Morác stood up, putting a light brown robe over his shoulders; then move out so he had room to manoeuvre. In his left hand Morác held a timpani drum the size of a lesser wheel; promptly he began chanting and dancing in a figure of eight, gently at first, working the drum with the stick in his right hand. At the first sound of the drum, people stopped talking and listened with rapt attention.

He intoned in a deep voice, 'O mighty Wáclaw. By the consecrated talisman from the sky above; I invoke thee. By the most sacred word-graph of heaven; I conjure thee. By the power of the meaning arising from these forms I make; I summon thee. I beseech thee; hear my form; mark my voice.'

The chanting rose and fell in a hypnotic fashion holding the listeners spell bound, capturing them in its rhythm. Then Morác asked the spirit, the questions he had been prompted to ask, 'Will the tribe reach the Golden Sea?' Dancing to the rhythm, the drumming increasing its hypnotic effect. 'Will the Schánda catch the tribe?' More drumming; more intense dancing. 'Will Bróda lead the tribe to safety?' The drum tapping reached a crescendo. Suddenly the drumming stopped. Morác dropped to the ground in a deep trance, holding his crystal talisman, allowing the spirit its voice—so it could answer the questions—through *his* voice.

Morác spoke with a contrasting high pitched inflection, '*The Bólani will reach the Golden Sea.*' Wáclaw was answering their questions. A hush descended, punctuated by night sounds. '*The Schánda will not catch the Bólani.*' Morác lay trembling, his mouth working, seemingly on its own. Then the next emission from Wáclaw, '*The Custodian will lead the Bólani to safety.*' Lying, twitching on the ground, perspiration flowed freely from Morác's forehead. Abruptly; he relaxed. His face reclaimed normality. Néra went to him and wiped his face with a cloth.

Bróda came over and helped Morác to his feet. 'Thanks,' he said quietly into his ear.

The relief on the faces of the tribes-people was clear. They heard the answers coming from Morác's spirit guide, Wáclaw. It was definite; they would succeed. They wanted to hear what Wáclaw told them. They *needed* to hear it, be reassured, and be told that everything would be all right.

93

Morác's exhausted form confirmed the veracity of the Spirit's words.

The tribe turned into to their beds that night, convinced now —all would be well with their trek; their journey.

10

STORM-FORCE

Nearing dawn, the wind picked up, ripping off the covers from the A-frame shelters; waking the people from their exhausted slumbers. Even as the tribe awoke, the ferocity of the wind increased. It howled through the trees, clashing leaves against leaves; branches against branches, impacting, snapping, crashing to the ground.

Wómak's voice was heard above the wind, '*Raise yourselves. Alarm! Alarm!*'

Then the thunderstorm struck. The stándy, tethered at one end of the clearing, began kicking their rear hooves into the air in distress; trying to stampede. Nearby the five kópis were growling in agitation; no whistling; always a bad sign. Bróda sent six warriors to round the animals up; the stándy were strung together, dragged under the trees, tied to the trunks. The kópi went to their owners.

The clearing was exposed to sudden gusts sweeping in from the east, laden with heavy raindrops.

Bróda and Wómak were shouting, '*To the trees; take your belongings.*'

People swiftly gathered their back-packs and bundles ran for the trees as lightening began to flash overhead. Peals of thunder followed, resounding in the twilight as the thunderstorm turned nasty and the wind picked up further, spiralling into a full blown storm. The heavens opened; rain poured onto the chaos of the emptying glade below.

Bróda yelled, *'Find sturdy tree trunks; lash yourselves to them.'*

Morác helped Néra to carry her bundle, pulling her towards the trees. Others ran, stumbling, falling, and picking themselves up. The elderly were being piggy-backed by warriors. Reaching the swaying canopy, they tied each other to the trees with the broadest girths.

With difficulty, Wómak went round checking the ropes were securely tied.

Morác was trying to tie Néra to a tree, but was having difficulties. Wómak came over, 'Let me help you.'

'My fingers are cold,' Morác explained.

Finally Wómak tied himself next to Ganúra, holding a kópi each.

Bróda was close by holding on to both kópis. The kópis were sheltering behind the tree, using the tree as a windbreak.

As the storm progressed, the tribe pressed themselves against the broadleaf trees, trying to sit on their belongings, backs to the trunks, facing west, away from the wind. Younger trees were uprooted, thrown to the ground. Above, the canopy oscillated tremendously. A few of the older weaker trees were sent crashing by the ferocious winds, narrowly missing people.

Dawn found the Bólani tribe cowering, shivering, lashed to tree trunks, the driving deluge soaking everything; everyone. Whooshing gusts of rain laden air were forced between the trunks, wrenching at the people, pulling at their clothes, trying to tear them free of their bindings.

The vehement outburst lasted well into morning. In the clearing, the remnants of their broken A-frames shelters were scattered to the west end of the glade. From the depth of the forest they heard violent detonations as trunks impacted against trunks. The foliage high above whip-lashed in the noxious wind; away in the clearing, flowers withered. Around, the forest floor hissed, erupting, hurling the decomposing ground litter into the air; then against anything solid.

Finally, close to mid-morning the storm abated, dying as quickly as it started. Dazed, windblown people untied themselves from the trunks, stumbling, muttering, sighing, and shaking.

'Píngo! Quick; light a fire.' Bróda's began to organise the recovery. 'Get people to help gather wood.'

A young girl screamed.

'Láila! What's the matter,' Émer demanded.

Émer's daughter pointed at her grandmother, hanging limp next to her, tied to the tree trunk.

'Oh, mother! I think she...she's dead,' she quivered.

People stared quietly.

'Let me through...let me through,' Émer's father insisted, pushing his way through the staring people.

He stood before his wife, tears beginning to roll down his cheeks. 'Émer, Láila; give me a hand,' he sobbed quietly, trying to undo the knots on the rope holding his wife.

Morác used his knife; the rope parted and the four caught the limp figure, gently lowering her to the forest floor.

Morác checked for signs of life. 'I'm sorry,' he told the grandfather. 'She's passed away peacefully.'

'*Not* peacefully—not in *this* storm. Not your fault though,' the old man added, sadness in his voice.

'With your permission; we'll bury your wife out there, in the glade—after you've said your goodbyes.' Morác pointed to a spot fourteen cubits away. 'Would that be acceptable to you?'

'I suppose...yes.' The old man knelt and took his dead wife in his arms; held her in silence one last time.

People stood nearby, willing their support to Sáor's family in their grief.

All three family members were holding each other, comforting themselves, standing by Sáor's kneeling father.

Morác ambled over to Wómak and took him aside. 'Station two warriors close by; when they're ready to put her to rest, get them to dig the grave. Call me when that's to happen.'

'I will,' the tall man replied.

'How did we fair...the storm, I mean?

'Apart from the lady, there; nobody's hurt. I'd say we came off pretty well—apart from...you know. Oh! We lost a kópi as well.'

'We were lucky,' Morác replied. 'Who's kópi?'

'Mine. The leash broke and he got blown away. Saw him flying.' A pained expression sat on his face. 'Yeah. A few bruises—people shook up. Yes, the Goddess was with us today. All it needed was one of the trees to hit us—and we'd have had a lot of casualties.' Wómak's grimace suggested he was thinking of the dead woman.

'The storm's nothing unusual for this time of season. If we'd been back in our dens, we'd have heard the wind; nothing more. It would have had little or no impact. We'd be forced to tidy a windswept mess up. That's all. Out here, in the open like this—'

'I know. You're right—we *were* lucky.'

All that remained of the mighty storm was a light breeze rustling the branches; sweeping the glade.

Soon a fire was roaring in the same place as the previous nights. The circle of logs had survived. People were returning with their belongings; warming themselves before the fire. The stándy and remaining four kópi were tethered nearby. The cooks had begun the delayed morning meal; which had to wait on the burial of Sáor's mother. The funeral service was kept short; a version of the battle service.

People gathered around the fire, a gloomy atmosphere permeating the clearing. Another of the tribe had gone to meet Húli, guardian of the gateway to the netherworld.

Morác brooded on his way to Bróda. *How many more are we to loose on this wretched journey?* he bemoaned. Whilst passing the log on which Cára sat huddled with Umára, the twins close with her, Morác overheard a scrap of conversation. Cára was telling Umára, '...Gárn never wanted to go on this journey—he got his wish didn't he?...I do *miss* him so....' She choked into her brown scarf, using the end to dab her face.

At least Umára kept his promise to Gárn, Morác mused, *taking Cára and the twins under his wing.* Not for the first time he marvelled at the good nature of the cook-come-warrior.

Bróda was saying a few words of comfort to Sáor and his family as Morác came up. Bróda hugged each family member before turning to Morác.

'We must make a move as soon as we can,' Morác advised.

'We will; shortly.' Bróda looked up at the sky. 'What do you think?'

'These things blow up—you know—out of nowhere. I think it's finished. Anyway, we've got no choice. There's that lot behind us. I hope it slowed *them*...if it hit that lot, that is.'

It was mid-day before the column reformed and trundled out of the clearing, the scouts taking the lead with Bróda's two kópis. In contrast to the grouchy tired sentiment on arrival; now the column had a melancholy feel to it. The idea that the trek might be simply a ramble through the forest, disappeared. Peoples' features set hard with the recognition the trek was clearly a fight for survival.

As the days passed, instinctively, people walked closer together, were more accommodating, less irascible. It took three uneventful solid days march to reach the Rími village. They all knew it would be empty, but they went there since the paths were less overgrown, and they might find provisions to refill their depleted supplies.

The scouts returned mid-afternoon of the third day to report that the Rími village was only half a league in front. As they marched on, a buzz of excitement filtered through the column. For most of the tribe, this would be their first encounter with the Rími tribe; their exotic neighbours to the south. The Rími had little in the way of items to trade; so the Bólani had little contact with them. The Rími traded with the Kárti through the Nólki, bypassing the Bólani.

Fúlmon with the two kópis out front led the march into the centre of the Rími village. Wild animals scattered in every which way. More came running out of the empty huts; others dispersed from beneath the high huts, platforms sitting on stilts, acting as the Rími storage larder. The scouts let their kópis off their leashes. Ganúra did likewise with her kópi. With the added help of the warriors, the village was soon cleared of wild animals.

The tribe stopped, stared—in horror at the desecration before them.

Shúta contemptuously uttered what was on most of their minds, 'May Aíne forgive them. These people live in dens made from dead trees; an outrage; sacrilege. How can civilised people destroy trees?'

'They're called huts here,' Morác's voice informed. 'I met the Rími a long time ago. They told me of themselves; I remember being shocked back then. They're different from us; that's all. We can't condemn them for being different; can we...?'

The scouts came back, kópis back on leashes, took Bróda aside, informed him they found a message from the Rími; addressed to the Bólani. Bróda's kópis nuzzled his legs. Bróda went to where the message was.

The column stayed in the centre of the Rími village; relaxed and began building a fire, as if they were staying there overnight. Bróda had said nothing of staying. Nevertheless, people began to unpack their bedrolls. They felt safer being back in a hamlet, any hamlet.

Bróda returned with the scouts. 'We've been left a pictorial message from the Rími. They say we can help ourselves to any supplies we might need. Fúlmon found the message in their Custodians den, etched into the table.'

'We thought we'd stay the night, here,' Morác told him. 'All right by you?'

'We ought to move on,' Bróda admonished. Then looked around at the tired people and said, 'Oh, what the Húli; we'll stay here tonight. Wómak! Post sentries.'

'Right away,' Wómak eagerly approved.

'Thanks,' Morác said.

'Morác; you should know better. Wómak; remember why we're here. I relented just now, but the Schánda will be at our throats, unless we outrun them. You do *understand* that?'

Both Morác and Wómak nodded, if a bit morosely.

'That means pushing ahead mercilessly. I look to the both of you, to *lead* in this; not behave as if this is a sort of game. I'm sorry to have to talk to you like this.'

'I'm sorry,' Morác said sheepishly, quickly realising.

'Me too,' added Wómak.

'Fine. We *are* the leaders—if we falter; the rest of the tribe won't stand a chance. Now let's see what the cooks have for us.' Bróda led the way to the campfire.

After the meal, Morác relaxed; he wasn't aware of it, but the village surroundings had sedated his unconscious. For a brief period, the worries lifted from his spirit. He searched and found the Rími shamán's hut and invited Néra to make it their den for the night. A few of the tribe did the same. Most refused to bed down surrounded by dead trees; they bedded down in the open, under the stars.

'It's a bit dim inside,' Néra complained when they entered their hut.

Morác found, strategically placed around the hut, six individual lamp-wicks floating in oil. He lit them all with a tinder from the campfire; stood back.

'Well? What do you think?'

'Needs tidying.'

'Fuss pot,' he teased.

'It's quite large—when it's lit. Still a bit creepy; dead trees.'

'It'll be all right. Well...make yourself at home.'

Unpacking his four notebooks, he began to thumb through them. The Bólani had an iconic script; simple, effective. It was as capable of communicating complex linguistic information as any cursive writing system. After a while he got Fándin's three notebooks out and tried furthering his sorcerer's studies. Néra prepared their bed-rolls after clearing a space in a corner.

He sat propped against the far wall from the door, Fándin's three notebooks by his left leg, and his own four by his right leg. Morác leaned back, closed his eyes and tried to memorise what he read. When he next opened his eyes, he thought he caught sight of a tiny loose scrap of paper in the spine of one of Fándin's notebooks he was reading. He lifted the book to the light. It was deep in the spine itself. He tried teasing it out with his fingers, but to no avail. He used his knife to ease it out, damaging the spine in the process. With difficulty he retrieved the scrap, unfolded it flat on the floor. He squinted at the minuscule pictograms—soon realising it was a spell.

From a distance to the East, there came a melancholy caterwauling, as though somebody was in great pain.

'What the Húli is that,' exclaimed Morác, startled out of his reading.

'I'm not sure I like the sound of that,' Néra agreed. 'What have you got there?' she asked. She came across looking over Morác's shoulder.

'Don't know...think it's a spell of a kind. It's in Fándin's hand. I'm having difficulty deciphering it.'

'My eyes are better than yours—let me have a look,' Néra reached over his shoulder. She held the scrap close to her eyes. 'It's about..."b-e-s-e-e-c-h t-h-e-e"...they really are tiny pictograms.'

'Read it *all* out to me—from the beginning.'

'All right, here goes..."I beseech thee...by the inverse reversion...of the sacred alignment...of the hand and eye...by the light...of the two suns of Kálar...make the word graph...of the pages within pages...known to your supplicant."'

Morác frowned. 'It can't mean what I think it means.' He stroked his beard, pulled at his moustache, getting agitated.

'Would you care to explain?' she stared at him.

'I'll show you.' Morác extracted his crystal talisman from under his tunic and held it in his hand, until it began to glow green, repeating, 'I beseech thee by the inverse reversion of the sacred alignment of the hand and eye, by the light of the two suns of Kálar, make the word graph of the pages within pages known to your supplicant.'

The melancholy caterwauling started again. They hadn't noticed when it stopped.

A rustle flurried through Fándin's three notebooks lying on the floor, startling Néra; as if a den sprite had skipped over the books. Morác picked up the top notebook and stared at the new pages.

'May Aíne protect me. Each page in the book has turned into two pages. Another page has been revealed— more spells!'

Néra had begun to be alarmed at Morác's behaviour; now she calmed. 'Is that all?'

'You don't understand. There are so many spells missing; spells I witnessed Fándin performing. I'd given up hope of finding them. Suddenly, I'm to double the number of spells at my command. This could be the difference between us surviving, or not surviving this trek.'

'Oh!' Néra wasn't impressed. She didn't seem to appreciate the enormity of the implications. She trusted

Morác to do the best for them both and didn't want to be too involved in his work.

'Let me read these for a while.'

Néra went over to their bed-roll and lay with a sigh. 'I'm so tired even the caterwauling won't keep me awake; all that walking. I wish we knew what that noise was.'

The occasional gasp escaped from Morác as he read the new pages. He was totally absorbed. Then after a while, 'Oh! Finally...so there it is.' He got up and went over to his back-pack and pulled out a piece of flat oval polished crystal the size of his hand. One side had black lacquer covering it. He stared at the clear side. Reciting the newly discovered spell whilst holding his talisman, the crystal began to shimmer. An image formed in the middle of the crystal as Morác stared inside; a picture of a swarm of vicious insects were surging over his green. Lándo trees in the background indicated it was the Bólani hamlet they left four days ago. Shock spread across Morác's face as the realisation sank in.

11

LETHAL LAKE

A hush descended on the Rími village as members of the Bólani tribe settled to their fifth night of flight from the advancing schánda. It was occasionally interrupted by a caterwauling coming from the East.

Otherwise, it was a quiet night, with a light breeze blowing from the North. Morác hurried across to Bróda's hut, stopping at the door, listening to the night; he almost said aloud, *damned caterwauling*. Bróda had settled into the Rími Custodian's hut where he sat gazing at the message etched for him into the table. Morác knocked.

'Come in,' shouted Bróda, 'It's open.'

Morác stepped inside.

'Well, what brings you here so late?' Bróda kept looking at the etching.

Morác joined him at the table. 'Look at this,' he placed the oval crystal on it.

'I've seen it before. If it doesn't work, it's useless.' Bróda said dismissively. 'You any idea what's causing that caterwauling?'

'No! Forget that—the crystal—it works—'

'If it works—then *why* did we have to send that scouting mission to the north, to the schánda? Answer me *that*?' Bróda was aggravated.

'Calm down. I've only just made it work. I found the right spell in Fándin's notebook—just a few moments ago. I hurried here as quickly as I could.'

'Oh! *Sorry* Morác—I'm distracted by that damn caterwauling. Is it threatening, do you think?' He turned his head eastwards. 'Frankly, I'm worried by our progress—and to top it, I've no idea how far back the schánda are.'

'That's what I'm here to tell you—I've just seen them.'

'Heh! What's that you say?'

'You heard me right. I've been looking at the schánda's progress. They're in our hamlet as we speak— swarming all over it.'

'Show me,' Bróda held Morác's eyes.

Morác placed the polished oval crystal on the table and took hold of his talisman hanging around his neck, fingering it gently. The amulet crystal began to glow with a deep green light whilst Morác recited the newly discovered "far-seeing" spell, *'By the power of the talisman I hold in the miracle of time, from the vantage of the northern compass point, through the eye of the great Racul, I seek to cast my sight onto the distant hamlet of the Bólani. Let the image be seen in the far-seeing crystal.'*

A mist began to circulate in the oval crystal, which cleared to show the familiar settlement, black with large hairy insects crawling all over it. The two stared at the abomination, their eyes captivated by the seething swarm.

'Look—to the right—there. Can you get this thing to close in on Mútani's den?' urged Bróda.

'By the power of the talisman—veer right—go closer.' Morác intoned.

The oval crystal zoomed in on eastern side where Mútani's Lándo tree stood. They saw that Mútani was in the top branches, out on a limb, claws trying to snip at him from inside the tree.

'How in Aíne's name did they get inside the tree?' Bróda wanted to know.

From inside, the protruding claws were trying to enlarge the hole, snipping at the edges of the bark, tearing pieces off. The close view through the crystal was as clear as looking at one's self in a pool of water; all the detail was seen. Below the limb waited a mass of schánda; a sea of claws extended upwards, snipping, trying to get at Mútani. The old man was doomed. The insects were climbing on each other's backs, trying to make a pyramid to reach the limb. It was desperate.

'Turn it off...turn it off...' Bróda pointed at the crystal.

'*By the power of the talisman—cease.*' Morác intoned.

'I warned everyone...I told everyone what would happen. Why didn't the old fool listen to me? That's no way to die...ripped apart by those claws...why the Húli didn't he listen?'

'It's not your fault,' Morác tried to console him. 'You did your best. He chose to go that way—near to his beloved Máda.'

Wómak burst thorough the door without knocking. 'You should have called me,' he complained to Bróda. 'I heard the commotion; the whole tribes listening to the noise coming from the East—*and* the noise coming from in here.'

'Morác's got the far-seeing crystal working,' Bróda said by way of explanation.

'We *all* know that. The den wall's thin enough to hear you breathing.'

'Then you know the schánda are in our hamlet—only five days behind us.'

'And that shrieking in the east?' Wómak stood his ground. 'The women think it's a bunch of Rími crones making the noise out there in the forest.'

'Well, if it is; then we have nothing to worry of.' Morác felt guilty at having caused his commotion. 'Now we know that, we'd better get to sleep. There's a long haul tomorrow.' He now urged everyone back to sleep.

Bróda began ushering Morác out of the room. 'Yeah, you're right. Back to bed Morác. Wómak, wait a moment.' When the shamán had left. 'I want you to lay a trap for those hags making the noise....'

Near dawn, there came an outburst from the direction of the sentries.

'Come on *you*—get a move on——move I say.'

The sentries were prodding three old women with their spears, driving them into the centre of the village.

'No more of that caterwauling—keep moving.' Wómak prodded the reluctant straggler.

Bróda came out of his hut. 'Ho! What's this? So our plan worked. Good job, Wómak. So our women were right.'

'It's a bunch of crazy Rími women,' Wómak explained. 'From what I can make out; they want us out of their village. They were trying to frighten us into leaving. Hoping we'd think they were lemurs on the prowl. We found them fifty cubits into the forest, howling like animals.'

'Why aren't they with their tribe?' Morác arrived quietly.

'*You go,*' shouted the old woman at the front. '*Our village,*' she proclaimed defiantly.

Bróda put his hand up for silence. 'We have an invitation from your Custodian in writing, to stay here; to take your provisions.' Then he turned. 'Why aren't you with your men-folk?'

The three Rími women were all dressed in black, loose hanging tunics, smudged with dirt. None were young. Their dark hair matted, unwashed—truthfully, they whiffed. All needed a good scrub. All had a wild look in their eyes.

The one in front spoke again, 'We stay. Men stupid!' Less loud this time.

The other two women nodded vigorously, agreeing with the speaker.

'You do *know* big insects are coming; you're in great danger.' Morác tried to explain to the old women standing before him. The stubborn bearing told him he was wasting his time.

'Forget it, Morác.' Bróda told him.

'Look at their faces. They don't care.' Néra had come up behind him. 'I don't think they're going anywhere. Leave them. We're going now—so they're either coming with us—or staying.'

'We can't just desert them to the schánda.' Morác was desperate not to abandon them to the huge insects.

'Néra's right. They'll quiet once we've gone,' Wómak advised. 'If their own Custodian couldn't make them leave—you're not going to succeed.'

Bróda shook his head, 'Get the people together—it's time we made a move. The suns are up.'

Back on the trek, replenished with fresh supplies, having eaten quickly, the tribe felt the need to put speed into their gait. Morác was congratulated by all, on getting the far-seeing crystal working—a real triumph.

Fúlmon went out front with the scouts and kópis. Now they knew where their enemy was; just the knowledge itself put their minds at ease. Fear always fed on the unknown —and the converse dispelled fear. They could now concentrate on the job at hand—putting distance between them and their foe.

The Spring weather was intoxicating, benign; the early morning freshness, invigorating.

'I think it's going to be a hot day,' Wómak ventured to Morác as they walked side by side.

'I simply don't understand those Rími women.' Morác was preoccupied ever since leaving the village. 'There's a wrongness, in their heads I mean.'

Wómak said nothing. There was nothing to be said; anyway, not by him. The women had refused to see sense—that was that. Who knows the mind of a woman? Wómak made an effort to understand Ganúra—but other women were beyond him.

Néra, Émana and Ganúra had taken to keeping each other company on the trek, talking on anything and everything. Ganúra was being pulled by their remaining kópi. They were poignantly giving each other comfort and support, soothing their fears in womanly chit-chat. They let their emotions gush out, feeling relieved by the process—instinctively knowing suppressing fear poisoned their physical system.

Morác and Wómak did the manly thing, they suppressed; marching in front, following Bróda. He was setting an example by setting the pace, striding out on sturdy legs, and letting physical exercise work out any poisons. Eyes sharp, pushing ahead as the leader of the tribe.

The terrain was flat, the trees well spaced, the going relatively good. They were pursuing the scouts up ahead on a barely visible path, following subtle markers. The path headed directly South, it had to lead—where—maybe to another village. Bróda didn't say anything to the others, but he had a glimmer of an idea which involved reaching the Golden Sea by re-provisioning at every village on the way; saving hunting time in the process; keeping well ahead of the schánda. He was hoping the path might lead to more provisions.

The column marched all day with only a short break for a mid-day meal. By late afternoon the scouts returned reporting a lake half a league ahead.

'Good! That's a bit of luck. Big is it—the lake?' Bróda asked.

'Oh, three-fifty by three hundred cubits,' Fúlmon told him.

'Decent size then...we'll camp by the lake tonight,' decreed Bróda.

'Maybe that's not such a good idea,' Fúlmon told him, pulling on the kópi leash.

'Let's keep moving—we're not there yet,' Bróda urged the people, who were beginning to bunch up. 'Come along, Fúlmon; walk with me. Why isn't it a good idea? Here —let me have the kópis.'

The two kópi jumped up on Bróda's chest, trying to lick his face.

'There's a kind of skull-and-cross-bone sign at the lakeside,' Huróyna put in, walking with Fúlmon.

'We've no idea what it might mean. Water poisoned? Danger in the lake? Could be anything,' Máyo added from behind.

'Damn! Could be *nothing*. We'll decide when we get there—I want to have a look at this sign before I make my mind up,' determined Bróda.

Fúlmon nodded, 'Right! We'll go ahead again—skirt the lake—check out the vicinity.'

Bróda gave the kópi leash back to Fúlmon. 'See you later!'

The scouts disappeared back from where they came. The rest trundled after. In a short while, just as the suns dipped to the tree line in the West, the column arrived at the lake. The far shore could clearly be seen. A medium sized lake. Reeds covered the shoreline, going way out into the water. The water looked clear enough. Spaced at a distances were signs planted on the shore. Bróda stood looking at the sign.

'Ah, Húli! I'm no wiser than I was. Morác—what do you think?'

Morác shrugged his shoulders. 'I think it means danger. The question is—what kind of danger?'

'You're exasperating at times. That's what I'm asking *you*? Can't you give me any suggestions?'

Morác had reached the shallow end of his indifference to the matter of the Rími women; not being able to help them. It now transferred itself into the current problem of the sign. He wanted to distance himself from *all* problems—in trying to do so, the slight depression created by the prior frustration turned into a mild case of apathy.

'What's the point of suggestions? You might as well ask that tree over there to give you a suggestion.' He swept his arm at the forest.

Bróda and Wómak stood there looking at him as if he were momentarily deranged.

'Are you all right? Néra! Come and tend to your husband.' Bróda turned solicitous.

'What's up?' Néra took Morác's arm, leading him aside. Morác had in the past told her how frustration turned to anger or depression. She now tried to remind him of his words, to jolt him out of the apathy.

'We're going to loose daylight if we don't get a move on.' Bróda was getting impatient. 'Wómak; set up camp a good two hundred cubits away from the water; back there where the ground is dry.' He pointed the way they had come. 'Post extra sentries immediately, mainly facing the water. I don't want to be caught out from that direction.'

As he talked, the rest of the column crowded around him. Unnoticed, a kópi went to the water for a drink. On the far side of the lake, Wómak watched their scouts moving along the shoreline—kópis sniffing the air. It would take a while before they rejoined the group.

'*Hey*! Get that kópi away from the water,' yelled Wómak.

Everybody stopped—looking in the direction of the kópi—expecting the worst. It was far too late to prevent the animal from drinking. Now they would know if the water was drinkable—or not.

'*Loti, come here*,' Súdair yelled at the young kópi.

'If that animal dies, I'm going to find a suitable reward for your negligence,' Bróda told the hapless Súdair.

'He's only young...he's nosy,' Súdair tried to excuse himself.

They made camp at a good distance from the lake, all the time watching the young kópi. It survived its drink. There were no signs of it going down with anything. To be on the safe side; they should wait at least a quarter of a day. They didn't have that luxury. As twilight settled in, Bróda declared the water safe to drink; still wondering what the skull signs were for.

Fúlmon and his scouts returned and reported they'd found nothing. Bróda took control of his kópis and told Fúlmon to tell his scouts to cut poles.

Since the water was declared safe, the stándy were allowed to quench their thirst. They were tethered close to a patch of good foraging, near the water. It would cool them.

Píngo lit a fire at the spot chosen by Bróda and Umára set the evening meal in motion. Most of the tribe retired to the forest to cut their A-frame poles for the night; a few of the women stayed to help Umára. Umára may have been in charge of the cooking but that didn't prevent the women giving him their advice—an extra bonus with their helping hand. He took it all in good humour; giving back as good as he got. Cára stood up for him. By the time the pole cutters returned, the food was ready—and plentiful, thanks to the Rími larder.

The tribe sat on an octagon of fallen logs around the fire, thirty-seven people in a huge circle, quietly eating, generally five people to a log. There was dried fish, reconstituted, added to a wild-seed millet porridge, washed down with plenty of herbal. Many went for a second helping. They had taken three varieties of fruit from the Rími larder, fruit they were familiar with. That was handed out after the porridge.

After the meal, the empty cooking pots were taken to the lake to be cleaned. The fire was built up into a bright roaring blaze. People relaxed, talked to their neighbours, and ate the fruit.

Bróda stretched himself, sitting next to Morác. 'You feel like a chat, Morác?'

'What's bothering you?' Morác asked politely, his earlier apathetic demeanour forgotten.

'There's a question that's been puzzling me ever since we began our journey. It seems to me we left it a bit late —leaving. Have you any explanations?'

Morác stared into the fire. 'I've been giving that thought,' he replied. 'My presumption is it had a bit to do with Fándin's early departure. Remember; in the normal run of circumstances, right now, Fándin would still be our shamán. I would be his apprentice. Him going off into the forest meant we lost a great deal—you had to put up with me as second best.

'Maybe his presence would have triggered the nightmares a lot earlier. It's speculation on my part—but maybe he would have cast a spell to spark the dreams. You're right; we're late in leaving. We're paying for it right now. A five day start on the schánda may not be enough—we still don't really know how fast they move.'

Bróda stared into Morác's face, searching for answers. 'The other thing that bothers me, *what* are the schánda? Why are they chasing us? I know you told us at the community meeting, they're on their way to the shores of the Golden Sea; a mating journey. But what else do you know? Tell me everything—it may make the difference when I have to make a rapid decision.'

Morác continued to stare into the fire. 'I'm going to tell you all I've discovered, all that's been revealed to me regarding the schánda. I've no way of knowing if the information is accurate. Worse still; I don't know where this knowledge is coming from.' He began his story with a heavy heart, as if it was troublesome for him to recall the information. 'The schánda stand a cubit high, have a two hundred year life-cycle and normally live up on the northern edges of the tundra. There, they feed on a moss called lichen, found up there in large quantities clinging to rocks. This moss seems to flourish in those extreme adverse conditions and the insects feed on this lichen.

'The adult form has no poisonous stinger and is definitely not carnivorous. When it's lived to its time of mating, it becomes a ferocious lichen eater, quadrupling in size, grows the stinger and large claws in its fourth and final moult, and then begins its long march south to its mating grounds. The schánda moult every fifty years. They have grippers on their feet enabling them to climb rocks, *and* smooth trees.

'The mating urge mutates the schánda into a swarm of ferocious carnivores. When they reach their breeding grounds in the South, on the shores of the Golden Sea, they're completely exhausted and starving. As you can see, their food, we animals, don't stay around long enough to be eaten. So when the schánda reach the sea, they're on their last gasp. They mate, dig holes in the sand, deposit their eggs, and then die.

'After a quarter of Kálar's season, a long gestation, the eggs hatch and are born as benign leaf eating grubs. The larvas emerge, feeding on leaves of the kerni bush, found only on the shores of the Golden Sea. After a season spent feeding, the larva begins the long crawl north to its normal habitat; burrowing underground for most of its journey. That takes three seasons. When they reach the tundra, the grub changes into a chrysalis and for four years lays dormant in shallow ground. It metamorphoses, and then emerges as a mature adult insect.

'I speculate they must have started life long ago on the shores of the Golden Sea and over time Kálar's climate, way in its past, pushed them into the Northern lands, where they've settled ever since.'

'That's it?'

'That's all I know.'

Without being aware of it, Morác had gathered a silent audience; the tribe around the fire was hushed, listening, straining their pointed ears at the story being told. It was a story that had forced them to this fireside. The tale was chilling, but entirely captivating.

'That part of "exhausted and starving" might be of use. It makes them more dangerous; if that's possible. It also makes them vulnerable; maybe?' Bróda stood. 'I think its time we turned in,' he announced to the listening audience.

'*Custodian!*' A voice from the distance halted Bróda. Wómak had called from near the forest.

The entire tribe turned to the outcry. Wómak had two struggling figures by the scruff of their necks and was leading them to the fire. Another figure followed. As the group reached the light, Bróda recognized his son, Fern and Wólni's boy Cóer being led towards him. Láila, Sáor's daughter, followed Wómak.

'What's all this?' Bróda put on a serious face.

'Found these two fighting back there,' Wómak informed him.

Now they were near the fire, Bróda could see smudges of blood, dirt, and bruising on both youth's faces.

'Explain yourselves,' he looked at them sternly.

They stood before Bróda, heads bowed, sullen and silent. Fern shuffled his feet uncomfortably. Cóer tried to twist out of Wómak's hold.

'Keep still,' Wómak snarled at Cóer.

'I'm waiting,' Bróda's voice took on a firmness that had turned most warriors into quivering heaps.

Fern was the first to break. 'I told him to leave her alone; but he wouldn't,' the youth pointed at his protagonist.

'He's got no rights to her, just cos he's the Custodian's son.'

'Sáor, Émer! Wólni, Málina! Come and stand with your young ones.' Bróda looked around for his wife. 'Émana! To be fair, you're needed here as well. Morác; since I'm a party to this, I have to stand down in judgement. I'm appointing you as arbiter in this matter. Clearly these two fellows think they have a claim on Láila. What do you say, Láila?'

'It's not my fault,' Láila objected. 'They keep following me around. If its not one, it's the other. It's as if they were on-heat.' She had a self-satisfied air to her; the centre of attention; two males fighting over her. It was a young woman's dream come true.

'That'll do, young lady,' Morác asserted his authority. 'I warrant you didn't try too hard to dissuade them; most likely strung them along.' He turned to the smiling tribe, who found the proceedings just a trifle amusing.

To his credit, Morác kept a straight face as he continued, 'We've all been young in our time. I think the situation is fairly transparent. But I want to make it clear, that we the tribe, and I speak on behalf of your Custodian, won't stand for this behaviour. We expect all three of you to stop this nonsense. Fern; you will stay away from Láila. That goes for you as well, Cóer. I forbid anymore fighting; is that understood?' Morác looked austerely at the two lads.

They each looked at Morác and slowly nodded.

'As for you, young lady; you will steer clear of these two. No more egging them on, which I'm pretty sure you did. Is that clear?'

'Yes,' Láila said quietly, directly realising she was the centre of attention for all the wrong reasons.

'Now, I'm not blaming you too much. It is spring and young blood quickens around this time. But we are in abnormal circumstances and I expect all three of you to help, not hinder. You're old enough to know better. Fern, Cóer, shake hands.' He watched as the two youths cautiously shook hands.

'Émer, you best take control of your daughter.'

Sáor and Émer walked Láila to their A-frames.

Cóer, still obstinately, followed Wólni and Málina.

'Right, thanks Morác.' Bróda turned his attention to the tribe. 'Time we turned in,' he informed them.

Bróda took Fern by his upper arm and marched him to their A-frames. The rest of the tribe made their way to their own A-frames, leaving the fire to burn itself out through the night.

12

POOR STÁNDY

The sentries facing the lake were the first to feel the little bites. At the beginning, they were an irritation; midges having a midnight snack. Then as the main cloud descended, they started yelling.

'*Alarm! Alarm!* Wake up!' as they ran to warn the camp.

Néra felt the little insects on her face, settling, stinging, and feasting. Morác jumped out of his A-frame; grabbed a groundsheet. Néra, thrashing around, did the same. They covered themselves against the bites. Other members of the tribe woke, urgently moving. Frantically swatting at their arms and faces, snatching at clothes, covering their heads.

Above the commotion, Bróda's voice could be heard. 'Run for the forest—leave everything—to the trees—hurry.'

People stumbled, their heads covered with whatever they could find, trying to make their way to the forest. Arms were beating the air in a demonic frenzy, their owners lashing out at nothing tangible, rushing to and fro. The swarm thickened, becoming solid. People lurched, fell, picked themselves up, and stumbled on; running around in circles, tormented by the tiny bloodsucking flies.

They blundered into each other, impeding each other's escape. Kópis growled with agony, instinctively running towards the trees. Shrieks of pain, distress, and anguish rose above the turmoil as the biting midges gorged themselves on Bólani blood.

It was a scene of utter chaos and wretchedness when the tribe staggered into the forest, floundering, limping, suffering. They had managed to scramble out of the maelstrom of stings into the safety of the trees. Why the tiny fiends refrained from pursuing them into the forest was a mystery. The beleaguered tribes-people were simply grateful they didn't.

Once the people had gone twenty cubits under the canopy, they were safe from their woes. No matter; the tribe trundled deeper into the forest, clumsily bumping into animals trying to rest, or evade the invasion. The discomfort of the bites now made themselves truly felt. Even in the darkness of the forest, grief was spread on everyone's face. Women unashamedly cried, joined by the younglings of the tribe. Some had got lost, separated from the main group.

'Everyone all right?' Bróda went round in the darkness, calling out names, noting who was missing.

It took a while before a semblance of order was restored, people found. Family members comforted each other. Younglings cried from fright as well as from the bites. Most people's skin had swollen where they were bitten. Older members felt faint from loss of blood.

'We know now what that damned sign was for,' Morác retorted gruffly to Wómak. Then in a more solicitous tone, 'How's Ganúra? Was she badly bitten?'

'The same as everyone. She's a strong woman; she'll survive.' Wómak said this gently, protectively.

Morác peered closely, 'You don't look so good yourself, even in the dark.'

'Here, use this on the bites,' Néra handed Ganúra a paste in a pot jar. 'I managed to grab my backpack in that confusion. Lucky I did. When you've finished, hand it round.'

'That was quick thinking. I left everything and ran. Ouch! Those little pests really hurt—don't they?' Ganúra spread the paste on her hands and face. 'Try this for the younglings first.' She passed the jar on. Her kópi lay whimpering in the darkness, by her feet, scratching and licking at its bites.

'We'd better try to settle, there's a long way to go before dawn,' Wómak advised.

Bróda added, 'Listen up everybody. There's paste coming round in a jar—for the bites. Use it sparingly. We'll try to make more when it gets light.'

'Why didn't the midges follow us into the trees?' Wómak asked Morác.

'I'm not sure. Probably an aversion to the plant life under the canopy. Some of the plants may be deadly to them —but I'm only guessing.'

'They didn't bother us last night—it's like they were waiting for a sneak attack.' A hint of irrational suspiciousness crept into Wómak's voice.

'They're nocturnal, that's all; probably hate the suns. The Rími knew what the sign was for; it was meant for them as a reminder. Strangers had no justification for being at the lake.'

'I'll be happy to be away from here; place gives me the creeps.' Wómak fidgeted, rubbing his bites. 'How can you fight that? You can't see them, their so tiny.'

Morác rejoindered, 'Yeah, small but deadly,' rubbing his own bites. His face was puffed up, his arms like long water skins.

'I don't think we lost anybody,' Wómak concluded.

'Thanks to the sentries,' Morác emphasised. 'We were ahead—only just, of the main cloud. A moments hesitation; we'd have had fatalities.'

It was a long wait till dawn. When light began to appear in the sky, the Bólani emerged from the forest into what looked like a battle field. A kópi lay dead half way between the camp and the forest. Near the lake the tethered stándy lay strewn. In the panic, A-frames lay toppled where they fell; the tribe's belongings were scattered all over, trampled as people tried to escape in the stampede. The smouldering ashes of the campfire adding to the desolate atmosphere.

Bróda pointed, 'whose kópi is that?' Then he came closer and recognised it. It was the young one, Loti, the eager drinker. Súdair's. His younglings, stung all over, Scuráia and Sadb were crying bitter tears over the body—inconsolable. Partly from the bites, but also from fright, as well as the loss of the kópi. Shúta came and took them away, having to drag them both by their hands; they refused to go. 'We have to bury him,' Sadb wailed. 'I want to go home,' cried Scuráia.

Bróda stomped off angrily towards the dead stándy. *Some people shouldn't have animals, if they're going to be that careless with them.*

Málina was already there, motionless, gazing at the stándy. All fourteen were lying on the grass, in various prone positions. Close up, Bróda could see that a few were still alive. Málina simply stood there—in shock. Wólni hurried up; went to Málina and put his arms around her. She gave a short shriek, startled by his touch, and then put her head into Wólni's shoulder. She gasped, shuddered, and then began to cry with heaving sobs.

Morác knelt and took a close look at each stándy. Émana and Ganúra helped.

After a while Morác reported back to Bróda, 'Looks like six confirmed dead; all the blood nearly sucked from them. Two might not survive; the rest have lost a lot of blood but are recuperating. Émana and Ganúra are bringing liquid, getting them to drink.'

'We can't stay here—not with those things out there,' he swept his arm at the lake.

'I'm with you there,' Morác agreed.

'Where's Robán?'

'Last time I saw him, he was helping Umára and Cára. The twins got badly bitten. Néra's looking for herbs in the forest; she needs to make up more of that paste.'

'Wómak; come over here.' Wómak hurried over. 'You look a sight. Are you all right?'

'I'm okay. Feel a bit puffed up—that's all.'

'Make sure everybody gathers their stuff. We leave *soon*. I want you to put two large water skins on one of the travois. I'll pull that myself.'

At that, Wómak gave him a hard stare.

Bróda continued, 'See if you can get Umára to forsake Cára for a while—get him to start the morning meal.'

'Right you are.' Wómak left.

Bróda turned to Morác, 'Ask Píngo to light...sorry, I forgot—you and Píngo don't get on. I'll tell him myself. Listen; instead, I want you to make sure that everyone drinks plenty of water before we leave. They've lost blood and will need to replenish their fluids. Do you agree?'

'Of course I agree; I was going to suggest that myself.'

'Thanks.' Bróda went over to the fire lighter.

Not for the first time, Morác brooded over his relations with Píngo as he went round the tribe urging them to drink lots of water. Píngo stayed out of Morác's way—having no use for lazy shamáns. Even when they were boys, Píngo had taken a dislike to little Morác. It was one of those things that Morác had no control over. Over the past decades, he had made great efforts to reconcile himself with Píngo, but the latter would have none of it. When Morác became the shamán, Píngo's dislike grew. Morác didn't enjoy the bad relations, but he cast the brooding thought aside as a fact of life he couldn't fix. He went to seek out Néra; help her make more anti-bite paste.

The six dead stándy were skinned, gutted and washed near the lake by Súdair, their carcasses hung up in the suns. It was a job the tanner was familiar with. The live ones were carried away before Súdair got to work, over to the campsite, well away from the lake. Málina had recovered her composure and tended to the sick stándy, bringing water, aiding their recovery, talking to them soothingly. Wólni gave his wife comfort and fetched the water. One more died soon after; he was given to Súdair. The others looked like they would recover.

Back at the campsite, Scéna erupted, shouting at Bréac, 'I've had enough; that's it; I'm not going another step. This is madness...leaving our dens like that. I insist we turn back. *I insist!*' Then she burst into tears, sobbing like a youngling.

Émana came over and comforted her whilst Bréac stood speechless at his wife's outburst.

'Don't just stand there,' Émana accused the hapless Bréac. 'Get her more anti-sting paste; can't you see she's at the end of her tether.'

Abashed, Bréac hurried away to look for Néra. He brought the paste back and helped Émana put more paste on Scéna's stings. She quietened after that.

Other members of the tribe picked up their belongings, stacking them on the ground in the order of the soon to be continued trek. Morác noted Scéna's outburst and resolved to reinforce the spell on both Bréac and Scéna. The tribe drifted over to Umára who was handing out plates of porridge covered liberally with sweet Orel sap.

After they had eaten, Bróda called a mini conference of Wómak, Fúlmon, Robán, and Morác.

'With the stándy in that state, I want half the warriors to take up the slack. Others will have to help. We're going to have to pull the travois ourselves for the rest of the day. The stándy are in no fit state. Even so, we've lost seven stándy. That's seven loads of travois to be distributed fairly amongst the tribe. Tonight when we stop, we're going to roast the stándy carcasses Súdair's preparing. We'll make a splash of things; dancing, singing. Try to overcome last night's fiasco;

boost morale. What do you think?' Bróda looked at their faces.

'Good idea, Bróda.' Fúlmon was the first to respond.

'Singing? Dancing? You sure people will go for that —I mean like this, still swollen from the bites—' Robán was particularly badly swollen. He was also known as a good dancer.

'Get their minds off it,' Wómak put in.

'I like it. We haven't had a roast round a fire for a long time. It reminds me...sorry. Forget it.' Morác was about to go into a story; then thought better of it.

'That's settled. Morác; you organise it for tonight.' It wasn't a suggestion from Bróda; it was a command. 'What we don't eat, we'll take with us for the next day.'

Having lost half the stándy, Bróda firmed up his decision to hop from village to village; make a virtue out of being late starting the trek. Use other villages as provisioning points. He was convinced the owners wouldn't mind.

They were late starting. The remaining stándy were groggy on their feet and needed nursing. People needed nursing. Néra had made up a large batch of anti-bite paste, easing the lot of the mauled tribe. Many were in pain with green paste all over their exposed skin. Their saving grace had been the tunics the tribe wore; only exposing the skin on their arms and faces, other areas were covered with sturdy material.

But it was only at mid-day that the column managed to continue their trek south. Bróda in front, pulling a travois with the two full large water skins on it. He made a show of sharing the tribe's heavy burdens. The going was slow, a lot of shuffling of feet with few people taking bold strides. There were objections and groans but no outright protests. There was no point; they had to keep moving.

To add to their sorrow, people were laden with extra cargo; the load the dead stándy would have pulled was spread amongst the grumbling tribes-people. Warriors were pulling six travois with the stándy carcasses, one doubled up. An appalling transposition of roles, making people grimace every time they looked at the bizarre sight. To the relief of many, those six travois were at the back of the column—out of sight, out of people's minds. All eyes were on Bróda, pulling his travois.

In the trees, on either side, animals jumped hurriedly, rustling in panic, heading in the same direction as the tribe, only faster. The afternoon went—rapidly, the same could not be said of the column. Roughly every two leagues Bróda halted the column and insisted people drink from the skins on his travois. He made a joke of it, saying "the more they drank, the lighter his load would be." Whereas they had usually managed a good few leagues in the previous days, this time, they could only manage five. Along the verges of their route, the women made an effort to look for wild millet, clipping the heads into a side pouch they carried. This would replenish the dwindling stocks of porridge. They had been doing this from the outset—from sheer habit.

The scouts returned and reported a clearing not far ahead, and Bróda gave way. At Émana's urging, he ordered a halt for the night. With many a sigh of relief, the wounded column stopped when they reached the intended clearing. It had been an exhausting afternoon and people just flopped anywhere they could. For while, they rested, lying on the grass, watching the sky, feeling the breeze dry their sweat.

Tirelessly Morác went around the prone tribes-people, appealing for them to agree to the evening's performance. All four musicians of the tribe were easily cajoled into playing their part—Morác was on timpani; a soft recruit. Persuading people to sing was just as easy. The dancing was another matter. Tired as they were just at that moment; nobody wanted to commit themselves to more foot work. He left that part of the programme till later—nearer the time.

Soon, fallen logs were dragged into a large circle round the fire and the cooks commenced to construct the spit roasts for the ready gutted stándy carcasses. The atmosphere began to ease; replaced by one of expectation.

Bróda approached Umára who was busily directing the erection of the spits, 'When you've got the roasts going, make lots of warm herbal for the tribe. I'm still trying to get people to drink lots of fluid.'

'Right you are, Custodian,' Umára kept working.

'*Morác!*' Bróda went looking for the shamán. 'There you are!' He found Morác organising the musicians for later on. 'How's it shaping up?'

'Fern here is eager to start.' Morác responded drolly.

'I should hope so. He's got our family reputation to maintain.' Bróda nodded to his son, one of the panpipe players.

It was the ancient wind instrument of the Bólani, consisting of a graduated series of short vertical pipes bound together, with mouthpieces in an even row. Fern had a talent with it, much to the consternation of Bróda, who wanted him to be a warrior.

The other panpipe player was the carpenter, Sáor, who made all the instruments. Finally there was Málina, their talented lyre player, using her plectrum to good effect. One moment nimbly weaving wool, the next moment nimbly weaving music. Morác pulled his sacred timpani out of a cloth bag and tapped it a few times, checking the tension of the stretched skin. The shamán was the only one allowed to play the round timpani due to its religious association with the suns and the moons.

The four musicians sat in a circle and tuned up. Throughout the ages, all the tribal music had been transmitted through performance; father to son, mother to daughter. The melodies had changed over the seasons as the individual creative impulses asserted themselves, each time giving a new flavour to their playing, but the melodies remained familiar to the listeners. Following precedence, the four played as a group since their adolescence and were used to each other's style. They began with a lively tune that immediately caught the attention of the rest of the tribe. It had a calming, yet uplifting effect on the listeners, who stopped what they were doing and attended to the notes filling the evening air.

As per direction, Umára came round, handing out pots of warm herbal drinks to the enraptured audience. The smell of roasting meat wafted throughout the clearing making the listener's stomachs grumble. Back in the hamlet, the Bólani were not big meat eaters, usually taking wild grains, legumes, berries, nuts, tubers, bulbs, roots, wild pulses, fish from the river, and the occasional cheese from the stándy.

That is not to say they were vegetarians, but they simply ate what the seasons provided. If meat was available, they would eat it, but they didn't go out on long hunting expeditions to chase it. Now, the abundance of meat as a result of their tragedy, turned into a blessing; people looked forward to getting stuck into the up-and-coming roast.

A few more tunes and one of the roasts was pronounced ready. The smell of roast meat wafted throughout the clearing. Noses twitched and stomachs murmured with anticipation. Morác said a prayer of grace for the stándy meat. People commiserated with Málina before they ate, for having lost the stándy, but thanked Aíne for the food they received in consequence.

Umára vowed to keep roasting all night, if necessary, so that all the carcasses would be thoroughly cooked, left overnight to cool, ready for transport the next day. Umára insisted on handing out large slices of the lean and succulent meat, that being the nature of the stándy. The slices were stacked high on the wooden plates. Second helpings were enthusiastically encouraged by the beaming cook. As people queued for the meat, stomachs could be heard growling all along the line.

In the benign ambience of a spring evening, people forgot their bitten skin, the swellings having gone down throughout the day. Full stomachs lulled people into a feeling of well-being. The musicians ate briskly, wanting to resume their playing. Sore feet were seen tapping in accompaniment to the music, despite their owners.

Looking round the clearing, Bróda's face assumed a benevolent smile. He was pleased with his judgement; his decision vindicated by what he saw. The tribe cheerful, morale restored, people in a happy mood.

Morác turned to Néra, 'Do you remember when we'd just started going out together, that time in the forest when we went alone camping? We were away for eight days, until Bróda had to send out Wómak looking for us. I don't know why, but tonight reminded me of it.'

'You dear sweet man. Yes, I remember—' For a moment her eyes glazed over. 'It's the memories of happier times, alone, courting—away from danger. The surroundings, here, brought back those peaceful memories, did they? Will we see them again?'

'I'll do all I can...everything in my power, to see we *do* see them again. I promise.' Morác held Néra around the waist, needing to feel close to her. 'Look,' he pointed surreptitiously at Bróda and Émana approaching.

'Come on you two; I know there's no moons but I want you to lead us in the moon dance.' Morác and Néra got up and stood with the Custodian and his wife where the circle would be made.

The circular moon dance was always led by the shamán, a prerogative of his position, symbolising the motion of the moon. Bróda could not begin without the medicine man. They joined hands and invited the tribes-people to join hands. Reluctantly at first, then with more enthusiasm, all of the tribe moved from the logs, out onto the selected open ground, and at a signal from Morác, the moon-dance tune was heard from the musicians.

Slowly at first the circle of people went in the clockwise direction, and then as the music paused—picked up again, they danced into the counter-clockwise direction. At the outset, it assumed a solemn religious expression, a moderate methodical rhythm. This was repeated ten times, each time with deliberate rhythmic bodily movements— promoting a feeling of unity among the dancers. By the end there was a feeling of relaxation as the tired muscles limbered up in an outpouring of free-flowing motion.

Morác, conscious of the days march, called a halt after ten circles. He wanted to maintain the good leisurely mood. Normally the dance was performed until half of the dancers were ready to drop—not this time. People stopped and stood, sweating, exhilarated. Morác whispered to Bróda, who proceeded to manoeuvre Émana behind him. Morác and Néra joined the chain, and as people watched the chain getting longer, they joined in on the end.

Bróda began to lead the chain in time to more music, firstly in a serpentine pattern, the chain rotating, bending, stretching and turning. Then he changed the pattern into spiral formations switching to the occasional straight-line as a variation. It became involved and complex, but all the dancers were familiar with the variations and eagerly followed their Custodian's lead. When Bróda had tired, Robán eagerly took over—leading the chain all around the clearing.

The simple physical pleasure of sharing these rhythmic movements unified the tribe, engendering a means of releasing their pent-up emotions, helping them express their previously felt pain in the vigorous motions of the dance. When the music finally stopped, people should have been fatigued by the exertions; instead they sweated profusely but were eager to continue. In a fit of enlightened circumspection, Morác demanded a rest and wanted everyone round the fire to join him in a song.

The Bólani singing had an instinctive open-throated, clear sound carrying the ancient unembellished melodies of the tribe. They began with a couple of songs of general entertainment, followed by a few comic songs, one even parodied the schánda, imitating the claw snipping by tapping wooden sticks together. The latter was composed by Sáor, who received a round of acclamation for his inventiveness. Finally, the evening was consummated with a couple of love songs, bringing the whole enjoyable event to a close.

13

OUT OF THE TREES

Dawn the next day found the column reformed after their morning meal. Bróda heard laughter where there was normally a surly reluctance to continue the trek. He felt gratified his decision to hold the musical evening had gone so well; content he had diagnosed the inner malady of the tribe and found the remedy. Most of the swellings from the bites had gone and a sense of relief pervaded the people that nothing really serious had happened. True, they had lost stándy; but they had not lost any more of their tribe.

Back on the trail, they moved further south, leaving the higher latitudes, entering the deciduous forest of the warmer climate. The burdens were lighter with a couple of the roast carcasses consumed, large quantities of water gone. Bróda had given his empty travois back to the stándy, who were again under harness. The warriors still carried extra, but they were not the ones who usually complained.

For four days the column marched on with little out of the ordinary befalling them. On the fifth day, the forest thinned out, making the going easier. For the forest people, this was a time of unease. Up North, the warriors knew the tundra had no trees, but the South was an completely unknown quantity. Even warriors had a nervy edge to their watchfulness. The three warriors on either side of the column had their hands on their axes and peered deeply into the trees.

At nearing mid-day, Fúlmon came back with the rest of his scouts, striding with purpose, kópis pulling at their leashes.

'I've news; don't know if it's good or bad,' he told Bróda.

'Let me decide,' Bróda told him.

'A league further on, the forest stops. No trees; just air. I looked over the edge and there's valley pointing south below. We're going to have to climb down a vertical drop. I've never come across anything like it.' He looked a bit lost in the new experience.

Bróda made Fúlmon repeat his story out loud to the people. Then he stood on a log and addressed his tribe. 'If that's the way we've got to go, then what choice have we? We know what waits for us behind. What ever's in front has got to be better. We must press forward.'

With those constraining utterances, the column moved on. Bróda felt he had to say a few words to calm people's fears; prepare them for whatever came. As the column got closer to the void, voices were raised; not in fear but excitement. The forest ended and a stretch of clear ground two hundred cubits long lay in front. On the edge stood Fúlmon, Huróyna and Máyo, staring into the distance.

The column halted of its own accord, out in the open, a hundred cubits from the edge. The people in the column sat on the ground where they halted, patiently resting, talking. Bróda went to join Fúlmon, taking Wómak, Morác and Robán with him. His kópi were tethered near.

They stood on the edge of a plateau facing a deep valley running north to south. A river ran curving down the valley with open scrub river meadows on either side backing onto the steep sides of the rock face. The rim of the valley walls were on a level with their plateau, but a long chasm separated the plateau from that rim, and the onlookers could see no way across.

'Lucky that gorge isn't running crossways,' Wómak commented with a measure of sarcasm.

'How far down is it? Have you searched for a way to the bottom?' Bróda asked Fúlmon.

Fúlmon shook his head, 'Stuck my head over the edge; can't see any path, or even a hint of one. It's a five hundred cubit drop, straight down.'

'Do you see that plume of smoke, in the distance; must be at the end of the valley,' Robán pointed.

'Yeah, I see it. It's too far to worry of right now. Wómak,' Bróda became decisive. 'Take warriors and search for a way down to the left; Fúlmon, you take your people and search to the right. Don't take too long, I don't want to be stuck up here overnight. We've got to find a way down.'

Both parties were away for a long time. People lolled around, waiting. Umára went round and handed out cold roast meat to anyone who wanted it. People were only too glad to eat and take it easy.

Wómak's party was the first to return, telling Bróda they had come to an edge running backwards. There was absolutely no way down going left. A short time later Fúlmon's party returned, reporting they hadn't found a way to get off the plateau to the right.

'I have an idea,' Morác spoke up. 'Bróda; get your two kópi. Prod them in the direction of the edge and see what they do. To help the kópi, I want us to think *find a way down* at them.'

'Can't do any harm,' Bróda replied.

'Could loose the kópi,' Robán warned.

'If you have a better idea, I'll listen? We can't stay up here. Wómak; go get my kópi. We'll use yours next time,' he soothed Wómak's eagerness.

They waited until the kópi were brought up. They were led to the edge and Wómak held them there for a while. Then he prodded the two towards the edge of the plateau, dangerously close to the edge.

The group thought at them as Morác had suggested. The kópi were startled, looking back to the forest. Wómak stood back and they all watched. First the two kópi moved to the left, keeping to the edge, with Wómak shooing them forward when they tried to escape back to Bróda. They went along the edge for a long distance, well out of sight of the main column, followed by Wómak, Fúlmon, and Bróda bringing up the rear of the group. Bróda stayed back so the kópi concentrated on the task.

Then they turned and insisted on going to the right, as if they'd both concluded going to the left was a dead end. The group accompanied the kópi to the right for a distance, and then Wómak stopped.

'It's no good,' Bróda said from the rear. 'They're just as stumped as we are. Good try Morác.'

While the rest were listening to Bróda's gloomy remarks, Robán noticed the kópi had strayed well away from the edge, back—to a dip in the ground. First one disappeared, then the other.

'*Hey!*' shouted Robán. 'Look at that,' he pointed to the spot where the kópi disappeared.

'Well I'll be—' Morác began.

Wómak urged, '*Quick!* Follow them.'

Robán was already at the camouflaged hole, scrambling into it, vanishing from sight. Fúlmon jumped in, too eagerly for safety. Bróda followed—Huróyna and Máyo were close behind. Other warriors, seeing the vanishing group, ran up and went down the hole in a rush. They found themselves in a short burrow leading to a roomy underground cave—running to the edge of the cliff. The nine present, could stand up comfortably in the cave; it didn't look like a natural cavity. Near the ledge, it led onto a precarious narrow path clinging to the side of the plateau, seemingly leading all the way to the valley floor.

As the group pushed to the edge of the cliff, they suddenly heard Bróda yelling, '*Halt!* Back up everybody. Fúlmon; grab the kópis. I want us back up top.'

When everyone had climbed back out of the hole, back onto the plateau, they stood waiting for Bróda to explain.

'I know you're eager to explore, but we have Fúlmon for that job. In our excitement, we forgot our duty to the tribe.'

People stood embarrassed, looking at the ground. They knew their Custodian had right on his side. What if they had all had a catastrophic accident in their rush to investigate —what then of the tribe's chances of survival?

'Well, Fúlmon. What are you waiting for—an invitation? Keep Huróyna back in the cavern with the kópis. Take Máyo and only go half way down; that should be enough to tell you what kind of state the paths in.'

Fúlmon led Huróyna and Máyo back down the invisible hole. Bróda led the rest of the group back to the waiting tribe.

Bróda looked on the recumbent people. Sáor and Émer with Láila in between them. Umára sitting with Cára and the twins. Súdair and Shúta with their younglings, close to their grieving Grandpa. Wólni and Málina on the edge of the group looking after the stándy; Cóer near. Bréac and Scéna trying to stay apart of the rest. Others lolling around, tired.

'Listen up. We've found a path downwards, to the valley floor. Fúlmon's investigating it right now. It's going to take us a while to make the descent. I want a show of hands whether to descend today, or stay up here overnight. We don't know what we'll find down there. What do you say? Do you want to go down now?' Bróda tried to put a benign smile on—he felt the fatigue.

Four or five hands went up reluctantly.

'That settles it. We camp up here tonight. Umára, Píngo, start the fire and get the food going. Píngo, keep the fire low and well back from the edge. Wómak; I want you to post sentries forward and back. Two on either side. I want your people to keep a sharp eye out on the valley floor. Lights. Fires. Anything that moves down there; I want to know in the morning. Is that clear?'

'Yes, Bróda.' Wómak saw the sense of it and didn't argue.

Wómak went away and passed on Bróda's orders to the sentries.

After a while Huróyna came back to camp, leading the two kópi. She handed them back to Bróda, who patted the two affectionately. Fúlmon and Máyo followed shortly.

'Well? What did you find?' Bróda was impatient.

'The path is good, if perilous. There's a resting shelf around a hundred cubits down.' Fúlmon told him. 'There's no reason we shouldn't make it tomorrow. We'll need to keep the kópis in check, and I suggest I go before the stándy, else they'll run too far ahead and we might loose them.'

'Good work. Go get food.'

A-frames were constructed and the reheated roast meat was again handed out by the cook. Only two of the carcasses were left. The kópis made a mess of the leftover bones. There were a few wry comments, people wanting to return to their porridge; but on the whole the meat was welcomed. People turned in for an early night, expecting an arduous descent the next day.

The ensuing morning, a bright treeless dawn found people awake and up early. The daybreak meal was rushed. A buzz of excitement permeated the tribe as they got ready for the descent. Wómak reported the sentries had spotted lights in the distance on the left, half way up the rim from the valley floor. More lights, further on the right, again half way up the slope from the valley.

Bróda addressed the tribe. 'We've seen smoke in the far distance and lights during the night down there, so I want everyone ready. This may be your chance to try out the bows and arrows. Fúlmon tells me the path down is rough at first, so be careful, go slow, and if you have to, hold on to the cliff face. Make sure what you're carrying is tied securely. Remember, take it easy—a step at a time.'

Bróda then turned his attention to his leading warriors. 'When we get down, we're going to have to be alert. Darts ready, warriors up front. I think we're safe from behind. The other thing is we may have to leave baggage behind in the tunnel for a second trip, just to be on the safe side.' Wómak, Robán and Fúlmon listened carefully.

'Fúlmon; not too far out in front today,' Wómak suggested. 'If there's trouble, I want us tight. Keep a sharp lookout—I know I don't have to tell you, but I feel better for having said it. Let's see if we can get through this valley in one piece. No heroics. Go!'

Fúlmon led his scouts away towards the concealed hole in the ground. The travois were dismantled and the provisions distributed. Morác waved to the scouts as they departed. The column reformed and followed Fúlmon to the hole, and down into the tunnel. A pile of provisions had to be left in the tunnel, waiting for a second trip.

Bróda with his kópis on leashes leading Wómak. Málina nudging the stándy forward out of the tunnel onto the narrow path leading steeply to the valley floor. As the tribe slowly sidled its way downwards, they dislodged stones and clumps of dirt, giving anybody on the valley floor lots of warning that people were on their way. It couldn't be helped.

Obliquely the tribe made its crabwise descent downhill, the vertical precipice always reminding people of the need to be conscientious where they planted their feet. The first one hundred cubits were the worst; stones and rocks inadvertently displaced. Minor landslips escalating to mini landslides. People could be heard "oohing," "aahing," with the occasional "ouch" over the most minor mishaps. Clearly everyone was scared and cautious of this new experience, but as the Custodian had informed them the night before, "What choice had they?" There was only one way to go.

When Bróda rounded a long declining z-bend, he found Huróyna waiting on a compact earthen shelf ten cubits wide, dug out in an overhang in the cliff. It had room enough for ten people and Bróda suggested that the elderly and young might want to rest there—if they wished. None took up his offer. They were all eager to get to the bottom.

At least, he got Umára to hand out water to anyone who wanted it. It would make the carrying of it by the warriors, less of a burden. They continued the descent for the whole morning, the declivitous path becoming less steep after they had traversed the shelf. The ground was more compacted past the shelf, firmer, giving the feet a more resolute grip.

Occasionally they passed large holes dug into the cliff face high above their heads and below the path; they heard shrieks emanating from deep inside the cavities, but whatever was causing the shrieks, stayed determinedly out of sight. Half way down, a body came flying out of one of the holes beneath the sidling column, rising upwards in the air.

'Look, there,' Wómak pointed at the huge black flying object.

'What the Húli is it?' Bróda asked, not expecting an answer.

'I think it's a Nester bird,' Morác informed him.

'And what the Húli is a Nester bird?' Bróda's sacrilegious language indicated alarm, but his face scowled.

'Fándin told me long ago, second hand; he'd heard it from a Rími he knew. I quote Fándin, "They're ferocious predators living in cliffs at the southern edge of Rími land. They have claws at the end of their wings and throw rocks at anything that moves." That's all I remember.'

As Morác was telling this, a rock flew at them from above, narrowly missing the splayed column of people. It bounced harmlessly off the cliff just below their path, plunging into the valley below.

Bróda pointed, 'Wómak; can you get that filthy thing with darts? *Warriors*! Try and down that Nester thing with your darts.'

The tribe stared in horror and fascination at this new danger. Warriors loaded their darts and fired a fusillade off at the Nester bird circling high above. None of the darts got their mark. The dark apparition swooped, and then spiralled downwards, landing on a platform below, and seeming to feed on whatever was there.

Bróda yelled past Émana at Wómak, 'Send the rearguard warriors back to that shelf we passed so they get a good vantage for firing at the thing. They're to stay up there until we reach the bottom.'

'Good idea,' Wómak shouted back.

'They can leave whatever they're carrying on the shelf. Later, they're to collect the rest of the stuff left in the tunnel,' Bróda told him.

'Right ho!' Wómak began shouting orders to four of the warriors. 'Leave your burdens on the path at the end of the column. Go back to the shelf and give us cover. When we get to the bottom; go back and collect the stuff in the tunnel.'

Another black silhouette shot out of a hole below the path, spiralling down to join the first bird.

'That one didn't even bother with us. What the Húli's on that platform.' Bróda strained his eyes trying to see that far. 'Morác; can you see what's on that platform below?' he shouted back at the shamán.

'Sorry, Bróda. Can't see clearly,' Morác shouted back. 'I can see there's something there, but not what. We'll have to wait till we get closer.'

Bróda goaded the column, 'Come on; keep moving. The sooner we're down, the safer we'll be.'

Slowly, carefully, the tribe shuffled down the narrow path all facing the cliff, clinging to it. Care had to be taken with the burdens people were carrying. As the descending column reached the final part of its journey, the path flattened and widened, giving the people a sense of relief. Just after mid-day, everyone reached the bottom, and to Bróda's utter comfort, without loosing anyone. Fúlmon was already tethering the last stándy. They now could see the platform with the Nester birds on it. The birds were so engrossed in their feeding that they took scant notice of the people coming onto the valley floor.

'It can't be,' Wómak was saying.

'I tell you it is,' Fúlmon insisted.

'Are those bodies on that platform?' Morác pointed to where the Nester bird was feeding.

'I was just telling Wómak. There are three bodies on that platform. And those damn Nester birds are eating them, stripping them clean. I also saw a lot of bones; more dead people. What the Húli's going on?'

Bróda joined in. 'Those platforms look like they're constructed specially for the job. Morác. Can you shed any light on this?'

'I believe that's how they dispose of their dead,' Morác ventured. 'I have a vague recollection of Fándin telling me of it, but I can't remember exactly what.'

'We'll have to wait here until the warriors come with the rest of our stuff, Bróda told them. 'Anyway, let's move away from that damn platform.' He led the tribe towards the river.

Fúlmon helped Málina and Wólni free the stándy from their lead ropes and harness them to the rebuilt travois. The burdens were replaced back on the travois, with many a sigh of contentment from those that were unburdened. Then they followed the rest of the tribe. They'd only gone a short distance when more rocks began to hurtle down on their heads. The Nester birds had finished eating, turning their attention back on the departing column. By an unheard signal, more birds began to come out of their holes; two, three. Five birds circled above, clawing rocks from the cliff, and throwing them on the retreating Bólani tribe.

As they watched, one of the birds gave a loud screech and toppled out of the sky. It dropped like a stone, rolling over and over. Just before it hit ground, it righted itself, furiously flapping its wings, halting its descent, swooping back upwards.

'There, look. It's got a dart sticking out of its leg,' Wómak yelled.

'Good shooting,' Bróda stuck up his thumbs at the warriors up on the shelf. 'Pity the thing didn't crash,' he added disappointedly.

Morác turned to Bróda, 'One of us is going to get hit by those stones they're throwing. We have to stop them. Gather the tribe round us, here, now. I'm going to conjure up an invisibility spell. It won't hold for long, but maybe it'll be long enough for those birds to loose interest in us.'

When the tribe came close round Morác, stándy and kópi in the centre, he began his incantation, holding the talisman round his neck. '*O mighty Wáclaw. By the consecrated talisman from the sky above; I invoke thee. By the most sacred word-graph of heaven; I conjure thee. By the power of the meaning arising from these forms I make; I summon thee. I beseech thee; hear my form; mark my voice.*' There was a change in the light above the tightly drawn-in tribe, pressing in on Morác—his talisman glowing in his hand. '*O mighty Wáclaw. By the sacred talisman—make us invisible from the sky above; I beseech thee.*'

Stillness settled in around the people. The birds continued to circle—but no more stones landed. The birds circled lower and lower, spiralling down until two landed nearby. They were puzzled. They looked around but ignored the silent tribe.

People could see the birds, but apparently the birds could not see the people. Within a short while the birds lost interest; that being the sum total of their attention span. They left, flying back to their holes in the cliff.

14

DOWN THE VALLEY

Leading the way, Bróda said, 'That's that. Well done Morác.' He looked satisfied at the outcome. 'Well, let's keep going. It's only a short distance to the river.'

Just before the column set off, Morác noticed Bréac and Scéna standing close together, whispering, sniggering.

Its time to re-enforce the spell, Morác thought. *I'll have to do it tonight, after we eat.*

The column resumed its progress. The noise of the river getting louder.

Fúlmon walked by Morác's side. 'Why can't you just throw a fire bolt at those birds, instead of all this invisibility thing? Why can't you be more direct with your powers?' It was Fúlmon the warrior talking.

Morác sighed. 'It's not that kind of sorcery. I simply don't have the ability to do such things. Fándin might have been able to do that; I can't. I'm really only half a shamán; a mere novice. I still had ten years of my apprenticeship to go when Fándin got into that tussle with that stranger. The other limit is that our sorcery goes back to ancient times, before we can remember. Over generations it's weakened. At the rate it's decreasing, there'll come a time not too far in the distant future, when we'll loose all our powers altogether.'

'You're not serious?' Fúlmon's shocked exclamation forced itself from him.

'Yes I am. It'll be a time of machines—and other kinds of wizardry. That aside—if I tried to use my powers now to harm, I might loose them altogether—at least that's what Fándin used to say. When I'd just began my apprenticeship, I asked Fándin why he didn't zap this or that with his talisman,' Morác reached for his talisman in memory, 'but Fándin told me I should never abuse my powers, never use them to do harm. They were for the benefit of the tribe, not my own personal gain—not there for me to abuse.'

'That's the part I don't understand,' Fúlmon said.

'Let me try to give you an example. You carry deadly poison darts—*right*?'

'All the warriors do,' Fúlmon agreed.

'And they can kill anything alive?'

'We haven't come across anything they can't.'

'So, how many people have you killed?'

'Heh; oh, only one. But it was an accident, I was young, you know that. You were there when it happened.'

'So you can kill people; but you don't. Why?'

'I can't go around murdering people just like that—it's against our tribal law,' Fúlmon protested.

'And I can't just go around zapping Nester birds for no good reason; even if I were able to. They have a right to survive. It wouldn't be fair. The powers I have, even limited as you see them are not a plaything. They are a scared trust—handed down from shamán to shamán. To be used wisely—for the protection of the tribe. A bit like your darts. Do you understand now?' Morác studied the scout's face.

'Yes, I do. You've expressed yourself well.'

The noise of the water became thunderous. The tribe arrived at the bank and found the river full of large boulders. The turbulence moved at a swift pace.

'Fúlmon!' Bróda shouted above the noise.

'Coming,' the scout shouted back.

When Fúlmon reached Bróda, he found the Custodian looking down the valley, in the direction of the flowing river.

'Take your group along the river bank a half a league, see what's up ahead. We'll wait here for the rest of the warriors—those bringing the stuff down from the tunnel at the top of the plateau. I'll keep the kópis here for now. Don't take any risks. All right?'

'I'll get my people.' Fúlmon went off.

Bróda continued, 'Émana! Come and take the kópi off my hands while I hold council.' He waited till she took them, and then shouted, 'Morác, Wómak, Robán! I need to talk to you.'

When he had his council around him, they witnessed a worried Custodian.

'The day isn't long enough,' he began.

They stood and listened in silence. Nobody said anything to contradict him.

Bróda went on, 'It's early afternoon and I can't see us getting out of this valley by night-fall. My guess is, we've already been spotted—by those,' he pointed in a sweeping arc at the valley walls. 'We saw their fires last night, so we know they're up there. They may be friendly—but I wouldn't risk it. When the warriors get back, I want us to be ready to move—fast. When we stop for the night—no fires. Cold rations. I don't want us out in the open, so the order is camouflage. Make sure everyone is well hidden for sleep. I'm saying this now, so when we stop, people can go quietly making their arrangements—since you'll have prepared them. Questions?'

'What happens if we're attacked?' Robán wanted to know.

'We defend; but press on in good order. So, let me be explicit. If we come under attack—we defend, moving swiftly off down the valley. Anyone separated, will have to catch up—further on, following the river. Is that clear? Make sure everyone knows this by night fall.'

Wómak and Robán went off to inform the rest of the tribe regarding the night's arrangements.

Fúlmon came running back, alone. 'I've found death. I think you should come and look.'

Bróda's face dropped. 'Nothing but bad tidings!' He shouted, 'Wómak! Take charge.' He told Fúlmon, 'Lead on.'

Fúlmon led the way downriver to a spot a quarter of a league along the bank. The party saw Huróyna and Máyo waiting way off from the river. The wind was coming towards them carrying a powerful smell of decay.

'I don't much like the smell of whatever you've found,' ventured Bróda above the noise of the river.

They reached Huróyna and Máyo. Both had a cloth over their noses. Nearby lay three decomposing corpses.

'My guess is, they're Rími,' Fúlmon told him. 'Those markings on their arms, remind me of marks I saw in their village.'

'Are those arrows sticking out of them?' Bróda wanted to know.

'They've been in a Húli of a fight,' Huróyna said. 'There's arrows all over the place. Those that won dumped these bodies in a pile like this.'

Morác had followed Bróda and the group, finally catching up with them.

'Looks like their throats were slit,' Morác commented when he joined them.

They had to shout to make themselves heard above the sound of rushing water.

'If those platforms are, as you claim, for the dead, for the birds to devour. Why didn't they put these bodies on the platform?' That loud contribution came from Máyo, directed at Morác.

'The platforms are for their own dead. The birds are sacred, venerated. They were desecrating these bodies twice by *not* putting them on the platform. That's as I read their beliefs.'

'They're supposed to be neighbours. Why the Húli did they attack the Rími?' Máyo wanted to know of Morác.

'We don't know they did. We don't know what happened here. All we have is the result; how it came to be, we can only speculate.' Morác answered, his ire rising.

Máyo appeared to be getting at him, at least Morác thought so.

'With this in mind, we have an idea how friendly these people can be,' Bróda concluded. 'Fúlmon, you continue way downriver with your scouts.' Then to Morác, 'There's only a league more before we have to make camp. Daylight ought to give out by then. Go back and collect the tribe and bring them here. And Morác; go round these bodies. Take our people round this stinking pile, over there, by those bushes. I'll wait and steer the column clear of this. It's a dead Caroó if anyone asks of the smell.'

'Right ho!' Morác disappeared back the way he came.

In a short while, Bróda heard feet approaching and saw the column heading towards him. He waved them away from the Rími corpses.

'There's a dead Caroó over here. Keep clear. It stinks to high heaven.' To himself, he excused concealing the bodies by contending it would be bad for moral.

Whatever the reason, Bróda didn't feel too happy at lying to the tribe. As the tail-end of the column passed him, he joined Robán bringing up the rear.

'That's not a Caroó, is it?' Robán whispered to him.

'What makes you say that?' Bróda replied cautiously.

'Caroó, here? Dead bodies more likely.'

'All right—keep your voice down. There's no fooling some people.'

Bróda was annoyed and pleased at the same time. Annoyed his ruse was so transparent; pleased Robán was so sharp.

'See that escarpment up there, high on the slope. It looks artificial to me,' Robán suggested.

'Yes, I see it. I've been watching it for a time now. It *is* artificial. Look, it's hiding that fortified wall behind it. I can't see any movement, but I'm sure we're being watched.' Bróda eyed the enclave above to their left. The column had halted on approaching the escarpment.

'I'm going back to the head of the column. Be watchful,' Bróda told Robán.

With that parting remark, Bróda ran to join Wómak at the head of the column.

As he came up, Wómak turned. 'Glad you here, Custodian,' Wómak informed him. 'I don't know what to make of that lot up there,' Wómak pointed. 'I'm not keen on going underneath that, not without preparation.'

'Quite right,' Bróda agreed. 'I see Fúlmon got past it.'

Fúlmon and his scouts were crouching near bushes, a distance past the escarpment. Just as the last remark left Bróda's lips, a boulder rumbled down from above, causing an avalanche of rocks and dirt two thousand cubits ahead. The large boulder maintained its momentum across the lengthy stretch of flat land and went crashing into the river.

'Why the Húli do they want to do that? Can't they see we're simply trying to get past?' Wómak demanded.

'They're being very defensive, that's obvious,' commented Morác sarcastically. 'Those up there are warning us off.'

'What do you think, Wómak? Shall we make a run for it?' Bróda looked anxiously at his tribe.

'Those with blisters and feet injuries might have a problem,' Morác reminded him.

'We can't just sit here. We've have to reach the far side of that fortification.' Bróda sounded determined.

Wómak agreed, 'I don't see we've a choice.'

'Right. Let's do it, before they send their warriors down. Get Ganúra to give Émana a hand. She's not as sprity as she used to be.' Bróda turned to the tribe, 'Listen, everybody. We're going to make a run for it across that patch of ground under the fort. You've just seen what they're up to. All those fit enough to run, go first. The warriors will help those with blisters and injuries. Give them your packs— they'll carry them until we're across. When I give the word— those feeling fit, make a dash for Fúlmon over there, near those bushes.' Bróda pointed to Fúlmon crouching by the bushes. 'It's a long run—so keep going until you're over there. You'll be safe then.'

'We won't make it!' wailed Scéna.

Bréac stood by, his face working into a sweat.

People removed their packs, handing them over to the sturdy warriors. They all breathed rapidly a few times to ventilate their blood. Then on Bróda's command, made a dash under the escarpment.

'What the....' Morác blurted out.

Málina was calmly pulling, one in each hand, a stándy dragging its travois. They were crossing the stretch under the escarpment, followed by Wólni and Cóer, both leading two stándy each. The last stándy followed meekly behind Málina. Those running kept going. Ganúra continued to pull Émana at a trot across the clearing; herself being pulled by her kópi. The scene turned into a farce. What was evidently a hazardous crossing with boulders plummeting, Málina managed to turn into a bizarre stroll.

At first, those above did nothing, probably amazed at the audacity of the lone crazed woman underneath, leading the stándy. Then belatedly, the boulders began to roll down the hillside. The less fit members of the Bólani tribe were stuck on one side of the escarpment, whilst the promenaders were almost across, making it safely to the far side.

Bróda's face was a confused picture. He could not decide whether to scowl or smile at the turn of events.

Morác finally said, 'I'm amazed they made it.'

'I can't decide whether to berate them, or hug them when we get across.' His face finally resolved into a smile. 'We'll wait until this avalanche of rocks stops. It's got to stop. Then we'll take the rest across. Better get your darts and bows ready. I think they may send their people—be ready.'

The dust got up everyone's noses. It settled on the hair, got into the eyes. They simply put up with it. Many covered their mouths with a cloth. When the avalanche stopped, only the rushing water made a sound.

'Right—go,' yelled Bróda, and then followed the rush of his kópis across the clearing.

Tribes-people—carried piggy-backed, other's running as best as they could, rushed across the clearing below the escarpment. Another volley of boulders and stones came tumbling, sent by those in the fort above. This time though, there was less loose material to join the plunging avalanche, most of it being dislodged in previous slides.

The crossing was successful, the measure being that nobody was hurt. The Bólani's first encounter with a hostile people was to have gone off remarkably well. That was the conclusion Bróda reached when he was mulling the incident over in his mind as the tribe continued their trek along the river bank.

'Keep it moving,' Wómak urged the column, standing by the side, counting numbers.

When Robán brought up the rear, Wómak joined him.

'I hope every encounter ends like that,' Robán ventured.

'Don't count on it. We're a long way from the Golden Sea. At this rate, not many of us will make it. Storms, deadly midges, loony birds and now that lot up there,' he gestured up to the left. 'We've lost five of the tribe already and we're nowhere near halfway.'

'You mean four, don't you?' Robán queried.

'Don't you count Mútani? He's gone. Máda, Gárn, Gara, and Sáor's mother in the storm. That's five. All down to the schánda.'

Wómak and Robán followed the column round a bend in the river, coming to another cliff in front, jutting out of the rock face. There was a natural arch in the cliff, suggesting the river was a lot more ferocious at times. Cautiously the column went through the arch, and then everyone came to an abrupt halt. In the far distance they could see plumes of thick smoke all along the distant horizon.

Wómak left Robán and hurried to the front of the column.

Bróda was in a huddle with Fúlmon and Morác.

'What's up?' Wómak asked as he came up.

'We can't go back,' Bróda was saying.

'But look at it,' Fúlmon pointed at the smoke.

'Bróda's right. We can't go back,' Morác agreed.

'Wómak!' Bróda acknowledged his arrival.

'So, what's up?' Wómak asked again.

'Nobody knows what that is,' Morác answered, pointing at the distant smoke. 'We don't know what's in front —but we simply can't go back to meet the schánda; not the way we came.'

'We've been going for a while now. What say you call a halt?' Wómak looked at Bróda.

'The light's holding. We'll go on for another league —*then* we'll call a halt for the night.' Bróda said that in a firm tone. 'I want to put distance between us and that cliff-fort back there. Anyway, I want us to bed down in a defensible spot, not out here—in the open.'

'Whatever that smoke is, we're going to find out soon enough. But I don't like it,' Fúlmon added.

'Let's get going then.' Bróda stood, took Émana by the elbow and led the column on.

Fúlmon went ahead with the scouts and Bróda's kópi.

Morác fell in with Wómak who now had the leash with his kópi. Ganúra kept Néra company. Twilight found them further along downriver, where the river bank narrowed considerably. Fúlmon was waiting. Bróda held his hand up to halt the column.

Bróda said quietly, 'Wómak, go tell Robán to take a couple of warriors back a way. Make sure we're not being followed by that lot from the fort.'

Then Bróda took Fúlmon's arm, 'What's the matter?'

'I think this is the best spot for the night,' Fúlmon told him.

Bróda looked around, a frown appearing on his forehead. 'What—here?' He looked around, puzzled.

'Look up there,' Fúlmon pointed to the left. 'See, there—sixty cubits up the cliff face. There's a ledge of sorts. I've been up there. It's not that wide but it's long enough to sleep our people. An added bonus; it's a good defensible position.'

'Hmm! Right, let's take a look.'

Fúlmon led Bróda up to the ledge. Morác went around quietly, letting people know what was being discussed. Folks craned their necks upwards, trying to discern the ledge in question.

Wómak returned, having sent Robán back along the river. He told Robán not to go too far, only back half a league. Otherwise, he joked; he'd miss a cold supper.

Once Bróda had confirmed the ledges suitability— the tribe began to make their way up. Many sore and tired individuals needed help getting up the steep hillside. Scéna was still complaining to Bréac. Once up—they found places and hastily spread their bedding, then settled to cold meals, huddled under a wall of rock.

Morác took the opportunity to search out Bréac and Scéna who had laid out their groundsheet on the southern edge of the ledge, almost apart from the rest of the settling people.

'Hi! Bréac, Scéna,' he said sitting with them.

They were uncomfortable with his presence, fidgeting. Without launching into pleasantries, Morác fingered his talisman, murmuring an incantation. He felt time was short so he murmured under his breath—*by the power of the talisman I hold in the miracle of time, from the compass points I invoke, Lord of all the sorcerers, strengthen the spell to make these two conjoin and scatter their malice asunder.* In a short while the crystal began to glow with a deep green light and a glazed look overtook Bréac and Scéna. They were put into a trance. Morác left them like that a moment or two, and then snapped his fingers, waking them up.

'Morác! How nice to see you—how long have you been sitting there? Scéna, get Morác a bite to eat. Sorry its cold food.' Bréac was beside himself with politeness.

Scéna rummaged in their belongings looking for the dried fruit and solidified porridge cake. They both looked fresh and invigorated, very unlike their old selves of just a while ago.

'Thanks Bréac, Scéna—I must dash, got to see Bróda,' Morác lied.

He wanted to get back to Néra and eat with her. Warriors crept around, strictly enforcing the silence, shushing at Bréac. After seeing the tribe settle, they set to guard duty according to their roster, and the whole tribe was soon sound asleep.

15

INTO THE FIRE

Near dawn, Robán gave a yelp, and then howled like a stuck Bári.

Fúlmon was next to give a shout. '*Alarm, alarm!*' he yelled.

Startled people woke from the slumbers. Warriors went scurrying down the hillside. A few hasty arrows flew over the heads of people trying to get up, landing harmlessly further up the hill.

'Fúlmon!' barked Bróda into the night.

As he neared the commotion on the northerly edge of the ledge, he could hear Robán cursing. Morác knelt over a prostrate figure clutching his left shoulder.

'Lie still,' Morác entreated. 'How can I get at this arrow if you keep moving—keep still I tell you.'

'What happened?' Bróda wanted to know.

'I'm not...' Morác began.

Bróda interrupted, 'Let's hear it from Robán,' he commanded. 'He can talk can't he?'

Robán coughed to clear his throat, and then launched into his account. 'The sneaky perishes crept up on us. Just when I was thinking that the night had passed off quietly...I got this arrow in my shoulder. Morác? Is it poisonous?' Robán looked worried.

'I don't think so—' Morác told him. 'Now the light is coming up—'

Robán shrieked with pain as Morác pulled the arrow from him.

'There! Look! It's a clean wound. Can't smell anything from the arrow tip,' Morác announced loudly, making a great show of sniffing the arrow.

He took a pot out of his medicine bag and put ointment onto a cloth, then dabbed it on the wound. It coagulated and the bleeding stopped.

'The rest of the warriors are chasing the culprits.' Robán told Bróda.

'Robán! How do you feel? Morác! How is he?' Bróda was worried of losing the third most important warrior in the tribe.

'I'm all right. It's just a nuisance—that's all.' Robán responded.

Morác chipped in, 'Oh, I think he'll survive...it's not a bad wound, as wounds go.'

Fúlmon reappeared, coming back onto the ledge from his chase. Other warriors followed.

'We managed to catch one—not alive though. The others have vanished back upriver.' Fúlmon almost spat the words out in disgust. 'Do you want us to chase them?'

'Definitely not! We haven't got the time. What happened to the one you caught?' Bróda queried.

'He took poison—it made him froth at the mouth. Convulsed once or twice, and was no more.' Again Fúlmon looked disgusted.

'Took his own life—heh? Peculiar people!' Bróda stood a moment and looked the way they had to go— downriver towards the smoke. 'Wómak! Get the people moving—we'll eat later on around noon.'

'Right you are.' Wómak hurried to get the tribe moving.

'Fúlmon—get warriors to help Robán.' Turning to Robán, 'Can you walk?'

'*Yes* Custodian,' Robán said defiantly.

'Well let's get moving.' With that, Bróda led the people off the ledge, to the riverbank.

Throughout the morning they walked steadily towards the smoking horizon, trepidation running through the tribe as to what they were to encounter. It was a blessing the noise of the river drowned out their thoughts. As they neared the rising dark fumes, warm air hit them from time to time, when the wind came from that direction. With the wind came a harsh sour air making people gasp and cough, increasing their anxiety.

At noon they reached the end of the valley and the river turned right, away from their intended route. There was a change in the colour of the ground. Where the river bent, it appeared to hit a raised solid black fine-grained rock that lay in large sheets, one on top of each other, as if thrown there. As they climbed onto the different soil, many commented on the change from a terra-cotta colour to a dark grey mass, wondering what it might mean.

Before them stretched a vast black-grey expanse, rising gently, as far as the eye could see; with only a gentle undulation now and again. The smoke was evidently bellowing out of a long hole in the ground—a rift that ran parallel with the horizon, blocking their southward journey. Black clouds rose from the fissure as if foul breath from a sleeping giant.

Bróda halted the column. 'Right, time for a rest and food—I hardly think the fort people will follow us this far.' A worried look sat evident on his broad face as he stared at the smoke. 'Morác, Wómak, Fúlmon. With me,' he bellowed, leading the way to where Robán had been lowered to the ground, sitting propped up.

'I can't say I like the look of that,' Wómak pointed at the smoke.

'What's your thought on the matter,' Bróda asked Morác, as they settled in a semi-circle around Robán.

Robán's face had gone ashen and he was suffering pain. As a warrior and Wómak's deputy, he made a great show of suppressing any outward signs of his discomfort— grimacing, and even trying to smile through clenched teeth.

Morác was rummaging through his medicine bag, pulling out an ointment jar. He unwrapped Robán's bandage and began cleaning the wound. 'I've no idea what that smoke is. We're almost there, so I suggest we send Fúlmon ahead with his scouts to have a look—then report back.'

'Just what I've been thinking,' said Bróda. 'All agree?'

Heads were nodded.

'Good. Get going,' Bróda looked at Fúlmon. 'Give the kópis to Émana.'

Fúlmon rose to his feet and went to find Máyo and Huróyna.

'What would make the ground smoke like that?' he looked at Morác hopefully.

Morác was putting on a new dressing on Robán's shoulder. 'I told you, I've no idea—and that's the truth. You'll just have to be patient until the scouts return.'

'Humph!' is all Bróda said, looking into the distance at the smoke.

Píngo made a fire and Umára gave out platters of wild millet porridge topped with sweet Orel sap. People sat eating in a listless manner. They made a grand display of relaxing, resting, but all wore worried faces and they talked in whispers. Everyone felt that this was likely to be their most onerous hurdle since they left their hamlet. A sense of foreboding settled and the mood was sombre.

When Bróda stood up, everyone stayed sitting. There was an obvious reluctance in the people to venture further.

'Come now!' Bróda looked at his tribes-people. 'You know we can't stay here.'

'Why can't we wait till the scouts return?' It was Ganúra who voiced everyone's thoughts.

Émana and Néra, standing with Ganúra nodded their heads. All three kópi lay quietly.

'Bróda. Let's wait for Fúlmon,' Émana said more gently to her mate. 'A few more moments won't make that much of a difference.'

Bróda gave way reluctantly. He sat again with Morác and Wómak. 'Don't they know what's behind us? We have to press on,' he said with a note of despondency in his voice.

They didn't have to wait long before Fúlmon appeared in the distance, leading the little trio of scouts. As they neared, there was fear clearly visible on Máyo's face. Fúlmon's features were set hard. He came up to Bróda and sat, indicating for his scouts to do the same.

'Well? What have you to report?' Bróda demanded.

'We went close to that long hole in the ground,' Fúlmon began, 'and were nearly choked by the foul air.' He rubbed his chest with the memory of it. Huróyna thinks that's where Húli lives—and it's the entrance way to the Netherworld.' Fúlmon looked embarrassed that he was quoting his woman's opinions.

'That's fine—but what do you think?' Bróda was getting impatient.

'It's a long deep rift with a red hot glow inside, as if the ground had melted. I've never come across anything like it. It might be the way down to the Netherworld—down to Húli.' His voice trailed off without conviction.

'That's not what we want to know,' Bróda exploded in exasperation. 'What I want to know is can we get round it? Which way do we go from here—left or right?'

'Oh! I see,' Fúlmon said abashed. 'From what could see, the only way forward is to the left. You can't see it from here, but there's a hillock down there. The view from the top shows that eastwards, the rift seems to end after a league and a half. We couldn't see the details, but the column should be able to proceed South if we can cross there. What we couldn't see, was if it really ended where we thought it did. If instead it continues, we're in real trouble.'

'Right, that does it. We'll have to take that chance.' Bróda stood, raising his voice. 'You might have heard what Fúlmon just said—and for those who didn't—we go left round the smoke.'

All the people stood, listening to this. Deep down, they knew they must go on. There was no alternative—there was no going back. They couldn't stay where they were, so—the reticence vanished and the column began to move, to the left. Wómak was supervising the assistance for Robán, Píngo and Láeg propping him up on either side like living crutches.

'Is that really the way to the Netherworld?' Ganúra asked Néra as they walked side by side.

'We'll never know—I hope,' she responded. 'Does it matter? Húli or no Húli. We can't ask the dead where they are. Everyone eventually is able to answer that question. Don't be in such a hurry to find out.'

'I suppose you're right.' With that they walked on silently, each deep in their own thoughts.

It took them the rest of the day, always veering to the left, closing in on the crevasse. There were many dead animals on the way, with no obvious injuries to show how they died.

Morác strode forward to catch Bróda up. He was striding out in front, making the column keep a good pace.

'Bróda! Wait up there. Let me catch up.' Morác puffed as if he were out of breath.

'Keep up! Keep up! We must press on.' Bróda replied.

'I want us to keep clear of the rift. Those animals,' he pointed at a few more carcasses. 'I think they're telling us to keep clear. I think the air from the rift can be poisonous. We mustn't get too close. Parallel the rift ridge until we get to the end, and then turn sharp south. Please Bróda,' Morác implored.

'Very well. But do try to keep up—and tell the rest to do the same.' Bróda was determined to push the pace.

Nightfall found the tribe silhouetted by the red glow from the crevasse, near the eastern end, still following the dogged footsteps of their Custodian. Morác insisted they move well away from the crevasse before he deemed it safe to stop. The wind was clear of dust particles and smoke coming from the chasm. The tribe finally halted for the night on groundmass that had a fine crystalline composition, with large crystals embedded. They were frightened and exhausted standing on the inner edges of the basalt plain. This was a new experience for the Bólani and they didn't like it.

At Morác's insistence they were had travelled half a league from the crustal rift—yet everyone was still scared witless they had camped at the entrance to the Netherworld, Húli waiting there to receive his due. People examined their consciences, rummaging through their minds in near panic, going over the various wrongs they thought they had committed, unable to take their eyes off the red glow, so close.

No sooner they settled, Píngo and Umára began the usual ritual of fire and food making. The fire made, the porridge boiling—when abruptly, without the lightest warning, molten lava came hurtling upwards with a mighty blast.

People jumped to their feet and ran from the red hot menace. The kópi raced ahead. Fortunately for the tribe, the lava was tossed southwards, away from the running people, ejected in a continuous stream onto the other side of the rift. Still, a mild wind blew north and hot sulphurous air blew towards them. The tribe raced north, spluttering and coughing, Robán was yelling with pain as two warriors pushed and dragged him to safety. More lava hurled out of the crevasse, propelled by the expanding crustal pressure eager to be released.

Bróda stopped and hollered, 'It's all right! You can stop this panic. We're safe. Look! Nothing is coming at us,' and he went into a spasm of coughing as a pocket of fumes hit his lungs. It was thus the Bólani flight was halted.

'Well I'll be!' exclaimed Morác, holding onto Néra. He'd been helping her, staying close, attending to her safety.

Even in the panic, families stayed together, helping each other. When they stropped, people cringed on the ground, expecting Húli to make an appearance. Many thought they were to be taken down into the Netherworld and feared for their mortality. Húli had been built up into a ferocious guardian of the Netherworld and invested with an appetite for all wrongdoers.

'It's all right! We're safe! Praise be to mighty Aíne for looking after us.' It was Wómak trying to pull the tribe out of their collective cowering. He was endeavouring to calm them, to put backbone back into them by reminding them of a force more powerful than Húli. The tribal protectress, their mother goddess to whom they prayed, whom they revered above all.

It worked. Fúlmon stood and glowered at those around him. His other two scouts joined him. Slowly, one by one, the warriors rose to their feet. It was a transformation. Seeing the warriors' example, the tribe unwound from their terror and rose. Even Robán forced himself to stand unsteadily aided by his living crutches. He was still weak from the wound but insisted on showing solidarity with his warriors.

'Let's get our belongings,' Bróda boomed, leading the way back to where they'd abandoned their gear and stándy in their hasty flight.

The molten lava was still being evicted from the crevasse, but with less intensity. It was a minor eruption venting the pent-up gasses trapped below. The Bólani saw it as Húli venting his spleen on them for daring to venture onto his sacred territory.

'The sooner we're away from this horrible place, the safer I'll feel,' voiced Néra to Morác, clutching his arm tightly.

'Bróda!' called Wómak. 'I think it might be wise if we marched through the night and get as far from here as we can,' he shouted over the din of the eruption.

Wómak caught up with the Custodian and repeated his suggestion.

'I'd already decided that to be the best course, but I'm glad you agree. We'll get our things and then keep going. Pass the word along.'

They reached the place where they'd intended to camp for the fourteenth night of their trek south and collected their belongings. Málina, helped by Wólni and Cóer, re-harnessed the stándy to the travois. Píngo doused the fire out of habit. Umára was helped by Cára and tubby Uílin to stow away the porridge for later. The three kópi ran around sniffing everything—they thought it was all just a big game. Their owners had to call them and calm them. Wómak put his kópi on a lead and gave the lead to Ganúra.

'Émana, put our kópis on leads. If they roam, they're bound to hurt themselves,' he told her.

Bróda raised his hand in the red glow of night and said, 'Right, let's get going.'

The column moved off again but this time in an orderly fashion. The light thrown into the sky from the rift was easily sufficient to let them see where they were going. They made their way parallel to the crevasse until they reached a point that indicated the rift had ended. The column halted whilst Fúlmon went ahead to scout the southern route.

He returned. 'We have to veer off further. There's still a rift down there that we can't cross. No more fire, but there's no way across. It's too wide.'

'Right, you heard Fúlmon. We're almost there. Follow me,' Bróda marched on. 'Fúlmon—you go ahead, but stay in sight.'

He watched as Fúlmon led his scouts ahead to guide them southwards. A while later, they reached the rift, or what was left of it at this end. There was still a shallow crack in the ground, as if it refused to give up so easily. It was now possible to cross but the light was almost gone and darkness had settled in around them. They could see the red glow in the distance but the ground dipped here and all lay in shadow. Cursing in the dark, Bróda led the stumbling column south, still veering off to the left, for now they were on the side of the rift where the lava was ejected. They needed to be as far away from the rift as possible.

As they moved south, gain the eruption intensified and lava was discharged, lighting up the sky. More flaming basalt hit the southern side of the rift. The tribe quickened its steps, almost running, but they had to be careful not to tumble in this unknown terrain. The last thing they wanted was broken limbs.

The fifteenth dawn of their journey found them well past the gaping wound in the ground and Bróda judged it a good time to resume their abandoned meal, the one they should have eaten before the eruption. He halted the tribe and with relief they all flopped on the ground, more tired than they could remember in the last fourteen days of trekking.

Píngo and Umára got to work, preparing the fire and food. Umára made fresh wild millet porridge and then baked the porridge cakes he'd stowed away earlier, into biscuits. To each platter he added lots of sweet Orel sap. There was little of the sap left, but he thought this time it was needed. People had been badly frightened and were now near the end of their tether. He made a mental note they'd need more water soon.

The food served—eaten, the tiredness made many eyelids droop. Bróda told Wómak to post sentries, to wake them in four hours, and then he joined the sleepers. The

Bólani tribe made a sorrowful presentation, spread in every which way, as if they had been blown there by the wind. They had flopped on the ground from exhaustion and only four lone sentries stood guard at the perimeter.

Before noon, Wómak gently shook Bróda's shoulder; waking him.

'Time to get up!' Wómak made his voice resonate in the morning air. He wanted to wake everybody while he was at it.

People stretched sleep out of their muscles. Others tried to close their eyes again, hoping it was a mistake. There was a distinct reluctance by many to face another day.

Bróda joined Wómak in an upright position.

'Well! How do you feel?' Wómak asked.

'Still a bit tired. But a lot better than before.'

'I wish we could spend a couple of days in one spot —really draw the fatigue out of us. But I suppose that's out of the question—' Wómak sighed.

'You know it is.' Bróda licked his forefinger and held it high—then suddenly sniffed the air. 'Can you feel it?'

'You mean the warm air coming from the South?'

'It's warmer than normal air should be—don't you think?' Bróda looked at Wómak quizzically.

'I took the liberty of sending Fúlmon and his scouts South to see what's there. I don't want another surprise like the rift,' Wómak told him.

'Good man!' Bróda clapped him on the back. 'How long's he been gone?'

'I sent him just after you fell asleep. Told him to go a couple of leagues—then report back.'

'Custodian! Come quick—' a voice exclaimed.

Bróda craned his neck to see who called him.

'Over there! It's Morác!' Wómak informed.

'Hmm! I wonder what he wants.' Both hurried over to where Morác was. They found him leaning over Robán.

'He's delirious. I'm not sure we can move him. Look at his shoulder.' He indicated exposed discoloured skin where the wound was. The shoulder was enflamed and swollen. 'I was wrong,' lamented Morác. 'That arrow must've had a kind of slow acting poison on it.' The look on his face was grim.

'What are you saying?' Wómak demanded.

'Keep your voice down!' Bróda told him.

Morác wouldn't look Wómak in the eyes, 'I'm sorry —'

Bróda's face took on the same grimness. 'How long?' He bent to have a closer look at the dying Robán.

'By evening—at the latest,' Morác whispered.

'It's a bad thing—this. We really can't afford to lose him. This is terrible,' he added bleakly.

'Keep it quiet as long as you can. Get the warriors to make a stretcher—I'm sorry, but we must move on.' This was the Custodian's job. Crisis or no, he had to keep the tribe moving. More than one life was at stake.

'I know,' Morác said quietly.

Wómak went and whispered with Umára, asking him to pass the message along—discreetly. Soon all the warriors knew of Robán's plight. The stretcher was made from one of the travois. Morác eased Robán's suffering by administering a bark extract to kill the pain. Four warriors volunteered to carry the stretcher. For them it would be like a funeral cortege.

Bróda went back to Émana and waited, expecting to see Fúlmon come over the horizon. There was a ridge running along the sky-line half a league South. Only when Fúlmon came over it would he become visible.

'He should be arriving soon if he went that early,' said Morác as he paced the ground with Wómak.

Not a few moments later. 'Look—there!' Wómak pointed to the far right. 'Is that him?'

Ganúra, standing close, confirmed the sighting, 'Yes it is—I'd recognise that outline anywhere.'

'You've got good eyes,' Bróda praised.

As Fúlmon neared, they saw a puzzled look on his face. Huróyna was arguing in undertones with Máyo. They both stopped their heated discussion when they reached Bróda.

'Well? What's up?' Bróda demanded.

'You're not going like this.'

'I won't know till you tell me,' Bróda responded with a measure of sarcasm.

'Beyond that ridge down there,' Fúlmon pointed at the ridge on the sky-line half a league south, 'there's a sort of shifting yellow ground. It's dry and hot from the suns. I've never seen anything like it. It's hard to describe.'

'So how much of it is there? I mean—how far does it go?' Bróda looked concerned.

'Remember, we started out from here, going to the left. As soon as we saw this barren area—we went along its edge, along the other side of that ridge, way to the west as far as we could, in the time—. It stretches as far as the eye can see. I'm sorry, but it looks like we're going to have to cross it —can't see any other way round.'

Bróda looked aghast at the prospect. He finally shouted— 'Council!' calling Morác and Wómak to him.

Together they squatted on the ground.

'There's a wasteland over that ridge—' he looked at Fúlmon, 'you tell them—'.

Fúlmon went into the whole tale, from the time he left them in the morning. The desert, for that's what it was, made no sense to him or the listeners. He told them of the arid conditions, the hot suns beating down on the scouts as they ventured into the barren landscape. A flat tawny desert littered with rocky scree for a great distance south, then even further south, into undulating sandy hills. A hot wind blew from the south, implying baking conditions that way. Why the Húli should it be so empty? Why weren't there any trees or grass? Had it anything to do with that rift back there? Wild guesses, morbid talk and thoughts permeated the discussion.

The Bólani were familiar with the cold desolate northern landscape, but down here in the south, they were expecting a lush tropical countryside.

'What are we going to do?' Wómak asked Bróda.

'What can we do? We go south. This isn't a stroll through nice scenery—we're running for our lives. I don't know how close the schánda are—but they're not hanging around. Umára!' Bróda yelled for the cook.

Umára came swiftly, hearing the urgency.

'How are we for food and water?' Bróda shot at him.

'Short on both, but we need water right now.'

'Wómak, I want you to let the three kópis loose all around here—let the seven stándy go as well. See if they can't find us water. We can't move south till we fill the water skins. Get to it!' It was worry that made him so abrupt with his second in command.

16

MORE DEATHS

Bróda turned to Morác. 'Get your crystal out. Find out where the schánda are right now.'

Sáor came up to Bróda. 'My dad's not feeling too well. Can we stay here a day or so?' He said it as if he was still back in the hamlet—a far away look on his face.

Bróda looked closely at him. *He seems dead on his feet.* 'Have you slept at all?'

'Not really—been watching dad.'

Morác got his crystal and was sitting on a groundsheet a way off, preparing, staring at it.

'That has to wait,' Bróda told him. 'Go with Sáor and have a look at his father.'

Morác looked in Sáor's direction and stood up. He went over and stared into Sáor's face. Didn't say anything, simply led the way to where Sáor's family was spread out— Sáor in tow.

'Émer! Láila! How are you?' he said as he came up to them. 'I hear your dad's not too well.' The old man was laying spread out on their groundsheet, seemingly oblivious to his surroundings—eyes open, staring at the sky.

'He's gone into himself—ever since mother died. He's hardly eating—doesn't say much. I can't get much of a response out of him.' All this was said in a flood as if a dam had burst. Sáor just stood gazing at his father.

Morác went and bent over the old man. He listened to his breathing, or the lack of it. 'When was the last time you checked him?' he asked quietly.

'Just a while ago,' Láila answered for them.

'I'm sorry. He's passed over—to the Netherworld,' he told them, assuming a kindly face.

Émer said, 'Oh!' and then burst into sobs.

Láila looked shocked—then put her arms round her mother and sobbed with her.

'If it's any consolation, he went peacefully—without suffering,' Morác added.

That set the women off even more. Through all this, Sáor just stood there, as if in a trance. Morác got up and took Sáor by the arm, sitting him on the groundsheet.

'He's taken it very hard, you know.'

Morác turned around and found Shúta frowning a way off. It was she with the comment.

'You mean his mother going in that storm the second night out?' Morác ventured.

'Yeah! His father took that hard. He watched his father deteriorate,' she got up and came over.

Morác took out of his pouch a vial—poured a dribble into his hand and then rubbed the ointment on Sáor's forehead.

'What's that?' asked Shúta.

'It's a balm—it'll put him to sleep,' he told her.

Shúta went and sat with Émer and Láila, trying to comfort them. Next, Málina arrived looking concerned. The news of another death was spreading fast. Then more women turned up to lend support. Men came and sat with Sáor, who had lay down and was now fast asleep—a look of peace finally replacing the stupefaction on his face. Wólni sat by the sleeping figure and placed a hand gently on Sáor's shoulder, assuring him of his presence.

Bróda arrived with Wómak. 'I'm sorry to see this,' Bróda said with a heavy heart. 'This is turning into a catastrophe.' He sat heavily on the edge of the next-door groundsheet, facing Morác. 'Wómak! Go and see how Robán is doing.'

At the mention of Robán's name, Morác remembered that he'd given him till nightfall—to pass-over. 'I know it's inconvenient, but we'll have to stay here the night.' Morác hung his head and felt the mood of the moment. 'We can't move—not right now.'

'Reluctantly, I agree—' Bróda trailed off. He was torn between his duty to the rest of the tribe, and his duty to the dead and dying.

Wómak came back to report. He shook his head, 'No change—he's getting weaker if anything. Néra is tending to him, trying to ease his passage.' He joined Bróda on the groundsheet.

Bróda rose to his feet and announced to the tribe, 'We're camping here the rest of the day—and tonight. It's now mid-afternoon and we need to gather anything that'll help us cross the wasteland. Those not comforting bereaved need to gather grass, or what there is of the dried clumps. Gather up those dried twigs while you're at it.' He turned to Wómak. 'How's the water gathering going?'

'Fúlmon and the scouts are following the kópi and stándy. The kópi might be onto a smell. They seem to moving with a purpose,' he reported.

Bróda shook his head in exasperation. 'This is bad— real bad. I hope it doesn't get any worse.' He shook his head again.

Máyo shouted from a distance at the far left of the ridge on the skyline.

Wómak jumped up. 'We better go see what he wants.'

Bróda rose lethargically to his feet. 'I could do with good news right now.'

Both sauntered off into Máyo's direction, leaving the sombre mood pervading the camp site. They'd nearly caught

171

up with the scout, who was heading back slowly the way he'd come.

'Well? Found anything?' Bróda called to Máyo.

Máyo turned and waited. 'Might have—' he said, trying to suppress any glimmer of hope. He turned and resumed his walk towards the distant Fúlmon and Huróyna.

'Aggravating fellow!' murmured Bróda.

'Are the kópi digging?' Wómak asked, pointing forward.

'Don't know why, but they've been at that spot, whining and digging for a good while now,' Máyo told them.

'If that's the case; they've found—what—hopefully water.' Bróda's mood picked up with the anticipation. 'Where's the stándy?' he inquired.

'Cóer took them westward with him, doing the same thing,' Máyo informed him.

The group neared where the kópi were digging. They'd made a hole in the ground, but not nearly to the depth needed if they were to reach the underground spring.

Bróda called the kópi to him and put them on leashes. 'Wómak, use the spades. Fúlmon, lend a hand. We'll be here all day if we use the animals to dig for us. The kópi were supposed to sniff the water out, not dig it out.'

The Custodian took charge of the situation. He grabbed the third spade and joined the dig. In a short time, when the hole was a couple of cubits deep, they hit moist ground—further digging and water began to seep into the bottom of the hole. More frantic digging produced a gurgle, a trickle, and water pushed upwards in a spout, filling the hole half way. Five happy faces stood on the edge, looking down, and exhilaration bursting from them.

'Let the kópi have the first drink,' Fúlmon suggested. 'After all, they found it.'

Bróda was only too happy to comply. The kópi were straining on the leashes, trying to reach the water. Bróda let them pull him to the water and they greedily quenched their thirst.

'Well done,' Huróyna came and patted their backs, stroking the ridges.

'That takes a load off my mind,' Bróda informed the group. 'Heh! We might make it after all.' It was the first time he admitted to himself that he'd had doubts on that score. Now he'd been able to give voice to that doubt—a burden lifted from him.

'Let the water settle, there's still a lot of silt floating in it. It's all right for the kópis, but we'd make ourselves ill,' advised Fúlmon.

'I wonder how the water's flowing.' Máyo slowly swept his red hair from his forehead with his hand.

'You mean "which way"—don't you?' Huróyna corrected him.

'It can't be from that river we passed—the rift's in the way. Unlikely to be from the direction of the wasteland.' Fúlmon ventured. 'Must be flowing parallel to the ridge— look at the spout, it's definitely flowing.'

Bróda interrupted the banter, 'Wómak! Go back and get the stándy with their travois. Bring all the water skins you can find. Fúlmon, I'm leaving you and the scouts the job of filling them all. All right by you?' Bróda was beaming. 'Wómak—hang on. I'll come back with you.' He was positively overflowing. With the kópis, he caught Wómak up. They virtually bounced back to the makeshift camp.

As they neared the site, they calmed themselves, remembering the situation they'd left. It would be improper to be so cheery in the midst of so much sorrow. In their absence, Morác had ambled over to see how Robán was doing under Néra's ministrations. They found Morác rubbing Robán's forehead in a concerned manner, seeming puzzled by Robán's deteriorating condition.

Whispering to Morác, Bróda said, 'We've found water!' he tried not to grin.

Morác maintained a solemn expression—but he winked an acknowledgement.

Wómak knelt to have a closer look at Robán. He looked at Morác and said, 'He's in a coma?'

There was surprise on his face—that his friend and right hand assistant would leave soon. He'd relied on him so much, that momentarily, he was confused at the thought of loosing him.

'He's not long for this realm,' Morác conceded. 'He's been slowly going downhill. I'm at a loss as to why. I've used spells on him; all the anti-poison salves I possess— yet to no avail.' He shook his head in despair.

'Don't blame yourself,' Bróda told him. 'If you want to vent your spleen, then vent it on the schánda—they're the cause of our misery and misfortune.' He spat their name out in real anger.

Wómak nodded in the direction of the returning stándy. Cóer was leading them back, head hung low, indicating he'd been unsuccessful in his search for water.

'Wómak!' Bróda said quietly. 'Go tell Cóer to re-harness the travois and load all the water skins—then take them to Fúlmon. That should buck Cóer up. If there's any water left, get the tribe to finish it. It shouldn't be too difficult.'

Wómak jumped to his feet and hurried to carry out the bidding.

Bróda stood and searched the camp until he spied who he was looking for. 'Scória!' he yelled in a throaty tone.

Bróda walked towards Robán's right hand man. They met in the middle of the camp.

'Sit, I want to have a quiet word with you.'

'How's Robán?' Scória inquired.

'No better. That's what I want to talk to you. Morác says he's not going to last long—and so, if you're willing, I want you to take over from him as of now. You'll be fifth in charge after me, Morác, Wómak and Fúlmon. You'll take over rearguard when we move. What do you say?'

'I'll do it—but with a heavy heart. I'm so used to Robán being there—that it's going to be strange not having him there. It's a bad business—this.'

'My sentiments exactly,' Bróda agreed. 'So you'll do it?'

'Can I pick my number two?'

'Of course!'

'Dalán?'

'If that's your choice?'

'Dalán! We've kept each other company on the journey. We get on well.'

'Right! That's decided. I'll tell the others.' Bróda got up and pulled Scória up with his muscular right hand.

Bróda went back to Morác—only to find that Robán had passed over. Robán lay still with a cloth over his face. All around, people were silent, subdued, shocked. They knew it would happen—but when it did, they were still stunned.

'It's now the end of the afternoon.' Bróda said solemnly, bending to whisper to Morác. 'We must bury Sáor's father and Robán. More to the point—we have to lift the tribe's moral. I'll get the warriors started on graves, over there—' he waved in a westerly direction, 'you get the "laying to rest" organised. After that I want to call a council.'

At that point, Fúlmon approached, leading a couple of stándy laden with water skins. He'd left Huróyna and Máyo filtering the water and filling the other skins.

Bróda straightened and called him over. 'How's the water coming? I want you to go round and make sure everyone has a good drink. If you see Umára, get him to make more wild millet cakes for crossing the wasteland—and tell him I want him at the council meeting in a while. Also tell Súdair to butcher one of the stándy—the weakest one. Málina won't like it, but it can't be helped. That's what they're there for.'

'I'll do that—but I came myself to make a suggestion —oh! and there's plenty of water,' Fúlmon explained. 'I think we ought to try crossing the wasteland tonight—travel all night. That way, the suns won't be so bad. What do you think?'

Bróda became thoughtful. 'Hmm! Sounds like a good idea. We'll start at midnight and keep going till dawn. Is that what you had in mind?'

Fúlmon nodded. 'Then we build shelters and bivouac through the day, sleeping. Start again in the evening—till we cross, till we come out the other side.'

'Good thinking! By the way—I've put Scória into Robán's place. Is that all right with you?'

'Yes it is. Good choice! Do you want me to tell the others?'

'Would you? Save me going round. I've got enough on my platter. Oh! And Scória's chosen Dalán as his aide. Include that.'

'I will.' Fúlmon continued his rounds with the stándy, going to people, handing out water.

Bróda coughed loudly, and gave voice to his dispirited kinsmen. 'This is a sorrowful time for us, and before we reach the Golden Sea, it may become much worse. This is the truth as I see it. But we will come through this; we'll reach the beach of the Golden Sea; far-seeing Wáclaw promised as much on the first night out—do you remember? I'm much grieved by the passing over of Sáor's father and Robán—but life begins and it ends—we all know that. The two who are on their way to Húli would have wished that we, the living, press-on with the journey. The schánda are not far behind.

'On a hopeful note—we've found water, plenty of it.' That news lifted people. Bróda even notice a few half smiles on faces—as if they were embarrassed to be cheery at such a time. He went on, 'We're going to bury the dead and rest here till around midnight. If the next stage south is to be through the wasteland, then I've decided its best we travel by night, when the suns beat down less on us. The point is, we've no idea how much of this wasteland there is. I have to tell you this now—so we can all agree on this. Raise your hand if you consent to this course of action.'

A bit reluctantly at first, hands appeared; then more, until all the tribe's hands showed.

'I'm glad! So, now get food down you, as much water as you like—and fill every container you possess with extra water—I have a feeling you'll need it.' Bróda sank back on his haunches for a moment. *Two more dead*—he thought *—that makes seven so far.* That weighed heavily with him, as if he'd been remiss with their lives. Yet he knew no blame attached itself to him for their deaths. *Cursed schánda!* He mouthed under his breath. He regained his feet and went to find Émana.

He found her sitting with Fern. In Bróda's absence, she was holding her son close, talking to him. Their kópi lay nearby, asleep. It was a scene that would have been a pleasure for him to see—back in the hamlet, in happier times. Now it simply reminded him of lost times; reminded him of what he had to do.

'You've found time for us, have you?' It wasn't said with malice, more of an unhappy statement of fact. She'd felt he'd neglected her. She knew he had to, but it still rankled. Back in the hamlet, she accepted it—here, now; she needed his support, his strength. Death all around, unknown dangers. She was scared—that was the simple fact of the matter.

'I'm sorry my love,' he responded morosely—hooking onto her mood. He sat heavily and took her hand. 'I know I've undervalued your patience,' he said disarmingly. 'Please forgive me. It's the pressure. I'm having a hard time coping.'

It worked. She suspended her sulking and became concerned. 'You poor dear.' She rubbed his hand and put an arm around him. 'I'm *also* sorry—I know you work hard.'

A sly smile flickered on his lips, and quickly vanished; replaced by one of sympathy. He needed to comfort her, but he also needed to go round the tribe; do his job. He'd taken the line of least resistance with her, and turned her mood round. They'd been together a long time and he knew her like Fern knew his panpipes. Fern joined in the hugging and the Custodian's family was once again united.

Out on the western perimeters of the camp, Wómak was overseeing the digging of two graves. Píngo and Némed were digging the old man's grave, next to that Scória and Dalán had volunteered to dig Robán's grave. The bodies lay on a groundsheet nearby, covered with another groundsheet.

Morác stood watch over the corpses, solemnly saying a prayer. 'May our Lady Aíne smile on your departure. May She guard and guide you past Húli's watchful gaze. May She help you choose the right path, so no harm befall you on your immortal journey to the Netherworld.' He was asking Aíne to intercede with Húli over their immortality—to ease their lemurs into the Netherworld.

Bróda led the mourners the short distance from the camp, in a silent procession to the gravesides. Sáor and his family behind the Custodian, followed by the rest of the tribe. The two bodies were lowered into the ground, fully clothed, and uncovered. There was no linen to wrap them in. It was not the way of the tribe, but these were exceptional circumstances.

Morác stood between the graves and cleared his throat. 'This is a sad time for us here. We have lost yet another two dear well beloved members of the Bólani tribe. That makes seven departed since the menace of the cursed schánda became known to us. We mourn their passing—we grieve at the loss to their families, their kinfolk. *We*—the tribe —feel their loss. May their lemurs find peace and happiness in the Netherworld.' He stopped, stood there in silence for a while—as did the rest of the mourners.

As the crowd began to disperse back to the camp, Málina caught up with Bróda. 'Custodian,' she began formally, 'Did you give permission for Súdair to murder one of my stándy?'

'Be reasonable, Málina. That's why we brought the stándy along with us—you knew that from the outset.' Bróda said this calmly.

'But—' she began.

'No "buts" now. By the time we reach the Golden Sea—there probably won't be a stándy left. I give you my word—*when* we get back to the hamlet, I'll get you more—as many as you want. Now, *we* have to survive, not the stándy. Its them or us—who do you choose?' he stared into her face.

'I...I...suppose—us.' She dropped her voice, almost tearful, then stopped and stood for a moment.

Bróda stopped and put his arm around her, nodded to Wólni, who'd been following them, to come and take over. Wólni and Néra took an arm each side of her and led her back to camp, to where Cóer was with the stándy. Súdair had already taken the weakest and was leading it to where the water hole was.

Málina dropped to the ground near one of the stándy and put an arm around its neck, hugging it—staring longingly after Súdair. Cóer and Wólni knelt with Málina and hugged her, all three rocking back and forth.

Bróda shouted out loud, 'Council!' and waited just on the outskirts of the camp for the group to gather to him.

Wómak arrived with Scória. They'd been establishing a new relationship, with Scória's promotion. Next Fúlmon came with Umára, shortly followed by Morác, who'd been talking to Sáor and his family—comforting them.

All six hunched in a circle at Bróda's invitation. 'It's now getting close to suns-set and I need to know how the food situation is.'

Umára coughed, 'We have enough wild millet for three more days, and then it's gone. Plenty of water thanks to your kópis, Custodian.' Umára smiled at Bróda.

'Súdair finished cutting up that stándy?' Bróda asked Wómak.

'He's just finishing—slicing the meat into strips. He's laid it out near the water hole,' Wómak answered. 'We now have six stándy left,' he added.

'Anything else I should know?' Bróda examined each face in turn.

Silence.

'Morác—now is the time for the crystal. Can you get it working?' Bróda asked.

'I'll try.' Morác pulled the polished oval crystal from his belt-pouch, laid it on the ground and fingered his talisman gently. 'Give me room,' he asked those present.

The circle enlarged.

The talisman round his neck began to glow with a deep green light whilst Morác recited the "far-seeing" spell, *'By the power of the talisman I hold in the miracle of time, from the vantage of the northern compass point, through the eye of the great Racul, I seek to cast my sight onto the distant schánda following the Bólani. Let the image be seen in the far-seeing crystal.'*

A mist began to circulate in the oval crystal, which cleared to show a seething black swarm in the distance. The view was from the sky, down on top of the cliff they had descended previously. Large hairy insects crawled all over it, with a few throwing themselves over the edge.

The circle stared at the detestation, their eyes enslaved by the seething swarm.

'Look—to the left—there! Focus this thing—get it closer,' urged Bróda.

'By the power of the talisman—veer left—go closer.' Morác intoned.

'They've found the hole to the cave—look, they're pouring down it,' bemoaned Wómak.

'That's it! I've decided not to wait for midnight—as soon as it gets dark, we're moving.' Bróda wasn't asking them, he was telling them.

They hunched there miserably and nodded. They watched spellbound by the schánda descending into the valley where the Nester birds had their platform.

'*By the power of the talisman—veer closer—go closer.*' Morác intoned.

The crystal zoomed closer to the cliff, showing the schánda going into the Nester bird holes. The rest of the carnage was left to the watcher's imagination. One of the birds came flying out, knocking the entering schánda off the cliff face. It screeched and Bróda squinted closer.

'One of the insects has that bird's foot by the claw,' Bróda exclaimed.

'*By the power of the talisman—pull back,*' chanted Morác.

Both bird and insect were seen to gyrate in the sky, locked in a struggle neither could win. On a larger scale, those picking up the pieces below would devour both.

'I hope those people in the hill fort, slow the schánda down.' Fúlmon gave voice to the groups wishes.

'Don't hold your breath,' Wómak advised them. 'They didn't slow us—did they?'

'What of the fire in the rift?' Scória chipped in.

'Now that might slow them,' Bróda said. 'If by an amazing stroke of luck they turn right instead of left—we could gain a day or so.'

'There's no use speculating and hoping,' Morác suddenly said. 'We'd better be on the move.'

Bróda gave him a glare as if to say, *that's my job.*

Morác ignore the glare and pronounced, '*By the power of the talisman—cease.*' At that, the crystal cleared of the image.

The group dispersed at Bróda's command and each returned to their posts. The suns were low on the western horizon and the column set out for the southern ridge in good order. Fúlmon way ahead with the scouts—Bróda had once again given Fúlmon his kópi. Bróda strode out purposefully, leading the tribe into the unknown desert.

17

INTO THE DESERT

They approached the long ridge, in a hush, with trepidation. Up until now, the terrain was familiar—unusual, dangerous—yes, but still they could recognise it. From Fúlmon's description, what was to come was beyond anyone's comprehension. That was more dreaded than the wasteland itself—the lack of comprehension.

Bróda was the first to climb the two cubit high ridge, followed by Émana, Fern, Wómak and Ganúra, she leading the kópi. Then Morác came with Néra. They waited on the other side for the rest of the people—standing on this *yellow sand*.

'If I didn't know better—I could swear this ridge was put up by people,' Bróda said to Wómak, looking the long heap of compacted soil up and down.

'Why do you know better?' Émana quizzed him.

'It isn't possible for people to have built it.' He stroked his face in thought. 'I mean, where are the people?'

'What of those in the hill fort?' Ganúra suggested.

'Simply not enough—I mean look at it—it goes for leagues and leagues in both directions.' He said it as if that was the end of the matter, it being self evident.

Then Morác nonplussed Bróda. 'What if this is very old? What if it was built a long time ago, when there were lots of people here?'

'There would be the remains of buildings. I don't see any! Signs to suggest people had lived here. Do you see anything like that?' Bróda voiced after thought.

By this time, all of the tribe had crossed the ridge and stood gaping at the vast emptiness. It was a moonless night; stars shone brightly and threw an eerie light onto the yellow emptiness before them.

Wómak bent and picked up a handful of sand; a yellow, waterless soil that seeped like water through his fingers. 'Won't we sink into this—this stuff?' he pondered out loud.

'Fúlmon says not. He says it's firm enough to walk on—if we're watchful,' Bróda told him. 'Look, there's Fúlmon's and the scout's footfalls leading off into the distance. If we're extremely observant in this light, we'll be able to follow them.'

Bróda waited till the whole tribe had crossed onto the sand, and then strode firmly in front, following the faint footfalls Fúlmon and the scouts had left. He clearly saw the paw prints of his kópis, and that comforted him. It was as if he were tracking friends, out on a pleasant jaunt. But the deception didn't last long.

Wómak came panting up, dragging him away from his revelry. 'Bróda—slow down a bit. People are having a hard time keeping pace.'

Bróda slowed. 'We have to maintain a fair stride if we're not to be a meal for those damned creatures. You know who I mean! Anyway, it's colder here than it was over the other side of the ridge. Have you noticed the temperature's dropped quite a bit?'

'Yes! But there's no point in loosing people in the process,' observed Wómak.

'Yeah! I suppose you're right,' he relented. 'Mind you, walking briskly will keep us warm.'

Bróda slowed, letting Émana, Ganúra and Morác with Néra catch up.

The column was heading up a shallow dune where the wind had piled sand into a hillock. People tried to hasten but were cautious walking on this shifting ground, fearful they might be pulled under—or put a foot into a hole and fall down it. No grass. No trees. Nothing familiar to lock onto. They didn't know what to expect.

Bróda, Wómak and Morác reached the crest of the dune and viewed the sea of sand in front. Sand was everywhere, covered everything, turning what at the ridge had been a barren rocky landscape, into a sand sea covered with gently undulating dunes. When a wisp of wind picked up fine grains in the eerie starlight, they danced a while, swirled around, and then fell back as the wind dwindled. It wasn't daylight, but all around appeared distinct as if in a clear half-light.

They walked on throughout the night, tracking the southern star, in the footfalls of the scouts ahead. Near dawn, as saffron light spread from over the horizon, Bróda spied the scouts squatting on the ground and he called a halt.

The kópi were overjoyed at seeing their food-holder and nuzzled round his legs.

'Why have you stopped here?' Bróda out front greeted Fúlmon.

'This is hard flat ground, rather than shifting sand. I thought you might be more comfortable setting up camp on a solid base after all that wobbling and slipping.' Fúlmon grinned as if he'd told a joke.

The other two scouts also found it amusing. Only the kópis maintained a serious demeanour.

'Well, yes—you're right! It's unsettling walking in this stuff,' Bróda admitted. 'People have queasy stomachs—not being on solid ground. We've been sinking into this sand every footfall. No wonder nothing lives here.' He swept his arm in an arc.

'Are we stopping here for the day?' Morác asked, as he came up with Wómak.

'Fúlmon thinks it's a good place.' Turning to Wómak he added, 'Get the travois dismantled. We'll use the poles as props for the groundsheets. That should provide enough cover from the suns.'

Umára ambled over and asked Bróda, 'Do you want me to make hot food?'

Bróda stifled a yawn— 'No! Not this time. We don't know how much more of this wilderness there is. Let's not squander the firewood right now. Cold rations!' Then he yawned again and said to Émana, 'Goodness, I'm tired.'

'We'll soon be bedded down, dear. Fern's helping with the shelter,' she told him.

Umára went away to unpack the travois containing the food. The rest of the tribe got to setting up the bivouac. They ate in silence in family groups and quickly bedded down. By the time the suns rose, the Bólani were dozing comfortably in oblivion. Most were so tired, that as soon as their heads lay on the groundsheets, they were snoozing. Only the four sentries sat awake under personal canopies, facing the four corners of the compass. They'd been given strict orders to stay awake at all cost. Wómak threatened them with the severest penalties if any fell asleep—penalties rarely used by the tribe.

Mid-day the sentries were rotated and they promptly joined the sleepers. By early evening as the suns began to dip to the west, the camp stirred. The bivouac quickly dismantled and the travois reassembled. The collective water from the skins was rationed out. People nibbled at a cold platter of biscuits washed down sparingly with their own personal water.

As the suns disappeared over the horizon, the tribe began their trek once more. Slipping and sinking into the sand with each footfall. Dragging their feet out and subsiding back into the sand, making the going intensely laborious. Yet with the firm knowledge of what lay behind, people didn't complain that much. Most bit their lips, and plodded on. The night went relatively quietly, without incident. A few thought they heard hissing in the sand—others put it to an overwrought imagination. The latter scoffed at anything being able to live in such hostile environment.

By dawn of the eighteenth morning of their flight from the schánda, the column found the scouts waiting for them in a dip between two dunes.

Bróda, on reaching Fúlmon asked, 'Have you found us firm ground again?'

'Afraid not this time.' Fúlmon told him, looking weary and tired, as did the other two scouts.

'You look all-in,' Wómak commented, showing concern. 'What's been happening?'

'Huróyna says she feels like she's being followed.' Fúlmon grunted. 'I've told her it's absurd—where's the proof?'

Máyo appealed to Wómak, 'I, for one, believe her.'

Fúlmon scowled. 'Use your head, not your emotions.' He repeated, 'Where's the proof?' He flung his arms out wide, 'Show me!'

Bróda snapped, 'I think we'd better keep a good watch today.' He wanted to end the bickering.

'We've been chasing around more than usual, trying to fathom Huróyna's intuition,' Fúlmon confided to Bróda. 'We've worn ourselves out. I admit it's got me edgy.'

Morác sighed and said, 'It's switching the sleeping pattern around that's adding to our tiredness. We're not used to sleeping during the day.'

'In spite of the cold at night, If we walked through the day, we'd bake. Stomping through this sand in the heat would make us far more tired than we are.' It was Ganúra who volunteered that tit-bit of advice. 'I think Fúlmon's idea of walking through the night was a stroke of brilliance.'

Looking round the gathered tribe, Bróda saw only nodding heads. 'It looks like everyone agrees with that—so we continue that way.'

'Right! Let's get the bivouac set up,' Wómak told the warriors.

Everyone lent a hand to spread groundsheets, disassemble the travois and put up the poles for the suns covers. Píngo and Umára were prevailed to start a fire and prepare hot food. Bróda's orders. This time it was for moral as much as anything. He wanted to take the peoples minds off their surroundings—make them thing on a full stomach. Life always appears better on a full stomach.

Light began to emerge in the distance. The tribe sat huddled together against the cold after the meal. Umára used the sand like water, cleaning the platters with it, scrubbing the pots, using cloth and sand as a scourer. The fire was doused as soon as the cooking was over, to preserve the precious firewood. They wanted the heat but simply couldn't afford the luxury.

Ganúra sat with Émana and Néra watching the isolated crescent shaped dunes slowly migrating downwind, horns forward. It was the first time they saw a beauty in their surroundings, watching the reasonably strong wind lift the sand grains, moving them in a series of bounces, above the soon to be fiery landscape. The men had their heads together, deliberating in the middle of the bivouac, trying to sort out what Huróyna had seen, or hadn't seen.

In contrast, the women looked at a dune to the left, and saw how wind had blown sand up the gently sloping windward side of the dune. When the grains reached the top, they rolled down the steeper leeward side. For a moment, they indulged themselves in an introspective reflection on the nature of the desert they had begun to loathe from the beginning.

It was thus, another night ended for the Bólani, and all eventually settled for another day's sleep, it being exceptionally welcome to tired worn feet.

18

THE ABOMINATION

The tribe, close to exhaustion, trudged on for another two freezing nights, always sleeping the succeeding day. The cold of the nights alternated with the heat of the days. Further and further they went into the inhospitable desert landscape.

If they were to cross this abomination, it would have to be done by plodding tediously, laboriously, monotonously, step over step through the shifting grainy yellow deposit. There was an unvoiced fear that the wilderness had no end—that they would run out of water, run out of energy—and perish deep in the Aíne's forsaken sand. Although the thought was writ-clear on everyone's faces, it was left unsaid —but *loudly*.

19

A DANGEROUS DESERT

On the morning of the fifth day in the desert, as the tribe began to ready for another days sleep, the silence was broken by a shriek of pain—followed by two ear-piercing screams. It came from the three women, Ganúra, Émana, and Néra. Startled, the men broke what they were doing and came bounding towards the disturbance.

Ganúra was up, jumping, shaking at a thing hanging from her behind. Néra was trying to get hold of it, but it was slippery, twisting and wriggling.

'Get it off—get it off,' screeched Ganúra, moving and shaking so that nobody was able to grab whatever it was.

'Keep still,' Néra appealed.

'For Aíne's sake, come and help us,' bawled Émana.

At that moment, Wómak was the first to reach his mate. He gave whatever it was a swift sharp whack, which managed to dislodge the wriggling thing.

Bróda arrived and hit it hard with a travois pole. 'What the Húli is it?'

Píngo had his blowpipe out and darted the thing in the middle.

'Good shot,' Morác observed on arrival.

Píngo glared at Morác as if to say, "Who asked you?" Morác shrugged and went to comfort Néra.

'What is it?' Fúlmon asked as he neared.

Huróyna spat out, 'There—I told you so,' as she reached the turmoil. 'That's what I've been feeling—that thing, there,' she pointed almost accusingly at the inert object. She wore a discernible expression of relief now her intuition had been vindicated.

Bróda again asked, 'But what the Húli is it?'

Morác bent to examine the cubit long life-form. He put his fist by the side and shook his head. 'It's as thick as my fist,' he articulated to those who listened.

'It looks like a long worm—but it's so thick,' Máyo exclaimed.

The tribe stood in a large arc round the shamán, bent over the worm, trying to analyse the still life form.

'Is it dead?' Ganúra wanted to know, rubbing her backside.

'Lucky you had thick clothing there,' Wómak observed.

Ganúra gave her mate a sly smile, and continued massaging her buttocks. She had recovered her composure quickly; now the object was no more.

Morác prised the mouth open with an axe and showed those watching, row upon row of backward facing teeth. 'Well look at that,' he said in astonishment. 'I'd say you were fortunate to have escaped so easily. Once those teeth are locked on, I shouldn't think they'd let go that readily.'

'Do you think we could use their meat for food?' Máyo asked.

'Can't take the chance,' Morác responded. 'Might be poisonous.'

Bróda turned to Ganúra and asked, 'Where were you sitting? Tell us the details. Where there's one, there's others. We now have to assume the worst.' He addressed the gathered tribe, 'Let's get onto ground sheets. They might find it more difficult to surface through fabric.' Again he looked at Ganúra, 'It surfaced from the sand, did it?'

192

Ganúra nodded. She rounded up her kópi and went to her sleep shelter.

The tribe retreated to their sleeping shelters.

'Can everyone hear me?' Bróda asked.

Fern was holding the two kópis on leashes, trying to quieten them. Émana had jammed up in a corner, terrified of the worms.

'We hear you...loud and clear...yes!' came from a number of voices, speaking on behalf of the rest.

'Good! This is a serious development. Now, Ganúra! Tell us what happened.' A hush descended.

People listened to Ganúra with one ear; the other was trained on any sound coming through the sand below.

Ganúra began, 'I was just sitting up there, on a dune, with Émana and Néra—when from nowhere, I felt it grab my bottom, from below. Wómak was right when he said that only my thick clothing saved me. It was so cold during the night's walk, that I put on extra clothing—that's what spared me from a viscous bite'.

'So you didn't hear it coming?' Bróda asked.

'None of us did,' sighed Émana, sitting by Bróda.

'It was so silent...no whooshes or anything,' Néra added.

At that point, Málina roared, 'There...by the stándy.'

Every face turned to where the stándy were tethered. One of the worm things had a stándy leg down its throat. Another worm was in a similar position with another stándy.

Quick as a wink, Wómak was leaping to where the stándy were. Warriors had their blowpipes out and were carefully aiming at the worms. A hail of darts landed near and on the two worms. The stándy were bleating from fear and pain. The two who were caught, were shaking their trapped legs, trying to dislodge the worms. The backward facing teeth were impossible to shake off.

Wómak set on the worms with a fury, smashing their mouths with a pole, attempting to loosen the grip on the stándy legs. Seeing his bravery, other warriors joined him with axes, chopping at the worms in the middle. More worm heads appeared out of the sand nearby—staring at the struggle. As the warriors dispatched the two gripping the stándy legs, the worm heads disappeared back into the sand.

'Well, I never!' snapped Fúlmon.

Wómak was splitting the mouth of the dead worm with his axe, so as to extract the stándy leg. Súdair was at the other worm, using his knife in an expert manner. The tanner had a way of dismembering any life-form. He'd achieved a knack at skinning anything that moved. Warriors watched Súdair's work with admiration.

'Did you see that?' Fúlmon asked. 'Worm heads sticking out of the sand—watching us deal with them—then disappearing back down.'

'I don't like the look of that,' agreed Bróda. 'It suggests a degree of awareness. It's almost as if they had intelligence.'

'I don't think we're safe here,' Morác added.

'Why attack now?' Néra inquired. 'Why wait five days—why wait at all?'

'It's as if they had a stratagem,' Wómak put in, extricating the stándy leg from the worm teeth.

All the leg shaking had cut the stándy leg to the raw and it was limping badly. The second stándy was little better off. Both bleated in agony from the suffering inflicted by the worms.

Málina ran up in tears. 'My poor dears,' she blurted out, as if they were younglings. 'Let me have a look at you.'

Morác bent to examine the legs, as did Súdair.

'Keep your hands off them,' she barked at Súdair. '*Leave them alone!*'

Bróda took a hand in the matter. 'Now, now, Málina!' He took a conciliatory approach, trying to make her see reason. 'You can see as well as I can—they're in pain. We can't stay here, and they're in no fit state to travel.'

She could see where he was leading—she screwed up her face and let the tears run freely. 'My poor stándy,' is all she wailed.

Bróda nodded to Súdair. Súdair understood and led the limping stándy away, guarded by two warriors, away from Málina, into a neighbouring dune. The noisy bleating ceased abruptly.

Málina sobbed uncontrollably. Wólni and Cóer made a fuss of her, trying to console her, leading her gently away to where the rest of the stándy were tethered. Attempting to distract her.

'We started with fourteen stándy,' Málina protested to the suns in the sky. 'Now, there's only four left. It's not right,' she blubbered loudly.

The warriors with her were alert, blowpipes at the ready—listening to her complaining to Aíne. They were to guard the remaining stándy.

'We can't stay here,' Bróda shouted to the tribe. 'This is one day we're going to have to forego sleep. Pack your gear and be ready to move off.'

People hurried to comply. All were eager to be away from the place—from the worms. Nobody thought the worms would follow. Súdair brought the butchered stándy carcass back, whilst the two warriors carried the second carcass between them. It had happened quickly, out of sight. The meat was loaded with the rest of the dwindling provisions on the remaining four travois and the column set off rapidly.

Bróda, Wómak and Fúlmon strode out front, poles and blowpipes at the ready. The column, in tight formation, moved as fast as they could. From time to time they glimpsed worms protruding from the sand, paralleling their direction, moving swiftly, ripples showing in the sand when they were near the surface. But all through the morning, suns beating on them, sweat pouring from the people, the worms stayed just out of reach, trailing the column.

By mid-day, everyone was worn out. Bróda called a halt and ordered the groundsheets to be spread in a tight square. All the tribe gathered on the sheets, jammed in tightly. Their weight on the sheets and other groundsheets hung like wall around the square, made it seem like a fort. All around them worms surfaced looking at the Bólani behaviour, seeming to study the situation.

'Look at the pests! They're inspecting us,' gasped Émana.

'Don't be silly, dear,' Bróda rasped. 'They're just worms. They're just puzzled by the groundsheets.'

As he was saying that, a worm sped along the surface and leapt over the cloth barricade, launching itself at Cára. Umára had the presence of mind to whack it mid-air with his axe, turning it to fall outside at the base of the protective groundsheet. It lay stunned for a twitch and then burrowed back into the sand. Another launched itself at Ádna, Úbor's wife, but Súdair thwacked that one with a pole, again turning it to fall outside. Two more worms came flying over the flimsy barricade; one was downed mid-air by a dart from Fúlmon, and Scória cleaved the other in its belly as it passed over, lengthways with his knife. One worm that managed to evade the defenders, landed in the middle amongst the kópis, who tore it to pieces with gusto.

'Steady your nerves,' Wómak yelled. 'Hold your guard—don't let them get inside.'

'Pull those groundsheets as high as you can—without exposing your feet,' Bróda roared.

The women were holding the bottoms of the sheet to the sand, making sure no gap appeared. The four stándy were held in the middle with the three kópi by Fern, Cóer, and Láila. Warriors and the other men stood at the make-shift barricades ready to repel the worms.

The worms ceased their attacks as suddenly as they'd begun them. One moment they were throwing themselves over the cloth ramparts, the next there was quiet. All the worms disappeared from view and an expectant silence hung in the air. The stillness continued, so Bróda had the warriors keep watch whilst the remainder rested on the groundsheets.

When Bróda felt the tribe had recovered from their ordeal, the column set off once more, heading south. The worms, although fewer in number tracked the tribe from a distance of twenty cubits, staying just insight, paralleling the moving group of people. That got on people's nerves—worms following them wherever they went.

The formation kept on the move for the rest of the day, into the night, and into the following morning, stopping only for short water breaks. By mid-day the dunes became more frequent and higher than they were accustomed to thus far.

Then as they neared a higher than usual dune running horizontally before them, the worms began to fall back. This encouraged the clan to further effort, thinking they were outrunning the worms. They climbed the high dune, sliding and slipping down every other footfall. As the leaders crested the top, they were struck dumb, stunned into immobility. They stood at the top—as if frozen.

Bróda's mouth was open in astonishment. Rarely was he struck speechless—this was one time he had nothing to say.

Morác reached the top and gasped, 'What—' and stopped mid sentence. He stared.

Others joined him and gazed in silence.

Huróyna finally voiced everyone's thoughts, 'What the Húli is it?' She'd picked up Fúlmon's blaspheming habits on the journey.

Folks gawked at the twin towers before them, and then looked at each other, unable to form a description of what they saw. The truth was none had seen anything like it. They had no experience to describe the vision. One moment they were running for their lives in an empty wilderness—the next, they were faced with a building unlike any they'd seen.

Sitting in a deep depression were two tall yellow round towers, wider at the base than at the top. The sides sloped two thirds of the way up, and then were topped by a lesser slope with a dome rounding the buildings off. From this distance, there were rings encircling both towers on the lower slope. The towers stood facing each other with a linking on the upper slope, near the dome.

Bróda remembered the worms and looked for them, but saw no sign. The warriors kept a sharp lookout.

Shaking his head, Morác finally said, 'I've never seen anything like this.' He displayed an arc in the direction of the towers with his right hand.

'I'm at a loss as to what to say,' Bróda said. 'I mean...what is it?'

'Look at the size of that,' Fúlmon muttered.

Prudently Wómak ventured, 'More to the point; who built it?'

'And further to the point; are there any inhabitants still left there?' added Ganúra.

'We're not going to find out standing here,' observed Néra.

'She's right!' said Bróda, nodding at Néra. 'Fúlmon! You don't have to—I'm not ordering you to. But go and scout that thing, will you?'

Fúlmon raised his eyebrows, and then said, 'That's my job!' He spun round at Huróyna, 'This time, please stay here. Me and Máyo will do this—please.'

Both scouts sped downhill, sliding and slipping down the sand, to the bottom of the dune. Then, as the assembled crowd watched from the top of the dune, after time they saw the scouts approach the twin towers. There was a kind of moat around the structures with only one breech. Both scouts went across the moat and began walking up the side of the nearest tower, where the lower rings circled it.

The scouts waved to show they were all right, and then continued to go out of sight round the far side of the first tower. Bróda decided that they could just as well wait at the bottom of the hill, and led the way down the slippery slope. No sign of the worms. People sat at the bottom and waited for the scouts to return. They were hot, thirsty, and near their limit of endurance.

For the last five days the tribe had slept during this time, and were now almost all yawning—trying to stay awake. The worms and novelty of the twin towers had their juices pumping, and frankly, that was the only reason people hadn't fallen asleep where they sprawled.

A while passed and others fell fast asleep, having covered themselves as best as they could.

20

THE ANCIENTS

A way off from those resting and sleeping, Bróda was holding a council.

'We can't decide anything until Fúlmon gets back with his report,' Bróda was saying.

'I know that,' Morác told him. 'It doesn't stop us speculating as to what that building is, does it?' He was puzzled why people refused to talk of the towers.

'Speculate away,' Bróda invited.

'What's it doing here, out in the wilderness?' Morác cast his eyes around. 'Who built it and why? It's the biggest building anyone of us has ever seen in our lives. It must have taken years to construct.'

Silence greeted his conjecture.

'Maybe they've found a way to escape the schánda? You know, up there in the towers.' He was met with blank faces. 'Oh, Húli! I give up.'

At that point a shout greeted them from the distance. Fúlmon came walking back, perplexed in appearance, gently scratching his head, talking with Máyo. He wasn't in a hurry.

Wómak remarked, 'Can't be much danger...look at them. They're out for a stroll.'

All looked relieved at the return of the scouts.

'Well? What have you found?' Morác couldn't contain himself and broke protocol by questioning the lead scout before the Custodian.

Fúlmon faced Bróda and gave him his report. 'We went onto a circular rampart going round the tower nearest to us. It leads almost to the top on the outside, and then the path enters a tunnel and continues upwards until it comes out onto a rope bridge—crossing to the other tower. That's as far as we went. We didn't cross the bridge up there.'

'For Aíne's sake, why not?' Bróda wanted to know.

'It didn't feel right. I don't know—neither of us felt we should. It was a feeling—call it a premonition.' Fúlmon was a bit downcast as he said this.

'I agree with Fúlmon—it just didn't feel right,' added Máyo.

'It wouldn't have anything to do with the height of the bridge—from the ground?' Bróda inquired.

Both scouts glanced at each other and cast their eyes to the ground, keeping silent.

'Oh, well! Never mind!' Bróda consoled. 'So tell me. Can we go camp near that moat?'

'I see no reason not to,' Fúlmon replied.

Bróda cleared his throat and bellowed, 'Those not asleep—please wake the sleepers. We're going to set up bivouac near the moat. We need to find water,' then as an after thought he added, 'and food. Let's get moving. The sooner we relocate; the sooner people can get back to sleep.'

Slowly, reluctantly, the tribe got itself moving. It was a quarter of a league to their destination and it took them a while. When they reached the moat, they found it contained a kind of putrid mush that looked distinctly evil. They moved the camp back a way, out of smelling distance.

'Right! We seem to have got rid of the worms,' Bróda beamed a broad smile at that, '—and I'm sure we're all glad of that. If there's no problem, I want us to camp here till tomorrow. Any objections?'

Nobody objected. More to the point, people had quickly spread their groundsheets and most were fast asleep, exhausted. It was mid-afternoon. Warriors went round and quietly set up covers on poles, over the sleeping tribe. Fear, tiredness, all contributed to the present state of affairs. If anything threatened the tribe just now, it's likely they would perish.

'Morác! Use your crystal. Tell me where the schánda are.' Bróda whispered this request.

'Can it wait till I've had a look up there.' Morác pointed at the towers.

'Suit yourself, but I must know the threat they pose.' Bróda was irked at being rebuffed. 'Don't be up there long. Oh! And since the scouts didn't find water or food, maybe you would be so kind—'

Morác had already made tracks for the bridge. Along the way he met Dalán and invited him along for company, and as a bodyguard. They crossed the moat in a cautious mood. Morác waved an acknowledgement at Bróda's entreaty to find water. The bridge was made of compacted sand. *Now how the Húli did they make that stuff stick together?* He speculated. *Apart from the mystery of the towers themselves, there's peculiar things going on here.*

On the other side of the bridge they found themselves on a wide path leading upwards, round the tower. As they ascended the circular path, the panorama of the depression became visible. It looked like the towers stood in an artificial depression, designed specifically to give height to the towers, yet for them not to stick out in the desert surroundings.

By the time they reached the top of the lower slope, they found the path ended in mid air. Evening was setting in and the suns were dipping downwards the western horizon. Dalán went closer to the edge and called Morác to him. He'd found a large arch to his right, going into the tower. Both entered and saw that the path continued upwards, but inside the tower this time.

Again, they proceeded on an internal pathway with a smooth thin yellow sand squared brick facing the walls on either side, and an arch fashioned of the same material above.

It's as if the sand of the desert was able to be made firm—for use as bricks. The people who constructed this were totally alien to their thinking—way beyond their comprehension. The Bólani lived in living trees, their beautiful Lándo trees, but out here no living thing existed, apart from those horrid worms, yet buildings had been constructed with a technology way beyond anything they'd encountered before.

Higher and higher they climbed along the circular path. The air below had been warm and dry at the beginning, but now was cooler and more humid. Night was readying to take over. The light was fading. The smell was musty as if decay was setting in. They eventually rounded a part of the path that led towards a distant dim light source ahead. As they neared, they discerned they were seeing the dim sky through another arch ahead. *This must lead to the rope bridge Fúlmon mentioned,* remembered Morác.

They came out onto a platform reaching out into nothingness, to which the rope bridge was attached. Opposite in the distance, a hundred cubits in front, there was another platform set in another arch, just like the one they were standing on. In between was a two cubit wide rope bridge. True, the ropes looked sturdy enough, but the distance down was dizzying. Both quite understood Fúlmon's reluctance. Morác was almost giddy himself looking down. Dalán was completely unaffected by the height.

'Would you mind testing that bridge?' Morác asked innocently.

'Not at all,' came the equally innocent reply.

With that, Dalán walked out boldly onto the bridge in the twilight. It wobbled and swayed moderately in the wind, but he was oblivious to the motion. Without much ado he reached the dipping centre, turned and waved at Morác to follow him. Morác centred himself, got a grip on his apprehension, and placed one foot on the bridge. Carefully, he proceeded to make progress across, holding onto the flimsy rope handrail. That only made things worse, as

Morác's weight was now on one side of the swinging bridge and that side sagged, making it more difficult to move forward.

Then for no reason, the bridge took on a firmness that it didn't naturally possess. It became almost solid, and Morác was able to walk on it as if it was made of brick. *A sorcerer's casting,* Morác bemused—*and it's not me.* The walk to the other side was now done at leisure, but with caution.

'How did you do that?' Dalán asked, as Morác approached.

'I didn't! Better let me go first from here on,' he advised.

'Hmm!' Dalán murmured. He stood a side and let Morác take the lead.

Morác approached the opposite arch steadily, trying to peer into the gloom with every step. He could see nothing that suggested anyone was watching. *Curious,* he muttered to himself. *So! You want to play games, heh?* he mumbled. Then he remembered what had happened to Fándin when he'd come across a wandering stranger, who'd turned out to be another sorcerer with far greater powers than himself. He was overconfident—and paid the price by being turned into a changeling; a fierce wild bári no one could approach, with no memory of his former self, destined forever to roam the forest.

That tempered his mumbling and he became quiet, thoughtful.

'Don't do anything threatening,' Morác whispered to Dalán. 'Just do what I do—slowly.'

Dalán nodded to indicate he understood. He pulled his hand away from his axe, which he'd intended to pull out.

They both reached the other side, one behind the other, walking further into the gloom—into a passage way, leading to a light source. Morác's face began to show surprise, as he closed the distance to another archway. This led into a huge circular room, two hundred cubits across, lit from a light source above, near a hole in the roof of the dome. Through the hole they saw the night sky and stars. Faded tattered tapestries lined the circular wall, going all round the rotunda. A long time ago, when they were new, they must have presented quite a spectacle, adding colour to the circular hall.

He peered at the hole above and saw that the opening was covered with glass. The size of the glass covering awed him. So clear, even the stars twinkled. Elliptical windows in the side walls showed the darkness outside. The artificial light from above highlighted a faded decorated purple carpet leading to a raised dais at the other end. As the two Bólani approached, on the dais they saw an ornate chair, carved from a dark wood they didn't recognise. Behind the dais was the outline of two gilded sun discs surrounded with ray bursts.

Dalán's mouth dropped open as he recognised Aíne's revered symbol. It was carved into stone in the Bólani sacred glade, in their open-air temple. Every Bólani youngling had it etched firmly into their memory from the first celebration in the place of high power in the forest. Six times a season he'd seen it ever since he could remember. What was it doing here?

Gingerly, Morác advanced towards the dais, walking beside the purple carpet, not wanting to tread onto anything that looked so fragile—like it might fall to pieces. Dalán copied his footfalls.

'Do you get the feeling eyes watching us?' asked Dalán in a whisper.

'Shush!' was all Morác said. 'I'm concentrating.'

The floor was dusty as if it hadn't been cleaned for a long time, but there were faint old footfalls criss-crossing everywhere.

'There's people been here.' Morác hissed.

They neared the dais and stopped, staring at the sunbursts on the back wall.

Morác raised his hands and intoned towards the sacred symbol, 'Oh mighty Aíne, I offer myself, a humble servant, to your judgement. May those who listen, show favour and forgiveness for our trespassing in this place of power.' He listened, and then continued, 'We mean no harm, but flee for our lives from the vicious schánda, seeking to devour us.'

An indistinct rustle came from the direction of one of the many faded and torn tapestries hanging from the side walls—to the left. Morác kept his arms raised, but pivoted his head in the direction of the noise.

A figure emerged from a vertical slit in the tapestry, creating a gentle shower of dust that shimmered in the suns light. The stooping figure walked serenely forward, towards Morác, almost seeming to glide along the floor. It was dressed in a long loose threadbare green flowing robe, decorated with intricate geometric designs, but the robe had seen better days.

Dalán had his hand back on is axe, ready. Morác turned to the advancing figure and put his hands down. Smiling, he indicated he meant no harm, looked sternly at Dalán, who again withdrew his hand from his axe.

The figure came to a halt ten cubits away from them. Morác beheld a tall wizened male, craggy face topped with a domed hat, covering white hair.

'Ehem!' was followed by 'Hum...hmm!' as the figure cleared its throat. 'Well? What brings you here?' the old man finally asked—staring down at Morác and pointedly ignoring Dalán.

'I beg your pardon for this intrusion,' Morác managed. 'We are travellers on the run from the schánda. Our tribe, the Bólani, is camped below for the while—resting. We were attacked by worms in the desert. We're looking for water, food, and a moments respite from our journey. May we stay for a short while?'

The old man gazed at Morác, examining him up and down like a prize specimen.

Finally he spoke, 'So you're what passes for a sorcerer on the outside—heh?'

'Only a minor one. My name is Morác, shamán to the Bólani. Whom do I have the pleasure of addressing?'

'I am Phèrlim, once Grand Wizard to the mighty ruler of Linkalúr, Lord Karlan. You are standing in the stronghold of Linkalúr, home of the now deceased Lord Karlan. And— yes—is the answer to your request. You may camp where you are.'

'That is gracious of you, Lord Phèrlim. If you will permit—I will send this one,' Morác pointed at Dalán, 'back to our Custodian to inform him of your permission. He has worried over trespassing on stranger's land.'

'I permit,' said Phèrlim offhandedly.

'Dalán! Go tell Bróda what you've seen and inform him I'll be along shortly. And tell Néra not to worry. That's all.'

Dalán was only too happy to go. The place made him nervous. He simply had no reference points to hook these new experiences onto. He turned and swiftly strode off towards the exit—and the rope bridge.

'Where is everyone?' Morác asked of Phèrlim. 'We haven't seen a person since we arrived. I assumed the place was forsaken. And how is it you speak our tongue?'

'It is a long story. I speak many languages. Would you care to join me in my accommodation? We can relax there.' With that Phèrlim led the way back to the place he'd appeared from—to the slit in the torn tapestry.

There, they went through a doorway behind the tapestry, down a series of steep steps to a large landing. Artificial lights were placed strategically on the walls. To the left off the landing were a number of closed doorways. Phèrlim went through the third door of the row of doors, pushing it open with ease.

Morác found himself in a large lit well furnished rectangular room, shelves all round the room stacked to the ceiling with books.

'I've never seen so many books in my whole life.' There was wonder in his voice.

'Come—have a drink,' beckoned Phèrlim, standing near a table flush against a wall. 'Have you ever tasted fermented Belem juice?' The table held bottles of coloured liquid.

'I can say with honesty—never,' replied Morác.

'You're in for a treat,' Phèrlim told him.

'If you wouldn't mind, at the moment I'm intensely thirsty and wouldn't appreciate the juice. If you have water, then I could drink a lot of that.' Morác didn't say so, but he was being prudent with any strange drinks, although he was telling the truth of being thirsty.

'As you wish!' Phèrlim poured a generous measure of a colourless liquid into a large glass, and handed Morác the glass and jug.

Morác consumed the glass of water after sniffing it. He poured another, and drank that more slowly.

'My—I needed that!' he exclaimed. 'We're short on water—have been for the last day or so.'

Morác looked around the room more carefully, taking in the details. At one end there was a large oval window showing the desert night on the far distant horizon, indicating they were extremely high up. He also noticed everything was worn, threadbare, dusty, and old. In fact it looked ancient, rather than simply old.

'Yes, it's old,' it was as if Phèrlim was reading his thoughts.

Morác looked away, thinking he'd offended the Grand Wizard. 'Beg pardon, Lord. I'm simply curious. Is that how you speak our language—taking the words from my mind?' Without waiting he continued, 'Where I come from, there is nothing like this.' He swept his arm around the room.

'I'm astonished that such a place even exists—out here in the wasteland.'

'Please sit,' Phèrlim indicated a chair. 'Brush the dust off—that's it. This wasn't always a wasteland—the desert you see before you,' he pointed through the window. 'Once, long ago, thousands of seasons in the past, were fields with crops growing out there.' Phèrlim's voice dropped to a whisper. It was as if he was remembering the sadness of the story he was recounting. 'Even when I was young, the desert was already taking over. People left, never to return. Some went north; others went south and crossed the Golden Sea. We spread to all four points of the compass. The encroaching sand clogged everything. The land died, suffocated by the yellow dust.'

Quietly Morác asked, 'But why did the sand come in the first place?'

'Which way did you come? Must be from the North.' Phèrlim paused, sighed, and continued, 'It's the time of the schánda migration—isn't it?'

Morác nodded.

'Then you must have passed the volcano?'

Morác furrowed his brow, 'What's a volcano?'

'The hole in the ground—the rift where the ground is on fire. Surely you must have seen it—passed it even?' Phèrlim looked at Morác in disbelief. 'There's no way you could have missed it?'

'Now I understand—yes, we went round it, to the east,' Morác explained. 'That's what you call it—a volcano? What causes it?'

'Pressure from underground. You've dug wells where water comes bubbling up—it's the same with lava. More to the point, did you see the river before the volcano, flowing down the valley?'

Morác nodded, 'Yes we did. We passed a fort there, sitting on an escarpment. It was a strong flowing river—why?'

'Well, that river used to flow straight here, before the volcano erupted. It was our lifeline, the blood of our land. We used it to irrigate all that is desert now. A vast network of channels running from the river. When the volcano erupted, a thousand seasons ago, we lost that lifeline. The river flowed into the rift for a while, then the lava build-up at the edge, diverted it to the west.' The old man sat heavy in his chair, the stoop more pronounced.

'Did I hear you right—a thousand seasons ago?' Morác couldn't believe is ears. 'And by the way—why didn't you stop the volcano, with your sorcery?'

'Yes! You heard right. As for stopping the volcano— even my prodigious powers are no match against the forces of Nature. When Kálar speaks, I listen. If ever you are forced to pit yourself against a natural phenomenon, be aware that it will drain your powers like pouring water from a jug.' Phèrlim smiled at the reference to the jug. Then, slowly, he enunciated the following words, 'I have already seen *two* schánda migrations—. Do you know how old that makes me?'

Morác gasped. 'But that means—you've lived at least...six hundred seasons.' Morác was stunned. 'How is that possible?'

'I am the Grand Wizard—the keeper of concealed knowledge. The holder of the ancient mysteries. I'm telling you this, since you are of the same knowledge.'

'I'm a mere lowly shamán—never to be compared with you, Lord Phèrlim. I felt your work when we crossed the rope bridge. You have power beyond anything I posses.' Morác was being honest.

'Be still,' Phèrlim commanded. 'You mentioned upstairs, standing before the sign of the two suns, the "Sacred and mysterious name of the True and Living Aíne Most High". That made the light of the darkness visible. When you crossed the rope bridge, I strengthened it so as to know whom I might strike down. When I heard you beseech our Holy

Lady, it was your salvation. I knew that the knowledge had come full circle.

'Listen carefully, Morác. I have told you I'm of a great age. What I didn't tell you is—my time is near. These walls will protect your tribe against the schánda. They have never breached the tower. These two towers were built to withstand their migration. They will get as far as the rope bridge—and no more. In the past, all of the surrounding population took refuge in this tower. Below, we have many floors like the big hall above. Enough to hold thousands of people, with their animals. The schánda take around six days to pass; during that time, the people sheltered here, and were safe. Then they came out and resumed their lives—in peace and harmony. This could be your life from now on.

'I want you to bring your tribe up here in the morning, into this tower. I will show you how to destroy the rope bridge, and how to re-construct it after the schánda have left. You will live here, clean the place up, and restore the majesty of the building, the tapestries. You, Morác will become my beneficiary, my heir, my replacement—the new Grand Wizard.' A fierceness sparkled in Phèrlim's eyes that hadn't been there before. He said this, willing it to be so. He took it for granted that Morác would *want* to be the next Grand Wizard. After all, who in their right mind would refuse such power.

21

MORÁC—THE WIZARD

'Lord—forgive me—I'm not worthy of such high office,' Morác appealed. 'I am but a simple forest shamán. We have lived all our lives in the forest. Please! Don't ask me to do this.'

A look of resignation replaced the previous sparkle on Phèrlim's face. 'Oh! Well. I had to try. I can't think of all this just going to ruin. It's been so long since anybody has come here, that I'd hoped—against hope. Deep down, I know you can't stay, won't stay. But an old man grasps at the slimmest chance. Well, at least before I leave, let me give you my insight. Come closer, give me your hand.'

Morác moved his chair closer to Phèrlim. Phèrlim took from round his neck a mighty pendant, hanging on a thick gold chain; his red stone talisman embedded in between two suns. As Morác gave him his hand, the old wizard put his red stone talisman in the palm of his hand and clasped Morác's with force, making Morác wince.

Then Phèrlim began to recite, 'Nothing resists the will of Aíne, for she is truth, and wills for good. She is the person of the law, of all that's good, the ritual of reason. To hold the right to possess the secrets for eternity, I offer Morác, my inheritor who—in his words, "is only a lowly shamán", but vows to glorify your holy name—Aíne.

'With the knowledge of his being a just man, conforming to the law of Nature, I, Phèrlim, Grand High

Wizard of Linkalúr, affirm by the word that creates form, spreading the veil of light over the shadows, making darkness visible, do pass the crystallised arcane mysteries handed down to me by Hrosim the Venerable Master that taught me my skills. May the corner-stone of truth guide his incantations, may his innate wisdom guard him from all evildoing. May my powers stir his magnetic nervous force and bring forth perpetual penetration of the darkness.'

A tingle passed from Phèrlim to his talisman, then to Morác through the crystal contact. Morác's eyes widened.

Phèrlim continued, 'By the Universal equilibrium of light and darkness, through the instrument of thought, I pass to this supplicant the infinite light of the body of Aíne. May he transcend his mortality—'

'No-o-o!' Cried Morác. 'I don't want your immortality—to live so long as to see my loved ones pass away. Please—spare me that!'

Phèrlim looked shocked—at the refusal. At the interruption. But then understood what Morác had shouted. He glanced at Morác—in a manner that dismissed him as a mere mortal. He had lived so long that he could no longer think in those short mortal terms. He calmed himself, and continued, 'May he *retain his mortality* and trace the light through his enhanced material instrument of thought.'

'Thank you,' murmured Morác, with great relief on his face.

Phèrlim hadn't noticed Morác's quiet gratitude and went on as if nothing happened, 'Aíne is the soul of light, writing on the great white book of night. Light is the source of thought that marks us out as a superior life-form. May this supplicant be worthy.' He sighed deeply, 'Aíne! Have mercy on my poor essence—as I depart this mortal turmoil.' He breathed another sigh. 'May Aíne watch over you and your tribe, Morác,' and his head slumped gently onto his chest. He was still. So passed away Phèrlim, the last Grand Wizard of Linkalúr. And Kálar was the poorer for his passing—at least

Morác thought so. A gentle tear welled up in his eyes, as he extricated his hand from the wizards grip, taking Phèrlim's talisman. He gazed at the red stone—so unlike his own green talisman. He placed the new talisman round his neck, hiding it under his shirt from view.

Slowly, with much sadness, Morác got up from his chair and went the length of the room to the window. He looked down but in the darkness, could not see where the tribe was camped. Anyhow, the other tower obscured his view. He felt strange, standing there, as if there was more energy flowing through him. He acquired many more memories than he had before the melding with Phèrlim. He was able to bring into his minds eye, the features of the last High Lord of Linkalúr, Lord Karlan. He saw and understood how the desert had destroyed a whole ancient civilisation. He understood the way the towers were constructed—the nooks and crannies of it. He'd gained words to describe many of the things that used to puzzle him. And the power of his sorcery, well he felt it almost throbbing in him, welling up, and ready to be used.

I must get a grip on myself—he thought—*to remember to use this only for good.* That calmed the throbbing inside. He came back and stood before Phèrlim's corpse. The skin had dried into parchment—tufts of hair had fallen out, those not held in position by the domed cap. Morác needed to give Phèrlim his due, to be laid to rest with honours. With this in mind, he made his way back to the rotunda above, up the steep stairs. Pushing the torn tapestry aside, he found Dalán waiting for him near the dais, sitting on the bottom step, back to Lord Karlan's royal seat.

'Dalán! I'm glad to see you. Come, give me a hand,' Morác said in a deeper voice than usual.

That startled Dalán. He looked up, expecting evil.

'You've acquired another voice,' Dalán peered closely at Morác, to see if it really was the Bólani shamán. 'It seems deeper,' he observed.

'Really? Well don't just sit there. Are you going to help me or not?' Morác walked back to the torn tapestry and waited.

Dalán got up and went to him. 'It is the middle of the night. Bróda sent me to see if you were all right.'

Both descended the steep stairs, back to the rectangular room with Phèrlim's body still sitting where he'd passed over. When they'd entered the room, Dalán just stood before the body, staring at it.

'Dalán! Can you find a container to carry the body in? *Dalán!*' Morác thundered.

Dalán shook himself back to composure. 'What happened?'

'I'll tell the story to the whole tribe when we get back to the bivouac. It's a long story. Do you mind waiting?'

'No! It's all right,' Dalán said, and wandered around the room looking for a way to move the corpse.

He wandered to a corner and shouted back, 'I've found two stout poles standing in the corner. Any good?'

'Perfect! Bring them here. We'll make a stretcher. Any cloth anywhere?'

'There's a kind of banner attached to the poles. Might be just the thing.' He carried the poles back to Morác, who was standing and staring kindly at Phèrlim.

'Let's see,' Morác said. 'Oh, yes. These are still strong. If we pin each banner to the opposite pole, we'll get a good stretcher.'

Dalán began to look around the room for pins. 'Here, on the desk. Will these do?' He picked up brooches and took them to Morác.

'Just the thing,' Morác told him.

They pinned the banners with brooches and laid the corpse gently onto the stretcher. To Dalán's surprise, the corpse was light; it had little weight to it.

'Careful!' Morác said, far more irritate than he'd intended. He felt upset by Phèrlim's demise, more than he cared to admit. 'Sorry!' he then apologised to Dalán. 'It's just —I was talking to him just a while ago. I feel he's still here.'

Dalán said nothing. He understood what Morác was getting at, and took no offence.

They lifted the litter and carried the corpse as sensitively as they could, upstairs to the rotunda. They laid him on the dais, at the foot of Lord Karlan's royal seat. To Morác, it was appropriate. Then, Morác went round and tore down two heavy age encrusted tapestries and covered what was left of the High Grand Wizard of Linkalúr with them.

Dust flew everywhere, but Morác was oblivious to it. Dalán coughed throughout, finally being forced to retreat to the rope bridge. There, in the night air, he breathed as if he was being suffocated. When he'd finished coughing, he sat and waited for Morác. It was a time before Morác finished saying his farewells to Phèrlim. He finally removed Karlan's royal seat from the dais and placed Phèrlim body on a table before Aíne's suns bursts.

Morác emerged from the arch onto the platform where Dalán waited. A light had lit above the arch, barley enough to see the rope bridge.

'Have you said your final farewells?' Dalán inquired.

'Yes! I think we'd better make our way back.' Morác stared into the darkness.

The other tower was an immense shadow in the moonless night. The desert below eerily lit by starlight, was a long way down. This time it was Dalán who hesitated crossing the rope bridge. Morác in contrast, walked boldly onto the rope bridge, which remarkably firmed up, as it had when they arrived.

'Is that your doing?' Dalán asked.

'This time, I'm doing it,' Morác replied.

When they got to the other side and stood on the opposite platform, Dalán asked, 'I thought it was supposed to be beyond your skill?'

'It was. That's changed, thanks to the late Phèrlim.'

'The Custodian will be glad to hear that,' observed Dalán.

They went through the arch into the tunnel leading downward along the internal path. The tunnel was pitch black and they had to feel their way along.

Morác continued in the darkness, 'This new knowledge will benefit the whole tribe. Now I'm confident we'll survive the schánda.'

'I can't see my hand feeling the wall,' Dalán complained.

Abruptly, a circular light shone in the palm of Morác's hand. He held it up to light the way, making progress much easier.

Dalán said nothing, merely gazed in amazement at Morác's hand held high, and followed. There was a tinge of awe mixed with fear on his face at the new power Morác acquired. He followed Morác meekly, entirely unlike the Dalán of earlier when they had trundled upwards along the same path.

This time it was easier, going downwards. When they came out of the tunnel, Morác doused the light. They followed the circular path to the moat bridge, where to Morác's surprise, Néra waited.

'Where've you been?' she complained. 'I was just going to go searching for you.' She nodded an acknowledgement at Dalán.

'Let's get away from this stink,' Morác referred to the mush in the moat. 'I'll tell you all of what's happened at the same time as I tell our people.' The three walked side by side, Morác in the middle.

Néra stared at Morác's face, a furrow on a brow between her eyes. She searched Morác's countenance.

'It's me,' Morác asserted, noticing the stare. 'Who else were you expecting?'

'It's only...you're different,' she replied.

'Yes! You're right. Still...it *is* me. I met a very powerful wizard up there,' he waved up at the towers, 'and he's passed on his knowledge to me—he died just a while ago. That's what's different.'

All three walked towards the bivouac. Bróda was waiting with Wómak, talking, standing a ways off, and doing sentry duty.

'Well, if it isn't our missing shamán,' joked Wómak. 'What have you found?'

Bróda looked stern, even worried, if that was possible in the starlight. It was a constant surprise to all at how much light there was in the desert. The starlight reflecting off the yellow sand, gave a sort of twilight feel at night.

'Morác!' hissed Bróda. 'I need to know where the schánda are at this moment. It's driving me nuts not knowing. Please, get your crystal.'

'They're one day into the desert—at the moment,' replied Morác, nonchalantly.

'You didn't take your crystal with you, did you? So how do you know?' Bróda was getting angry.

'Take my word for it—I know. Don't need a crystal anymore.' Morác said this as if it was self evident.

Bróda looked hard at Morác, then at Néra. To her he said, 'What's he talking about? What's happened to him?'

'He says a wizard up in the tower has given him new knowledge—he says he's going to explain it to us all.' Néra simply stated what Morác had said. What could she add?

'They got held up by the rift—now they're moving rapidly across the desert, five days behind us.'

'Who are? You mean the schánda?' Bróda asked.

'I do! The night's almost done,' Morác observed. 'If you wake the tribes-people, I have food and drink for them.'

That got their attention.

'Where?' Wómak wanted to know. 'I can't see anything.'

'Wake the people, and I'll show you,' Morác insisted.

'Go quietly, wake everyone up,' Bróda told Wómak.

When the people had woken, stood outside their makeshift tents, Morác addressed them. 'I have good news for you—plenty of herbal drink and good solid porridge—with syrup.'

Morác concentrated, waved his hands in a dramatic manner, and a morning fire appeared way off. More waving and a pot of porridge sat on the fire. Another pot with herbal sat next to the porridge pot. Out of thin air, logs materialised neatly arranged around the fire so people could sit.

Mouths dropped open, people stared, amazed. Then they looked at Morác as if he was a stranger—fear clearly visible on most faces. People even shuffled back, as if Morác was to harm them. It looked like their shamán, but how could it be? Why did their innocuous, friendly shamán, behave like this? They perceived what he'd done as threatening. He'd never done anything like this—ever. Píngo threw Morác a dark stare for lighting *his* fire—usurping *his* prerogative.

'It's all right,' Morác tried to reassure them. 'Please—Umára, serve the food. It's perfectly safe! You have my word.'

Umára looked at Bróda, who nodded for him to serve the food. Cautiously, people lined up for the platters of porridge. They were famished and hadn't eaten porridge for four days now, ever since it ran out. They were existing on the slender pickings from the two stándy Súdair butchered after the worm attack. By the fire, Umára was ladling out the porridge and from a nearby pot, sweet sap from their precious Orel tree, pouring it over the porridge. Uílin, Umára's assistant handed out wooden mugs of herbal to each person.

Mouths were watering at the prospect of eating their staple food. Drinking their normal drink. And Orel sap? Disbelief was painted on everyone's' faces. They took their platters and sat on the logs provided—expectant. The hungry ate greedily, others waited for an explanation. Not entirely trusting to this good fortune—wary of sorcery on such a scale.

'I'm going to wait until you've all finished eating— so those holding back had better get on with it. Then, when we're all clasping our full bellies, I'm going to tell you the story of Linkalúr—of the great Grand Wizard to the Lord of Linkalúr, Lord Karlan. His name was Phèrlim.'

Those hanging back looked at each other and gingerly at first, began to eat. Soon they were queuing for seconds and thirds. The pots were bottomless. Porridge, syrup, and herbal were endlessly handed out by a beaming Umára. He particularly made sure Cára and the twins were well supplied. When all had eaten their fill, Morác began to relate the whole story in great detail.

By the time he'd finished, the morning suns were high in the sky. People didn't care. For the first time in a long time, they were content—more than that, happy. They had slept well, and now eaten their fill, and even the threat they were running from was less urgent. They gazed admiringly at Morác—at their transformed shamán. They felt confident that he could deal with anything. Had they not seen with their own eyes, his powerful sorcery?

'So!' Bróda finally gave voice to his thoughts. 'We can stay here, and avoid the schánda, up there in the tower—' he looked in the direction of the imposing structure. 'Or...we can keep going—' he trailed. 'What's it going to be?'

People stared at the Custodian, puzzled.

'I'm for going on!' Wómak declared.

'So am I!' It was Ganúra, supporting her mate.

'No! We have to stay!' Sáor yelled.

'We want to stay!' shouted Émer, in support of her mate.

More people shouted in favour—and against.

'That's it! I'm calling an emergency meeting of the tribe—out here, in the open.' Bróda spread his legs in the sand, folded his arms, indicating he was adamant.

Morác joined Bróda on one side, Wómak on the other. People stayed sitting on their logs.

'Wómak! Since you're in favour of moving on—let's hear your reasoning. Sáor can speak for those who want to stay.'

Wómak shifted his weight in the sand, cleared his throat and began. 'We have managed to outrun the schánda so far, and I feel confident we can continue to do so. These strange towers behind us are empty. The people have gone— probably running for their lives—from the schánda.' He paused for effect, to give his words more weight. 'I have no trust in their ability to hold the schánda off. I *have* trust in my ability to outrun them. I intend to keep going, and I urge the rest of the tribe to do the same.'

Wómak had just broken the rules of the meeting by insisting on an ultimatum, and the surprise it caused didn't go down well.

Bróda grimaced as he heard the ultimatum, but ignored it for the moment. 'I call upon Sáor to back his proposal.'

Sáor got up from his log and gazed round his audience. 'Did you enjoy the food?' he said casually. 'Well if you did, it was Morác's work. Now Morác has told us how his friend the Grand Wizard what's-his-name, assured him that the ancients were safe from the schánda up in the tower. I for one believe him. When the nasties have gone past, we can all go back home. Sure it's going to be a long journey back, but how long's it going to be if we've to keep running? I'm fed up of running from them. I miss our hamlet...my home. I'm all for going up into the tower. That's all I've got to say,' and he sat.

Émer and Láila clapped his performance—no one else did. The silence was disquieting.

'Anyone else want to speak?' Bróda asked. 'What? No one else?' Nobody moved. 'Come now! There were enough people making a noise when I asked which way we were to go. You, Úbor. You were for staying. Don't you want to give us your reasons?'

Úbor shook his head and said, 'I've changed my mind. I want to go on.'

'Won't you tell us why?' Bróda appealed.

Úbor just shook his head again.

'Oh, Well! Let's get on with the vote, then. All those in favour of staying?' Bróda scrutinised the hands going up, counting them. 'One...two...three...' he counted them out loud so everyone could hear. 'Fifteen...sixteen...seventeen. That's it then, seventeen in favour of staying. Those for going on.' Again he counted the hands. 'Eighteen...nineteen...twenty. Twenty in favour of going on. That's decided—we go on.'

Sáor started to argue with Úbor, Ádna defended her partner, whilst Émer tried to support Sáor.

'*I want you to stop this—right now!*' Bróda was thundering at those arguing. '*It's been decided!*' he roared at them.

22

LEAVING LINKALÚR

When the acrimony died, people gathered their groundsheets, dismantled the bivouac, and made ready to continue their journey. A few in a better humour than others. Sáor and a few similar kept looking at the towers, loathe to leave what they perceived as a realm of safety.

The travois were reassembled, loaded, and the four remaining stándy were re-harnessed. Kópis back on leashes, Fúlmon and the scouts out front and Scória bringing up the rear with Dalán. It was thus the column set out again on their journey south. By mid-morning they reached the high dune that gave shelter to the towers, almost like a wall, and scrambled up the slippery slope.

After cresting the dune, then walking way out, they spied the first worm—as if it was waiting for them. Bróda halted the column, and the two life-forms stared at each other in what was a stand-off. Morác strode forward, looked hard at the worm. It appeared to shake its tiny head and disappeared back into the sand.

'It's all right now,' he said aloud, as if announcing to all. 'We won't have any more trouble from them.'

'What did you do?' Bróda wanted to know.

'I thought to that one, that if they kept after us, I would make them all rigid. No more slithering in the sand.'

'And that was bad, was it?' Bróda had a hint of sarcasm in his voice.

'It's the worst thing that they can contemplate.' Morác didn't notice Bróda's attempt at irony.

The column continued. Bróda, Morác and Wómak were striding out abreast, the column trundling behind.

'When we stop for food and drink—you going to do your trick again?' Wómak asked.

'No! I've filled the sacks with millet—and the water skins. They're on the travois now. I saw how frightened people were when I did that thing. I think it's best to let Píngo light the fire and Umára do the cooking—normally,' Morác told him. 'When I did that, you know—I was trying to show them... They didn't take to it. From now on, I stick to a semblance of normality.'

'That's considerate of you—I mean that,' Bróda asserted. 'I appreciate that you've decided to be moderate with your newly attained powers. It'll be easier on the people.'

Morác nodded.

'So, are you now as powerful as Fándin was?' Wómak inquired.

'No!' Morác answered. 'A lot more powerful! I never really knew before how little power I had. Or for that matter, how little power Fándin had. What I have now is much, much more. There's no comparison!'

'I see,' said Wómak, raising his eyebrows, not really seeing at all. He hadn't any idea of the powers Morác had before, so had nothing to compare them with.

*   *   *

Morác cast his mind back along the people, seeing them for the first time in their true light. Warts and everything. In the past, he'd been kind to them in his mind, but now reassessed them ruthlessly. He fingered his new red talisman surreptitiously under his shirt, and permanently changed Bréac and Scéna as he walked—entrenching them in their better personas.

He took Sáor's mind off the towers, and soothed his disposition over the loss of his father and mother. He appeased Émer's thoughts in parting with Sáor's parents. Stilled Láila's loss of her grandparents. He contrived it so Málina was less intense over her stándy. He calmed Cára over the loss of her partner, Gárn, and their daughter Gara. He quietened the twins over the loss of their father. Made Scória grieve less over Robán. He relaxed Émana so she fussed less over thinking Bróda ignored her. Even got Bróda to be less worried over the schánda. He was going to pacify Néra, but stopped himself. *No! I want her just as she is*—he decided.

He excused his meddling by insisting the people would be more likely to survive with what he'd done, on the whole. At the back of his mind, he knew he'd done it to show off. He was stretching his mental abilities—testing what he could accomplish. Trying to calculate his limits.

*   *   *

They had walked during the day, the hot suns beating mercilessly, mainly to escape the towers. Bróda thought if they stayed near the towers till nightfall, the tribe might split into those wanting to remain and those wanting to go on. So he'd made the decision to walk away from the reminder—to walk in the heat throughout the day.

At mid-day they stopped for a water break. They discovered they had biscuits again, and these were handed out to everyone's' delight. As they ate, people from time to time, glanced appreciatively at Morác. They knew it was his doing.

After the break, the desert wind picked up, coming from the east. Sand flew, getting into everything. People covered their faces with scarves, kerchiefs, anything that would keep the sand out. Only narrowed eyes were left exposed. Málina even put make-shift covers on the stándy orifices. By mid-afternoon, the going had become almost intolerable.

'*There's a storm c-o-m-i-n-g—we've got to s-t-o-p!*' yelled Wómak at Bróda, trying to make himself heard above the wind.

'*I know!*' Bróda yelled back at him. '*Morác! What do you say?*' Bróda shouted at Morác, deferring to his new position of power.

Morác stared into the east—straining to see what was coming. '*I think we should find a hollow and dig in—until it stops,*' he shouted back.

'*Wómak! Where's Fúlmon?*' Bróda bellowed.

Wómak pointed forward, '*I think that's him, just ahead.*'

The sandstorm increased in intensity and threw sand at the people. It twisted and swirled, surging and curling, grabbing clothes, trying to deprive the owners of them. The tribe was forced to halt, crouching, holding animals in the centre to avoid being tossed, and waiting for Bróda to issue orders. Fúlmon, followed by the scouts, came back doubled up against the gusts and eddies.

'*Down the other side, t-h-e-r-e. It'll protect us!*' Fúlmon screamed at the tribe.

Bróda followed Fúlmon, who led them to the other side of the dune, using the hump against the wind. The people, seeing their Custodian waving for them to follow, trailed after him. Tumbling, stumbling, people and animals plunged into the depression, where they herded close around the animals to avoid being grabbed by the fiercest of tempests.

Even so, the ferocious blustering got worse.

'*D-o s-o-m-e-t-h-i-n-g!*' Bróda shouted at Morác in desperation—he was afraid for their lives.

Morác recalled Phèrlim's warning as if he were hearing it there and then. "If ever you are forced to pit yourself against a natural phenomenon, be aware that it will drain your powers like pouring water from a jug." He even remembered the smile on Phèrlim craggy face as he said it. What was he to do? If he did nothing, and the tribe was shattered, scattered by the sandstorm? He'd not be able to face himself, or the survivors. No! There was no choice. He would have to pit himself against this natural monster.

With the remnants of reluctance, he sought the red talisman under his shirt; gripped it tightly, and projected himself, his powers—Phèrlim's powers, at the storm, but not dissipating them, trying instead to find its focal point. At first, it was all just a big twisting muddle—no form or substance to converge upon. Plummeting, then up, lurching sideways, and then falling. Being picked up again by forces he didn't want to fight, didn't want to waste his powers on. Further and further he went inside the coiling winds; ever upwards into the gyrating miasma, always searching for the eye of stillness.

After a series of lengthy oscillations he reached the angry darkness, high up in the sky, pulling and contorting the air around, and around; a viscous procession of serpentine meanderings leading back to the battered desert. If he could nip this apex, then the storm might dissolve. He manoeuvred himself in an axial to and fro until he flittered to the vertex then darted in on the epicentre and projected c-a-l-m with all the power at his disposal. Again—c-a-l-m...and he could feel the power draining from him, Phèrlim's gift, stilling the turmoil. Sadness formed deep inside Morác, an intimate loss in the core of his heart. Yet, he put more force into his projection, and unleashed a *c-a-l-m* that imploded the vertex, collapsing the epicentre in on itself, forcing it to undergo a violent compression.

What the huddled people saw and felt on the ground, was that the storm declined with a peculiar cut-off effect.

One moment the hurricane was raging—the next, sand flopped back to the desert. A stillness descended all around— a thunderous tranquillity.

Morác slumped to the sand at Néra's feet. She screamed, which pierced the strange stalemate of inactivity. She quickly bent to him and checked he was breathing. He panted shallowly as if exhausted. She undid his shirt collar and didn't recognise the gold chain with the red talisman. A charcoal burn was on Morác's skin where the talisman touched the surface. She didn't know what to make of it.

Morác twitched, and then stirred. He opened his eyes and tried a weak smile at Néra.

'You gave me quite a fright,' she berated him softly.

The tribe gathered around their prone shamán, standing in silent concern.

'Is he all right?' Bróda voiced everyone's' thoughts.

'It must have taken a lot out of him, stopping this storm,' Ganúra opined.

'I didn't think he would—' Bróda didn't finish.

Néra gave Bróda a look of bitterness—which cut him off in mid sentence. She'd heard Bróda yell at Morác to "do something". This was the result. Behind her anger there was fear and concern for Morác—and herself. Out here, all alone, what would she do—how would she endure? It was her unconscious survival instinct at work, reproaching the Custodian for Morác's state.

'Spread a groundsheet,' Ganúra appealed.

That was done and Morác was gently lifted, protesting, onto the sheet.

'I'm all right now,' he muttered. 'I can get up.' He tried and sat back heavily.

'There! You see! You're not all right,' Néra told him. 'You're just being stubborn.'

Morác sat, gazing around, brow furrowed, checking himself, looking at the onlookers. Málina came and handed him a tumbler of water. The more he examined how much he'd been drained, the sadder his face became.

'I...I...I've lost so much—' he bemoaned. 'You can't *begin* to realise,' he told Néra.

'There, there! You're still here. Don't torment yourself. You'll get it again.' She was trying to comfort him, without really grasping what he was talking of.

'You don't understand—' he moaned.

'You're alive— that's all that matters,' she insisted.

Morác lay back on the groundsheet and closed his eyes.

'Everyone—check the damage, if any. See if you've lost anything.' Bróda the leader was evaluating whether the storm had wrecked anything.

People went back and inspected their belongings, counted numbers, made sure everyone was present.

Morác sat up and said to Néra, sitting on his left, 'I'm sorry—you're right. We're both still here, together. That's all that matters.'

He put a reassuring arm round her shoulder and hugged her. She laid her head on his shoulder, and sighed tenderly.

'We'll be all right—I promise.' He squeezed again, sensitively.

'Here, have this water,' he handed her the tumbler.

'Thanks,' she responded.

People had overcome their fright, had survived. They now spread their groundsheets and were having a picnic under the peaceful mid-afternoon suns. The desert was serene again; the sky was clear, and the storm nearly forgotten.

Néra got up to fetch more water.

Morác got to his feet and said loudly, 'I'm sorry to inform you, that dealing with that storm...means...that we're going to have to be careful with the food and water again. I can't conjure things up out of nothing anymore. My apologies!'

He sat back, less dejected than before, mainly due to Néra's ministrations. After a while, Huróyna came over and sat by Morác.

'Morác! When you still had your powers,' she said innocently, 'were you able to whisk us back home, back to the hamlet?

The question struck Morác like a thunderbolt. He banged his temple with the flat of his right palm, and said, 'There's no fool like an overconfident fool.'

'By that I gather you could've....' She sat without a word, and then said, 'I don't know if I'll ever forgive you!' She wasn't angry—more dejected if anything. She continued, 'Fúlmon and I have been planning a nice Lándo tree for our new home together—' she left the rest unsaid, got up and walked off, fighting back tears.

Huróyna's visit put Morác into a foul mood—with himself. *How could I've been so blind? Why the Húli didn't I think of that? Too busy showing off, wasting my powers and time. I could kick myself! For Aíne's sake, we could all have been back home right now—ugh...stupid...stupid!*

At that point Néra returned, carrying two tumblers full of water. Seeing a different Morác to the one she'd left, she became concerned again.

'What's happened? Why the dumps again?' She handed him the tumbler and sat.

'I don't know if I should tell you,' he groaned.

'You'd better! I won't speak to you for a whole day if you don't.' She was half joking and half serious. She'd carried out such a threat in the past.

'Well, all right,' Morác gave in. 'I've just been talking to Huróyna. She asked me if I could've transported us all back to the hamlet—you know, when I had my full powers, before the storm.' He shook his head at the painful thought. 'I could've, you know. I just never thought of it. Too busy playing the fool—' he trailed off and hung his head.

'My poor Morác,' she put her tumbler down, embedding it in the nearby sand, then rubbed his shoulder. She clasped him by both shoulders and turned Morác to face her. 'Look! What's done is done. I can't say I'm happy to hear what you've just told me, but there's nothing we can do —is there?' She looked into his eyes.

He shook his head, avoiding her gaze, 'No, there isn't. It's too late.'

'Well then? Let's not worry over spilt water in the sand. We still have to outrun those wretched schánda, don't we?' she kept her stare steady.

Morác nodded.

'Better not spread this around, you know, that we could have—' she didn't need to finish the sentence.

Morác nodded again, agreeing with her.

23

BLESSED OASIS

A while later, they were on the move again, trudging in Fúlmon's footfalls, making good progress in the shifting ground, now all was peaceful. Everyone had become an expert in walking on this strange loose material called sand. The dunes were diminishing and the ground firming up. The day waned and evening approached, suns dipping in the sky.

Máyo came running back using long strides, a grin on his face.

'Keep going—this way,' he yelled from a distance. 'We've found water.'

As he came to Bróda, brushing particles off his face, he couldn't contain his joy. 'Trees!' he panted. '*Real* trees—up ahead!'

'Slow down a bit,' Wómak advised. 'How far ahead?'

'Over that rise—see! There!' Máyo pointed to a distant rise in the darkening desert. 'Fúlmon and Huróyna are waiting for us—drinking water.'

The column visibly speeded up on hearing the news, Máyo out front, leading the way. Wómak and Bróda hastening after the scout, spurting on towards where he claimed there were *real* trees. Ever since the tribe descended the cliff with the Nester birds, eleven days ago at the head of the valley, they hadn't seen any proper trees. For forest people, that was close to a calamity. They were like fish out of water. Volcanoes, deserts, worms—all alien and entirely frightening. Now, they were to be reunited with a forest. At least that's what many envisioned.

By the time they neared the incline, the tribe was all but running. Máyo sped over the gently sloping rise, followed by the others. Everyone eager to see the forest—the expected forest. What they saw was a miserly few trees in the descending distance. All halted, disappointed at investing such high hope on such a meagre return. Even at that distance they saw no more than six sparse trees and a few half withered bushes surrounding a water hole.

'Call these trees?' Émana berated Máyo, as if he was to blame.

'It's not his fault,' Bróda defended his scout.

'But look at them—' Ganúra couldn't finish, lost for words.

'They're still trees,' Néra put a positive spin on the meagre offering.

'Well, anyway, let's go have a look,' Wómak ventured, moving off again.

The column converged on the fiasco, unable to believe their shattered expectations. The oasis stood in a large depression; Fúlmon and Huróyna were already relaxing by the water, having spread their groundsheets. Seeing the two already lolling around, pacified many of the disgruntled, and they soon joined the reclining scouts.

The bivouac was erected and people lounged around, resting after rushing to the *trees*.

Morác called for their attention, announcing, 'You'll be pleased to hear—the real forest isn't far off. A day's journey south and we'll be under a canopy again.' Having said his say, he went and sat with Néra by the pool.

That news went down like Orel syrup, improving everyones' disposition. Píngo made the fire and Umára made the evening meal. By nightfall, there was a roaring fire from the brushwood, including bits of fallen tree.

'We're staying the night here in view of what Morác's just told us,' Bróda informed the relaxing tribe.

That was more good news. No more travelling through the night. At last, things were beginning to return to a semblance of normality. They hadn't been desperate for the water when they arrived, but they filled the water skins out of respect for their needs.

What really fascinated people were the peculiar trees. Many of the tribe lay on their groundsheets, reclining in the moonlight, staring up at them. They were unlike any trees they'd seen before. All had a single tall unbranching trunk with a thick cluster of large dark-green feather-like leaves at the crown. The large leaves were fan-shaped, seemingly resembling an outstretched hand. The trunk had rough rings and at the base was an interwoven mass of roots. All in all—a peculiar tree. But the main point, all agreed, was—they were trees. Then, of course, according to Morác, there was the promise of more trees, *proper* trees, in a day's time. The people felt, things were definitely looking up.

'Morác! Tell us the story of our creation.' It was Émana who called—from over where she lay with Bróda.

'Yes, Morác. We haven't heard that story in a long while,' encouraged Ganúra.

'Are you sure you want to hear it, at this time of night?' Morác teased.

A clamour arose from those present for him to tell the story—but he was reluctant at first, then acquiescing with a smile. He tease was an appeal for as many people as possible to press him to tell the story. That way he got attentive listeners.

Morác made himself comfortable next to Néra, who smiled at him encouragingly. Thus the scene was set in the inspiring moonlight for the telling of the story. He cleared his throat—coughed once or twice, then began.

'This is the wonderful story of our creation,' Morác embarked, 'as has been passed from shamán to shamán in the

234

Bólani tribe, from time immemorial. It opens at the very beginning of time—when the skies above were not yet named, nor the ground below pronounced by name... It was in a distant time when from the void sprang Aíne. She had existed for an extremely long time, but then felt the need for a companion, and so gave birth to Húli. He was dear to her and kept her company, whilst she treated him in fellowship. They were the only ones who lived in the dark disorder of nothingness, frolicking in the haze of non-existence, before the time of the naming of names.

'Then, Húli began to be consumed with jealousy—mainly due to Aíne's fair looks. She had a nimbleness of thought, intelligence, and was full of the joys of life. And so, a tormenting poison begun to devour him from inside, and he began to plot the overthrow of Aíne. She was aware from the start, of the changes in Húli, and of his plot—after all; she was all seeing and all knowing.

'She waited and hoped he would never attempt to carry out his evil plan, but there was little hope from the jealousy that was devouring him. It was then that she gave thought to the outcome, over a measure of time, and eventually named Kálar—and with a great deal of sadness, she exiled Húli into the bowels of Kálar, locking him in the far reaches beneath the ground, with great spells and incantations. He was never to rise into the world again, destined to be the keeper of all dead things.

'For a long time, Aíne was in deep mourning for her lost companion—it was then that she decided to name many things, bringing them into existence. She earnestly reflected on a great variety of names, and after long thought, she began. She named the stars that gave starlight. She named mighty Búla with her face a strong bright yellow-orange; shyly peering through the haze, for Búla was only young. Immediately after came Mára, smaller with a yellow countenance, heaving herself into existence.

'Aíne spent many seasons naming all the trees, bushes, flowers, and creatures. After a long time and much careful thought, she named the various tribes of Kálar, and all that we see—and for that we, the Bólani, and all the other people on Kálar, worship Aíne, and are grateful to her for her hard work—of creation.' Morác finished the story and all was quiet amongst the listening people.

Many of the folks sighed, longing for the sanctuary of their distant hamlet. Others fell asleep quietly. Morác lay deep in thought, yet again regretting having not had the foresight to transfer his people back to their hamlet when he had the power to carry out such an undertaking.

After a good nights sleep, they were fully rested and restored. At dawn they rose and carried on with their ablutions. A hearty breakfast was prepared, and eaten; then the people were ready to face the journey again.

'Morác! Is there any chance of reaching the forest today?' Bróda queried, finding him tying up his bundle.

'If we really push it—but why? I mean, it's not as if the schánda are bearing on us. They've made good time on reaching the desert and are now only three and a half days behind. There are no obstructions in the desert, so they've put on speed. But we've still got a good head-start. That gives us sufficient time. I estimate we're roughly eight days from the sea.'

Bróda beamed. 'That close, heh! That's good news. But I'd feel safer in the forest.'

Morác left his bundle and faced Bróda; laid a hand on Bróda's arm. 'Listen! The forest we're to enter isn't like the one we know. It's a tropical forest; that's what I get from Phèrlim's residual memories, with its own dangers. I'd be happier if we went in during daylight. That's what I sense!'

Wómak arrived and joined in. 'Is that right, what I hear? We're almost at the journey's end?'

Morác nodded, 'But we're not safe yet. We have to build a raft when we get there—the coast of the Golden Sea. Build it large enough to hold all our people, then sail it from shore.'

'What of two rafts?' Wómak suggested, wiping a smudge of leftover porridge from the corner of his mouth.

'Could be! Tonight, when we pitch camp, I want us to hold a special council—to plan what kind of raft we need to build, and how many. I'd like,' Morác looked at Bróda, 'for you Bróda, to allocate each warrior a task, so that when we arrive on the shore, everyone gets on with their assigned chore, so the work runs smoothly.'

'How're we going to build this raft?' Fúlmon came up and added his bit.

'You know—we might have to destroy trees,' Bróda voiced the sacrilege. 'I mean, we might not find ready fallen trees—might have to chop trees.'

That brought a silence.

'We *have* to use already fallen trees?' Fúlmon appealed. 'I mean, we *can't chop* trees down. It's...it's never been done—not by the Bólani.'

'That's the type of thing I meant...the things we have to sort out,' Morác asserted. 'I don't have the answers. We don't know what we're going to find—do we?'

'But we're not going to chop trees, are we?' Fúlmon persisted.

'If it gets too difficult to sort out amongst ourselves,' Bróda meant the council, 'then we may have no choice but to let the tribe decide. The trees or us? Let's leave it for the moment. Fúlmon! You're on point.' Bróda tried to get the scout's attention away from chopping trees. 'Be extra vigilant since we're close to this southern forest.'

'Right! Gather your belongings,' he said loudly to the people, 'and let's make a move. Today we might reach the forest. When we get there, we'll decide whether to camp the night before going in—or whatever.' He went to Émana and took her gently by the arm.

Since he usually strode out front, this surprised Émana. Even Fern gave him a strange look. Bróda took the leashes with the kópis and handed them to Fern, as if to say; *don't look at me like that.*

As they left the oasis, people tended to look back longingly, not wanting to leave behind the sheltered haven with trees. This went on till they were out of sight of the oasis. Then the formation proceeded at a rapid rate, Wómak and Ganúra out front, being pulled by their kópi, leading. Bróda and Émana following, with Morác and Néra behind. Then the rest of the tribe, followed by the four stándy; Scória and Dalán bringing up the rear.

The suns beat down mercilessly on the contingent, intent on baking them. Around mid-afternoon, Fúlmon, looking serious, returned with the scouts.

He approached Bróda, 'We've come across tracks out front,' he said, breathing hard.

'People or Animals?' Bróda asked.

'No—it's people. I wouldn't rush back like this for animals.' Fúlmon sat on the hot sand.

'Not even for worms?' joked Wómak.

Fúlmon ignored the jibe. Bróda crouched with Wómak and Morác.

'How many? Come, give us details,' invited Bróda.

'I estimate around twenty,' Fúlmon answered.

Huróyna opened her water bottle and handed it to Fúlmon.

'The strange thing is,' Fúlmon continued, taking a sip, 'they come from the south, as you might expect; go as far as where we found them—then return; almost as if they'd forgot an item and turned back.'

Bróda thought for a moment, and then said, 'This might be serious. Everybody's under pressure from the schánda—it makes them aggressive. Remember that fort in the valley, the one near the river. We need to keep pushing ahead, but we've got to be prepared. Wómak! Make sure the warriors have their blowpipes ready—and the people have their bows and arrows handy. Well Fúlmon—take the kópis and head out again.'

When the two scouts had rested and watered themselves, they headed back the way they came, and the Bólani formation followed.

'What do you make of it?' Bróda asked Morác.

'It's clear! We've been spotted—that's why they've turned back. To warn their people!' Morác ventured.

'Yeah! That's how I see it too. Though we've no choice but to keep going. Be prepared!'

Fúlmon waited by the strange footfalls. The column halted as they reached the scouts.

'There they are,' Máyo quipped, pointing at the footprints.

Bróda responded irritably, 'I can see for myself.'

'I've been staring at them,' Fúlmon told him, 'and I've concluded they're taller than us—see, bigger feet. All heavier, too!'

'Could be!' Bróda conceded.

Wómak looked peeved at the information. Being the tallest, barring Píngo, and certainly the biggest in build, he considered himself the giant of the tribe. Here were twenty or so who were supposedly bigger than him. In reality, he saw himself as the defender of the tribe and was frightened that he wouldn't be able to carry out his self imposed role.

With a touch of false bravado he asserted, 'We can handle them—I'm confident our warriors will deal with them.'

Bróda stared at Wómak in surprise. He'd never heard Wómak boast like that. 'I'm glad you're confident, he said, 'but still—be on your guard.'

'I'm going on!' Fúlmon announced. 'We can't learn any more here.'

The scouts began their way back south; Fúlmon stopped and came back. Without a word, he took the leashes from Fern, and departed again with the kópis.

The Bólani resumed their trek in the footfalls of the scouts. By evening, to the south, stretched a vast green horizon—as far as the eye could see. The last rays of the suns slanted on the vibrant canopy where remnants of a slight lazily haze hung above it. Smells of moisture from the southern forest danced in the nostrils; exotic sounds came to the pointed Bólani ears from the distant fauna inhabiting the inviting vastness. Flying things lifted, and then settled in the far distance. A few even came to inspect the approaching contingent. Vivid coloured birds circled inquisitively above, spying on the people below—who increased their pace in eagerness.

As the party reached the edges of the forest, they encountered sparse grassland, bushes that tenaciously defended ground from encroaching sand. Stunted, awkwardly branched trees insisted on carving out a niche away from the security of shelter.

People's faces bore wide grins, smiles partly due to being back in the forest, but also due to the proximity of what they perceived was journey's end. There was an exhilaration not felt for a long time. Twenty four days after setting out from their hamlet in the north, they had reached the haven of another forest.

'How far would you say we've travelled—I mean from the time we left our hamlet?' Néra asked Morác as they walked arm in arm.

'Ooh! That's difficult to say—I mean precisely. I would guess between three hundred and fifty to four hundred leagues.' He gently squeezed her hand to distract her from the enormous figure.

He wanted to tell her the truth, but also wanted to dull the massive figure, so it didn't create such an impact. In living memory no Bólani had journeyed so far, seen so many things, and been in so much danger. He wanted to soften the jolt on her of their immense expedition. Even so, the walking was still not at an end.

At the very edge of the looming thick forest canopy, Bróda called a halt for the night, as Morác had advised. He ordered Wómak to pitch camp with sentries posted facing the forest. He was eager to be under cover; under the safety of the canopy as he thought, but he had to admit, the forest smelt different from any forest he'd ever come across. Maybe caution was the better path to travel. Morác had called it a tropical forest—but what did that mean? After all, a tree is a tree—isn't it?

Píngo and Umára soon had the fire and food under way, whilst the rest of the tribe stood and stared into the darkness. The moons were up, throwing an eerie light on the proceedings. An air of expectancy hung over the place, camped so close to the new forest, mixed with moon light, generating an atmosphere that overflowed with the buzz of excitement. For a change, wood was available in plenty for building their usual A-frame night shelters—missing since they came down from the cliff containing the Nester birds. Gathering the wood and erecting the structures worked off the excess stimulation. Tiredness did the rest.

Over their evening porridge, folks energetically speculated on what lay ahead. Indeed, they even anticipated a swift return to their hamlet, as if the worst was behind them. It made people edgy, apprehensive. Yet mostly, with enthusiasm, they looked forward to the morning.

As soon as the meal was consumed, Bróda called the special council—the one agreed on earlier, to decide what to do when they reached the coast. They gathered round the smaller fire, a ways off from the chattering people—wood was no longer a problem.

Morác sat quietly, waiting for the serious discussion to commence.

Bróda began. 'Right! Let's get our heads together. I think the first thing we have to decide is how to build this raft. Morác—it was your idea, so lets hear your proposal.'

'Before we talk of building, I want to know if we're going to chop down trees!' Fúlmon was back on his own bugbear.

'Fúlmon! We'll come to that in a while,' Bróda told him sternly. 'I'm setting the course of the discussion—and right now, I want Morác to explain the raft construction. Is that clear?'

'Yes Custodian,' Fúlmon said half contritely.

Morác looked around the gathered group—Scória hunched beside him to his right, Dalán next, then Fúlmon, Wómak, and finally Bróda. Morác steadily eyed each member of the council, trying to make it clear that he wasn't there to argue. When he'd asserted his authority by staring into their eyes, he began, 'This isn't done lightly—chopping trees.'

Fúlmon glared at him.

'But if we are forced to, since there may be no other way to save ourselves—then it is *I* who will bear the brunt of Aíne's wrath. It is *I,* your shamán, who will appease her for our sacrilege, not another member of the tribe.' He pointedly locked eyeball-to-eyeball with Fúlmon—staring him down. 'We'll try to find *ready* fallen logs in the first case—but if we're not able to, then I will nominate the warriors who will be the tree choppers.'

Morác had Dalán hold up a burning branch for light, and then used a twig to draw a diagram on the ground. It was a simple structure with logs lashed in parallel, then underpinned by four large logs at right angles; two at either end and two in the middle. A rudder at one end and a central mast for sail was held in place between the two middle logs.

'That's the design of the raft,' he said, pointing at the drawing. 'And if we have to build two, as the logs may be too small, then we build two of these.'

Bróda began, 'Well—'

Morác interrupted, 'Just one more thing. Any warrior can refuse to chop trees, but if they do chop a tree down—I take the responsibility. I want to make sure they understand that. That's all I have to say.'

'Thank you, Morác,' Bróda began again. 'You stated your piece well. When we get to the coast, we'll make a model of the raft, so people can see what they're going to travel on. Anyone wants to make any points?' he glanced sideways at Fúlmon, but the scout was quiet—having had the fear of sacrilege extracted from him, by the only person who could have performed the miracle; Morác.

The council broke up and the members retired to their chosen sleep places. Peace descended on the Bólani camp, only broken by the night sounds coming from the tropical forest.

The precocious dawn chorus coming from the nearby canopy was music to the pointed ears of the Bólani. They roused to the noise of birds in full song, strange animal sounds, and another hot day readying for them. The morning porridge was set onto Píngo's fire and the herbal liquid sat brewing, tended by Uílin, almost ready for consumption. People woke full of enthusiasm for the expected entry into the forest, anticipating being surrounded by trees again.

Bróda called for attention. 'The sentries inform me they felt they were being watched all through the night. This morning, before we leave, I want us all to do bow and arrow practice. Over there,' he pointed to standing poles not far away, 'the warriors have set an upright to aim at—use them as targets. Once we've eaten, I want you to show those watching what we're capable of.'

Umára ventured, 'Won't that invite a fight?'

'I hope not. We're trying to tell them to leave us alone,' Wómak explained. 'It was my suggestion—if it goes wrong,' he insisted, 'you can blame me.'

Umára gave Wómak a look—which told him, that's exactly what he would do.

The target practice was treated as a bit of fun, producing mixed results. A few showed an unusual proficiency with the strange implements. The person who made the bows and arrows for instance, Sáor, was a natural marksman. To everyone's surprise, Láila also had a knack with the bow, the only one of her gender to try. Fern and Cóer were good shots, but others were entirely hopeless. Bréac fumbled his shots, unable to get the hang of the instrument. Úbor was just as useless, but was all right with the blowpipe.

Most of the warriors had a go, and as expected, turned out reasonable shots. To nobodies' surprise, Morác cheated and directed the arrow with his sorcery. By now, they expected such tricks from their shamán, especially in the light of recent events. Súdair turned out to be the same as Wómak —absolutely brilliant, and in a best-out-of-three, Súdair beat Wómak, who visibly, took it in good spirit.

By the time the trials were declared over, the fire dampened, mid-morning was upon them. The people's attention turned on the nearby forest.

24

TROPICAL FOREST

People broke camp. Scouts went ahead as vanguard, and the column entered the tropical forest. The four stándy became extremely jittery, making those close by nervous.

'What's with the animals?' Wólni demanded of Málina, who was leading them, two in each hand.

'Whatever it is, they're not happy with,' she replied casually.

'Any idea what?' he appealed.

'I've been looking—can't see anything,' she responded.

He walked briskly ahead, throwing over his shoulder, 'I'm going to tell Wómak.'

'Suit yourself.' She didn't seem concerned.

Morác's meddling with her mind in the desert, before the storm, had intended to make her less intense regarding the stándy. But it made her more careless at the same time—and that wasn't good.

Along the way, the Bólani formation passed a wide range of exotic plant life, making their mouths drop wide open in astonishment. For size and colour, they had never seen the like. Not long after entering the forest, the scouts were spotted ahead—all in a tizz. Huróyna was holding a kópi on a leash, while it strained to get at an enormous red flower. The flower stuck out high from an enormous bunch of curled up purple leaves hugging the stem in a bulge. As the column reached the scouts, Bróda noticed tears in Huróyna's eyes. Máyo was in shock, and Fúlmon was ranting angrily. All stared at the red flower.

'It...it...ate the kópi,' Máyo blurted out.

Bróda looked at him—as if he were crazy.

'Talk sense lad—it's a plant. How can a plant eat a kópi?' Bróda simply refused to believe what he'd heard.

'It's true!' Fúlmon said heatedly. 'The kópis were loose and Latish got to sniffing that flower over there. When I looked at the noise, I saw his tail vanishing inside the leaves. There's nothing I could do. The leaves just curled around him and pulled him in.'

He looked ready to do battle with the bunched up purple leaves. With a cry of anguish, he pulled his axe out of his belt and went to hacking at the curled up foliage— oblivious of the fact the axe made little impression. It cut in, and as he withdrew, the wound closed. He might as well be hitting water.

'May Húli curse you—' he shouted at the plant in frustration.

Morác tried to calm the raging scout. 'Leave it! Come away,' he said to Fúlmon. 'Néra...come and give me a hand. Huróyna! Stop bawling and help Néra.'

By this time people gathered round in a semicircle near the flower, curious at the commotion. Most didn't understand what had happened, despite the mix of explanations coming from the scouts.

Bróda was pacing up and down; not at all clear what to do in the situation. Should he deal with the flower? Ought he to call the tribe to order? Was there anything to be done for his beloved kópi? His emotion over the devoured kópi was getting in the way of his thinking. It was suppressed grief. Wómak saw the confusion his Custodian was in, and set to getting things to rights.

'There's no use hanging around here,' Wómak told the tribe. 'Might as well move on. Scória! You take the lead

—let's get the column going. Huróyna, Máyo, will you take Fúlmon away from here.'

Slowly, the column reformed and Scória led them away at a funerary pace. Fúlmon was helped away, gently but firmly, by his two scouts. Finally, Wómak took Bróda by the arm and focussed his attention on following the rest of the tribe, disappearing into the foliage.

Soothingly he told Bróda, 'There's nothing we can do here—I'm afraid he's gone!'

Bróda let himself be led away, still stunned by the sudden demise of his faithful companion. On went the tribe, into the tropical jungle. It was well past mid-day before Bróda called a halt for food. He'd regained possession of himself—was a bit sad, but otherwise back in control. He'd lost tribe members—and now a personal loss of one of his beloved kópi.

The remaining kópi was at a loss; restless, constantly looking for her brother. They had been together, brother and sister, from whelping. Now the female felt it was alone, and it didn't cope well. Fern took charge of her, petting her, trying to console her. It helped, but the poor thing was disconsolate. She whistle-grunted in a forlorn way, calling for her companion. Nothing could be done and Fern had his hands full. Morác was of the opinion that the kópi might pine soon away if she didn't pull out of her depression.

As the food halt came to an end, the sound of crashing and breaking branches came from deep in the foliage. Warriors were sent to find the cause. They reported back, a person unknown had tried to climb a tree, but a weak branch had given way, causing the noise. All agreed whoever was spying on them, had been visited by Aíne, and sent hurling to the ground. It reaffirmed the tribe's view the goddess was looking after their welfare.

The excitement over the strange commotion ended, the scouts moved off, followed by all the people in single file. On either side of the moving column, imperceptible distant rustling sounds came from the undergrowth. Bróda consulted with Wómak and both agreed they were being tracked by the unseen natives of the forest. There was little they could do. The best they hoped for—was to be left in peace to finish their journey. All said silent prayers to Aíne, seeking protection to complete their passage to the shores of the Golden Sea.

They travelled in this manner, well into dusk before the scouts reported finding a suitable spot to spend the night. The exhausted column was called to a halt by Bróda, and the people simply flopped on the forest floor. The spot was a clearing of low brush with strange twisting trees overhead.

'Go check the perimeter—station sentries,' Bróda ordered Wómak.

Wómak took warriors and hurried to carry out the custodian's bidding. Umára got busy with the pots. Píngo chose a clearing and crouching over his equipment, busied himself with making fire. Half the warriors were finally stationed on the edge of the clearing facing out into the forest, the other half dispersed into the forest as guards for the people who went to collect material for the A-frames.

From above, in the canopy, there came a constant rustling sound as though the branches were unsettled with the alien presence below. Morác found himself standing alone in the clearing where the proposed bivouac was to be, staring at Píngo's crouched back, wondering, not for the first time, how to ease the childhood animosity that had grown up between them. If only he could get past Píngo's guard, somehow reach under into the innocence, below whatever it was that had soured the big albino, before he'd assembled the wall he put up against the rest of the world. Musing distractedly in this fashion, Morác brushed off the first tendril that stroked him on the left shoulder. The next tendril grasped him firmly round his waist knocking the breath out of him. Shocked, he twisted trying to unravel the strong pliant branch, whilst even more runners corkscrewed on to him seizing him round the neck, with more encircling his body. He tried to cry out but he was already being lifted off the ground, chocking.

Píngo glanced round at the disturbance and promptly leaped to his feet. He rushed for Morác and just managed to grab his dangling legs, pulling him back to the ground. In an instant, he had his knife out and began hacking at the tightening tendrils. Finally, Morác managed a piercing scream. Umára heard and saw what was happening, rushed to help Píngo, shouting the alarm on the run. By this time, Píngo had managed to cut through the snare round Morác's neck, yet the one round his waist held firm. Struggling on the ground, other tendrils were descending from above, trying to pull Píngo off of Morác.

Umára reached them axe out, and commenced hacking at the thick branch around Morác's waist; this produced thick blue-green ooze that came seeping out of the wound. It released Píngo to slash at the other twining branches. The alerted sentries arrived, and soon dismembered tendrils were lying in mortal profusion, withering, leaking with the blue-green life-fluid, saturating the ground where they lay. The message was getting through to this hanging life form that it was losing the battle and rest of the coils began retreating back up in the canopy.

Morác sat massaging the enormous weal on his neck, breathing heavily. Píngo was staring at Morác quizzically, as if he had a profound decision to make. Néra came rushing back out of the forest, anguish spread wide across her face.

'What happened?' she demanded, voice furious with emotion and fear.

Morác tried to swallow, still couldn't speak, so he pointed unsteadily upwards. Píngo was not the one to explain, being a bit slow and lost for words, which left Umára.

'The damned trees, they attacked Morác,' he told Néra, sheathing his axe in his belt. 'Just dropped on him.' — He added thoughtfully, 'Píngo saved his life.'

Néra handed Morác a water pouch to clear and ease his throat. At the mention of Píngo, Morác turned and gazed at the big albino with admiration—then smiled at him in gratitude. He held out the water container to Píngo, who accepted it. Píngo's eyebrows rose in question. At this, Morác shakily got to his feet and stumbled the single step to where Píngo sat. He stooped, took him by the shoulders and pulled the big lunk up onto his feet. He took the untouched water pouch from Píngo's hand and passed it back to Néra. Then he put his arms around him and hugged him. At this, Píngo seemed to soften and he returned the hug bashfully.

'I'm forever in your debt—I owe you my life—and that's a debt I cannot treat lightly. Without you, Píngo, I would be up there—dead,' he pointed at the canopy. 'You are my blood brother as of this moment on, and I call on all the Bólani to witness that Píngo is a member of my family.' Then he hesitated, and added, 'if you wish.'

This speech brought tears to Píngo's eyes—and astonishment to all the onlooker's faces, those that had rushed back and now gathered round to observe the momentous bringing together. Everyone was aware of the old-standing animosity between the two.

Slowly, Píngo pronounced, 'Yes, you are my brother,' and tightened his hug on Morác.

The scene was greeted with prolonged cheers—a resounding endorsement from the whole tribe at the overdue reconciliation.

'Well, I never,' Wómak exhaled.

'I never thought to see the day,' added Bróda, his arm around Émana, the dead kópi temporarily forgotten.

Néra beamed at the new member of her family, and Píngo at long last released his grip on Morác, who exhaled a long sigh of relief.

'Clearly, this is no place to spend the night,' Bróda finally interjected. 'Wómak, form the column—dark or no dark, we must find another place. Fúlmon, take the scouts and find us a different location.'

Carefully the tribe moved off, Píngo now walking between Morác and Néra, both his arms round their shoulders as if they'd always been like this. Píngo's face showed happiness, so much so, that Ganúra, walking with Wómak and being pulled by her whistle-grunting kópi, remarked on how she'd never seen Píngo so happy.

Finally, Huróyna returned and reported a safe clearing not too far ahead. No covering canopy and a clear visibility of the night sky above them. This is where once again Bróda called a halt for the remainder of the night. The A-frames were put together by the warriors and the rest of the tribe settled to their evening meal round a relit campfire. Píngo sat next to Morác and Néra, as if they were bonded— and in a way they were. The atmosphere was subdued whilst ears strained to pick up sounds of their watchers. They were there; everyone could feel a myriad of eyes observing every move being made.

Bróda got Morác to stroll round the resting folk and inform everyone they were to pay no attention to those scrutinizing their progress from deep in the forest. He was still hoping not to provoke them into precipitate action. The sentries were specifically told not to react to, or pursue any noise. They were to *protect* the encampment—that was all.

The Bólani tribe spent a restless night in this strange forest. Animal noises nobody recognised kept many awake— and it seemed the brief night ushered in an early dawn. It had rained a number of times during the night—in short but furious burst—and the ground was well and truly damp.

Without waiting to have their morning meal, Bróda made the bold decision for an early start. He informed the disgruntled tribe that they would stop halfway through the morning and have an early midday meal. Unhappy, but mindful of the danger, compliant, the column began its trek southwards—just as a heavy rain began to fall.

Now they were travelling in the southern tropical zone, they came upon more of the giant flowers, variants of the one that had gobbled up Bróda's kópi. They also kept a sharp lookout for any more hanging tendrils from above. All through the morning the rain fell, soaking many of the tribe. Those that had the wit used the wide leaves of the tropical plants to cover their heads as they walked. Eventually everyone copied this form of protection against the rainfall.

When Bróda finally called a halt for the much delayed meal, the rain was as heavy as ever and warriors built a large frame covered with the wide leaves as a shelter to build a fire. It allowed Umára to dish out portions of the porridge relative free from the downpour. When they were about to resume their journey, there came a break in the incessant rain and the suns reappeared in the blue sky. Búla gave a strong bright yellow-orange light, when they glimpsed her; whilst Mára when seen, was smaller with a yellow countenance, always keeping Búla company in their constant journey. This familiarity gave the travelling group below those suns a measure of continuity; some confidence and a mental link with their faraway hamlet back up in the distant north.

The forward scouts came back in the middle of the afternoon and reported a wonder they were to reach in a short distance ahead. The structure of the trees in front changed radically, with exposed aerial roots shoring up long branches, whose buttressed crown of foliage, in some cases, were as much as four hundred cubits across. The aerial roots descended from the outlying limbs of the trees, growing earthwards as mere threads at first, these roots eventually developed into stout auxiliary trunks that enabled a single tree to extend its canopy of leaves to cover an enormous area. The area underneath amongst the roots turned out to be an ideal shelter for the whole tribe for the night.

The first question that sprang to peoples lips was, "Is this place safe?" They had no wish to repeat the business with the tendrils.

This time Morác did a short incantation to check if the Bara trees were hazardous. He named them "bara," for they reminded him of the Bara shrub near their hamlet—only this was a colossal relative.

They chose a camp under an angular limb to the left of their approach, which spread across a span of one hundred and six cubits, palatial in its expanse. Almost snug, as if they were all in a huge Lándo tree back in their hamlet. Sentries were posted and latrines dug. People spread themselves on the ground as if to be closer to the nourishing earth. That night the encampment was subdued as if they were in a holy temple—and soon all was quiet in the camp.

The next morning people claimed they'd slept just as well in this 'temple' as if they'd been at home in their hamlet, snug in their own bunks. It lightened their spirits and lifted the burden of the journey, reinvigorating them for what was to come.

After their usual morning meal, they set off on the trail south once again. They travelled without event for the next four days, always aware of being shadowed by an unseen escort on either side of them. They followed a barely perceptible path, clearly made by some animal that used it regularly. It led directly south and there had been a long heated discussion as to whether it was wise to expose themselves like that. They might meet whoever it was who used it and have to explain why they were trespassing.

The counter argument by Morác was that it was far too late for such prudence. They were already being followed —and so why hide? At least the path made trekking easier. Their followers and the path made them jumpy and cautious, with everybody whispering to each other. No one strayed very far from the column, even when they needed to stop for ablutions.

On the fifth day around noon, the two suns high in the sky, a commotion ahead encouraged Bróda to speed up the column—to establish what the noise was. He rounded a bend in the path and found Fúlmon, Huróyna and Máyo sitting back to back in the middle of the trail, hands clasped on their heads, spears pointed at them by a large group of tall dark-skinned warriors all dabbed with subdued paint for camouflage. All were at least a head above the Bólani in height and wore decorative strings of shells round their necks. There were some fifteen of these grass skirted strangers, six pointed spears at the sitting Bólani scouts, the rest with bow and arrows drawn, faced Bróda and the approaching column.

Bróda halted ten cubits from the lead hostile. It was as if that was the signal for others of the tall dark-skinned band to announce their presence. All around the Bólani column, these strange warriors emerged from ambush. The Bólani were surrounded by at least a hundred warriors with drawn arrows pointing menacingly at them. All was done in an eerie silence, the normal tropical forest hubbub a backdrop to this tragedy.

Bróda leisurely turned to face the Bólani column and raised his hands. 'Do not make any belligerent moves. If they'd wanted to kill us, they'd have fired first—instead of this.' He swept his arm gently at the situation. 'Put all your belongings on the ground—slowly! Then raise your arms as I've done.'

Some hesitated, but eventually all copied their Custodian.

25

PRISONERS OF THE RHALPI

Fear was spread tight on all the faces of the Bólani as they trudged along the same path as before, this time surrounded by sparsely clad painted hostile warriors—who prodded them with spears to encourage them to keep moving. No attempt had been at communication by the leader of the dark-skinned warriors who had a thin straight bone piercing his nose. He gestured and jabbed them with his own spear—shouted at them in a language Morác could not distinguish—and looked mightily pleased with himself at his handiwork.

The Bólani were marched as prisoners, thoroughly dejected, until late into the afternoon, when Wómak whispered to Bróda that he could smell smoke. A short while later, the path opened onto a large clearing. In the middle stood an immense stockade with high walls and a guarded gateway. As the prisoners and escort neared the entrance, some of the inhabitants adorned with a variety of shell necklaces, came streaming out to gaze at the unusual procession, pointing and making incomprehensible remarks, to each other and out loud at the prisoners.

'If we could talk to them, we might come to some kind of understanding,' Morác whispered to Néra.

'Can't you communicate with them?' Néra asked.

'I'm waiting for a chance—the leader seems full of himself, and it suggests he's bringing us to someone else. I want to know who—before I make my move. We may have only one opportunity to escape—and we'd better time it right.'

'I hope you know what you're doing.'

Néra fell silent as they entered the timber stockade. Round wooden thatched huts stood neatly in a large semi-circle, leaving an open communal space before a larger hut with an elaborately carved ornamented façade. They were herded towards a podium where a large dark male sat imposingly on a throne. He was decorated with various feather adornments, wearing a beautiful multicoloured cloak —a large bone ring pierced his nose and the skin on his chest bore patterned scarring. By his right side at his feet sat a wizened old man covered with a tan kóira fur skin cloak.

The leader of the ambush came and prostrated himself in the dust in front of the podium—the large male regarding this with some contempt. To Morác, the seated chief seemed to be their 'Custodian' or its equivalent. Words were exchanged amidst a lot of pointing in the Bólani direction. The Bólani in their turn dumped all their belongings on the ground where they stood. The four stándy were taken from them and herded into a small corral with the travois contents dumped at the entrance of the enclosure, and the two kópi tied to nearby posts. The chief abruptly waved his hand and the prisoners were prodded out towards another gate to the left, still within the stockade. When they attempted to take their belongings with them, they were mightily discouraged.

As they were being ushered into the second compound, an overpowering stench reached everyone's nostril; a mix of urine and vomit. This disgusting odour emanated from the entrance to the main wooden hut within the prison stockade. They were pushed inside the hut and forced to crowd into its limited space—all thirty-five of them. Bróda raised his voice and called for a council meeting in the centre of the hut, which resulted in forcing the rest back to the outer rim. It was intended to quieten people's fears, show something was about to be done. Wómak, Morác, Fúlmon, Scória and Umára crouched around Bróda, and waited.

Bróda began, 'I'm inviting Morác to assess the situation, since he's been in more strange situations than the rest of us, Morác!'

'We're in a húli of a fix—I'll not pretend otherwise. I haven't fathomed their intentions yet, which is why I've not made any move. They haven't hurt us—but that doesn't mean they won't. I really need to have a quiet word with their 'Custodian,'...' and Morác stopped—staring at the ground thoughtfully.

'Ehm. Is that it...Morác?' Bróda inquired calmly. '... Anything to add, Wómak?'

'I was all for fighting it out—there then—but you told us to give in—and I'm not going to argue with you.' With that Wómak shrugged his big shoulders as if to say, now it was out of his hands.

'They came out of nowhere—I never saw them—no warning or anything,' Fúlmon was trying to explain how come he was caught off guard. 'One instant we were creeping forward, the next I had an arrow at my heart...I'm sorry Bróda—I feel I've let you down.'

'You did your best,' Bróda reassured him. 'Don't blame yourself—that goes for the rest of you. What we need is to be out of here in one piece...that's the big question— and how to achieve that. So—anymore *constructive* suggestions?'

They discussed for a long while without result, until exhausted, they sat silent, trying not to breathe the foul air. The council ploy had subdued the initial tense mood—but it was only a stratagem designed to calm. For a short while it had taken people's attention away from their dire circumstances. Now all squatted gloomily trying not to breathe.

Some time later, the door to the hut was wrenched open and five guards preceded by spears, began poking those spears at the prisoners, shouting something. They prodded until they spied Píngo—and it was clear they wanted Píngo to come with them. Píngo resisted, and the Bólani shielded him, until Uílin was stabbed in the right thigh, trying to shield Píngo. All turmoil ceased in a stand-off, the guards still near the door, but Píngo seeing the injured assistant cook, gave in and went with the guards voluntarily. The big albino surrounded by the dark-skinned warriors made a strange sight. The contrast couldn't be more outstanding. It was the disparity that explained why they wanted the big albino. He was just about their height.

'I think they're curious—' Morác ventured. 'I hope they're curious. They've never seen anyone like him. No point in speculating what they're going to do—it won't help us. It's a pity we're spending our thirty-second night on the journey in this goddess forsaken place.'

It was now evening, and for the rest of the night all was quiet. By the following morning people complained they were nauseous with the smell—but even so—they were thirsty and hungry.

'Are they going to feed us?' Cara was desperate to know.

Umára tried to pacify her. 'I don't think it's any use wanting things just right now. Cara my dear, you'll just have to be patient—and hope we get out of this in one piece.'

'Morác!' Ganúra called. 'Uílin's getting worse. Is there anything you can do for him? We've used his spittle to try and cleanse the wound, but conditions in here are simply filthy.'

'I'm sorry, Ganúra—all our medicines are out there.' He was genuinely distressed but could do little. He tried to ease the delirium by chanting over the injured man—and he relieved the pain a bit with the incantation, putting him to sleep—but it was only temporary.

Ganúra was nursing the assistant cook, who had become delirious over night. She feared for his life if the situation didn't improve—and the situation didn't improve. They were left like that in the stinking prison for the rest of the day and for the second night. No visitors. No food or water. Now they understood why the stench was overpowering, for they had to add to the stench with their own toilet. There was no help when nature demanded it. Grit their teeth and bear it. Morác told stories to ease their plight —repeating the legends of the Bólani tribe. It took their minds off of their predicament—their immediate condition. Only their release would alleviate their troubles, and that was in the lap of their captors.

In the middle of the afternoon of the third day of their captivity, Píngo returned to them healthy, with a silly smile on his face—telling stories of how they fed and entertained him—whilst all listened enviously. Next, the guards wanted Morác, mainly as a result of what Píngo had told them about their tribal shamán. Somehow Píngo had managed to make himself understood, and that amazed his listeners—for he was a bit slow with words. How did he do it, they asked themselves? Bróda raised his voice and insisted on going next, but the guards refused him.

Morác didn't resist, and was taken out of the prison stockade—to see not the chief, but the shrunken wizened old man who'd sat at the chief's feet. This took Morác by surprise. The guards escorted him to a hut off the main open space, but near the chief's hut. Morác was bid to enter. Inside, near a fire, seated on the floor was a half naked youth poking the embers with a stick. He didn't look up. Morác moved near to the warming flames and then heard movement from the shadows. Unlike the others of the tribe, this youth's skin was unscarred.

The old man bare to the waist, bearing a number of decorative scars, shuffled forward to stand behind the youth. Round his neck he wore a green stone pendant. He nudged the youth in the back, who somewhat reluctantly rose and gave way for the old man, who took his place. The old man shouted what sounded like an order at the youth, who again slowly went and brought a pitcher to the old man from somewhere in the shadows of the hut.

The old man gestured to Morác to sit near the fire—then handed the pitcher to Morác after smelling and tasting the contents. Morác did the same, smelling a sweet liquid. The old man bid him drink—and cautiously Morác took a small sip. This settled warmly in his stomach and encouraged him to take a larger swig. What with hunger gnawing at him and the pungent liquid warming his insides—Morác went into a fit of shivers, perspiring freely. He couldn't stop shaking and the old man ordered the youth to bring the kóira fur skin cloak to help control this sudden onset. The shivers abated somewhat. With difficulty, Morác was disrobed to the waist of his green shirt and the youth began rubbing him with a cloth. The youth built up the fire increasing the heat in the hut.

Later when Morác told the story to Néra, it was at that point as he was being disrobed that the old man's eyebrows shot up at the sight of the pendant Lord Phèrlim had given Morác. Although Morác was again shivering uncontrollably, he was watching the old man carefully. The old man's eyes were riveted to the mighty pendant, hanging on a thick gold chain; a red stone talisman embedded in between two suns which hung round Morác's neck. As the youth rubbed Morác's sweat away, the old man continued to stare at the pendant. Finally, Morác stopped shivering. The youth brought Morác a clean dry shirt and helped him to put it over his head. The old man ordered the youth to leave—and sullenly the youth obeyed.

When alone with Morác, the old man pointed at the pendant round Morác's neck, and then performed a rubbing movement with his hands. He wanted Morác to activate the stone with an enchantment—at least, this is what Morác understood.

Morác held the pendant in his right hand and began, 'I beseech thee by the inverse reversion of the sacred alignment of the hand and eye, by the light of the two suns of Kálar, make the word graph of this old man known to your supplicant.' And he waited till the red stone began to glow.

A little time went by, and then from the old man's thoughts came a hesitant question—*who are you?*

Morác understood the old man's mind through the power of the glow of the red stone in the pendant.

My name is Morác of the tribe Bólani. Morác thought at him. *We come in peace. We are running from the schánda.* Morác waited for a response.

What is that—round your neck? It was a simple blunt question.

I am the shamán of my tribe and this is my emblem, given to me by a mighty wizard, Lord Phèrlim, who lived in the desert up north—in the big twin towers. Morác didn't know how to explain to the old man—about the Grand Wizard of Linkalúr. In truth, Morác was still too emotional at the memory of the experience, of the death of Phèrlim, and it made any explanation difficult.

Back from the old man came the thought, *You wear the sign of our Holy Lady, how is that?*

That startled Morác. Did they…could they also…was the True and Living Aíne Most High…known to these people? Had she shone the light which made the darkness visible even down here? Then he shrugged, well of course she had. Wasn't she all powerful? Didn't Phèrlim say that belief in her went wide, throughout all the lands on their planet?

Yes…our Lady Aíne…the two suns in the sky… these thought interrupted Morác's own reminiscences. He realised the old man had listened to his thinking about Aíne.

You know of the sacred and mysterious name of the True and Living Aíne Most High? She who made the light of the darkness visible. Morác thought at the old man.

Yes of course. I even know of the terrible and great Lord Phèrlim—he of the sand. It is his pendant I recognised round your neck. Many seasons ago we met when we travelled north into the wasteland. I needed to know how you obtained it—that you had not stolen it somehow. How is the mighty wizard? The thought from the old man now came through strong, almost as if he were a different person.

Morác's face was sad as he thought; *I laid him to rest not ten cycles ago—up in the twin towers. Lord Phèrlim is no more—may Aíne preserve his lemur.*

I'm sorry to know that. He was powerful. It was a simple thought—a sad thought. Then the mood shifted. *I must leave you for a while—I must try and put an end to this terrible injustice we have perpetrated on you and your people. We cannot sacrifice you to Aíne if you are a believer.*

With these parting shots, the old man rose quickly and left the hut. Shortly thereafter the youth reappeared and produced some food for Morác, cold roast meat and a variety of exotic fruit. He ate ravenously—didn't care what kind of food it was—his first meal in three days. He drank cautiously, more of the pungent sweet liquid, until he gently dozed by the fireside.

He was shaken awake by Néra, who sat by his side with tears running down her face. He put his arm around her.

'They've just let us go. Just came and unlocked the hut we were in—and all our people—are in the main arena outside—eating and drinking as if…' She couldn't finish.

'Yes my love…I was hoping that's what he'd do.' Morác said gently.

'Who do you mean?' She asked. Without waiting for a reply, she continued, 'the tribe is looking for you—they want to thank you—they know it was you who…'

He jumped in, fingering the talisman thoughtfully, 'I think this pendant saved us—not I. It would seem once again we owe our salvation to our Holy Lady Aíne. It is a knowledge that has come full circle to me. By the way, how's Uílin?'

'Ganúra is nursing him. I've put on a poultice of medication right after we got our belongings back. He seems stable but the swelling isn't going down—one more night in that foul prison and he'd have died for sure. I think he might have blood poisoning.'

The old man re-entered the hut, a big smile on his face. He looked at Morác with his arm around Néra. *I am glad—is this your mate?* His thought came over strong as ever as he pointed at Néra.

Morác stood and went to embrace the old man—to thank him for releasing his tribe. *I thank you from the bottom of my heart. You have made me very happy—and yes this is my mate—her name is Néra.*

The old man repeated aloud, 'Néra.'

That startled Néra, but she smiled, stood up and bowed to the old man, honouring him for what he'd done.

'What is your name?' Néra asked instinctively.

Morác gave her a sharp look, but in his mind he repeated the question. *What are you named?*

Hnar'ad—I am Hnar'ad of the Rhalpi. My chief apologises for holding all of you prisoner—but we thought maybe if we sacrificed you to the Holy Lady, then she would spare us from the insects. You called them the schánda—we know them—and their time is due. We prepare for their coming. Suddenly the old man was pushing a whole gush of thought at Morác and he began to understand what had happened to his people—why they'd been imprisoned. It all had to do with the damned schánda.

Morác looked closely at Hnar'ad; *Why are the men of your tribe so scarred—and what are those curious shells you all wear round your necks?*

The old man smiled indulgently. *When we reach warrior age, we are initiated into the tribe by undergoing ritual cuts on the skin. The mark of a brave warrior is the number of scars they carry, how many cuts they were able to endure in silence—without crying out with pain. As for the shells—we are close to the sea and these are simple seashells. We all wear them—they look pleasing don't they?*

All explanations were simple, thought Morác. His curiosity satisfied—and free at last, he was in a mood to celebrate. *Before I go to meet my tribe I need to ask you one more question—how far are we from the Golden Sea?*

A puzzled frown broke the old man's features. He smiled and thought, *Is that your destination? We are only two days from the Great Sea. If you wish, we will go together to the water?*

I think that would be excellent, Morác replied with his mind. *I must talk with my chief about this—I will try to get all our people to join you on your journey to the Great Sea—if that is permitted? One more question. One of our people has been injured, in the prison. Why is his wound not healing.*

The old man's face saddened. *Yes, I've been told one of our warriors stabbed one of your people with a spear. I'm sorry. We Rhalpi are all sorry for your loss. He will die.*

This brought a moment of disbelief at the certainty in the old man's thoughts. *Why will he die? Surely not. Can you not cure him?*

I'm sorry. Our spear points are dipped in our waste —you know—our excrement. If Lord Phèrlim was here, he could save him. But we have never known anybody survive a stabbing. You must prepare yourself for the worst. He nodded in encouragement—but his face held no hope.

Morác took Néra's hand and both went sombrely to find Bróda and the rest of the tribe. They decided not to tell the Custodian of the old man's prediction. Uílin might still pull through—against the odds. They didn't have far to go. In the middle of the open space outside, a huge campfire roared, throwing a warm glow into the evening. It was just after dusk, and Morác breathed deeply of the fresh evening air—free of the foul stench of his former prison. He spied Bróda sitting on the ground on the far right of the fire circle. Bróda got to his feet as Morác approached.

'Bróda! Glad to see you.' Morác shouted as he ambled up, hand in hand with Néra. 'Émana,' Morác acknowledged. 'Wómak, Ganúra. I see they've given you back the kópis.'

'I've been delegated by the tribe to offer our official thanks to you— for getting us released, Morác.' Bróda beamed at him. 'They've given us back our belongings and assigned us this area,' he swept the open space around, 'for the night.' Then he sat.

One by one, the grateful tribe came and thanked Morác for his efforts—and Morác understood they needed to do that. To show gratitude to someone for escaping the foul prison—escaping the uncertainty of what people imagined lay ahead of them as prisoners. He didn't mention the pendant out of respect for their needs.

'Well, what do you think of this place?' Morác asked the Custodian. 'Have you had time to look around?'

'It's the biggest village I've ever come across. D'you know they number some two and a half hundred in their tribe? And this enclosure's massive. How do they manage to feed all their people?' Bróda seemed quite impressed.

There was more banter in this vein until finally Morác asked to see how Uílin was getting on, finding him still struggling with his injury, trying to sleep behind Wómak and Ganúra.

'How is he?'

Ganúra smiled, 'He's not really improving—I can't understand it. We've tried all the right things for a wound. The remedy Néra put on his wound worked for a while. Then he started sinking again. I tried giving him some food but he brought it up. He's in the lap of Aíne now. She seemed resigned to his fate.

Morác kept his council as he'd agreed with Néra. He was afraid they would lose another of their number. It needn't always be fatal. He bent over the suffering assistant cook and said an incantation, enjoining Aíne to help him get well. That's all he could do. When all the rest of the Bólani had settled—people fed—Morác led them in a prayer of thanks to Aíne.

All stood round the fire, hands joined in a circle. Morác's voice carrying in the night air. 'O Mighty Aíne, we give thanks to you for our salvation. Hear now our plea to you Holy Lady. You from where all good comes, continue to protect us and guard us from harm. Guide us back to our hamlet, safeguard us on the remainder of our coming journey. We are grateful supplicants!'

They stood for a while in silence to reinforce their plea. It was at this point Morác noticed the old man watching them from the darkened entrance of his hut. It made the prayer they'd just offered up all the more essential. It reinforced the bond they'd established between the two tribes, with Aíne as the mediatress. Then they spread their blankets and made themselves comfortable under the tropical sky, feeling most thankful to be in the clean open air again.

Early next morning, around dawn, a general movement around them in the open space had every member of the Bólani awake. A fire had been started and members of the Rhalpi tribe were roasting meat on spits—the odour making people's mouths water. The Bólani were invited to join the Rhalpi in their meal—and this was enthusiastically accepted.

Morác dug around in his possessions until he located the polished oval crystal he used for the "far-seeing" spell. He wrapped it in a cloth and took it to the old man's hut. He knocked on the entrance post and coughed his presence.

A voice said something from the inside which Morác took for an invitation to enter. He found the old man seated near the fire and he joined him, facing him. Unwrapping the cloth he placed it between them. It was evident he had the old man's interest. Morác took hold of his talisman hanging around his neck, fingering it gently. The amulet crystal began to glow with a deep red light whilst Morác recited the "far-seeing" spell, *'By the power of the talisman I hold in the miracle of time, from the vantage of the northern compass point, through the eye of the great Racul, I seek to cast my sight onto the distant schánda. Let the image be seen in the far-seeing crystal.'*

A mist began to circulate in the oval crystal, which cleared to show the seething swarm crawling across the desert, a line of black abomination pushing forward, large hairy insects scurrying in their direction—three or four days away.

The old man's eyes were captivated by the image in the crystal. In a flicker of an eyelid, Morác saw horror, disgust, and finally determination each in quick succession on the old man's face.

His thought came over strong, *You have the eye! Yes, those are the rasch'a we fear—from who we must flee. We call rasch'a—you call schánda. You are a great wizard, Morác. You see the rasch'a—in the wilderness. We must flee—go today, we have rafts to build. They come soon.*

Morác agreed, *Yes we must go.* Although Hnar'ad had approved the Bólani should join the Rhalpi the previous day, Morác needed to confirm it again—now—for his own peace of mind. *We are still invited to come with you? I know you said we could, but have you changed your mind?*

No! I have talked with my chief and he agrees—we did you a great injustice and we must make amends. The old man didn't mention Uílin—or his prediction of his demise. Both knew of this unsaid burden between them. *We want to help you build your rafts. You do intend to build rafts?* The old man's face turned quizzical.

Morác's heart lightened. *Yes, we intend to build rafts —and we would be grateful for any help. I must go and tell my people that we go today. Thank you.*

Morác was about to go when the old man's thoughts again broke in on him. *Before we go, we will hold a big rejoicing today to celebrate our two tribes coming together— so you can meet our chief—properly.* A twinkle crept back into the old man's eyes—*and it will be an excuse to eat and drink everything we cannot take with us.*

Morác left the hut and went to find Bróda. Émana was with Ganúra trying to feed Uílin—who was sitting up and looking much better.

'Bróda, I have some urgent news for our tribe.' Morác crouched by Wómak facing Bróda.'

'I'm worried about Uílin,' was Bróda's response. 'He doesn't seem to be improving. Can't you do something?'

Morác ignored the assistant cook. 'Look Bróda, I've just used the far-seeing crystal—and the schánda are only three days away. The old shamán of this tribe has told me that the Rhalpi intend to go to the Sea today, and he invited us to join them. They want to help us build our rafts. What do you think?'

Bróda's face changed—and lit up. 'What do I think? I think we should jump at the chance. I think we should thank them and be quick to join them—that's what I think.'

'Well done Morác,' Wómak joined in the praise.

'Yes, Morác. You've turned a nasty situation into what looks like becoming a real blessing,' Émana joined in.

Morác felt relieved at his friend's reactions. He had half expected them to insist on getting away from the Rhalpi as quick as possible—away from a bad experience and from worse memories.

'Their chief invites us to join them today in festivities—to rejoice at our tribes meeting—in communion with Aíne. He wants to scoff all the food and drink in the village in one massive binge. At least that's my reading of what's to happen. And he wants us there.'

'Tell him we'll be only too happy to oblige,' said Bróda, a large grin on his face. 'I rather like all their strange tropical fruits. As for that sweet drink they have…' He winked at Wómak, who nodded with a heavy head.

The festivities started mid-morning, with the Bólani gathering together in front of the chief's hut—waiting for the big man to arrive. He sauntered in with his retinue, their old tribal shamán by his right side. Hnar'ad came and joined Morác and together they cast a language spell, combining their powers so the spell would be strengthened from both languages.

Morác and Hnar'ad intoned together, Morác having rehearsed the spell with Hnar'ad just before; both gripping Morác's talisman with their right hands, 'We beseech thee by the inverse reversion of the sacred alignment of the hand and eye, by the light of the two suns of Kálar, make the word graphs of our tribes known to your supplicants.' Both waited till the red stone began to glow. Morác indicated to Bróda he should speak.

Bróda squared his shoulders and looked the chief in the eyes. 'My name is Bróda of the Bólani, I am their Custodian. I greet you in on behalf of our tribe and thank you for your present hospitality.'

The chief's reaction seemed to indicate he understood what the Bólani Custodian was saying—the enchantment was working.

Others of the Bólani were a bit uncomfortable at those words with the prison stench and Uílin's condition still fresh in their minds—they shuffled about a bit but kept silent.

Bróda continued, 'We come in peace and would be pleased to join you in building rafts to escape the schánda.'

At those kind words, the dark-skinned chief rose and cleared his throat. 'I am Frah'nud, Chief of the Rhalpi and I welcome you to our village. We apologise for your earlier treatment, and especially for your injured warrior, and wish to make reparations by...' he clapped his hands, and a warrior stepped from behind with a multicoloured cloak, similar to the one he wore. '...bestowing on your chief this royal cloak.' He stopped while Bróda strode forward to accept the gift. The chief continued, 'But we feel this is still not enough and we wish to add to this by showing you the way to the sea and helping you build your rafts to escape the rasch'a.' The chief could see he'd overwhelmed the Bólani chief, so he quickly added, 'But now, we wish you to join us in our festivities.'

The chief sat, clapped his hands again, which was the signal for a large number of Rhalpi to appear from the huts, bearing platters stacked high with many kinds of roast meats, and a variety of exotic fruits. Both tribes ate, seated in the large open space, as if it was their last meal, and maybe some thought it would be. By noon all had been eaten that could be eaten—and then some. The merriment was high with all the drink and people sang and laughed loudly.

Bróda had given instruction for the ancient wind instrument of the Bólani to be unearthed and instructed his son, Fern, to ask the musicians to begin with some lively tunes. Fern had a chat with the carpenter, Sáor, who was the other panpipe player, and Málina, their talented lyre player. The four musicians sat in a circle and tuned up. Morác pulled his sacred timpani out of a cloth bag and tapped it a few times, checking the tension of the stretched skin. Then the four of them began. The two panpipes played an energetic jig, Málina using her plectrum with gusto. The music immediately caught the attention of the Rhalpi. The effect had the Rhalpi tapping their feet, and Fúlmon jumped up and took Huróyna in his arms and they danced vigorously wherever there was space.

Soon the majority of the Rhalpi, more than a two hundred people were leaping and dancing in the large open space in front of the chief's ornate hut. Even the chief was seen stomping around with some of his females. The festivities went on till mid-afternoon in this manner—when there was the sound of a loud horn.

Frah'nud, the chief, had his hands raised, standing tall beside the horn blower on the dais. 'We must get ready,' he boomed across the heads of his audience. It is time.'

All knew what he meant and the Rhalpi immediately ran to obey, going to their huts to gather what they were to take with them. People rushed about with purpose, and soon a large crowd assembled near the gate of the wooden stockade. Bróda's people, being seasoned travellers, simply had to pick up their belongings to be ready. They reharnessed the travois to the two remaining stándy and Bróda collected his kópi, at the same time bringing Wómak his.

26

THE GOLDEN SEA

The almost three hundred strong column of the two combined tribes left the stockade, marching purposefully south into the jungle four abreast. Bróda and the Bólani followed Frah'nud's large retinue, and then came the rest of the Rhalpi, many carrying large bundles. They only had to lug them for two days unlike the long trek of the Bólani. But what made the Bólani curious was the amount of braided rope being transported to the sea by the Rhalpi. Around twenty warriors were overloaded with huge bundles on their heads, all carrying this coarse rope. It was intriguing.

Frah'nud, his conscience still bothering him, assigned four of his warriors to carry Uílin's stretcher. He was no better. People pleaded to Aíne on his behalf. Málina reasserted her ownership of the four remaining stándy and insisted on looking after them for the last leg of their long march. She was adamant. A further six sturdy Rhalpi warriors went out front, hacking at anything that obstructed their path. Fúlmon went with his two scouts hot on the heels of the Rhalpi scouts.

They spent their first night by three pools in a large clearing. The number of people meant they over spilled into the forest, Rhalpi hammocks strung between trees, contrasting with the Bólani A-frames in the clearing. Worried faces queried the location so close to the pools until they were reassured by Hnar'ad and Frah'nud that the area was quite safe.

'You're sure there aren't any plagues of biting insects?' Wómak asked Frah'nud, both outsized warriors were quickly becoming friends.

'Most assuredly we would not have camped here if there were,' replied the chief.

Ganúra fussed over the deteriorating Uílin, who had passed into a coma. 'The poison in his blood is ebbing his life force away.'

Néra and Émana were busying themselves around the ailing fellow tribesman trying to make him more comfortable —with little to show for their worry.

'I'm afraid he's not going to last the night,' Néra commented softly to Émana. 'Nothing is helping.'

Not far away in a huddle by one of the pools, Morác wanted to know of Hnar'ad, 'Why aren't there any animals in the forest? We haven't seen a single animal since we entered the forest way back from the desert. Is it the schánda—I mean the rasch'a?'

'But of course—you must have guessed.'

'Sort of.'

'They've all fled many suns ago. They have more sense than we people,' he cackled merrily.

Morác furrowed his brow, 'Also I am curious as to how you know of the rasch'a—their time of coming. The last time was many many seasons ago. You cannot remember *that* time.'

'Wait—I will show you.' The old man turned to the youth who was his shadow. 'Fetch me the Sacred Scroll,' he commanded.

The youth rummaged in an enormous backpack he'd carried since they'd left, and pulled out a long brown roll. He ambled back to the old man and handed it to him.

'Look at this,' Hnar'ad said unrolling the scroll. 'We've put it all on this sacred roll so we don't forget.' He laid it on the ground and the youth went to obtain a burning branch from the fire, without being asked, to Morác's astonishment.

When light was brought, Morác saw the roll contained diagrams and finely drawn pictures of the entire two hundred year life cycle of the schánda. There was no sign of writing and Morác assumed they didn't have it. Starting in the left corner of the scroll and running horizontally, there were pictograms of the schánda's birth on the shores of the Golden Sea, marks indicating a quarter of Kálar's season, the long gestation, the eggs hatching and then their birth as benign leaf eating grubs. The larvae emerged, feeding on leaves of the kerni bush, found only on the shores of the Golden Sea. After a further season spent feeding, the pictograms showed the larvae beginning the long crawl north to their normal habitat; burrowing underground for most of its journey.

'That's roughly were we come from,' Morác pointed excitedly to the spot where his hamlet lay.

The old man nodded. The diagrams indicated that burrowing took three seasons. Then it showed them reaching the tundra, the grub changing into a chrysalis and for four years this lay dormant in shallow ground. The chrysalis metamorphosed, and emerged as a mature adult insect.

More pictograms showed its time of mating, when it became a ferocious lichen eater, quadrupling in size, growing the stinger and large claws in its fourth and final moult, and then beginning its long march south to the mating grounds. More pictograms indicated the schánda moulted every fifty years. It illustrated the grippers on their feet enabling them to climb rocks, *and* smooth trees.

This mating urge mutated the schánda into a swarm of ferocious carnivores. When they finally reached their breeding grounds in the South, on the shores of the Golden Sea, they were caricatured as completely exhausted and starving. When the schánda reached the sea, they mated, dug holes in the sand, deposited their eggs, and then died.

'This is magnificent,' enthused Morác. 'You don't need our nightmares—it's all here. You can pass this on from generation to generation. Ehm…do you think we could make a copy of this scroll?'

He knew it was a big request—it was clear the scroll was sacred to the Rhalpi.

'I must ask my chief—if he agrees, then you may make a copy.' Now it was Hnar'ad's turn to look embarrassed. 'Would you mind looking into your crystal—finding the rasch'a? I feel in my bones they're closing on us.'

'But of course,' and Morác rose to go find the crystal, giving Hnar'ad a chance to approach his chief for the permission to copy the scroll.

A little while later they met up at the same spot as before.

'My chief agrees. He says you are of the same belief as the Rhalpi and he still feels guilty for locking you up and for your injured warrior. So yes, you may copy the scroll.'

'Néra,' Morác called over to where she sat with Ganúra and Émana tending Uílin. 'Please come over here.'

When she'd come, Morác explained what he wanted her to do. She was far better at drawing than he was.

'Well of course I'd be only too happy—and Ganúra will call me if she needs me—but I don't think we have the paper. Can I do it in one of your books?'

'If you can find one empty.' Morác was guarded about his precious books.

Néra went away to look through Morác's belongings. She spent the rest of the evening and part of the night near the fire working on the copying. She was aware of the importance of the commission. Morác was aiding her by being helpful to Hnar'ad. He put the crystal he'd brought on the ground between them and cast the far-seeing spell. He was shocked to find the schánda only two days behind, moving rapidly on the abandoned Rhalpi village.

'But how? They were three—maybe four days away and in the desert, yesterday. How have they managed to be virtually a day away from your village?'

'The mating urge—did you see them, they were in a frenzied hurry. They can smell the sea. They know they're almost at the end of *their* journey.' Hnar'ad sat worried for an instant and then said, 'I must tell my chief.'

This bit of news unbalanced Morác. He decided he needed to consult with Bróda when he'd finished talking to the old man—he wanted Bróda, in the morning, to put a sense of urgency into their pace.

The two tribal shamáns talked like that well into the night, each telling the other of their tribe and its customs, exchanging information.

*   *   *

The next day was a sad day for the Bólani tribe. During the night, near dawn, Uílin passed over into the netherworld. Ganúra and Émana sobbed quietly until the rest of the tribe was awake. Morác was the first to know of the tragedy, sensing the sadness emanating from the two women. He was joined by Néra and soon, by the rest of the tribe, who gathered round the corpse.

When the suns came up, the Rhalpi chief arrived to express his sorrow.

'We are deeply saddened by your loss—and no words of regret or comfort will bring him back,' said Frah'nud, visibly moved by this discord reopening between the two tribes. 'I am sorry we were the cause of his death—and I wish it were not so.' He stopped, unable to say more.

Bróda looked at the gathered mourners and made a bold decision. 'I was chosen to lead the Bólani and now speak on their behalf...' He raised his voice. 'Why are we here?' He glared at his own people, defiantly demanding they trust him. 'Why are we standing so far from our hamlet, from our homes?' Again he paused, making sure they were focusing their attention on him. Then he spat out, 'The schánda…that's why. We would not here but for them…and so, I believe the schánda were responsible for the death of Uílin…Robán…Gárn, Sáor and the others. Frah'nud and the Rhalpi have become our friends and I do not blame them for what's happened to Uílin, no more than I blame the dárgh or the kóira for the death of Máda, Mútani, Gárn, and Gara.' He stopped and lowered his eyes to where Uílin lay before him. 'Now—we must bury him—and move on…' He turned to Morác, and appealed with his eyes for the shamán to intervene.

'I agree with Bróda,' responded Morác. 'We elected him—and he speaks for us. We must be quick and bury Uílin —and move on to the sea.'

Scória had been entrusted with finding a burial spot in the forest, and now waved his hand to Bróda, indicating he had found one. Umára, Uílin's friend, lifted the stretcher, with Wómak, Píngo and Dalán—and the subdued Bólani procession made its way into the forest.

'We invite our Rhalpi friends to join us in our grief,' said Bróda, looking at Frah'nud and Hnar'ad, 'please.'

There was relief on both the Rhalpi leaders' faces that an awkward moment in intertribal relations had been swiftly overcome. They followed the Bólani into the forest.

Morác saw the grave dug and the body of the assistant cook laid to rest—and all threw a handful of gravel into the grave. Then Morác called for attention, so he could perform the oration.

'It is with great sorrow that we put into the ground another of our tribe. We throw sand into the eyes of Húli on behalf of Uílin, so his lemur may sneak passed the guardian of the netherworld—to take his rightful place in everlasting repose.

Standing over the grave, ringed by the gathered warriors, facing outwards as a guard, their blowpipes raised in salute to a fellow warrior; they listened to Morác reciting the shortened battle version of the oration to the dead. When he'd finished, the gathering dispersed, the column reformed ready for the days hike.

The convoy moved out at a rapid rate with a number of Rhalpi warriors assigned the task of bullying the slothful ones in the rear with spears. It was brutal but effective—and it seemed the warriors delegated to the task, thoroughly enjoyed their work. They put far too much enthusiasm into it, prodding and pushing the hapless laggards, forcing them to keep up.

At around midday the tribes were brought to a halt by the scouts on the edge of a clearing. People milled around until Frah'nud gave orders to his warriors. The scouts stood facing a vast expanse of what Bróda had named "the kópi eating flowers." The whole clearing was full of them, purple leaves spread out wide from enormous stems, itching to curl onto some unsuspecting prey. For the Bólani this was as menacing a scene as they'd come across in their travels.

Most of the Bólani were shocked to be facing this purple monstrosity—yet the Rhalpi seemed bemused by the Bólani's' reaction.

'How are we supposed to get through that,' Bróda pointed a shaky finger at the impenetrable mass.

'Their scouts say it's not a problem,' offered Fúlmon, shrugging his shoulders.

'What d'you mean not a problem…'

'Calm down Bróda,' Morác urged. 'I know how you feel but there's bigger things here than your poor missing kópi.'

Wómak yelled, 'Look!'

And all the Bólani were surprised to see the Rhalpi scouts poking the base of the flowers with long poles they'd cut while the Bólani were staring in shock. The poked flower closed its foliage as if it had been ordered to do so.

'You have to know where the closing spot is,' Hnar'ad was telling Morác, as they watched other flowers being poked and closed to order.

Rhalpi warriors with long poles were out in a wide arc closing flowers so the column could cross the deadly glade in safety. Once the flowers were closed, all that was left was a tall purple forest with plenty of clear space in between the flowers for people to pass.

'Well I never!' exclaimed Bróda, scratching his head. 'Just like that, hey.'

The shock on the Bólani faces had turned to bemusement as they watched the Rhalpi deal with the problem.

'If only we'd known,' lamented Fúlmon.

Huróyna and Máyo were laughing with relief, and this infected the rest of the Bólani, who were joining in the laughter. With that the tension evaporated for all except Bróda, who was finally able to lay the ghost of his kópi to rest in his mind. He was subdued all across the clearing, passing the closed flowers, remembering his recently deceased, but sorely missed kópi.

'Poor sweet Latish, I should have looked after you better,' Émana heard him mumble.

The clearing was crossed without fuss and in good order—and soon the lengthy procession was back in the forest, racing on towards the sea as fast as they could go. By late afternoon they could smell the sea air, but the trees and bushes became more impenetrable, not because there was no path, simply due to the size of the column. So many people spread across a small path leading to the ocean. It was as if the tropical forest was fighting their passage, trying to prevent them reaching their goal.

Eventually, by evening they could hear the waves breaking on the seashore—still the undergrowth held them despite ferocious efforts by the Rhalpi warriors hacking on either side of the trail. With the sound of the sea roaring in their ears and the smell of salt filling their nostril, they broke through onto the shore of the Golden Sea. The vast blue green ocean lit by the light of the two moons beat against a steep declining shore, spilling foam onto the golden sand at the bottom.

The view was breathtaking and the Bólani, open mouthed and speechless—but only temporarily.

'Thirty five days it's taken us to get here,' Ganúra burst out, 'and it's still not over. We've rafts to build and then…' She broke off choking her words back.

The long voyage had taken its toll. People had died, animals had been killed, worms were faced and even killer plants overcome. It had been a long passage—some just flopped onto the grass verge above the sand and stared out to sea, unwilling to move. There was a relief of sorts they'd finally arrived at what some considered falsely—journey's end.

'Right Wómak, get the latrines sorted. Early night. We have work to do in the morning.' Bróda was trying to organise his people.

The Rhalpi started a big fire above the beach and soon, roasted meat smells were being blown back into the forest. The sea, now they could see it below, was extremely squally and the idea of going out onto it was only appealing when the schánda were kept in mind. What surprised Bróda and Morác was that Frah'nud immediately set half of the Rhalpi warriors to chopping trees for the rafts in the morning. One half ate whilst the other half worked, then they alternated. A few held burning branches to light the work of the others. The chopping was particularly noisy in the near distance, probably because it was done at night.

'How in the name of all that's holy can they see what they're doing,' commented Wómak to Fúlmon.

'It's sacrilege,' Fúlmon replied, resigned to the deed but still far from happy.

In this atmosphere the Bólani spent the thirty-sixth night camped on the edge of the forest facing the steep shoreline within sight of the turbulent sea, listening to the incessant chopping sounds of the Rhalpi. They were in the company of newly made friends who knew the area, were doing *their* work—but gazing out into the distant horizon—none were comforted.

When the camp had settled and the food eaten—again the Rhalpi shared their provisions with the Bólani, making Bróda most appreciative, Morác received a message from Hnar'ad for Bróda and Morác to join him in his tent. Both went to find the old Rhalpi shamán. Bróda wanted to discuss the raft building for the next day. He wanted his people to contribute to the building.

Standing guard near a small tent placed in an undersized clearing, they came across the large patrol leader who'd taken them in ambush four days earlier. He smiled a wide grin at them, but they could see he was still antagonistic. The youth, whose name Morác still didn't know, standing outside the tent guarding the tent flap itself, holding it closed with both hands.

'Is Hnar'ad inside?' Morác asked the youth.

From inside came an invitation. 'Come in, come in, but disrobe first.'

Intrigued, Morác and Bróda removed their shirts and were about to enter, when the youth motioned they should remove their trousers as well. Further puzzled, both did as they were bid, and the youth parted the flap he'd been holding shut.

Into Morác's unexpecting face, from inside, there came a whoosh of steam that almost bowled him backwards. Morác followed by Bróda, pushed their way in and readjusted their eyes to the dim light. Round the fire sat Hnar'ad and Frah'nud dripping with sweat. The tent seemed to be a boiling cauldron and the steam was being increased by Hnar'ad pouring water gently into a pot containing hot stones from the fire. The old man motioned for Morác and Bróda to join them round the fire.

Cautiously the two Bólani sat as the heat penetrated their bodies and they began to perspire freely. All the time in the background, the chopping was heard.

'What are you doing?' Morác quizzed the old man.

Lethargically Hnar'ad answered, 'We're cleaning our minds—and the pours of our skins. Wait—in a little you will feel the benefit. You will begin to relax.'

Morác looked at Bróda, who shrugged his big shoulders.

'It's true,' added Frah'nud. 'You will experience peace within—it will clear your wits. The time for decisions is after a long cleansing.'

'We have learned many things from the Rhalpi, and this may be one of them.' Bróda was being diplomatic. 'I will enjoy this,' he insisted.

Morác could see his Custodian was uncomfortable but intended to last it out as best as he could.

'We had a message you wanted to see us.' Morác was beginning to get pleasure from the heat, but the raft building bothered him.

'We thought you would benefit from this experience. We wanted to share it with our new friends.' Hnar'ad interposed.

'I see you've started the raft building—but why at night?' Bróda interrupted.

'We cannot wait—the rasch'a come.' Frah'nud bluntly stated.

'But we want to help,' insisted Bróda.

'And you shall. But first—the anusha,' Hnar'ad waved the water ladle at the steam.

'Anusha—is that what you call this?' Morác asked.

'Anusha…' repeated Bróda, sluggishly.

'I think this…may be too much for my Custodian,' Morác said reluctantly. 'He's not used to the steam.'

'Belh'od!' Shouted Frah'nud at the top of his voice.

The flap of the tent opened and the big warrior guarding the tent thrust his head through. 'My chief,' he kept his head low, eyes averted.

'Help the Bólani chief outside—he's had enough.'

'I obey.'

Morác took one arm and the ambush leader took the other and they heaved Bróda to his wobbly feet.

'We're going for some fresh air Bróda,' Morác reassured.

The two—half dragged half carried Bróda to the nearby verge at the top of the seashore where an astonishing sight greeted them. All along the long steep shoreline, rafts were being assembled in the moonlight by Rhalpi warriors. Blazing torches mingled with the moonbeams casting an eerie light on the frantic activity. There must have been well over twenty rafts taking shape.

'But…we…' Morác couldn't get the words out with amazement. 'We wanted to help…'

Bróda sat with his head in his lap. Morác wasn't talking to anybody in particular, but Belh'od took it he was talking to him. He didn't reply.

27

RAFT BUILDING

At dawn, those Rhalpi and Bólani not working were lined up on the steep shoreline, staring at the half finished rafts. After throwing off the effects of the steam bath, Bróda woke all his warriors and set them working alongside the Rhalpi.

The morning found him in the midst of lashing logs with ropes made by the Rhalpi women, ordering his men to hurry.

This activity by a chieftain amused Frah'nud, who couldn't understand why Bróda felt the need to get his hands dirty.

'Why does your Chief work?' Asked Hnar'ad of Morác.

'For that—' he replied, 'you would've had to have been with us on our long trek south. We've discussed this…' he waved his hand at the rafts, 'many times. Some thought it sacrilege cutting down trees—that is one of our beliefs— others wondered if we would get this far, to be *able* to cut trees. It's been a long voyage, distressing in so many ways. Even I had doubts.'

'But did you have a choice?'

'Not really. We can see that now—we even knew it then—but…' Morác broke off. He was suddenly deep in thought.

'We've built three rafts for your people,' Hnar'ad burst into Morác's contemplation. 'They're at the far end on the left of the shore. Your Chief wanted it that way. We'll go along the coast to the right—as is our tradition. Your chief wants to go to the left along the coast—it's his right.'

'What you said about "choice," I was thinking. The Rhalpi living here have it easier. You wait till the rasch'a come—build the rafts—sail along the coast a little way. When you land, you're almost home. But we—we have the same distance to go back, as we travelled down—before we're home, back to our hamlet. Maybe…we should stay here—with you.'

'My chief and I have discussed this, and we'd be pleased if your tribe would join ours. Why not talk it over with your people.'

That startled Morác. The idea was revolutionary—the tribes were so different, physically. He was surprised the Rhalpi had discussed such a plan—*he'd put it to his tribe—but time was running short. He'd do it just before they sailed.* Hnar'ad was waiting to see what Morác thought of the proposition.

'I'll talk to my people before we push the rafts into the sea.' Then as an afterthought Morác asked, 'You haven't seen any other people here—I mean people like us?'

The old man looked at Morác with interest. 'No. Why do you ask?'

'We have neighbours up where we live—Nólki, Hánum, Kárti, Grónda, Rími. It's curious we haven't come across any of them on our long trek down. I know the Kárti, Nólki and Rími went south-west—so I didn't expect to see them, but the Hánum—unless they went south-east.'

'I'm sorry, but I can't help you.'

Just at that point Rhalpi warriors rushed over to where Frah'nud was sitting and prostrated themselves before him.

'I must go see what our scouts report on the rasch'a. The patrol has just returned.'

'Can I come with you?' Morác wanted to hear what they had to say so he could inform Bróda.

'But of course. I don't think the report is good, not from what I can see on my chief's face.'

'Ah! Shamán—good you come.' Frah'nud had grim features. 'The scouts report the rasch'a are closing fast. They're just over half a day away. They will be here by nightfall. Have you had a close look at the rafts—are they ready?'

'Almost my chief. We will just make it—I think.' Hnar'ad was being cautious. 'We're having difficulty making enough rope. All the rope we carried from the village has been used. Now our women are braiding rope as fast as the hanging twines are being brought in.' He repeated, 'I think we'll just manage.'

'Good. Make sure everybody is doing something to help—no shirkers—I won't stand for it, not now.' Frah'nud resumed his conference with the scouts.

'Come; let's see how the raft-making is progressing.' Hnar'ad led Morác back to the steep shore.

They reached the first raft a third of the way along the shoreline. They found Fúlmon with Scória and Dalán finishing lashing the rudder into place to the top logs placed on four large logs underpinning the structure at right angles.

'Yo Morác. Come to lend us a hand?' Behind the banter, Fúlmon was still nervous at handling the dead trees.

'Who designed the rafts?' Morác wanted to know.

'Oh, the Rhalpi. But your right, they look like the same design we had in mind.'

All the rafts were of a simple structure with logs lashed in parallel, then underpinned by four large logs at right angles; two at either end and two in the middle. A rudder at one end with a tiller. A central mast with a cross spar for sail was held in place between the two middle logs with rope braces. All the rafts were done but only nineteen masts were reaching out towards the morning sky—and they were at the western end of the beach—those assigned to the Rhalpi.

'They look solid enough,' Morác told Hnar'ad as they walked along the beach towards the east—the Bólani end. 'Do you build many rafts?'

'We don't encourage our warriors to go to sea. It's far too dangerous. There are all sorts of things out there—monsters, serpents…'

'But you're so close to the water. Don't you fish?'

'Not if we can help it. Only if the game is scarce—we sometimes build rafts and go fishing.'

'It can't be that treacherous—surely…' Morác had trouble believing the bit about monsters and serpents.

'It's not just what's in the sea, but the sea itself.' Hnar'ad motioned Morác to walk to the top of the long beach and sit with him on the verge. He'd something to tell. When they'd settled, he continued. 'We have two suns and two moons pulling on Kálar. This was explained to me by Lord Phèrlim long ago, when we visited him. And I'm sorry to hear he's died—may his lemur rest in peace. But because of the suns and moons, the tides on this sea are dreadful, especially when the suns and moons are almost in line.' He drew a small diagram in the sand. 'The pull of the suns and moons causes the sea to lift, and as you can observe, there is a steep difference between forest and sea. How big a drop do you think there is between the forest and the sea?' He looked at Morác quizzically.

'Oh, I don't know.' He measured with his eye. 'I should say about thirty cubits. Why?'

'That's the tide rise and fall—but when the suns and moons are in line, the sea can overflow into the forest. What d'you think of that?'

'Surly not! You don't mean actually *into* the forest. But that's incredible!' Morác was astounded.

'Luckily, the suns and moons only rarely come into line—but this is one of those times—they'll line-up in the next three rotations of Kálar.'

'But that means we'll still be on the sea—then. How long do we have to stay out there?' He pointed at the water.

Morác now saw all their troubles were not over. This news was just as bad as the closeness of the schánda.

'We'll stay three days on the raft—to make sure. That is what our sacred scroll advises.' Hnar'ad had not intended to frighten the Bólani shamán, and was distressed he'd done so. 'If you and your people decide to join our tribe, there will be nothing to be frightened of. We're sure we'll be safe.' He smiled reassuringly at Morác.

'That's not a decision we have yet taken. I better go and talk with my Custodian. The time is short for such big resolutions.' Morác thanked the old man and went to search out Bróda.

He found him near the three craft allocated to the Bólani—giving orders to Sáor for a hut to be built on each raft.

'We need to have some place which is drier than the rest,' he was telling Wómak. 'Keep it low,' he added to Sáor.

Morác saw the time wasn't right to inform him of the Rhalpi offer. 'Bróda, how's it going?'

'I'm told we're launching the rafts late afternoon. I don't think we're going to be ready by then. Frah'nud sent a message saying the schánda will be here by evening. It's getting chaotic. Just now I sent Fúlmon and his scouts to check how close the schánda really are—I know what Frah'nud says—but I want it verified by *our* scouts.'

Wómak shrugged his shoulders, as if to say, *what a waste of time.*

Bróda saw this and was irritated. 'Wómak, make sure the food gets loaded on each raft—and water.'

'Yes, Bróda. I'll do it now.' Wómak went to look for the supplies.

But Morác was straining his pointed ears as if he was hearing something. 'With all the sounds of the waves, I can't hear…'

'What are you listening for?' Wómak was intrigued.

'Now don't get worried but I think I can hear a muffled snipping in the far distance.'

Bróda heard that. '*What*—it's too soon—I only just sent Fúlmon to…'

'I know,' Morác interrupted, but I'm sure I can hear them. Remember the nightmares—and the snipping sounds. It'll haunt me for the rest of my life. I'm *sure* I can hear it now—again.'

Fúlmon returned at a run, the other two scouts panting up the beach. 'Bad news—away from the sea noise you can hear them coming. Like a nasty buzzing, snapping, about a league inland.'

'You're certain?' Bróda demanded.

'If you get away from the water, you can hear them for yourself—they'll be upon us soon.'

'Right! Wómak, go gather our people—*make haste*. Morác, go help him. Sáor, tidy up—we're leaving. Put logs on the rafts and we might be able to put something up when we've launched them. I want the rafts tied together—I mean a strong rope two cubits long, each raft to the other.'

Morác and Wómak rushed up the beach and found the others ready to descend. Huróyna had grouped them according to rafts. The furthest east was "Raft One," then "Raft Two," and "Raft Three." Warriors had been building and the women braiding rope from twine. Now that was abandoned and those not on the beach were waiting with Huróyna in three short lines.

Émana, Cára with the twins, and Ádna were for Raft One, Néra, herself, Málina and Scéna, Raft Two, and Ganúra, Shúta holding the hands of Scuráia and Sadb, Émer and Láila, Raft Three. Their men folk would join them on launching. At a glance Wómak took in the grouping and hurried back to the beach to inform the men folk as to which raft they were to embark. It wasn't complicated—there were only three rafts.

A commotion animated the Rhalpi. They were also allocating people to rafts. They'd made twenty-two rafts and now were in a hurry to complete and board. Obviously their scouts reported what Fúlmon had. Everything was in a panic. The swarm was closing in on them. It was going to be more a frenzied launch than they'd hoped for.

'*Come on*, warriors report to Wómak for allocation— then help launch the raft you're allocated to.' Bróda was rushing around trying to get people to board.

Their meagre belongings were piled on top of the log platform. Sails of sorts were thrown on—to be raised at sea. Kópi and stándy were shared out in case they needed to be used as meat reserve. Two went on Raft Two with Málina. One each on the other rafts.

The sounds from the forest was beginning to punch thorough the noise from the sea—overpowering the splashing of the waves. The snipping was getting louder—as if the forest was rustling loudly and protesting at such abuse. An incessant relentless force was reaching out at them.

'Quick—get the women aboard,' Bróda was beginning to push his raft towards the swell.

Rhalpi warriors arrived to help the Bólani push their rafts into the water. Bróda's kópi stood on Raft One and grunted excitedly. Émana tried to pull him back from the edge.

Píngo and Morác, side by side, were pushing for all their worth. Fúlmon next to Morác and Máyo was pushing Bréac. All trying desperately to launch Raft Two. Some Rhalpi had their shoulders to the logs—bit by bit the raft slid forward into the swell. The slope of the beach helped, but the rafts were heavy.

The other two rafts were moving similarly into the water. Some of the Rhalpi were already afloat; cheers of encouragement were heard from them.

'*Watch out!*' Ganúra yelled at Wómak pushing below her, his shoulder bleeding from the exertion. 'I can see the schánda—at the top of the beach.'

Indeed, huge insects were climbing, falling over the grass verge onto the beach. Luckily, most of the rafts were in the water, but only just. One was still stranded with Rhalpi pushing wildly, horrified they were still on land—panicking. One insect managed to reach the raft just as it eased into the water, followed closely by others. A Rhalpi lost his leg while climbing onto the raft. His companions pulled him aboard, his severed stump spouting blood onto the water. Some of the Bólani onlookers were forced to avert their gaze—sickened by the sight.

From the safety of their vessels, now drifting out to sea, the occupants watched as the beach filled with loathsome insects, mesmerised, blackening the shoreline, snipping at each other, in a mating frenzy.

28

THE TREACHEROUS SEA

From Raft One Bróda shouted to Píngo standing on Raft Two, '*Come on lad, throw the rope again.*' On their respective rafts they'd viewed the spectacle, and were relieved to have managed to escape with their lives; no more damned insects. Others looked out to the turbulent sea. Morác watched the Rhalpi rafts being pole pushed by warriors towards the west. The prevailing current was drifting the Bólani rafts to the east. The two tribes were barely visible to each other.

Because of the frantic nature of their departure, many things were left undone. Now the problem was to link the three rafts with stout ropes—to prevent them drifting apart.

Píngo was seen to heave the heavy rope as far as he could from Raft Two, but it fell short of Raft One and he was forced to haul it in again. It was one throw among many and each time the throw just wasn't far enough. Scória and Dalán on Raft One were attempting to use the rudder to close the gap between the two rafts but the violent surge and ebb of the waves prevented them holding the tiller still or making any headway. They were in danger of breaking the tiller.

Cára and the twins were being shielded by Umára in the middle of the raft, Émana was holding onto a stándy and Fern, who in his turn was nearby, restrained their kópi by the collar. Sea water was washing over the deck, soaking everything and everyone. Their belongings were tied high on the pile of logs in the centre round the mast. Ládra, Úbor and Ádna were holding and tying the logs to prevent them from shifting. All three were frantically using more rope to bind the logs to the raft.

Finally, Píngo's last throw reached Bróda and he dragged the soaking rope on board, tying it quickly to a fixed log. Dalán rushed over to help and both made the knot tight.

'Thank Aíne for small mercies,' exploded Bróda.

'Now all we have to do is put the spar on the mast, and tie the sail to it,' observed Dalán gruffly.

* * *

On the other side of Raft Two Fúlmon was trying to reach Wómak on Raft Three with an equally soggy rope throw. Although the sea was just as rough, he held off as Raft Three seemed to be drifting closer. He waited till it closed the gap and then threw again. Wómak grabbed the rope and made it fast. All three rafts were now joined. At least one danger had been averted. The Bólani would stay together come what may.

Máyo yelled, '*Great throw,*' at Fúlmon, whilst hanging onto the tiller with all his might.

Málina and Cóer were each clutching a stándy inside the small hut in the centre of the raft to prevent them being washed overboard. Bréac, Scéna, and Huróyna were helping Morác and Néra to fasten more brace ropes to the mast, making sure the mast stayed upright. The sail was still furled under the spar due to the heavy squall. Unlike Raft One, Raft Two and Three were almost complete. Each had a low hut built round the mast. Raised seats inside meant their belongings were relatively dry.

* * *

Wómak stood on Raft Three looking pleased. 'We've got to keep within sight of land—crawl along the coast. And don't tell me; I know we're losing the light.'

Ganúra didn't hear him; she was bossing Némed and Láeg to brace their spar with more ropes. Sáor was working hard to put some form of rail round their raft—he'd intended to do it with all the other rafts but the hurried departure put a stop to it. He kept the rail low, knee high. If people were lying down, they couldn't roll off. Any higher and it would break. He'd improvised a drill and was hammering wooden pins into cross joints.

Because the carpenter was on Raft Three, it was in a better state than the other two rafts—as might be expected. Shúta had Scuráia and Sadb inside the low hut with Émer and Láila. Láila held the collar of Wómak's kópi, who was straining to join his master.

The tanner volunteered to man the tiller and was partly responsible for steering the raft closer to its neighbour, bringing it near enough for Wómak to grab the rope.

'Good work, Súdair,' Wómak praised the tiller-man.

'Thanks,' he groaned, the undercurrent swaying the rudder trying to jump the tiller from under his grip.

'Sáor!' Wómak called the carpenter. 'We're going to have to find a way of getting you to the other rafts so you can finish them off. Especially Raft One. How are you in water?'

Sáor crawled to where Wómak sat. 'I'm good—only it's rough out there,' he gestured at the ocean. It was getting late and the suns were dipping towards the horizon. Dark clouds were gathering.

'Can't be helped. The evening is creeping on us. We'll wait till morning. Then we'll tie a rope round you and you can go arm over arm along the rope linking the rafts. If we start early, you might finish by evening. What'd you think?'

Clearly unhappy at the prospect, but resigned to the inevitable. 'I'll give it a go.'

*   *   *

Since all the rafts were linked, the passengers gave themselves up to the job of making them ship shape. On Raft One Bróda had the same dilemma in mind as Wómak on Raft Three. He was concerned about losing sight of land, and pensively, from time to time kept glancing in that direction in the dimming light.

'Úbor, can you get on the tiller and release Scória and Dalán,' Bróda requested.

To keep people from worrying, Bróda had Scória, Dalán, and Ládra help him secure the spar to the mast and tie the furled sail to it. Then they set about building the hut out of the logs in the centre.

The commotion and banging with the mast spooked the stándy Émana was holding and she lost her grip. It ran for the edge—and in panic jumped into the ocean.

'Oh no,' she screamed and chased after it—into the turbulent sea.

Bróda couldn't believe what he saw—aghast—but only for a moment, dropped everything and jumped in after her. The stándy went under, followed by Émana—closely followed by Bróda.

The occupants of Raft One were too stunned to do anything. The raft was bobbing about. They looked and looked—but no one surfaced. There was no sign of them— stándy, Émana or Bróda. The violent sea had swallowed them whole.

Fern was in shock and just stood staring at the sea.

Nobody knew what to do. Cára began to wail and Ádna joined her. Umára was left comforting the twins.

Scória shouted to Morác, *'Bróda's gone—Bróda's gone.'*

*   *   *

Fúlmon watched the catastrophe helplessly from Raft Two, the stándy, Émana, and Bróda jumping in the water—but waited for them to surface. Finally he grabbed Morác by the arm and pointed at Scória on the other raft.

'Bróda's jumped in the water.' He was in devastated.

'*What!* Where?' He was looking where Fúlmon was pointing—at Scória.

'No, *there*,' he pointed to the spot where he'd seen Bróda go in. '*There*. I can't see him. He's disappeared.'

'What d'you mean disappeared?' Morác repeated.

'Émana too, went after the stándy. *Émana too*,' he repeated almost hysterically.

'I can't see them. You sure?' Morác couldn't take in what was being said—it was too horrible.

Píngo started shouting at the top of his voice, '*Bróda...Bróda...Bróda.*' Over and over.

Huróyna stuck her head from out the hut, 'What's all the shouting?'

'I think we've lost Bróda...overboard.' For Morác, it was beginning to register that they'd just lost their Custodian. 'And Émana,' he added as an afterthought.

Everybody on Raft Two was now standing up and staring at the disarray on Raft One.

*   *   *

The occupants of Raft Three were still unaware of the tragedy, Raft Two obscuring their line of sight. All they saw was that everybody on Raft Two had their backs to them and that something had their attention on Raft One.

Wómak shouted at those on Raft Two, '*What's going on?*'

Ganúra sensed something was amiss. All of Raft Three were on their feet, trying to see what was happening on Raft One.

'Don't know what's going on over there, but it's something bad,' Ganúra told her listeners.

Finally—they heard from Huróyna what had happened. She shouted to Ganúra the whole distressing episode. That put everyone into shock. They might as well been kicked in the teeth. When Huróyna finished, tears were streaming down Ganúra's face. Shúta was holding onto the hut roof, crying. Scuráia and Sadb wailed inside the hut without knowing why, just because their mother was crying. Émer and Láila held each other in their arms and wept. Sáor had stopped working and sat dejected on the logs.

Súdair insisted Némed take the tiller, 'Come on, hold this. I've got to go to Shúta and the kids.'

Láeg joined Némed on the tiller, both subdued.

The sea heaved up and down, lifting and dropping the linked rafts with each swell.

*   *   *

Throughout the night, a collective wailing was heard from Raft One, women wailing—men crying. Their Custodian had left them—abandoned them. What were they to do?

Fern sat on the raft, dumbfounded, still holding the kópi by the collar. Nothing showed on his face. He stared at the dark sea, at the spot on the raft from where his mother and father had disappeared into the water. Just sat and stared at the blue-green ocean.

Ádna saw how he was taking it, or denying it, and came, sat by his side and put her hands round him, pulling him to face her. Fern held tight onto the kópi. Then without warning, he cried into Ádna's shoulder, sobbing like a small boy. Even Cára handed care of the tearful twins over to Umára and went to join Ádna and Fern. She could see the boy needed to let out his grief. In reality the whole raft was afraid Fern might do something foolish like jump into the water after them.

'I don't understand why Bróda jumped in—it doesn't make sense,' Ládra was saying through tears.

Dalán asked him, 'She's his partner, mother to his son—don't tell me you wouldn't have done the same?'

Ládra had no answer. No one did. Bróda had acted instinctively. He went where she went—to rescue her.

The rafts bobbed about, drifting east all through the night. It was morning before anybody thought of getting on with any work.

Umára managed to put some food together in difficult conditions. He fed the twins first, and then went to see if he could induce Fern to take some food. He left the dried porridge cakes with Ádna and Cára both still trying to comfort the weeping Fern.

Scória took charge of the raft and put Úbor back on the tiller, Dalán back to finishing the hut. It was a resumption of life, of survival. What could they do? Life had to go on.

*   *   *

By mid morning, the occupants of Raft Two were huddled in and around the small hut, Morác saying words to try and comfort them. The sail had been unfurled and the wind drove them eastwards. They couldn't understand how the Rhalpi had managed to go west when everything on the ocean seemed to drag or push them east.

Morác rose from his prayers and suggested Fúlmon organise some food. He knew from past experience that mourners were hungry people. The work, the sea air, all conspired to make the stomach growl. It would take their minds off the disaster.

Néra went to help Fúlmon and Huróyna prepare a cold meal of porridge biscuits with water. Anything to be doing something.

Cóer kept looking at his old adversary—Fern, from where he sat by the hut entrance.

'I wish there was something I could do for him,' he confided to Málina, his mother, sitting further inside.

'Hush, let him grieve in peace,' she responded.

The light was strong and the two suns beat down on a choppy ocean. After the meagre food, Fúlmon organised a rota on the tiller.

He sat near the hut entrance. 'Cóer! I need your help. I want you to count to twenty thousand then get Píngo to relieve Wólni on the tiller—can you do that?'

'Sure, no problem.' The boy looked pleased to be doing something.

'When you need to rest, get another person to do the counting,' Fúlmon added.

Cóer snapped back warrior style, 'Right ho.'

*   *   *

The Raft Three sail was up and as a result, it was now the lead raft pulling the others east. The order of the rafts had reversed—but it made no difference to those on board.

Wómak had Ganúra doing a similar count. The tiller-man had to have a rest. The length of the count wasn't important—the rotation was.

Raft Three settled after their meal into a subdued melancholy. The twins were sleep, as was Shúta. Ganúra was near the entrance to the small hut, Émer and Láila were inside. There was no room for anybody else. The rest, Láeg, Némed, Súdair, and Sáor were sitting in the sun, backs against the wall of the hut. Wómak was on the tiller.

No one had slept a wink except those in the huts. It was one of the most frightening days anyone could remember. The surface motion of the large body of rough water crashed waves on the raft with every swell. Only their overall fitness allowed them to overcome the fatigue and hunger—but the discomfort coupled with distress made every member of the Bólani miserable.

The evening arrived with no further mishap and was greeted with relief—another day had gone—one less on this accursed sea. When the moons rose—the cold added to their discomfort. The cold supper was doled out in silence, and eaten in that manner. The lack of a fire was their joint complaint.

The dawn found everybody stiff and complaining of the buffeting. Sáor got back to work completing the rail, working off his stiffness, securing the logs so they didn't end up in the water.

'I want you to go to Raft Two in the early morning and finish it off. They've probably done most of the work themselves, but you can check it and…well…you know,' Wómak informed the carpenter. 'Then go on to Raft One and do the same.'

*   *   *

All of the second day on the sea, the people on Raft One give out a sullen disposition, brooding on the terrible tragedy that befell the tribe the previous day. Fern turned to music; an incessant dirge on his panpipes was wailing along with the wind, mournful and keeping the mood gloomy. The kópi was tied to the mast.

'I don't want to get heavy,' Scória told Umára, 'but his music is irritating the húli out of me. 'I don't think I can put up with much more of it.'

'I know it's annoying, but he's just lost his whole family, and he's coping in the only way he knows,' Umára responded.

'I'm not the only one,' Scória shot back defensively.

'Look, give him some leeway for a couple of days. I think he's getting over it, coping well as a matter of fact. If he's still putting out that noise after that, then I'll have a quiet word with him, what d'you say?' Umára was pleading for Scória to back off.

Apart from melancholy, people were on edge, the slightest thing could set them off. They were scared. What would they do without their Custodian to guide them? They still had a long way to go. Then there was—the sea. Heaving undulations, rogue waves crashing over the rafts. People clung to logs or anything that seemed secure.

'I think we'd be better off closer to shore,' suggested Dalán. 'It might not be so rough.'

'What if we're beached by the wind, driven on shore? Then we'd be in trouble.' Ládra pointed out.

*   *   *

Mid morning Sáor arrived on Raft Two, after much delay patching up a damaged tiller, and was impressed by the work they'd done.

'There's little I can add to this,' he told Morác. 'You must have watched me put up the rail on our raft—because this one is solid. The best thing I can do is try to reach Raft One, seems they've neglected putting up their hut—lots of work there.'

'I think you're right,' agreed Morác.

'How's Raft Three holding up?' Fúlmon asked.

'We're all sad, but that's to be expected. People are scared.'

'Look. I've been thinking.' Morác took Sáor by the arm. 'We should elect a new Custodian.'

'*You can't—not yet*. Wait till we get to shore,' protested Sáor. 'A few days won't make a difference, surely.'

'You said yourself—people are scared.' Morác had a determined look on his face. 'Since you're going from raft to raft—I want you to carry the result. Wait a little, while I go and ask who our raft wants as the next leader of the Bólani.'

He went round and talked rapidly with the ten others —people protested as Sáor had. Sáor looked puzzled and agitated sitting with his back against the hut.

Morác came back and announced, 'This raft votes Wómak be made the next Custodian. Will you tell the people on Raft One when you get there—and ask them who they want.'

Sáor looked bemused at the speed this election was progressing. He suspected Wómak was going to be pushed into it. On the other side, Morác was right—they needed to move on. An election would take peoples mind off their misery. *Clever of Morác to do this*, he thought. He stood, just as a big wave washed over and almost had him in the water.

'Careful there. We don't want to lose you as well.' Morác chided.

Fúlmon got his blowpipe ready, as did the other warriors on Raft Two. They'd seen Wómak, Némed and Láeg take aim with their weapons at the sea just in case of sea monsters. Sáor slid into the sea his tool-bag round his waist, pulling himself arm over arm along the rope that linked the two rafts.

Yet again Sáor risked himself sliding gingerly into the turbulent sea—heading for Raft One hand over hand.

*   *   *

'Come on, give me your arm,' Scória was shouting at Sáor as he approached the raft.

Sáor reached him—gave him his hand and was pulled aboard.

'Glad to see a different face,' Ládra commented.

'What's that noise,' Sáor asked, hearing Fern's panpipes. 'It's so sad.'

'Forget it. It's Fern—he's driving us crazy with that sad music,' Scória informed him.

'I want to start on the hut. Can you get the muscle to sort the logs?' Sáor was eager to use the light.

Scória had Úbor take the tiller. The women went to sit near Úbor but Cára took the twins to sit on the opposite side. She led Fern to sit with her—she liked his playing. Even with all the waves, they made good progress and the hut was up in short order. Sáor worked hard—but made time to tell Scória what Morác wanted to be conveyed.

By mid afternoon the roof of the hut was finished. Scória came and sat with Sáor, who was resting after storing the rafts belongings inside.

'I've gone round everybody. They all think it's too early—but—all agree Wómak would be the best choice. He was Bróda's deputy, so in a sense, Bróda chose him for next in line. All we're doing is confirming Bróda's choice—right? Can you tell Morác when you get back to Raft Two.'

'You can count on it,' Sáor replied.

Sáor's crossing back to Raft Two almost cost him his life. The heavy pouch with his drill, hammer and tooth saw dragged him down and he had to abandon it—or go under. The choice was simple.

*   *   *

The sea buffeted and pummelled Sáor as he reached Raft Two. Píngo and Fúlmon waited to haul him aboard.

'I lost my tools,' he moaned as he climbed up and was dragged onto the raft. 'What am I going to do?'

'Blow the tools—you're more important,' scolded Morác as he helped Sáor to his feet.

'But we need the tools—*I* need the tools.'

'They're gone, forget them.' Morác paused to let Sáor catch his breath. 'Well? What did they decide? Did they agree to Wómak?' Morác was anxious to confirm their new Custodian.

'Yes, they agreed. I need a drink—I've swallowed half the ocean.'

'Good. That just leaves Raft Three to vote. Píngo, can you get Sáor some fresh water please.'

'Right ho!' Píngo stuck his head inside the hut and returned with a water skin. 'There you go,' he said as he handed the skin to Sáor.

'I can't imagine his own raft voting against him—can you?' Morác continued. 'So it's settled—almost. I wish him the best.'

Sáor felt the raft heave to one side and was thrown against the hut wall. 'Better take the sail down or you'll lose it,' he advised. 'Raft Three's already taken down theirs.'

Morác nodded, 'Good idea. Píngo, Fúlmon—could you?'

The two warriors climbed onto the roof of the hut and with difficulty lashed the sail tight to the spar in the howling wind.

Fúlmon cursed as he came back and sat with his back against the hut. 'Crossing the Márka was bad enough but this…' he pointed accusingly at the sea, 'this is the limit. This rotten water's already killed two of our best.'

Píngo positioned himself between Morác and Sáor listening to Fúlmon, nodding and smiling. The two former foes were now inseparable. Píngo anticipated Morác's every wish—making Morác a bit embarrassed. He accepted it with good grace, always remembering what it had been like before. This was far preferable.

'I'm thinking Wómak's election was necessary,' Morác sighed. 'Does it make you feel more secure?' He turned to gaze at his companions.

'Not secure exactly—but better.' Fúlmon was hesitant.

Morác looked at Sáor. He needed a reply—a reassurance he'd done the right thing.

Sáor shrugged, and took another swig of the water skin. 'Yes, I think it makes me feel better knowing we've got a Custodian again. You were right, Morác. It needed to be done.'

Morác's face relaxed. People might resent the speed with which it was done—later—but for now they had a new leader.

'I'd better get back to my raft,' Sáor muttered. 'Give me time to dry off. You know—I don't like this rotten sea all that much. What am I going to do without my tools?'

*   *   *

Wómak watched Sáor slide from Raft Two into the water and start the laborious overhand journey back to Raft Three. *He's tired*, Wómak thought, then: *where's his tool bag?*

Sáor made his way ever nearer and finally reached the bobbing raft. Wómak held his hand out and grabbed Sáor by the elbow, helping him out of the water. Sáor lay on the logs on his stomach, panting with the exertion.

'You've left your tool-bag behind,' Wómak reprimanded.

Sáor heaved himself to his feet and wiped his face with his hand. 'I lost it in the water.' He wasn't happy about it.

At that moment a thick grey tentacle grasped Sáor round his right ankle and pulled—trying to drag him into the sea. Sáor threw his arms out to Wómak who seized Sáor's left arm and a tug of war ensued.

'*Help me*,' Wómak yelled.

Némed and Láeg were behind Wómak and saw the tentacle come out of the sea. Both grabbed Wómak and Sáor's other arm—pulling with all their might. Súdair left the tiller and joined the struggle.

'*Father!*' screamed Láila. His daughter was there to welcome him back and watched the struggle—helpless.

A mighty wrench by whatever it was, of enormous strength, and Wómak's grip was broken. So was Némed's. Sáor shrieked. He was pulled in and his head went under the water screaming. The strength of the wrench almost pulled the remaining three in with Sáor.

Émer couldn't contain herself and would have leapt in after Sáor had Láila not held her back. Both were in shock. Súdair saw what Émer was intending and blocked her path to self destruction. He joined Láila in holding Émer in check.

'*No!*' Wómak shouted. '*Not another—no!*'

It was all Némed and Láeg could do to stop Wómak also diving in after Sáor.

Némed and Láeg made sure Wómak wasn't going to jump then began jumping up and down on the raft in sheer frustration. Wómak brought his impulse under control and guardedly stared at the eddying spot where Sáor had gone.

Émer and Láila were sobbing loudly.

'*My poor Sáor,*' Émer wailed over and over.

Súdair helped by Ganúra, guided Sáor's distraught family towards the hut and made sure they went and sat inside. Shúta and her two kids made room for Émer and Láila and joined in comforting the bereaving women.

'*This damned rotten sea,*' Wómak ranted. '*May Húli curse it forever—and everything in it,*' he added for good measure.

'Calm down,' Ganúra demanded, having left Súdair guarding the hut entrance. 'You can't do anything,'

'Oh yes I can,' responded Wómak. '*Láeg!*' he bellowed, '*Get on the rudder, and aim the tiller for the shore.* In the mean time, Ganúra,' he became determined but calmer, 'can you make sure everybody keeps away from the edge. Whatever's following us is still down there.'

'You sure?' Ganúra questioned. 'What about the schánda? I don't think we can land yet—and it's getting late.'

'I know that,' he snapped back. 'We're not staying out here—*that's final.*'

The suns were making for the western horizon and the light was dimming with grey clouds overhead. A sudden streak of lightening struck far out to sea. To add to their misery, it began to rain heavily.

'Does that answer your question?' Wómak told Ganúra, pointing at the flash.

In the mood he was in, Ganúra didn't argue with him anymore. She went round and made sure people were clustered near and inside the hut.

Wómak turned to his warriors. 'Némed, shout out to Raft Two what's happened—and that we're heading to shore. Make sure you're clear—get their rudders to head that way.'

'Yes, Wómak,' Némed snapped back.

'And don't holler from the edge—do it from the centre of the raft.'

* * *

Morác had a hard time hearing Némed's shouting over the pouring rain and thunderclaps. It was Huróyna whose ears were sharpest. She and Fúlmon finally agreed what Némed was trying to impart.

'We've lost Sáor overboard to some sea creature,' Fúlmon told Morác. 'Wómak insists we set a course for the shore—immediately.'

'Damn it to húli—*Sáor*—another one?' Morác was shocked. 'I saw the commotion but with all that bobbing about I couldn't see what was happening. And you're sure he means us to head for land?'

'Positive,' responded Huróyna.

'Go tell Máyo please—he's back on the rudder. And oh!' Morác held Huróyna back, 'And get Fúlmon to shout back that Wómak is the new elected Custodian, can you. We don't know Sáor told him before the tragedy.'

'We'll get it organised,' she assured. 'I'll get as many as we can inside the hut.'

What ever they did, they couldn't change course for land. The sails were furled but the howling prevailing wind insisted on pushing all three rafts out to sea. All through the night the downpour made it more difficult, and an almighty struggle developed aboard the three rafts. Three or four warriors were moving each of the tillers back and forward on each raft, doing their utmost to propel the flimsy vessels by vigorous to and fro movements of the rudder, trying to drive the rafts against the wind. None expected the rudders to hold.

As dawn spread reluctant thin cerise streaks in the sky, the rain finally ceased. They thanked Aíne for small mercies. Those on the tillers were near to exhaustion—and those in and near the huts were bitterly cold. Then with the suns beginning to show, the wind capriciously changed in their favour. One moment they were being pushed out to sea —a short lull—and the wind changed to push them towards land.

Néra groaned to Málina, 'It's been one disaster after another out here—give me a forest any day. I shudder to think what's at the other end of those tentacles.'

'At least we'll get to land now. Look at the men, their done in.'

'There's that—you're right, poor things. We better get some food ready for them.'

With the wind driving the raft to shore, the tiller was left to mighty Píngo, tired but far from worn out. They didn't raise the sails for fear of landing too suddenly without control.

Morác stood near the tiller, keeping Píngo company. He began to worry. *Had the schánda finished with their mating? Were they gone off the beach? First the schánda and now sea creatures. What kind of creature's attacking us? Is it big?*

Néra brought them biscuits and the water skin, breaking into Morác's thoughts.

'Thanks Néra,' Píngo went to it ravenously while Morác took a turn at the tiller.

'There's more if you want it,' she offered.

'Let me finish this first,' Píngo protested.

'I'm not sure—but I think I can see land, there in the distance,' he pointed with his left hand in the direction the wind was taking them.

At that instant a grey tentacle shot from the water and grabbed his left wrist. Morác clutched the tiller with the crook of his right elbow, which prevented him being pulled overboard. Píngo, normally slow witted, instinctively pulled out his axe and hacked furiously at the grey tentacle—trying to sever it below Morác's wrist. The axe simply bounced off the tough grey outer covering after each chop and Morác was rapidly losing his hold on the tiller.

'*Help! For Aíne's sake, someone help me!*' Morác screamed.

Néra joined in the screaming as did Málina and Scéna. Huróyna and Fúlmon rushed over and seized Morác's arm—the one round the tiller.

Píngo saw they were going to lose Morác—and in a split second, lifted the axe above his head and brought it down on Morác's wrist—above the tentacle's grip. The blade severed the hand—the tentacle snapped back into the sea with its small prize. Morác was thrown into Fúlmon, staring in shock at the stump gushing blood. Néra rushed over and began tearing her skirt into strips, binding a tourniquet around the stump.

Píngo was in tears, sobbing, 'I had to do it—I had to. It would have taken you into the water.'

Morác felt momentarily weak but, now the blood had been staunched, looked weakly at Píngo and told him hoarsely, 'Thank you Píngo—I mean that. You did the right thing. Hush there now! You did the right thing—you saved my life.'

Píngo didn't hear him. He kept babbling for some time, over and over how he couldn't help it. Fúlmon supported Morác under one arm while Huróyna supported the other side. Máyo and Wólni relieved them on the tiller.

Morác was taken inside the hut to be nursed by Néra and the other women.

'I'm amazed he's still with us,' Málina voiced.

'Píngo saved his life,' Néra said with a tinge of admiration.

29

ON BLESSED LAND AGAIN

'**I** can't see any movement,' Fúlmon told his skittish listeners. He was peering hard at the beach—trying to make out if any of the schánda littering the shoreline were stirring —were alive.

'Are you sure,' Bréac asked for the umpteenth time.

All three rafts were being held back offshore some hundred cubits from where the breakers crashed onto the seashore. The wind was blowing gently from the land, filling their sails.

Fúlmon signalled to the other two; he was going to scout the beach.

'Huróyna, Máyo—you know we have to do this for the tribe.' He looked steadily at them.

They nodded unenthusiastically.

'Píngo, take the tiller.'

Fúlmon jumped in the water, swam until he could wade ashore—followed by Huróyna and Máyo. Cautiously they explored the beach, trying not to step on the schánda carcasses.

'Morác said we'd only find corpses—you know— after their mating.' Máyo whispered to Huróyna.

Fúlmon jibed at Máyo, 'Why're you whispering— afraid you'll wake them?'

Máyo grimaced as he stepped round a group that appeared to have fought each other to the death over something. Black bits and pieces of schánda lay scattered—most of the bodies badly mutilated.

'Get a peek at this lot, they look like they've done each other in,' Máyo was more upbeat.

'Morác said they fought over the females—trying to mate,' Huróyna explained—then added, 'Look at the size of them, they're huge.'

Fúlmon led the scouts in a long ellipse along the rim of the forest and then back along the water's edge. He came back to where Raft Two waited to beach.

'*Bring her in Píngo,*' he yelled at the top of his voice. '*They're all dead. Tell the others.*'

He went to where Wómak's raft had come in closer to shore and gave them the same news—Wómak shouted the news to Scória on Raft One. Wómak then jumped overboard and waded up the sandy foreshore, reaching Fúlmon and grasping him by the shoulders.

'Good to be able to touch you again, Fúlmon. And you Huróyna—Máyo,' he clasped their hands in turn. He then stamped the sand in affirmation of landing on firm ground after their nightmare voyage. 'It's good to be back on firm land. I don't want to see another raft—ever again—I mean that.' To Fúlmon, 'You confirm they're dead?' He waved a hand at the schánda.

'I do.'

'Then let's get the rafts landed. We'll pull Morác in first, then the others.'

Píngo threw a rope to the beach and the four hoisted it over their backs and pulled the raft to shore. Néra jumped down and Morác was lowered over the side into Wómak's arms by Píngo. Wómak carried Morác up the beach and laid him gently on the warm sand. Píngo was close behind. Néra tended to Morác's seeping stump, changing the dressing.

'Píngo, can you get a fire going. We need to cauterize the wound as a matter of urgency.'

'Right-ho! Custodian.'

It was strange to hear himself called thus, but Wómak smiled encouragingly at Píngo. Raft One landed with the help of a turning gust of wind—and Raft Three had to be pulled to shore with rope. The reluctant sailors disembarked with enthusiasm, glancing round and loudly cursing their former mode of transport—happy to be rid of it. The stándy, although malnourished, had survived and Ganúra led Wómak's and Fern's kópis onto land.

'Can we clear a few of the schánda corpses into a heap and make a clearing where we can rest for a while,' Wómak was talking to Fúlmon and the warriors.

'Ládra! Scória! Come on Máyo, lend a hand,' Fúlmon encouraged the others to join him. He and Píngo were hoisting bits of insects, making a small hillock. Huróyna was smoothing the sand in the clearing with a branch. Other tribe members were piling their belongings into the cleared area.

Wólni, Cóer and Fern had got some firewood from the nearby forest and stacked it well away from their possessions. Fern then drifted off to where Láila sat.

Píngo was on his knees and began the process of fire making whilst Umára busied himself with organising the food.

Néra helped Morác to where their belongings were piled. He was on his feet, walking slowly with her aid, and smiling in a silly way.

'What're smiling about,' she demanded. She saw no reason for merriment.

'I'm alive. Don't you understand? If Píngo hadn't done what he did—you know, I'd be like…Sáor or Bróda…' He chuckled, more as a relief of tension and past stress. They were on land and the schánda—the causes of their misery— were all dead, scattered around them. The threat was over. They had survived—well, some of them had.

The two sat on their personal effects, Morác had his good arm round Néra and she rested her head on his shoulder.

A fire crackled in the clearing with the sound of waves gently crashing on the seashore. The weather had softened now they were back on land, and the tribe rested, exhausted after their watery ordeal.

Wómak came and sat by Morác. 'Well old man—it's time we cauterized your stump.' He said it as gently as he could.

'Thanks for the offer—but we'll do that only if my own remedy fails.'

'What remedy?' Néra wanted to know.

'I'm going to try some growing magic on it. I might be able to regrow the hand. It'll only work if we don't seal it off.'

Wómak looked quizzical and doubtful. 'You sure you want to do that?'

'Positive!'

'Well, call me if you change your mind,' and Wómak walked back to Ganúra scratching his head, mumbling, 'Bloomin Wizards!'

Fern sat with Láila, both comforted each other with the recent loss of their parents. Láila had lost her dear father and Fern, his whole family. They now sought solace in each others company.

Umára made some hot drink and asked Málina if he could take one of her stándy to feed the tribe. Reluctantly she relinquished the scrawniest and Súdair took him behind the insect mound and cut its throat. Shúta gathered the blood in a bowl and Súdair butchered the emaciated stándy, cutting it into the communal pot. Umára added the blood and water and a few spices were added to the pot over the fire. They ate the Rhalpi biscuits with the sparse boiled meat and determined they would replenish their porridge or procure an alternative. The Rhalpi had offered to provision them for their return journey.

Cára and the twins sat waiting for Umára to finish with the food. Úbor and Ádna comforted Émer, who couldn't stop crying. Málina had Wólni help her feed and check the two remaining stándy. She sat with her arms around the stándy necks, hoping this would somehow protect them from Súdair and Umára. Wómak and Ganúra sat with the two kópi nearby, holding each other. The members of the Bólani tribe were re-establishing their bonds and silently grieving for their lost companions.

By the time they'd finished their meal and rested, it was early afternoon. At this point Néra was asleep and Morác held his talisman, chanting quietly to himself, looking at his stump. He got up and cleared his throat—it woke Néra with a start.

'Dear sweet tired people, I know you'd rather rest, but I think it's time I said a few words for our dear departed Custodian—Bróda, may Aíne guide his lemur. We have elected a new Custodian,' and Morác nodded in Wómak's direction, 'but on the cruel ocean we couldn't pay our respects to Bróda, Émana and our brave carpenter. I beg your indulgence and ask you to observe a moments silence in their honour.' People bowed their heads while the close-by forest noises joined the sea splashing coming from the beach.

Morác continued solemnly with a prayer. 'May our Lady Aíne smile on their departure. May She guard and guide them past Húli's watchful gaze. May She help choose the right path, so no harm befalls them on their immortal journey to the Netherworld.' He was asking Aíne to intercede with Húli over their immortality—to ease their lemurs into the Netherworld.

As Morác finished he nodded again at Wómak, who released Ganúra and rose to his feet.

Wómak coughed a few times to clear his throat. 'I want to add my voice to Morác's in grieving for Bróda, Émana and Sáor. It's been a big tragedy for us all—losing them. I still can't believe he's gone.' He paused and took a deep breath, gulping down emotion. 'He was like a father to me—no disrespect to Fern.'

Fern was seen to wipe away tears.

Wómak continued, 'What we must do to commemorate his passing is to complete this terrible journey.'

People nodded their approval at this.

Wómak paused…'And this brings me to something that we have to decide before we take another step.'

That got everybody's attention.

'We have to decide whether to join the Rhalpi—or head back home. Most of you don't know this, but the Rhalpi, before we boarded our rafts three days ago, gave us an invitation to join their tribe. It came up when we were complaining of the long journey we had to make to escape the schánda. All the Rhalpi have to do is go down to the sea and get on their rafts—nothing compared to our long voyage.' He stopped to see how the tribe reacted to the news. 'We could join the Rhalpi—and our children would never have to make such a journey again. What do you say?'

Almost as one, a great chorus of, 'No-o-o!' was heard in the clearing. Everyone was against it—they wanted to go home—back to their forest life.

Wómak smiled and held his hands up. 'Well I never. I felt sure some would want to stay. But I'm with you—I too want to go back up North, back home to my Lándo tree. This is the thirty-ninth day of our journey, and I can't wait to get back to see our hamlet.'

The whole group cheered and clapped their hands. A unity had been established under their new Custodian. Wómak and Ganúra sought Fern out, and found him sitting with Láila. Ganúra sat with Láila and Wómak took Fern aside and commiserated with him on his loss.

'If you ever need advice or help of any kind, I would feel it a privilege if you'd turn to us first,' Wómak told the young man.

Ganúra was saying pretty much the same to Láila. Both seemed to appreciate the extra gesture.

Wómak and Ganúra went to where Morác and Néra were sitting side by side, holding on to each other.

'How's your arm?' asked Wómak.

'I've been talking to it,' Morác replied, as if it were normal. 'Take a look.' He began to unwrap his stump overriding Néra's objections.

'Fúlmon!' Wómak shouted for him to join them.

Morác had unwrapped the stump and Wómak stared at it—unable to believe what he saw. The stump had a clean covering of new skin.

'Will you look at that,' he said to Fúlmon as he crouched nearby. 'That quick heh? Well bowl me over with a feather. I've never seen the like. You and your bloomin magic. Glad we got you on our side, though.'

'It's only just starting. Might not work—but I've got to try.' Morác was almost apologetic for not allowing Wómak to cauterize his stump.

'I'm telling you formally in front of Morác,' Wómak told Fúlmon, 'that you're my choice as second in command—that's if you want it.'

Fúlmon looked sharply at Wómak, and then a smile spread on his face. 'Thanks. I'm grateful. When we get back —can I have your Lándo tree? You know, for Huróyna and me.'

That startled Wómak. 'I suppose, but where am I going to live?'

'Why Wómak,' Morác chided, 'you're the Custodian now—and you'll move into Bróda's old tree.'

'Yes, I suppose you're right. Hmm! So many changes. It'll need getting used to.'

'But first we have a long way to go to get home. Early start tomorrow.'

The suns were making their way towards the distant horizon bringing a long eventful day to a conclusion.

'One last thing before we turn in,' Morác announced. 'I've made a momentous decision, with your approval, to write down our whole experience, the journey and all that, in the manner of the Rhalpi sacred scrolls. I intend to relate how when the Schánda come—you know, the timing, and what the tribe should do. What we can expect to meet on the journey, how long it takes. What do you think…?' he was looking at Wómak, wanting him to comment.

'Why I think that's the most sensible thing I've heard this entire trip—I'm all for it. Please, Morác, do it for the tribe and our children. It'll help us plan our future—well not exactly ours—but our offspring's future.'

30

EPILOGUE

The return journey north to their old village was arduous and took almost fifty six days. Runners were sent to the Rhalpi who were as good as their word and supplied them with provisions for the long trip back. They were disappointed the Bólani didn't want to stay but wished them a safe journey home. Morác and Wómak promised they would stay in touch.

On the way back they travelled through swamps, came across other villages attempting to reconstruct their lives after the devastation caused by the predatory insects. A couple more people were lost but to counterbalance the tragedies, Umára and Cára got together and the twins acquired a new dad.

In this time Fern had matured beyond his eighteen summers and had been invited to join the warriors *and* become engaged to Láila. Both had lost parents and their mutual grief bonded them firstly in sorrow, comforting each other, then later it transformed into the deepest feelings of affection culminating in Morác pronouncing them "man and wife."

By the time they returned to their Lándo trees, well over four months had been ripped from the lives of the occupants of the Bólani village. Fifty days it had taken them to get to thc Golden Sea; fourteen days spent on the infernal rafts; then the long difficult trail to return to their dwellings.

In this time Bréac and Scéna were a transformed couple as they resettled their Lándo tree on the southern edge of the village. The two became pillars of the community, helping wherever they could without any sign of their former whinging. All the Bólani became better people for their journey of suffering, more tolerant to each other, kinder. Bréac and Scéna were certainly permanently changed for the better. They were symptomatic of transformation of the whole area. Neighbours became better neighbours—trade flourished.

The life of the peaceful Bólani village continued into deep summer and then more reluctantly into Kálar's winter. The villagers settled into their former routines with enthusiasm, getting on with their regular lives.

One evening in late summer, Morác sat in his favourite basket chair spreading sweet wild-berry preserve on freshly baked wild-seed bread. He blew on his favourite herbal brew, took a sip and then tucked into his a meagre evening meal. Food was still at a premium.

Néra had brought his dusk meal served on a bark trencher, smiling at him with her hazel green eyes. For the umpteenth time, her smile made his heart skip a beat.

'No matter how far you go, no matter how long you travel, it's almost axiomatic that you end up exactly back where you started,' Morác told her with his mouth full.

'That's very profound of you,' Néra answered, biting into her bread. 'Any other pearls of wisdom while you're at it?'

'As a matter of fact I think there is; while we were on that nightmare journey you stood by me as a trusted friend and companion and I've come to realise how much I owe you —and love you, more than ever before.' He reached out over the table and placed his good hand over hers.

A tear blossomed in Néra's right eye and she dabbed at it with her free hand. 'I married you for better or for worse;

and I'm happy to say it's been for the better most of the time.'

After the dishes were cleared, Morác climbed the narrow stairs to the top of his living Lándo tree. Gazing out onto his favourite idling spot, carefully and gingerly using his good arm, he climbed out onto the sturdy branch into the evening air. He had told Néra he was convinced that out of the stump, he could conjure his arm to regrow just as good as new, given a little wizardly encouragement and patience.

He sat and watched mighty Búla, her face a strong bright yellow-orange, dipping back over the horizon, slowly and majestically counterpoised by Mára, smaller with a yellow countenance. The binary suns were returning to their slumbers and the stars shone as an orchestra of light twinkling in the deep-blue dark sky. Perched on the hardy branch, enchanted and entranced by the kaleidoscope of flowing colours, Morác felt an aura of contentment coming from the peaceful night time sounds of his fellow villagers as they settled in for the evening.

All was contentment——until the next time.

End

Murder in Hattusas

Sasha Garrydeb

This is the first volume of the Hittite Trilogy. At the close of the Old Kingdom in 1420 BC, the realm of the ancient Hittite Empire is in chaos. Muwatallis, the king has been assassinated in the capital, Hattusas, by the feared Kaska Assassin's Guild. Muwas, the dead king's brother blames the two sons of the previous king, Huzziyas, and he insists he be the one to succeed his brother. The two sons of Huzziyas, Kantuzzili and Himuili, insist the next king be Tudhaliyas, son of Himuili, since rewarding Muwatallis' previous assassination of Huzziyas, is unthinkable. Neither side is prepared to give way, and the scene is set for civil war. Tagrama, the High Priest of the temple of the Storm God Taru, tries to broker a peace, but is up against outright stubbornness.

Muwas then hires Harep, of the same Assassin's Guild, to kill Tudhaliyas. Only Mokhat, the former spiritual adviser to the Assassin's Guild, knows what Harep looks like, and he is determined to stop all the damnable assassinations. He's had enough of the Guild's murdering ways.

Muwas calls upon his Mittani allies, the Mittani King Saustatar, who sends his son Artatama with an army to Muwas' aid. The Kizzuwatna King Shunashura changes allegiance and abandons the Mittani in favour of Kantuzzili's faction, sending an army to help Tudhaliyas. The Pharaoh Amenhotep II threatens to invade Mittani unless they pull their army out of Hatti. Saustatar refuses.

When Tudhaliyas meets Nikal, he falls for this daughter of the Kizzuwatna king. They announce their engagement. Harep, the hired assassin, makes a number of attempts on Tudhaliyas' life, but is foiled. The major Battle of the Wide Plateau settles the civil war but in the mean time, Harap manages to kidnap Nikal.

The protagonist, Mokhat, is in search of himself after his sordid ministrations to a bunch of murderers. It is a bronze-age thriller, which includes a romp through the Hittite landscape, a civil war, and chariots in battle. This is a tale of love and adventure set in the most fascinating recently discovered culture of the ancient world. 2nd Volume of this trilogy is due out Easter 2011.

A must for all fans of the Hittite civilisation. Volume 3 is scheduled to be published in 2012.

Madduwatta's Rebellion

Sasha Garrydeb

This is the 2nd Volume of the Hittite trilogy. It is now three years since the Battle of the Plateau (Vol 1—Murder in Hattusas) put Tudhaliyas on the throne in the realm of the ancient Hittite Empire, yet instead of feeling secure, he feels menaced. His chief spy, Satipilli, has vanished, and trouble is brewing in the west, possibly from Ahhiyawa. The Mittani are threatening Ishuwa in the east. All this needs reliable intelligence reports. Tudhaliyas turns to the unknown faces of Mokhat and Palaiyas and asks them to go to Millawanda and discover the truth.

At the close of the Old Kingdom in 1417 BC Madduwatta, the Governor of Lukka, a nominal vassal of Tudhaliyas, has plans of his own. He wants to be a King in his own right and will use any means to achieve that. He has his eyes on Arzawa. He badly needs friends, and will ally himself with anyone prepared to help him achieve his goal. But who has stirred him up? Who has gone to these lengths to create a rebellion for the Hittites?

Meanwhile, Ahhiyawa is in the grip of Civil War, with two brothers fighting it out for the throne in Millawanda. The outcome of the war will impact on their neighbours, Arzawa, the Hittites, *and* Lukka.

From Milllawanda, Palaiyas, a Prince of Tiryns, decides to cross the water and go home to make peace with his father, the king. While in Tiryns, he's arrested by his uncle, the Mycenaean Wanax (king), taken to Mycenae to account for his desertion, and then forced to complete his tour of duty on Keftiu (Crete). Mokhat follows to rescue him and they end up in Khemet (Egypt), then Ugarit, then Lukka and back to Ivalanda, all in an effort to stay alive and search for Satipilli. Someone keeps trying to kill them, and with each failure, their attempts become more desperate. Somebody doesn't want them to complete their mission.

Volume 3 is scheduled to be published in 2012. A must for all fans of the Hittite civilisation.

Worlds Beyond Ours

Sasha Garrydeb

In the fourth millennium humans finally invent the warp-drive and set out to explore the Galaxy. The first mission is sent to our nearest star, Alpha Centauri, and the starship returns to a stormy acclaim by earth's population. It then comes as a shock to our planet when aliens visit earth and announce that the Galactic Federation intends to lift its quarantine around the Solar System. Since humans now have warp drive capability, would they like to join the Galactic Federation?

This story brings humanity for the first time into contact with a variety of alien life-forms: elfin-like creatures, dinosauroids, insectoids, and many more, when Earth's Embassies are sent to other worlds. As the humans fan out from their home world they encounter a number of adventures which shape humanity's future for generations to come. Wonders like floating cities in the sky, terraforming other planets and genetic advertising.

The story at the end comes full circle when it culminates in another first contact, but this time from our neighbouring galaxy for this Galactic Federation.